Praise 

"*One Click* pulls you in and
one sitting. It's a page-turner
will make you stop and thi
again." – Patricia Gibney, au

"*One Click* is menacing from the start, surprising to the end. Makes
you think – hard – about what we share and reveal, and who might
be watching." – Emily Hourican, author of *White Villa*

"A cracking read!" – Stella O'Malley, author of *Bully-Proof Kids*

'Gripping – it will keep you guessing until the last page.' – Sarah
Breen, co-author of *Oh My God What a Complete Aisling*

Praise for *The Other Side of the Wall*

"A masterful debut, which combines the ordinary themes of working
mothers and modern suburbia, with all the foreboding malevolence
of a Jeffery Deaver novel ... a gripping read that is hard to put down
and would make a great movie." – *The Independent*

"I read this in one sitting and thoroughly enjoyed it – the right side
of chillingly good." – *Woman's Way*

"A twisting tale of evil lurking behind a suburban hall
door." – Sinéad Crowley, author of *One Bad Turn*

"This is a prime example of a superior grip lit book. From the first
eerie chapter to the very last page it is quite literally unputdownable
with an abundance of 'oh!' moments throughout. The characters
are well developed and the subplots all deal with everyday-life
issues that everyone I know will relate to. Honestly, a very, very
superior debut." – Margaret Scott, author of *The Fallout*

ONE CLICK

Andrea Mara

POOLBEG
CRIMSON

Published 2019 by Crimson
an imprint of Poolbeg Press Ltd
123 Grange Hill, Baldoyle
Dublin 13, Ireland
www.poolbeg.com

A catalogue record for this book is available from the British Library.

ISBN 978-1-78199-809-0

f www.facebook.com/poolbegpress
@PoolbegBooks

Typeset by Poolbeg in Sabon
Printed by CPI Group, UK

www.poolbeg.com

About the Author

Andrea Mara lives in Dublin with her husband and three children. She's a freelance features writer for newspapers and magazines, and blogger at *OfficeMum.ie*.

One Click is her second novel. Her first book, *The Other Side of the Wall,* was shortlisted for the Kate O'Brien Award 2018.

Also by Andrea Mara

The Other Side of the Wall

Published by Poolbeg

To my mum. She's not any of the mothers in this book, but I think she'd have enjoyed all this.

Prologue

If I'd known what would happen to all of us, I would never have taken the picture. Was there even a decision? Or just an unconscious microsecond between seeing the woman and reaching for my phone. A whisper of a pause during which I could have uncurled my fingers. The uncurled fingers, the unflapped wings of the butterfly in the unrippled water.

But I did it. One small motion. Like the hose lying flat and lifeless on the ground, before the tap is turned. Just one twist, and the hose takes on a life of its own, spraying water into the sky and drowning everything in sight.

One small motion. Just one click.

LAUREN

Chapter 1

The woman is where she is every day. Her eyes closed, her face turned to the sun, and she has no idea I'm here. Turquoise waves lap around her feet and the low frame of her deckchair. Dark-red hair glints in the morning light and her book hangs loosely in her hand. It's Utopia wrapped up in a single square shot and I can't resist.

My phone is on silent, and there's no tell-tale click when I take the photo, but still she glances up. Does she know? She looks at me for a moment, then down to her book.

I turn and take some more shots, out to sea this time. My arms drop to my sides and I stand for a moment, breathing in the sea air, letting the babble of accents wash over me. Then a wave splashes across my feet and the spell is broken.

My wet trainers squelch on the sand on the way back to the campsite. I should run, but it's too hot now, and I'm tired. Or maybe old. Older than yesterday when I'm sure I ran for longer.

"*Caffè? Pasticcini?*" comes the familiar call from the kiosk.

"*Cappuccino, per favore,*" I say, feeling only slightly guilty that I don't have enough money with me to take pastries back to the girls. I'll drink my coffee on the walk back so they don't get cranky. Especially Rebecca, I think, picturing the raised-eyebrow look she's been perfecting since we arrived in Italy. The coffee is strong and hot as it hits the back of my throat, and the morning ritual is complete.

"Mum, did you bring us anything?" Rebecca asks as I walk up to the deck, not looking up from her phone. Her hand hovers absentmindedly over a plate of toast.

"Are you on Snapchat again? It's going to cost a fortune, Rebecca."

Now she looks up, and there's the raised eyebrow. "Did you bring us pastries?" she asks, and takes a bite of toast.

"Nope, I didn't have any money with me," I tell her. "Where's Ava?"

"Still in bed," she says, going back to her phone.

Pulling up a chair beside her, I scan through my photos. Fourteen taken this morning – the girls will have a field day. They never take photos of the sea, or anything that doesn't have a pouting human in the foreground, and they can't understand why I do. I stop when I get to the girl with the dark-red hair. There's something about her expression that radiates an easy indifference to the sunbathers and paddlers around her. The way the book hangs from her hand, the tilt of her wrist. Her upturned unlined face. The blush-coloured dress against nutmeg skin, a turquoise bracelet the only flash of colour. A sun goddess dressed up as a carefree millennial. Clicking into Instagram, I upload the photo. It doesn't need a filter – the girl on the beach speaks for herself. I type a caption.

All the envy on my morning run – this is #howIwishIspentmytwenties

I hit share, and put down my phone as Ava pads out of the mobile home and flops into a chair.

"I'm starving – did you bring us anything? Hey! Rebecca, did you eat all the bread?"

And just like that, I'm back to the real world of ever-hungry teens and bickering siblings.

It's after lunch before I check into Instagram. 354 likes already. I share it on Facebook and Twitter too, and Rebecca catches me smiling.

"Mum, are you obsessing over your blog again? *You're never off that phone*," she says, mimicking me.

"It's not my blog, it's Instagram, and I'm just checking it. *I haven't been on in hours actually*," I say, mimicking her back.

She leans in to have a look.

"Who's that in the pic?"

"I don't know – just a woman I saw on my run this morning. Doesn't she look so happy and chilled?"

"Yeah . . . does she know you took her photo though? Did you ask her?"

"No, but it's just a photo of the beach – people take pictures like that all the time. With strangers in them, I mean."

"Sure, but this picture is very much about her, and now you've put it online. Like, you can see her really clearly – she's not just one of the crowd. Ha – you're constantly telling us not to post photos without permission, and now you've just gone and done it!"

"Excuse me, it's not the same thing – photographers take pictures like this all the time. It's a candid shot – a study of a person having a moment in time, that's all." I'm aware of how defensive I sound and, watching my daughter do her perfect eyebrow-raise, I see she is too.

"Whatever, Mum, but maybe practise what you preach?" she says, picking up her plate and walking inside.

I can hear her telling Ava about it and I can picture the eye-rolls. Shutting out their voices, I look down again at my phone. It's just a good photo. That's all. And the woman will never know I took it. Even if she did, she'd surely be flattered. She's beautiful, and she has 354 likes now too.

At the pool, the girls jump straight in the water while I stay on a sunlounger with my book. It's odd to think of all those times I wished for this when they were small – now they don't need me any more, and I miss it. I watch as Rebecca stands under a fountain of water, shrieking that it's cold. Memories of a similar pool in another campsite surface – a much smaller Rebecca standing under a stream of water while Dave held her, the two of them laughing hysterically. I close my eyes to block it out but it doesn't work. Dave did all the holiday bookings – he was rubbish at lots of things, but great at finding just the right campsite in just the right part of France. That's why we're in Italy now – because I needed it to be different.

Still thinking about Dave, my eyes move across to the next pool and that's when I see her – the woman from the beach is lying on a lounger, reading her book. Shit. I had no idea she was staying on the campsite. Then again, what does it matter? She's hardly going to see the photo. I wonder where she's from? At the beach I assumed she was Italian, but now I'm not sure. I squint to see the name of her book but I can't. Did it show up in the photo? I click into Instagram to check. *The Goldfinch* by Donna Tartt – so she's an English-speaker, or at least someone who can read books in English. A splinter of unease digs into the pit of my stomach. Maybe I should take down the photo . . . But it has over 600 likes on Instagram now and almost a hundred between Facebook and Twitter. I'm being silly – it's not doing any harm. There are dozens of new comments about what people wish they'd done in their twenties too and, as I scroll, I spot one from Rebecca.

So much for 'don't post pics online without permission', Mum.

She's followed it with a smiley face but it still makes me defensive.

It's a candid shot of a beach, smarty-pants, I reply before scrolling on.

A message interrupts my browsing – Dave wants to know if he can let himself into the house to collect some more stuff. He's thinking of booking a week in the sun, he says. With Nadine, of course. Closing my eyes, I take some deep breaths and only start to type when I know I can say the right thing.

Of course, any time. Weather great here.

I hit send, and stuff my phone in my bag. My book is on the ground beside me but I don't feel like reading any more. How ironic, after all those years wishing I could do just this. I close my eyes.

The night-time humidity is a muggy blanket, and the only light on the deck is our candle, glowing in the centre of the table. Tonight's game is Pontoon, and Ava is winning. My wine is crisp despite the heat, but it won't be long before it's lukewarm – taking a deep swallow, I check my phone. The photo of the woman has been picked up by an entertainment website and shared on their Facebook page – they've asked their thousands of followers to post their own answers and photos with the hashtag #howIwishIspentmytwenties and they're doing so in droves, each one trying to outdo the last with funnier and pithier responses. They should have asked me first, but they do credit my blog name so I can't complain really. Strangers are tweeting me with their answers to the question, and notifications light up my phone every couple of seconds. Someone called Jess122 says I'm being presumptuous about millennials, and a user called Maxx wants to know if I got the woman's number. There's a tweet from a VIN saying the beach looks lovely and asking where we are, and another person called Sharon would like our campsite details so she can book for next year – I can't remember posting that we're on a campsite but maybe I did. EmmaB says she's in her twenties like the woman on the beach, but it's too late to do anything – she wants to go back to her teens.

I wonder if any of us mean it – would we change things if we could? Would I? I certainly got married too young. Twenty-four and barely out of college, with nothing seen of the world. Me the strait-laced psychology graduate, and Dave, the cliché: the handsome junior doctor who – more cliché – swept me off my feet. I had never met someone like him. He didn't care what people thought and he didn't take shit from anyone. I remember when I first took him home to meet Mum – I was so nervous about what he'd say or do. But he flipped like a light-switch as soon as she opened the front door – turning into this charming template of a perfect boyfriend. Less than a year later she walked me down the aisle and into Dave's arms, and ten months after that Ava came along. So would I change it? I look over at Ava, studying her hand of cards. Not if it meant changing the girls. But if I could have had those same children when I was older, then yes, maybe I would change how I spent my twenties – going straight from college to marriage to nappies wasn't how I expected things to go.

I shake my head and Rebecca looks up.

"Are you okay, Mum?"

"Yep, just thinking."

Rebecca touches my phone screen. "Wow, Mum, is that your beach photo on *TheDailyByte.ie* – oh my God, it's practically viral! What are you going to do if the woman finds out?"

I pull my phone away. "Oh come on, it's not a big deal, and she's hardly going to see it – she's probably Italian. I doubt she follows my blog or *The Daily Byte* somehow."

"She doesn't look Italian – Italians don't have red hair, do they? Ha, she's probably Irish! I'm just amazed at the double standards, Mum. You'd literally kill me if I did the same thing."

"That's a completely incorrect use of the word 'literally'," Ava tells her.

"I don't know . . . maybe not," I mutter, clicking back into Twitter.

The person called "VIN" has tweeted me a second time asking what the name of the beach is, and someone called Oliver says the woman looks older than twenty, completely missing the point. But most people are focused on giving their own suggestions about how they wish they'd spent their twenties. Beer, wine, and sun feature heavily. My Twitter friend MollyRants72 wishes she'd spent her twenties having her kids so she'd be out the other side now.

"It's not all it's cracked up to be," I reply, then feel guilty when I look at Ava and Rebecca.

CatherineW says she wishes she'd known she looked good, instead of worrying about losing weight – now she wants to look like she did in her twenties. This is all getting a bit serious, I think, replying to tell her she looks amazing. At least I assume she does – I've never met her in real life.

Then I see a third tweet from the account called "VIN". Three less friendly unpunctuated words this time:

Where are you

I click into it to look at the details. It's a new account – only one tweet so far – the question to me. No profile picture, no details at all. The display name is "VIN" and the underlying username below that is @Vin_H_O_Rus. Someone's initials? I must be staring because Rebecca notices.

"What's up, Mum, is something wrong?"

I put down my phone. "Nothing. Just an odd message."

Ava looks up now. "It's not that weird guy from last year again, is it? The one who was sending you the horrible 'I am watching you' messages? Leon?"

I shake my head. "No, God, nothing like that, love – don't worry. Leon is long gone. He got bored when I stopped replying. He's not back, I'm certain."

But I'm lying. Really, I'm not sure at all.

Chapter 2

There she is again, in the same deckchair in the shallow waves. I stop running to look out at the water and, although my phone is full of sea-blue photos, my finger swipes instinctively to the camera. Swivelling so that my back is to the sea, I stretch my arms to take a photo of myself. I'm usually cautious with selfies in case anyone from work sees one, but I'm pretty sure Lauren-the-runner in sunglasses and ponytail won't be identifiable as Lauren-the-psychologist with make-up and a carefully groomed bob. Imagine if Brian realised I have a blog – he'd be purple, and adamant it's against clinic policy. It isn't, I've checked the handbook. But still, I can see why clients might not like it if the person in whom they confide their innermost thoughts is also running a photography blog.

My phone vibrates as I close the camera – another Twitter notification, and from the same account as last night – VIN.

Ignoring me won't work. I can see you're in Venice – who is the woman in your photo?

The morning sun is beating down but suddenly I feel cold. '*Ignoring me won't work.*' That's exactly the kind of thing Leon used to say. Shit. Of course he's not gone away – why would he? '*Ignoring me won't work.*' I thought it did, but maybe he just found someone else to torment for a while. I hit the block option so he can't tweet me any more – something I should have done much

12

sooner first time round, wondering what 'VIN' means, and why Leon changed his name.

The narrow Venice streets are restless and bustling – busier this afternoon than during our first visit last week, and humidity cloaks us at every step. Rebecca says we should have stayed on the beach, but it seems daft to come all this way and only travel into the city once. We cross a tiny stone bridge and stop to look down over the water – more to get a breather than to see anything in particular. Lines of coloured shirts and backpacks stretch down the canal-side street, on to the next bridge and beyond, like a determined but slow-moving Chinese dragon dance. We watch for a while, resting our elbows on the stone parapet, then I get the girls to face me for a photo. On auto-pilot they smile and, just as I'm about to take it, a man crosses between us. He turns to face the camera when I press the button, as though posing with the girls, then walks on. Instinctively I laugh, though I'm not sure if I get the joke. The girls want to see the picture. The man is wearing a bright-red baseball cap and sunglasses and he's not smiling, though his head is inclined towards Rebecca, as if he's meant to be in the shot. Then Ava points out that he's wearing a Guinness T-shirt – probably an Irish tourist who spotted we were Irish too, she says, and decided to photobomb. It makes sense, though why he looks so serious I don't know. That's part of the joke, Ava says, shaking her head at me. I'm obviously too old for the joke. I want to crop him out of the photo before I share it on Instagram but the girls want to keep him in. There's no accounting for teen humour, nevertheless I do as I'm asked, then we slip back into the throngs of tourists weaving their way down the sweltering street.

At the next laneway we duck away from the canal in search of shade. It's not much cooler, but in the small square up ahead I can see an ice-cream café, which more than likely means air-conditioning. My phone buzzes as we shuffle behind a tour group – another tweet from VIN. How did he do that if I blocked him? It takes me a moment to spot that he's set up a completely new profile with a similar username, by adding a "1" at the end. @Vin_H_O_Rus1. I stop to open it.

Nice to be so close to you

My stomach lurches – what does that mean? I stand still as people jostle against me, my head swivelling left and right, but nobody is looking at me. My phone buzzes again.

I could almost smell you

Jesus, is he here?

Another tweet:

What's that perfume you're wearing?

A man bumps against me and I flinch – he mutters something under his breath and keeps moving. All around, tourists push their way towards the square and there's nobody standing still or watching me.

Another tweet pops up:

And nice to be so near to your daughter. Rebecca, is it?

Oh my God, where are the girls? I start pushing through the crowd, apologising as I force my way towards the square, until I see Ava standing outside the ice-cream shop. But there's no sign of Rebecca.

"Where's your sister?" I ask, half shouting when I get to her.

Ava looks confused. "Is she not with you?"

"No, I stopped for a minute, I didn't see where she went."

My eyes scour the crowd as it passes, looking for red curls.

"Mum, just ring her – there's no panic – she knows we're coming here, doesn't she?" Ava says, pointing into the café.

Of course, I just need to ring her. I take out my phone and find another message from VIN.

She's very pretty. I like her red hair.

Oh fuck. I think I'm going to throw up. My fingers rattle over the screen as I pull up Rebecca's number, but it goes straight to voicemail. I try again, and still the crowd trails past, oblivious to my rising panic. Again it goes to voicemail. Oh my God, where is she?

Two policemen come out of the restaurant next door.

"Excuse me, can you help?" I hurry over. "My daughter's missing!"

I show them her photo – the one I just took on the bridge.

"Does she have a phone? You can try to call her?" one of them asks in accented but perfect English.

"I tried but it's going to voicemail. And this man has been sending me messages." I pull up the VIN tweets. They look

14

confused. "I'm afraid he's here and that maybe he –" My voice breaks, swallowing the end of the sentence.

"*Mum!*" Ava is calling me.

I look behind me and see Rebecca standing beside her, outside the café.

"Rebecca, my God, where were you?" I march over, cross and relieved and foolish.

"Eh, in the toilet of the café? What's the panic?"

"But I phoned you – it went to voicemail?"

She shrugs. "I don't have any missed calls. The toilets are downstairs, probably out of coverage."

I check my phone – two more tweets have come in from VIN while I was searching for her.

She smells nice too.

I liked being in your photo on the bridge. It makes me feel closer to all of you.

Jesus. I pull up the photo again and look at the man in the baseball cap. VIN? He found us?

"Rebecca, did anyone speak to you? That man?"

"What man?"

"The man who stood into our picture on the bridge – did you see him again?"

"God, Mum, it was just a photobomb – people do stuff like that all the time."

Glancing behind me, I put my arms around the girls to herd them into the ice-cream café and we take a seat by the window so I can watch people going past. The girls babble about ice-cream flavours and I smile and nod but my eyes are on the crowd. Then I see him. The red baseball cap, the dark glasses, in among a group of tourists following a flag-wielding guide. Pushing back my stool, I dart outside and before I can stop to think about what I'm going to say, I squeeze my way through the tour group and grab the man by the elbow.

He yanks his arm away and jumps back, then starts yelling at me in Spanish.

"*Who are you?*" I yell back. "*Did you send me those messages?*"

He takes off his sunglasses and bewildered eyes stare at me. He backs away, jostling the woman behind him. She links arms with him, and asks him something in Spanish. Pointing at me, he shakes his head.

"*No hablo ingles*," he says to me.

"My husband doesn't speak English. I think you mix him with someone else?" the woman says, looking me up and down.

A small circle forms around me and suddenly I want to be anywhere but here – a frazzled, half-manic woman accusing strangers on a Venice street.

"But you were in my photo – on the bridge," I say to the man. "Have you been following me? Messaging me?"

He looks confused, and his wife says something to him in Spanish.

He laughs and replies to her.

"The photo was a joke," she says. "My husband is sorry if it offends you. He doesn't send you any messages. How would he do that?"

I don't think her husband is sorry but it's a moot point – it's clear he's not the person who's been tweeting me. With as much dignity as I can muster, I mumble an apology and turn back towards the café, ignoring the muttering and laughing behind me.

Ava and Rebecca stare open-mouthed when I return to our table and immediately want to know what it was about. I don't want to tell them about VIN, so I go for a watered-down version of the truth.

"I think someone back home saw the photo of you two with the guy on the bridge and thought it would be funny to message me pretending to be him."

The girls look confused.

"But it wasn't him," I continue. "He's a Spanish tourist with no idea what I was talking about. The messages are from someone playing a trick on me. Easy to do when you think about it. No big deal."

I smile to reassure them that I'm not losing it but, as I sit eating melted ice cream, still shaking from the encounter, I wonder if perhaps I am.

The girls are tired after the trip to Venice and there's no card game on the deck tonight – by ten they're in their rooms. I'm reading my book outside except I'm not really, I'm scrolling through Facebook. A tweet comes in from VIN.

Did you enjoy meeting me on the bridge? Or was it me? I guess you'll never know.

Then another:

Blocking me won't work by the way, I'm not going anywhere until you tell me about the woman on the beach. And perhaps we can have more fun in the meantime.

Jesus Christ. Could it be Leon, watching my holiday through what I post online? It doesn't sound like him though – not with the questions about the girl in the beach photo. Then again maybe that's just a sideshow and the main aim is to freak me out . . . God, it's all just speculation – I don't even know if it's him.

Right, block. He's gone.

I switch off my phone.

Chapter 3

She wasn't on the beach this morning and, unexpectedly, I missed her. She was like a cornerstone, with swimmers and walkers flowing around, while she stayed perfectly still, just being. The sea was as blue as it is every day but it failed to lift me – I'd slept badly, dreaming about Leon, and when I got up I argued with the girls over the mess in the mobile home. So, on my way back to the campsite, I stopped to pick up coffee and pastries. My mother would say I was feeling guilty. But it was worth it – the girls were happy, and the sugar and caffeine are giving me the lift I need.

Sitting on the deck, drinking the last of my coffee, I feel better. Then my phone vibrates, breaking the mood, and I know who it's going to be before I look. VIN with another new account, @Vin_H_O_Rus2. All he needs is a new email address each time and he can keep setting up accounts indefinitely. Christ.

You are obviously used to obsessing about yourself, but NEWSFLASH – not everything is about you. Who is the woman?

My mouth goes dry as I read the message a second time. This doesn't sound like Leon. Shit. I should never have posted the photo. My fingers race to press delete – from Instagram, from Facebook, from Twitter. It's too little, too late, and I know it. The irony catches me – how often have I drilled it into the girls – once you share something online, it's there forever. Deleting it afterwards is useless. But it feels better than doing nothing. I need to ask *TheDailyByte.ie* to take it down too, and while I'm searching for their contact details, another tweet comes in.

Deleting it is a waste of time – I saved the photo. It doesn't change anything, I'm not going away until you tell me who she is.

What the hell does he want with the woman in the photo – does he know her? But then why is he asking me about her? I block him again but I already know he'll be back.

Ava and Rebecca want to go to the beach for the afternoon. I try to talk them out of it – the sun is hotter than it has been, and they've both got Dave's fair skin. But they insist, and tell me that's what sun cream is for.

My phone rings as we're about to leave, shrill in the quiet afternoon air. Work. Great. I consider not answering but it'll hang over me all afternoon if I don't. Ignoring the look Ava's giving me, I pick up.

"Lauren, it's Brian. I'm sorry to call you on holidays but I need you to do a quick interview with a journalist about the impact of redundancy on mental health and everyone else is too busy. You're very good with these things – she'll call you at 3 o'clock our time. So that's what – an hour later or an hour earlier wherever you are?"

Wow, thanks for working that out for me, I want to say. But I don't.

"I'm just about to head out with the girls – maybe someone else can do it, once all the appointments are done?"

"Sorry, I wouldn't ask if I had someone else – we're all stretched at the moment while you're on leave. And we need to take any opportunity we can to get Steps to Wellness a mention in the media – it's all about the clinic's profile. Thanks, Lauren, I appreciate it."

I glance up at Ava. She's glaring at me and tapping her foot.

"Can you give me the journalist's details and I'll call her this evening when I'm free?"

There's a hint of petulance when he passes me her number, as though I'm putting him out and not the other way around.

"And listen, we may need to look at your hours, Lauren. It's difficult to manage the clinic when you're working shorter days than everyone else. I'm worried about *you* more than anything – it must be hard to fit everything in, and you need to focus on self-care too. So we'll talk when you're back."

Way to ruin a holiday, thanks, Brian. I force a smile into my voice. "I'm sure I can make it work – I was thinking of taking my paperwork home with me at night – sure we'll chat when I'm back." I hang up before he can sound any more death knells.

Ava is still glaring. "Mum, don't be such a wuss – just tell him you're on holidays and can't do the call."

"It's fine, I don't mind chatting to journalists," I tell her, stuffing a beach towel into my bag.

"But not on your holidays – you're meant to be spending time with us!"

I manage to suppress what I really want to say about dealing with a sulky child as well as a sulky boss, and instead promise her it's the one and only work-call I'll do.

My phone beeps again but I know better than to check it and, by the time we get to the beach, Ava has forgotten she was cross. The two of them stretch out, determined to tan, Rebecca with a book on mythology and Ava with something depressingly dystopian.

On any other day, I'd lie down too, but unease keeps me upright, my eyes combing the umbrellas and sunbathers that line the sand in higgledy-piggledy rows. Something catches my eye – the girl from the photograph, sitting in a deckchair just a little to my left. Her hair glints in the late-afternoon sun and a pale-blue sundress sets off her tan. In a sea of bikinis she looks apart. I must be staring – she glances over. Turning away, I rummage in my bag for my book but instead my hand closes around my phone. Two emails, a missed call from my mother, and two tweets, both from a new VIN account.

You're so self-obsessed. I don't actually care about you. Who is the woman?

And another:

I'm not going anywhere. I'll see you very soon.

I look over at the girl, then back down at my phone, and start to feel sick.

Chapter 4

In the end, the call with the journalist is easy. I phone her while the girls are getting ready to go out and we bond over a shared love of Montepulciano when I tell her I'm in Italy – a wine neither of us can pronounce, but both of us like to drink. I give her what she needs for her article and she says it reminds her of her own redundancy and how anxious she felt, even though her partner had a good job. Not for the first time since Dave left, the fear of losing my job hits. I never thought like this before we broke up – even in the downturn, we were fine. People always need doctors. Not so much psychologists in private practice, but it didn't matter because Dave was there. And then he wasn't.

My stomach is rumbling as I say goodbye but the girls are still getting ready. Calling inside to tell them to hurry up, I wait on the deck, watching barbecues light up all around as dusk falls. My phone buzzes. Another Twitter notification. The now familiar dread sets in as I open it.

Listen you spoilt, self-obsessed narcissist, this isn't about you. Tell me where you are.

Jesus. My cheeks burn as though I've been slapped, and though I know better than to engage with trolls, my fingers start to tap out a reply. Maybe I can make it stop if I explain.

I don't know her. She's a stranger. I haven't seen her since.

The response is immediate.

I know you've seen her before – she's in the background of photos from another day.

Shit. Seriously? I scroll back through my beach photos and spot her in two pictures from earlier in the week. She's much further in the distance, just another person on the beach, but once you know what she looks like, it's clear it's her.

I type another reply.

It still doesn't mean I know her. She's a stranger.

He comes straight back.

Ask her for her surname and where she's from.

What the hell is this?

I'm not asking her anything. Why would I do that? Who are you?

The answer comes in seconds:

Just do it.

Jesus Christ. I take a screenshot of the tweets and block him again, if only to get a break until the next account is opened. An uncomfortable question takes root – do I need to find the woman from the photo and tell her what's happening?

The girls come out bickering about make-up and don't notice I'm upset, and I'm grateful for the mundanity as we set off for the restaurant. The sky is navy by the time we get there, and candles glow on the tables. We sit outside – Irish enough to choose the still-humid outdoors over air conditioning. White tablecloths give a hint of luxury, but we've eaten here most nights – we know they're disposable. We know the menu off by heart too though the girls still take their time to read it. I watch their faces in the candlelight. The dark circles under Ava's eyes have faded, and Rebecca's normally pale face has colour.

"Can you believe we've only one night left after this?" I say, looking around for someone to take our order. "Then it's back to school in another week and a half."

Ava's mouth opens in protest. "Ah come on, Mum, don't mention school!"

"Sorry, I won't bring it up again. School, I mean. I won't bring up school again."

Ava shakes her head. I'm not funny. I roll my eyes at Rebecca but she doesn't react.

"Rebecca, are you okay?"

A forced smile greets me, then she's saved by a harassed-looking waiter coming to take our order. I ask for a glass of wine, and Ava does a wonderfully casual "I'll have the same" nod at the waiter. He looks confused when I tell him to ignore her and indeed, moments later, he drops two glasses of wine to us before rushing to take another order. Ava is delighted but I pull both glasses over to my place setting.

"No chance," I tell her.

The food takes longer than usual to arrive and the wine is going to my head – I'm only half listening to the conversation about some band both girls like. When my phone buzzes, I'm not surprised to see another VIN tweet.

You're running out of time. Find her, get me her name, and where she's from.

I screenshot again and wonder if I need to file some kind of report with the police. How would I even do it from here? I try googling but my brain is fuzzy with wine.

"Mum, are you okay?" Ava asks.

"Yes . . . I'm just going to go to the bathroom."

I make my way between the tables towards the restaurant toilets, feeling dizzy and slightly sick. Inside, shrill white walls greet me and the smell of air freshener makes my stomach turn. Jesus, I need to pull myself together. Deep breaths. Three stall doors hang open, but I don't move. I'm still leaning against the door when suddenly I'm pushed forward. The unexpected movement shocks me but it's just someone trying to come into the bathroom. I turn to apologise, and it's her.

She looks at me, dark-brown eyes appraising me, at odds with her auburn hair, an interested, slightly amused look on her face.

"That's all right," she says, in an unmistakable American accent, and moves to a sink. "Chicken wings," she says then, turning back to me, holding up her hands.

I don't know what she means.

"I should really order Italian when I'm here, but I can't resist the chicken wings," she says, putting her hands under the tap.

The water rushes down over them and I'm oddly transfixed as she rubs them together in the stream. Her red-and-white-striped cropped vest looks very like the one I wouldn't let Rebecca buy in Top Shop before we left. My mother always says red-haired people can't wear red, though that's not why I wouldn't buy it for Rebecca. The woman shakes her hands in the sink and pulls a lipstick out of an unseen pocket in her jeans. Looking in the mirror, she traces the cherry-red colour around her lips then pauses and turns again to me.

"Are you okay?" she asks.

I nod but don't say anything.

"Are you here with anyone? Do you want to sit down?" She steps towards me. "You look very pale."

There's a wooden chair against the wall, and she takes me by the arm to lead me to it. I sink down, wishing I'd eaten some of the breadsticks on the table before drinking two glasses of wine. But it's not just the wine, I know what I need to do.

"You don't know me, but there's something I have to tell you."

She looks only mildly curious. I imagine she thinks I'm slightly touched. But I've started now.

"I take photos on the beach when I go for a run every morning and, a few days ago, you were in one of my photos."

Now she looks more interested.

"And . . . I posted it on Instagram."

She shrugs, and in a way I can't explain the shrug reminds me of a mermaid.

"No big deal, I don't mind. I have been a prolific Instagrammer in my time."

"It's just that it went a bit viral and then I started getting a lot of comments."

"Viral? Why, what kind of photo was it?"

"Well, not properly viral, but I have a photography blog and a big social media following, and people really liked the photo and then a media site picked it up too. Your chair was in the shallow waves, you had your eyes closed, enjoying the sun. I hashtagged it with 'how I wish I spent my twenties' and it got a lot of interest. People started sharing their own photos too."

She's staring at me now and I can't work out what she's thinking.

"Right. What's your blog?"

"It's called Le Photo. The 'Le' is a play on my initials – Lauren Elliot. So it sounds French, but it's not. I'm Irish."

"No way! I'm from the United States but living in Ireland right now. Long story, best served with tequila. What part are you from?"

Oh God, so much for assuming she was an Italian I'd never see again.

"I'm in South Dublin. Monkstown."

"Oh sure, I've heard of it. I live in Dublin city, on Aungier Street. Do you know it?"

I nod. She pronounces it "On-jeer" street instead of "Ain-jer".

"It's a tiny ground-floor apartment not worth what I pay in rent but it's in Lafayette House." She stops, waiting for me to understand, but I just look blankly at her. "Oh, you don't know it? It's this beautiful period building at the end of the block, and really close to everything, so I suck it up on the extortionate rent. You're here on vacation, I guess?"

"Yes, I'm here with my two daughters. My husband and I just split up and I thought a holiday would be good for us, so here we are." I have literally no idea what prompted me to tell her my life story.

"Sorry to hear that. But glad you're enjoying your trip. And don't worry about the photo. Are you feeling any better now? Should I get your daughters for you?"

I shake my head. "No thanks, I'm fine. I'll go back out to them now." I take a deep breath. I have to tell her about the messages. "It's just I've been getting some weird comments. I thought you should know." Even as I speak I feel like a hypocrite. It's clear I'm only telling her because we met like this.

"Oh right. What was it – the usual gross, lewd comments?"

I shake my head and hold up my phone to her.

"No, it's someone who wants to know where we are, and what your name is. And the messages are quite intimidating. I was half-thinking about contacting the guards but that seems over the top . . ."

"The who?"

"Sorry, I mean the police – the Gardaí – we call them guards."

Taking my phone, she screws up her eyes to read the latest tweet.

"Hmm, I don't know anyone called VIN," she says.

"Take a look at the username too – do you know anyone with the initials H. O. Rus? Or maybe it's O'Rus like some version of an Irish name?"

"No, I can't think of anyone," she says, handing it back. "It's all a bit odd but I guess it'll taper off when he gets bored?" She opens the bathroom door.

I smile for the first time since meeting her, and stand up to follow her out.

"You're right – if I ignore him, he'll go away. But sorry for putting up the photo – I did take it down in the meantime."

She holds the door to let me out and shrugs. "That's okay. Was it a nice picture? Do you still have it on your camera roll?"

I nod and pull it up for her.

"Hey, I like that! You're good at this. Would you send me a copy?"

I nod, and she types her number into my phone, then presses the call button.

"There you go, you have my number in your phone log now – just send me the photo on that. I'm on WhatsApp if you want to do it that way. I'm Cleo by the way. Cleo Holloway."

This isn't how I pictured the conversation going, and relief floats around me in a giddy haze as I say goodbye and make my way back to the table, where the food has finally, thankfully, arrived.

Chapter 5

On Friday, the girls want to do everything one last time – a final swim, one more ice cream, and dinner in their favourite restaurant. I've been staying offline all day, but just before dinner I check my phone. There's nothing from VIN, just a text from my mother asking what time our flight arrives tomorrow – a highly irrelevant question since she lives in West Cork and won't be anywhere near Dublin – and an email from Brian checking that I'm back in work on Monday. Hello, real world. It's after five at home and Brian will be gone, but I reply anyway.

An email pings back a couple of minutes later – Brian's still there. Jonathan Oliver has been looking for me, he says, and it took him a while to get him off the phone. Christ. That's my last bit of holiday peace well and truly dismantled. Brian says Jonathan insisted on booking an appointment with me on Monday at three, and wouldn't take no for an answer.

Fantastic. Brian knows well I finish at three and, if it was any other client, he'd say no. But because he's intimidated by Jonathan, I'm stuck working extra hours. My reply says exactly that, but I delete it. In any given week, about a third of the emails I write to Brian end up deleted. Imagine if some hackers ever released all the deleted draft emails in the world. I'd be so screwed. And fired.

I rewrite it, keeping it brief. Jonathan has now managed to

bookend my holiday, and not in a good way. He was my last client the day before we flew out here, and sent me home with a throbbing headache. I actually have no idea why he comes to therapy at all – he refuses to open up about anything, but instead dances around every conversation, dropping tantalising crumbs about his ex-wife, then pulling away again. Or, at least, I think I'm supposed to find them tantalising. And that day was the worst to date; every time I asked a question, he turned it back on me, getting more and more personal – asking about my husband with a nod to my wedding ring, and asking if I have children. When I didn't answer, he said he knew I didn't have children, because I still had a "fine, tight figure" for someone my age. It wasn't just the words, it was his eyes, crawling all over me as he spoke. Eyes like a fish. Susan on reception thinks he's handsome but I can't see it at all. Fisheye Jonathan. That's what I call him, but only in my head. Outwardly, I'm the polished professional – warm, but not too warm; an occasional smile, but I'm not here to smile – I'm here to help you fix yourself. That's the message I give my clients, and most of the time it works well. But not with Jonathan. Sometimes I think he sees through my mask and is laughing at me, but mostly I think he's too caught up in his own world to have any grasp of what I'm saying.

Ava comes out on deck to see if I'm ready to go for dinner, pulling me out of my thoughts.

"Mum! You're not even dressed – come on!"

I look down at my shorts and vest top. "Am I not fine like this?"

"Well, I don't mind, but what if one of your Instagram followers saw you?"

My children think they're hilarious. Well, actually, they think the fact that their mother has a blog is hilarious. Blogs are dead, they tell me. So last century. Why can't I just embarrass them on Facebook like their friends' parents do, they wonder. I am very good at ignoring my children, but in this instance Ava is right – I'm not really a shorts-and-vest-top-to-the-restaurant person. Hauling myself off the chair, I go inside to shower.

The girls' insistence on doing everything one last time includes stopping in to check out the Friday-night entertainment in the bar. A lone guitarist sings Ed Sheeran songs to an audience more intent on knocking back cheap Chianti than listening to ballads, but the atmosphere is warm and buzzy, and I don't mind being here. Ava and Rebecca get chatting to a group of English kids and soon they're moving towards the pool table. Ava sends me a questioning look, and I wave her away. I'm perfectly happy in my own company. Tables all around are full of couples and families, some singing along, most chatting, faces lit up by candles in old spirit bottles. Mine is Baileys – I pick at the candle wax, letting the music and the wine wash over me.

A chair scrapes against the tiled floor and when I look up Cleo is sitting opposite me.

"Hey, how're you doing? Are you here on your own?" she asks.

I nod towards the pool table where Ava and Rebecca are posing for a boy taking a photo. "My daughters are over there with some people much cooler than me. Are you here with anyone?"

She shakes her head and her hair flows like a mane around her shoulders. Tonight she's wearing a floaty jade-green dress – my mother would approve. If she could, my mother would have me dress Rebecca in green and only green since the first moment we realised we had a red-haired child. Though she might not approve of the turquoise-blue bracelet Cleo is wearing, its silver elephant charm rattling against the beads. *Blue and green must never be seen*" is another of my mother's top fashion tips.

"Yes, all alone tonight," Cleo says. "Well, I'm travelling alone, but I did meet a nice guy from Sweden who kept me company the last few evenings. He's gone back to Stockholm. I say Stockholm, but actually I've no idea where he was from. He was beautiful . . . Hey, you still wear your ring, I see?" She points at my finger.

My hand covers it instinctively. "I know. It's silly."

She shrugs. She shrugs a lot, but it suits her.

"I haven't told many people about the split, so I keep the ring on."

Eyebrows arch at me. "Wow. Why's that?"

A sip of wine slows my answer. "I suppose I'm just not ready to announce to everyone what a failure I am."

Cleo laughs. I don't know what's funny about a marriage break-up. Maybe it's an age thing – she can't be more than twenty-nine or thirty. Or an American thing. I guess lots of people over there split up and I sound a bit dramatic

29

"Look, sorry, I don't mean to make fun. It just makes no sense to me. Why not tell people and start looking forward, moving on? It's not a failure, it's just life. Relationships break up all the time. Believe me, I know all about that."

My eye drops to her ring finger, but there's no gold band. Could she be married and divorced at such a young age? I must seem archaic to her.

"Oh, it's not that I think everyone whose marriage breaks up is a failure. It's just so far removed from how I pictured my own life panning out and I'm still wondering what I could have done differently."

Cleo signals to the waiter for another glass of wine and asks what mine is. My protestations are ignored, and she points out that my daughters are very happily hanging out with their new friends and unlikely to be interested in going home yet. Oh feck it, another glass of wine won't kill me.

"So let's see a photo of him," she says, once the wine arrives.

"Who?"

"Your husband."

Why she wants to see him I have no idea, but I pull up a photo on my phone and hand it to her. She studies it for a moment, then hands it back.

"You are so far out of his league, you know that, right?"

I laugh and then choke a little on my wine.

"Seriously! You are a beautiful woman. How old are you?"

I'm so taken aback by her directness I don't even consider not answering. "Forty."

"Wow, you look amazing for forty. Your husband, not so much. He's older than you, right?"

"Only by five years. I think he looks pretty good for his age . . ."

"Nah, he looks like a man who enjoys his wine and steak too much – you can tell by his skin and his eyes. You take good care of yourself, I can see that. You'll meet someone new."

"Jesus, I'm not looking to meet anyone new! I'm a forty-year-old mother of two teens with a busy job, a falling-down house, and a time-consuming mother. Meeting someone new is the last thing on my mind."

She swirls her drink, staring at me as she does. It's awkward and

I drop my gaze to her wine, wondering if it's going to spill over the side. But Cleo doesn't seem like a person who ever spills wine.

"Don't sell yourself short. I suspect you already have, so maybe don't do it again."

My mother is the only person I know who is this direct, but somehow with Cleo it doesn't make me want to tear my hair out. In fact, I almost believe her. Touching my phone screen, I make the photo of Dave appear again. Maybe he has gone to seed a little.

"Anyway, enough about me," I say out loud. "What has you living in Ireland?"

"Oh, I got restless in New York, and there may have been a spot of boy trouble." She does one of her shrugs. Mermaid shrugs. "I like it there, people just leave you to do your thing."

"From New York to Dublin – that must be a culture shock. What do you do? For work, I mean?"

"This and that. A bit of bar-tending, some graphic design. I manage social media for a couple of restaurants near where I live too. It's cool – nothing that ties me to an office five days a week, you know? I'd hate that. What do you do?"

"Well, I guess I'm tied to an office five days a week."

She grins. "Oh sure, each to their own – what kind of office?"

"I'm a counselling psychologist, so basically I spend most of my day with clients. It could be bereavement, work-related anxiety, anger management – whatever comes my way really."

She cocks her head to one side and looks at me over the top of her wineglass. "I can totally picture you doing that. I bet you're like this really serious, professional therapist on the outside, and inside you want to scream at your clients sometimes, right?"

I'm about to say no, then I laugh. "Yeah, sometimes I want to fucking *throw* things at them."

She laughs now too, loudly, throwing back her head.

Ava looks over, and I realise it's close to eleven, and we still have to finish packing. The protests I'm expecting don't materialise when I call time; they say goodbye to their new friends without fuss. They're all following each other on Snapchat and Instagram they tell me, so it's not like really saying goodbye. Right so, maybe I'll ask Cleo if she's on Snapchat, I tell them. That earns me eye-rolls. To their relief, it's one social media platform I haven't gone near

31

and no matter how often they tell me how it works, it makes absolutely no sense to me. Why would you bother posting a photo that disappears after twenty-four hours?

Back at the table, Cleo is watching the singer. Somehow I feel bad leaving her there to walk home on her own, but that's silly – she's travelling alone so must do that every night. Or at least when she's not with beautiful men who may or may not be from Stockholm.

"We're going to head off now, we're flying home in the morning," I tell her, not sure whether we're at the hugging stage or not.

She stays in her seat.

"Well, it was nice meeting you, and who knows, maybe we'll bump into each other in Dublin some time."

"Exactly!" I say, but I suspect we don't run in quite the same circles.

I wave as I follow the girls out of the bar and she watches me, still with that half-smile and I wonder if I asked her now would she even remember my name.

It's cooler on the deck tonight and the candle flickers in an unfamiliar breeze. Ava and Rebecca are talking online to their friends from the bar but soon decide it's too cold to sit out. I tell them to go to bed, but I don't take my own advice – I want to eke out the last few minutes of the holiday all on my own on the deck. Pulling my cardigan tighter, I take a sip of my wine and sit back. It's after midnight and, apart from the chirping of crickets, there isn't a sound. I don't want to think about what's ahead, about Dave and Brian and Jonathan Oliver, I just want to enjoy this peace and think about nothing at all.

Then, as it always does, my phone breaks the silence. The noise seems louder than usual, and my hand fumbles when I turn over the phone. The little @ symbol at the top tells me it's Twitter and my heart sinks. I think about ignoring it but my fingers move to do otherwise.

I can see you

Just four little words, but my blood runs cold. I pull my cardigan closer, scanning the darkness, and instinctively I lift my feet up onto the chair. I know I should go inside but I can't move. Everything is heightened, and I can hear nothing beyond blood rushing in my ears. In my head, a voice tells me to get up, walk inside, and lock the door, but still I can't move. I jump when my phone buzzes a second time.

I see you, sitting on your deck in the dark

I'm shaking now and freezing cold and I know I have to go inside. Holding my phone, I move to get off the chair but somehow my foot gets caught between the slats and I land on the deck, stunned and sore. Without stopping, I crawl to the door of the mobile home and reach up to yank it open. Pulling it behind me once inside, I turn the key and pull the curtain, then run to check on the girls. They're both asleep. Back in the kitchen, I sink to the floor, trying to slow my breathing.

Jesus Christ. That can't have just happened, can it? I look at my phone, waiting for the next message, listening for noises outside. But there's nothing. No tweets, no footsteps. I pull myself up to standing and put my hand through the gap in the curtains to check the door is locked. I don't want to look outside. I switch on the porch light and the kitchen light, and check the girls again, and all the windows.

In my own room, I lie on the bed and wait for another message but nothing comes and eventually I pull the blanket over me and fall into a fitful, jangled sleep.

Chapter 6

The flurry of the journey home pushes the VIN messages to the back of my mind and, by the time we arrive in Monkstown, it all seems like a surreal bad dream. And it's really, really good to be back inside our house. Well, for about ten minutes, then we discover the radiator in the spare room has leaked on the carpet. Sometimes I'm surprised the house is still standing at all – loose floorboards, cracked ceilings, and a hunk of plaster missing from the kitchen wall. We had such plans when we first moved in – it had everything going for it – a Georgian mid-terrace with high ceilings and bay windows, huge rooms and lots of light. I was the one who held back about buying it, worried it was too big and too expensive, but as always Dave swept me along. And I couldn't help getting caught up in the excitement – the pale yellow outside walls, the gravel path and the granite steps up to the raincloud-blue front door. The hallway with its glittering chandelier and black-and-white tiled floor. The wide stairs, up to the bedrooms, and the narrower one, down to the basement. Sure, it needed work, but we'd get there he said. And here we are, in a house that looks just as it did fifteen years ago, only more faded, and no Dave.

The unopened letters on the kitchen table stare up at me, their plastic windows announcing nothing good. They can wait. Instead I shout up to the girls that I'm going out to pick up dinner. Bracing myself as I open the front door, I check to make sure there's nobody going in or out of Nadine's, then rush down the steps to my car, frustrated again at the unfairness. Of all the people he had to run off with, how could he end up living two doors from us? Well, that's exactly how, I suppose: she was near to hand. All those dinner parties, all the barbecues, all the popping in and out of one another's houses to borrow hedge trimmers or fix radiators or sneak upstairs for a quick shag. And now he thinks it's fantastic he's living so close to us – for the girls, he says. For fuck's sake is what I say, though only when no-one is listening.

The rest of the neighbours fall into two camps: the ones who've taken my side and are therefore just about civil to Dave and Nadine, and the ones who are carrying on as normal, afraid to get involved. And apart from Clare next door, nobody says anything about it to me. We chat about the weather, the kids' school, the pothole at the end of the street, but never about the fact that two months ago my husband walked out of my house and moved in with our neighbour. If it wasn't for Clare, I'd go insane.

My mother calls just as I put the key in the ignition. I start to tell her about the holiday but she cuts me off – she wants to know if we've seen Dave yet. She's certain that this is a mid-life crisis and we'll be back together any day now.

"People from our family don't get divorced," she says. "You muddle through, Lauren – marriage isn't meant to be easy. Your dad wasn't always easy, God rest him, but we got on with it."

"I was perfectly happy to muddle through," I tell her, "but it's pretty hard to do without a husband there to muddle with me. Mum, Dave is gone. We need to get used to it."

There's a sharp intake of breath, then silence. Is she crying? I don't think I've ever heard her cry.

But her voice is steady when she replies. "I see. Well, you never know what might happen when he gets tired of that woman. Don't let yourself go in the meantime, Lauren, that's the worst thing you could do."

Sure, Mum, that's the worst thing I could do. Jumping off a cliff or running away would be fine, but for the love of God don't gain a few pounds or stop wearing lipstick.

"Right. I'll give you a call during the week," I tell her,

35

disconnecting and resisting the impulse to bang my head on the steering wheel.

When I look up, they're there. Dave and Nadine, carrying shopping up the steps to her front door. I watch her rummaging in her bag for her keys, her blonde bob swishing forward as she dips her head. She's the same height as him, I realise. Dave hates that he's not tall – I think it's one of the things he always liked about me – I'm smaller than him. Even as I watch, he pulls himself up straighter, conscious of her height. Ha. I bet she doesn't wear heels any more.

She's still searching for keys and he loops his arm around her waist, kissing the back of her neck. Slinking lower in my seat, I look away. Only when they're inside do I start the car, wishing for the millionth time that he'd found somewhere further to stray.

By eleven, Ava is asleep but, when I put my head around her door, Rebecca is lying in bed reading. I nudge her and she slides across on her belly to let me lie down beside her, but doesn't look up from her book.

"What are you reading?" I ask.

She flips the cover up to show me – a book on Greek mythology, her current obsession. Last month it was the Romans. Thank God for the library or I'd be broke.

"How does it feel to be home?" I try.

"It's fine," she says, turning a page.

"Was it strange calling down to your dad this evening after being away?"

"Not really."

"I know it's weird that we were away without him but you'll get used to it, I promise." I reach out to rub her back.

She turns another page. "It's fine, Mum. I'm not a kid. I get it."

I change the subject again. "Are you looking forward to starting second year? Are you going to meet up with the girls before you go back?"

She doesn't reply but I feel her shoulders tense under my hand.

"Is everything okay?"

"Everything's fine. Mum, I'm just really trying to concentrate on my book, okay?"

I kiss her cheek and roll back off her bed. "All right. Don't stay up too late reading though – we have to get back on track before school starts."

Nothing. I leave her, wistful for the days when she always wanted just one more story.

Downstairs, it's just me and TV I don't want to watch and a bottle of red from Venice. I switch the TV on for comfort and open the wine, then click into Twitter and start scrolling. There are all sorts of conversations going on but I'm late to the party and don't feel like jumping in. I look for my usual online buddies – MollyRants72, CatherineW, AnnaRose and LillGalwayGirl but none of them are around. That's the downside of Twitter friends – you never know when they might all disappear into the real world. There's nothing on TV to distract me either – after a redundant flick through the channels, I scroll back through Twitter, and suddenly I feel lonelier than any other time in my entire life. Tears threaten and I don't try to stop them; I'm just too bloody tired of pretending. I need something to make me feel better but I can't even think what to do. Chocolate won't help – I still can't shift the 5lbs I put on at Christmas and I'm starting to think this is not Christmas, this is forty. I get off the couch and walk behind it to look in the mirror. Red-rimmed eyes, drippy mascara, pale cheeks. Not too many creases on my forehead but they're coming. Stepping closer to the mirror, I examine the fine lines around my eyes. The cracks are literally starting to show.

I can hear my mother's voice now: you spent too much time in the sun, the damage is done. And as for drinking my glass of wine – she'd have a field day with that. Never drink on your own, she always says, it's a slippery slope.

Cheers, Mum, I think, sitting back down on the couch – that's from me and all the other single people out there who shouldn't have wine at home ever if we follow your logic. Although much as she drives me crazy, I wouldn't hate it if she was here now, sitting across from me prattling on. It's so bloody quiet. Pitch dark outside, and the only sounds are the creaks the house makes all night long. It's cold too, but I'm being cautious about heating bills, and the lack of insulation is bitingly evident. I pull a blanket off the back of the couch to wrap it around my knees. Oh my God, this is pathetic – huddled on my couch under a blanket, drinking my wine, tears rolling down my face, all on my own.

And then finally my phone chirps up – there's someone to talk to after all. But it's not Molly or Catherine or Anna or Lill – it's VIN.

I freeze, staring at the screen.

All good in that old house of yours? I'm not gone away, you know. I'm never going away.

Chapter 7

Just before three, Brian sticks his head around my office door.

"Oh, good, you're back. You've been missed! You're not going away again this year, are you?"

I smile and shake my head even though part of me wants to throw my stapler at him. I bet he doesn't begrudge annual leave to any of the others. But because I don't work full-time hours, he seems to think I shouldn't get holidays at all. The drama when I put in for two weeks – like I'd asked for a year's paid leave. Humming and hawing, stroking his wispy little beard, studying me with his tiny, piggish eyes. And now I'm being punished, via a three o'clock session with Jonathan.

"No, not going anywhere, and straight back into it here." I nod at my laptop screen. "Just getting some notes done before my next appointment."

"Oh, Mr Oliver's here already, I'll get him for you," Brian says, with a glint of satisfaction, and seconds later he's ushering Jonathan in and closing the door behind him.

Deep inside I sigh, then plaster on what I hope is a welcoming smile as I gesture for him to sit, and walk around to take the seat opposite him.

The chairs are Brian's idea of what should be in a therapist's room – oatmeal in colour, bland, utterly free of any kind of

39

personality. They're too low and too deep, so I can't sit back properly – I end up perching on the edge, which probably doesn't put clients at ease. I tried asking for new chairs once, but Brian just laughed. He also laughed when I asked if we could paint the walls something other than stark white, but I've since managed to warm them up with paintings I brought from home. I glance up at my favourite – a small print of the bandstand on Dún Laoghaire Pier – and get ready to do battle with Jonathan.

"You were away," he says, and it sounds accusatory.

"I was, yes, on annual leave, but I'm back now. How are you, Jonathan?"

"Who did you go with? Your husband?" he asks, pulling up the knees of his suit trousers so he can lean forward.

His suits always look expensive, and at odds with his boyish features – he's tall, but when he's sitting down he looks like a little boy who's raided his father's wardrobe.

"Jonathan, as we've discussed in the past, we need our sessions to be about you. How have you been feeling over the last two weeks?"

He locks his eyes on mine and holds my gaze for longer than is comfortable, his expression unreadable. I shift in the seat and tug my dress down over my knees.

Finally he shrugs. "Not great, to be honest. It was tough missing therapy. I thought about Sorcha a lot."

"What kind of thoughts?" I ask.

"About the day she told me she was leaving. Wondering what she's doing now. With him."

The parallels with my own life are not lost on me.

"And how did that make you feel?"

His voice is tight when he answers. "Angry. When I think of his hands all over her, I want to kill him. Both of them. In my head sometimes I stab them, over and over." His breath is coming faster now and his cheeks are mottled red.

I'm trying to keep my expression neutral but he must see something there. His shoulders go down and he barks a laugh.

"Jesus, your face. I'm joking! I'm not a psycho. Though if I was having mad thoughts, you couldn't tell anyone, could you?"

"Anything we discuss here is confidential, of course."

He grins at that and I squirm. My eyes go discreetly to the clock on the wall behind him. It's only ten past three. Jesus.

I spend the next thirty minutes trying to draw him out about his ex-wife, and he spends most of that time skirting my questions, going silent for periods of time, then diving back in with something dramatic about what he wants to do to Sorcha and her new boyfriend. He's baiting me, but I do a reasonable job of staying neutral. When I tell him time is up, he brings up the holiday again.

"So where did you go anyway? Somewhere hot, I bet?"

"Yes, hot and sunny – it was lovely, thanks. Now, can you ask Susan to book –"

"Italy is lovely this time of year."

"I'm sorry?"

"I said Italy is lovely this time of year. Particularly Venice."

My mouth is open but I can't think of anything to say as he gets up to leave.

When the door closes, I stand stock still, trying to order the thoughts that are barrelling through my brain. How did he know we were in Italy? Does he have something to do with the VIN messages? I'm careful with clients; I never reveal personal information, and particularly with someone like Jonathan who makes boundary-crossing a recreational sport. Could Susan have said it, when Jonathan tried to book a session?

On my way out, I ask Susan. She shakes her head and looks a little put out – of course she wouldn't tell a client where I was on my holidays. I should have known that. But she and I did have a chat about whether or not there are mosquitoes in Italy, and maybe Jonathan overheard that, or maybe he spotted the Venice travel guide in my handbag. Or could he have seen my photos online – does he know I'm behind the LePhoto blog? I need to be more careful.

When Dave calls that evening to pick up some paperwork, suddenly, more than anything, I need someone to talk to, and I invite him in for coffee. He glances to his left – checking to see if Nadine is watching? – and steps in.

We sit at the kitchen table, both of us gravitating instinctively to our own chairs, and I ask him about work. The new registrar is an idiot, he says, and today he mixed up two patients who were both called Anne Wilson. Someone could have been killed if a nurse hadn't spotted the mistake. Then Dave remembers doing something very similar when he was a reg and starts to laugh. He always had a great ability to laugh at himself. He asks me about my day, so I tell him about Jonathan and his Italy reference, without mentioning Jonathan's name.

"I'm not sure how exactly he knew, and maybe he just overheard something," I tell him. "Either way, I was a bit creeped out."

But the sympathy I've been craving doesn't materialise. Dave just shakes his head.

"Jesus, Lauren, you put so much on social media all the time, how the hell can you be surprised when people know what's going on in your life?"

My cheeks flame. "Hey, that's not fair! I'm careful not to share personal details online, and nobody knows 'LePhoto' is me."

Dave is still shaking his head. "And yet, here we are – you put stuff online and now you're creeped out when someone at work has obviously seen it. This is the same old conversation we've had dozens of times."

"Why is it always like this? Instead of giving me a bit of sympathy, you use it as a stick to beat me with."

He stands up. "I'm not going to pretend I think it's fine that you share too much, because I don't. I think it's the wrong message to give the girls too."

He puts his cup in the dishwasher, something he never bothered to do when he lived here, and somehow that annoys me even more than his lecture. I bite my lip.

"Do you want to go on upstairs to the girls – they probably don't know you're here."

With a curt nod, he leaves the kitchen, and half an hour later he leaves the house without coming back in to say goodbye.

By ten, the girls are gone to bed, and again it's just me and the flicker of the TV screen. This is the part I can't get used to – the quiet at night. Dave never stopped talking when he was here – now there's only the ticking of the clock above the low hum of the TV and an occasional car outside. A dog barks, or maybe it's a fox – there are always foxes slinking around here at night, looking for open bins. I shiver.

My phone buzzes with a Twitter notification and I know that on some level I've been waiting for it.

So now that you're home, let's get back to the woman in Venice. I know she's American. I need her name.

I block the account again, and open WhatsApp.

Hi Cleo, it's Lauren from the campsite. How are you? Just getting in touch to say I'm still getting weird comments on Twitter about you re that photo (so sorry again). The person seems to know you're American? So maybe it's someone who knows you in real life? Not sure if that gives you any insight into who it might be? Lauren x

A few minutes go by before her reply arrives.

I think I've worked out who it is. Maybe I should give you a call.

Before I can reply to say I'm free to talk, my phone is ringing and it's her.

"So who is it – who's been sending the messages?" I ask as soon as I pick up.

"It's a long story," Cleo says, "and it goes back to Memorial Day weekend last year. Have you got time?"

I do, I say, and she starts to tell her story.

CLEO

Chapter 8

It was the start of Memorial Day weekend when he walked into the bar, and everything changed forever. Cleo was carrying a tray of beers to a group of guys in the corner, ducking to avoid the red, white and blue bunting Gina had strung through the wooden beams above. They passed one another as he made his way to the bar, and when a beer wobbled on her tray, he reached out a hand to steady it. She flashed a smile of thanks. He didn't smile, he just looked at her with slate-grey eyes as he squeezed past and took a seat at the bar. This one might be interesting, she thought, watching him push a mop of dark hair out of his eyes and raise a hand to get Gina's attention. It was a busy night – humid outside, and the after-work crowd swarmed in for cold drinks and cool air. The high spirits were converting to cold hard cash for Cleo; she was making double her usual Friday-night tips, and thinking about calling Ruth and Erica to meet up after work. But she never called them in the end, and afterwards she wondered what might have changed if she had.

He sat at the bar all night, paging through a dog-eared paperback and slowly drinking his beer. That stood out. People didn't read novels in The Cornerstone – it was more of a dance-on-the-bar kind of place. And, every now and then when Cleo looked over, she found him watching. He never looked away when she caught him, and he never smiled. Bit by bit, people rolled out the door to the hot Brooklyn night in search of parties, but still he stayed, reading his book. She tried to see what it was, but it was flat on the bar, cover down. When Gina called time, he closed the book and looked straight at her. Nothing much unnerved Cleo but, with this guy, it was different. She was wiping down a table near the door when he walked by. He came close and leaned in. She didn't move.

"I'll be outside," he said, almost in a whisper, and walked out the door.

Cleo stuck her apron behind the bar and grabbed her phone and keys. Gina was counting money from the till, and muttering something about takings being down. Gina always assumed takings were down until she counted them.

"Do you need anything else?" Cleo asked.

She held up her hand in an unspoken *don't interrupt*.

"Sorry, okay, I'm leaving now, I'll see you next week," Cleo said, walking out onto Lorimer Street.

He was there, like she knew he would be. And they didn't say a word, they just walked together, both of them knowing exactly what would happen. That was the first time. A chance meeting, the flapping of the butterfly's wings, with a chain reaction nobody could foresee.

And so it went. Every now and then he'd call in during her shift, and on those nights they always went home together. In the bar, they never spoke, and on the short walk to her apartment he said little. In the beginning, all Cleo knew was that his name was Marcus and he smoked a lot. She didn't mind. He never stayed over, and she didn't mind that either. When he was leaving, he'd ask about her next shift at The Cornerstone, and sometimes he'd turn up. On the nights he didn't, that was just fine too.

At least at first it was. She'd never been the girl who watches the door, wondering if the guy will walk in, yet slowly it was starting to happen. She told her girlfriends about it and they laughed. Cleo, the one-night-stand queen, finally getting serious. Only she wasn't – serious is two-sided, and she didn't even have his number. She had never been to his apartment. If he was to stop showing up at The Cornerstone, she might never see him again.

But he did show up, and they continued with their series of one-night stands right through June. By the end of the month he was showing up for most of her shifts – three nights a week – unless it was Sunday. He wouldn't say why, but he never came to the bar on Sundays. And still she knew nothing about him. She asked where he lived, and he said near Union Avenue, but nothing more specific. When she asked what he did, he said he worked in banking, then changed the subject. Usually she was the one being coy and the role reversal took getting used to. She hated it and she loved it. She wanted him in her apartment on the nights he wasn't there, and once, when he didn't show up at the bar, she could feel unfamiliar pangs of anxiety. What if he was gone? But he did show up eventually, and they went home together, and for the first time as they walked he took her hand. Much later, she still remembered the feeling when he did that. They'd slept together dozens of times by then, but when he took her hand there was no going back.

The morning after the handholding epiphany, Cleo woke earlier than usual. Marcus was gone hours by then, but something had changed. A switch had been flicked. On her phone, she opened her Norwood Girls group text, wondering if anyone was up. None of her friends were the kind to get out of bed before it was absolutely necessary, though ironically she was the only one who didn't have an office job – unless you counted designing logos from her apartment for sporadic clients who needed a cheap graphic designer. She started typing a text.

So. I'm officially smitten. I held his hand. Kill me now.

She pressed send and sat back. Ten long minutes went by, so she got up to make coffee, then got back into bed, balancing her laptop on her knees. Jude had replied.

I knew you'd join us eventually. Welcome to the dark side of love and happiness. (It's not as great as we told you) (OK ignore me, Nate and I had a fight last night)

Erica replied next.

Go, you! So tell us more about the mysterious Marcus – where's he from, and what does he do for a living?

Erica always liked to weigh up Cleo's dates based on their net worth. Since she mostly dated aspiring playwrights and starving artists, Erica rarely had high hopes.

Cleo chewed her fingernail for a moment, then started typing.

He's from Texas originally, I don't know much about his work except that it's an investment bank, he lives off Union, and seems to have a thing about not drinking on Sundays. And is very beautiful. That's all that matters, right?

Ruth jumped in then, always Cleo's defender since they met in second grade at Norwood Elementary. An older kid had knocked her over, and Cleo had helped her up. Ruth was still paying her back.

It's wonderful, Cleo. I'm really happy for you and Marcus xx

Then Erica asked Jude about the fight with Nate and the conversation moved on and she sat back, drinking her coffee and wondering if this was what it was like to have a boyfriend. All those years she'd been feeling sorry for Erica and Jude, thinking they were staying in because they had to. Finally she understood – they'd found people who made staying in worthwhile.

Chapter 9

"You know, you can stay over if you like," Cleo finally said, one night in late July, two months after they met.

It was too hot to open the windows and even with her creaky old air conditioner running at full blast, the apartment was sweaty.

Marcus was standing by the side of the bed pulling on jeans, and at first he didn't turn around. And Cleo thought back to all the guys who'd said the same to her, and all the times she'd brushed it off with a breezy smile. So this was the other side of the coin.

Finally he turned around, though in the dark she couldn't read his expression.

"I can't stay, Cleo. I have to work in the morning, and I need to sleep."

"Well, what do you even do at work that's so important? You hardly ever talk about it." The irritation in her voice was palpable and she regretted it as soon as the words were out.

"I've told you before – I work in an investment bank and trying to explain it further would be very boring. But I do have to be on my A-game every day, so . . . " he shrugged.

Cleo nodded, summoning up a casual smile, invisible in the dark. Shit, how had she ended up here? "Sure, I get it. Actually I have a lot on tomorrow morning too. I've got some designs to finish for a client and I'm meeting my mom to go shopping . . . "

Without answering, Marcus went out on the balcony to smoke. Cleo turned over and when he left a few minutes later she pretended to be asleep.

Cleo's mom knew immediately there was something up that day. They met in a Venezuelan restaurant in the East Village – a new place Delphine's neighbour had been raving about. Delphine lived in Garden City, Long Island, but always liked to come in to the city when meeting her daughter.

"There'll be plenty of time for staying home when I'm old," she said when they sat down, smoothing a hand over her dark-red hair, the mirror image of Cleo's.

They ordered – roasted pork shoulder with a spicy mango sauce for both of them – and, as soon as the waiter walked away, Delphine asked Cleo what was wrong.

"Nothing, why do you ask?" she replied, picking at a speck of something on the bright-green oilskin tablecloth.

"Cleo, I've known you since the minute you came out, squawking and screaming, and you're not going to tell me now there's something wrong. Talk."

"Okay. I met a guy."

Delphine's eyes widened. This wasn't what she was expecting.

"And the thing about it is . . . I think I like him."

Delphine smiled and reached across to put her hand on Cleo's.

"Oh, my darling, you are the only person I know who could make falling in love sound mournful."

"Whoa! Nobody said anything about falling in love."

The waiter arrived with their iced teas and Delphine took a sip before continuing.

"So what is it – what's wrong? Are you pregnant?"

Cleo spluttered her tea onto the table. "Mom! No, I am not pregnant. Believe me, I know how to not get pregnant."

"That's what everyone thinks, Cleo, right up until they pee on the stick. Remember, I know all about it."

"Yes, Mom, I know I was a 'surprise', but that's not it. It's just what I said, nothing more dramatic than that: I think I like this guy, but I'm not sure he feels the same way."

"Okay, sweetheart, tell me about him."

And Cleo did, in a dramatic monologue that was interrupted by the waiter bringing their food – and if her mother was grateful for the break, she hid it well.

"So, Cleo," she said, once they'd started eating, "it seems to me this will go one of two ways. Either he will realise he's just as mad about you as you are about him and you will live happily ever after, or that will not happen and you will eventually go your separate ways. So you can push him to spend more time with you, or give him space and see what happens. Only you can decide what's best."

Cleo chewed her pork, thinking about her answer, then burst out laughing. "Mom, that's the biggest load of bull I've ever heard! You've basically said nothing. I could have given myself that advice."

Delphine threw up her hands. "But that's the point – nobody can tell you what to do. Stay with him, keep things as they are, push for more commitment, leave – those are all options but there's no silver bullet. You know that, right?"

She did know that. And really, she knew Delphine wouldn't be able to fix it but she felt better having let it out. As Delphine might say herself, since Cleo came out squawking and screaming, she'd always known how to make her daughter feel better.

Cleo was supposed to be working that night, but Gina cancelled her shift at short notice, so she messaged in Norwood Girls to see if anyone was around. Jude was staying in with Nate (again) but Erica and Ruth were free. They decided to meet for beers in a dive bar near Prospect Park, and see where the night might take them.

When Cleo arrived at O'Shea's, Erica and Ruth were already perched at the bar, sucking froth off the tops of their beers. Immediately, they wanted to know the latest developments with Marcus, and if it was getting serious. That made Cleo laugh. No chance, she told them, she still never knew for sure if he'd even show up at the bar.

"So will he be there tonight, or does he know your shift was cancelled?" Ruth asked.

"Oh crap. He doesn't know."

"So just call him and tell him," Erica said, waving at the bartender to order Cleo a beer.

"Yeah, um, slight problem there. We haven't actually swapped numbers yet."

Two jaws dropped at that little nugget, and Cleo could see it sounded insane.

"You can't be serious?" Erica said. "You've been dating for, like, two months now?"

"Well, that's just it," she explained. "I mean, he comes back to my place at night but never stays over – it's not like we're really dating."

"Oh, come on, Cleo!" Erica said. "Even you can see that's not normal."

And of course she was right; it wasn't normal. But it wasn't simple either. Cleo had asked for his number once, just to call his cell-phone when he couldn't find it in her apartment, but he'd said *no, not necessary*. And something about the casual refusal to give her his number even for the most functional of reasons held her back from asking again.

"Well, it's just a different kind of relationship, and that's okay," Ruth said, though Cleo could tell even she thought it was odd.

"Yeah, that's it," she replied. "He's a different kind of guy. He's doesn't say much, and he's obviously not big on commitment, but oh my God, I'm borderline obsessed with him. And if that means not swapping numbers, so be it." She took a deep swallow from her beer.

"But what are you going to do about tonight – will he be in The Cornerstone waiting for you?" Erica asked.

"I guess. Maybe no harm if I don't turn up, right?" But even as she said it, she knew she didn't mean it.

Ruth rescued her again. "Well, we could grab a drink at The Cornerstone? They do good cocktails?"

Cleo nodded. "They do. And Gina will probably give us a few drinks on the house . . ."

Erica wasn't convinced. "Isn't that chasing him though? How about playing hard to get?"

And Cleo knew she was right, but she couldn't not go. And, afterwards, she wondered how things might have gone if she had listened to Erica that night – or if perhaps it was a shortcut to an outcome already ordained.

Chapter 10

As they weaved their way between the crowded tables, Cleo's breath quickened and her eyes scanned the bar ahead. There he was, in his usual spot. She searched for some sign that he was disappointed by her absence, but saw none. He was deep in his paperback, one hand around his glass of beer. Marcus only ever drank craft beers – one of the few things she knew about him.

As they drew near, Cleo slowed, and started to wonder if it was a mistake, but before she could change her mind those grey eyes looked up at her, and she was hooked.

"Hey," she said, leaning in to kiss his cheek. "I'm off tonight but my girlfriends wanted to come here –" she gestured behind her. "So here we are. Erica, Ruth, this is Marcus. Marcus, these are two of my best friends from when I was growing up in Norwood."

Marcus leaned back on his stool and looked at them, assessing them – for what? Then, with a half-mocking smile, he stretched over to shake hands.

"Marcus, nice to meet you – the first guy who ever managed to hold on to Cleo for more than a month," Erica said and, although Cleo knew she meant it as a compliment, she was suffocated with self-consciousness. Did it sound like she'd said they were in a relationship?

Marcus didn't react. Instead he pointed to a small table in the far corner, and suggested they move there. Maybe everything would be okay.

And it was okay. Not amazing, but okay. Marcus answered questions when asked, but mostly he sat back and watched. Erica was beside him and made a big effort to include him in every conversation. Ruth was beside Cleo, and was much quieter than usual. At the time, Cleo thought it was because of work – she'd been having some trouble with her boss. After, she wished it had been that simple.

At last call, Erica suggested they go on to a cocktail bar on Union Avenue and Cleo realised she had a dilemma. She and Marcus had never gone anywhere other than her apartment together – this would be new territory. Looking over, she caught him staring at her, and started to get that familiar fluttery feeling. There was no question about another bar, they were going home. When she told the girls, Erica winked and Ruth smiled, though there was something not quite real about it. Cleo promised they'd catch a movie Sunday night to make up for leaving early, and they said goodbye.

On the way home, she asked Marcus what he thought of her friends.

"They're fine," he said, his voice neutral. "Very normal women with very normal lives."

Somehow he made the word *normal* sound like an insult and Cleo was hurt on their behalf.

"Not like you, Cleo," he added. "You're quite different. I'm becoming very distracted by you." And as he took her hand, she forgot all about being hurt and wondered if tonight perhaps he'd stay over.

He didn't stay over. But he did pick up her phone and type something in. His number, he said, in case she had a cancelled shift again. Then, as cool as always, he got dressed and smoked his cigarette on the balcony. But, before letting himself out, he leaned across the bed and kissed her cheek.

"Distracted," he whispered, then left.

Progress, she thought, then slept.

In the morning, Cleo spotted a text Ruth had sent the night before.

Can you call me before work tomorrow?

Almost nine – Ruth would be waiting in line for coffee at the cart outside her office. She sounded anxious when she picked up Cleo's call, tripping over her words, but one thing was clear – it was about Marcus.

"You're worried about the lack of commitment, I get that," Cleo said. "But I'm a big girl. And hey, I'm pretty sure we're heading towards settling down."

"Oh, Cleo," Ruth said, and went quiet.

"I'm kidding, I'm not settling down – I just mean I like him. Is that so bad?"

Silence again.

"I recognised him."

Oh. That didn't sound good. She continued when Cleo said nothing.

"From a profile picture on Facebook."

Cleo swung her legs out of bed and padded through to the kitchen. "Well, he's allowed to be on Facebook. Though – confession time – I've totally searched and never found him, so maybe it's not him?"

"It is. It's not his account – he's in the photo with a friend of a friend of mine. Shannon. It's her account. He's in her profile photo."

Cleo was aware of a slightly sick feeling in her stomach as she answered Ruth. "Well, that doesn't mean anything."

But even then, in that first moment, she knew that of course it meant something. She sank down on the couch.

"I'm so sorry," Ruth was saying. "But I had to tell you. I don't really know Shannon but I looked at her account and it's pretty clear she has a boyfriend and his name is Marcus."

"Can you send me a screenshot?"

"Sure. I'm about to step into the elevator now but call me later, okay?"

Cleo didn't answer. She disconnected the call and sat in her apartment, staring at the wall. Her phone buzzed, with a new message – the photo of Shannon and Marcus. There was no doubt – it was him. And suddenly it was all so painfully clear. Of course he didn't ever bring her back to his apartment – he was living with his girlfriend. How on earth had she not seen this? All along, she thought he was so mysterious, so unattainable, the ultimate commitment-phobe, and really it was the oldest story in the book. Well, screw him. Before she could stop to think about it, she searched for his number and sent on the photo, with a short but clear message.

I don't know who you think I am, and I certainly don't know who you are, but this is not how I do things. Don't come into the bar again.

She pressed send, and slumped back in the sofa. And then she called her mom.

Chapter 11

Cleo checked the clock above the fireplace, squinting to see the time. Just before ten. Her mom had picked up the clock at a thrift store and insisted it would look perfect on the exposed brick wall above the fireplace, but the face was too small and Cleo could never read it without scrunching up her eyes. It was pretty though, with a birdcage and pink flowers filling the centre of the face, so she kept it. Delphine had visited earlier, making the journey from Garden City to bring flowers and a shoulder to cry on. Cleo didn't cry, she was too pissed at him to cry. And Delphine didn't tell her she should have spotted what was going on. She said bad things happen to good people and that you have to be able to trust those around you – to live your life by the many who don't let you down, not the few who do. There was something raw in her voice when she said it and Cleo wondered for a moment if Delphine was still talking about Marcus, or something else entirely. And after she left, Cleo stayed right there on the lime-green sofa her mother always said hurt her eyes, and for a whole hour she didn't move. When she did get up, it was to fix herself a vodka, then she flopped back down to do some more seething and self-pitying. In all that time, Marcus never replied to her message.

And she was still there at ten o'clock, vowing she'd never let something like this happen again. That's when he banged on the door. Not a knock – a loud bang that made her jump. As soon as she opened the door, the familiar flutter was back, but she made herself turn and walk to the couch without looking at him. Following close behind, he sat beside her. She shook her head – there was no way she was going to be the first to speak.

"Cleo, I'm sorry."

He sounded different. Not so aloof. He ran his fingers through his hair, pushing back the bit that always hung down across his eyes.

She shrugged and waited.

"I should have told you about Shannon. We're together since I was sixteen, and I realise it's been coming to an end for a long time, but when you're with someone almost half your life, it's hard to break away." He ran his fingers through his hair again, and looked down. "I was afraid of hurting her, and it's complicated – my parents and hers are long-time friends, and they can't wait for us to get married. Wrecking this wrecks everything."

This was truly the longest speech she'd ever heard Marcus make, and he was barely recognisable without the air of detachment. Part of her wanted to laugh, then she remembered that she'd spent two months sleeping with a liar.

"But I've done it now," he said quietly. "I've told her it's over. She can have the money we've been saving for a house, I don't want any of it." He looked up. "I just want you."

That gave Cleo a jolt.

"Are you serious? You left your girlfriend of fourteen years? Just like that?"

He nodded, still holding her gaze, and oh, those eyes.

"Yep, and I felt like a complete asshole doing it, but part of me thinks she was waiting for one of us to say something."

Cleo's head was spinning. "But don't you live together?"

"No. Her parents are strict Catholics and don't believe in what they call living in sin. So we've been saving for a house."

That didn't sound credible. "If you don't live with her, why didn't you ever suggest going back to your place?"

He looked down at his hands again. "I share an apartment with her brother Chris. We were both house-hunting at the same time, and it was cheaper to share. So obviously, I couldn't take you there."

It had seemed so dark and mysterious, and all this time the broad daylight truth was oh so mundane.

"Do you think I could stay here tonight?" he asked, looking up at her from under his eyelashes.

"I'm sorry, what?"

"I don't feel comfortable going home with Chris there – things are obviously a little raw – I imagine he wants to punch me and I suspect Shannon's dad feels the same. I doubt her mom will ever speak to me again. We have dinner with her grandmother every single Sunday night and have done for years – I'm like a part of the family already. They're going to be furious after what I did today. So can I stay?"

Cleo threw up her hands. "I'm not going to toss you out on the street at this time of night." Getting up, she nudged him off the sofa, and bent down to pull the lower part out to make a bed. "I'll get some extra covers and a pillow for you." She turned to look at him.

His mouth was open and Cleo felt the first small hint of satisfaction.

"Oh . . . I thought I'd be . . ." he nodded towards her bedroom.

"Marcus, we're not together, and you are not welcome in my bed. You can sleep on my sofa tonight and, tomorrow, you go."

She marched into her room, and for the first time since she met him, she felt like the old Cleo was back.

Chapter 12

Unfortunately the old Cleo didn't stay long. Within weeks, Marcus slipped back into her life and into her bed. Before she knew what was happening, they'd fallen into a routine – he'd go to his office each morning while she worked on graphic-design projects at home and, in the evenings, if she was pulling a shift at The Cornerstone, he came by. On her nights off, they went out and did all the stuff normal people do when they first start dating – except they'd skipped the dating part and gone straight to living together.

Cleo's friends were entranced – they couldn't believe she'd settled down. Cleo couldn't believe it either. And, for a while, it was nice having someone around, but it took some of the mystery out of it too. Once she'd seen him in his pyjamas, flossing in her bathroom, a little bit of the magic evaporated. She messaged about it in Norwood Girls one morning, after a particularly uninspiring evening watching him do laundry.

So I'm not sure how excited I am to have Marcus here as a permanent fixture. I mean, the whole thing has just lost some of the allure, you know?

Sarah, who was hardly ever online, was the first to reply.

Seriously, Cleo, you are never happy! You spent two months wishing things would move up a notch and you nearly fainted over him holding your hand. Now he's interested and you're not?

Jude jumped in then.

Hey, that's totally normal. The honeymoon period absolutely wears off when you see them all the time. When our first argument was about the amount of toilet paper we were buying I really did question my relationship with Nate. But you get past that, and realise it's normal.

Erica agreed with Jude – the gloss comes off when you live together, and that's okay. Ruth was quiet. Ruth was the only other single person in the group, and she was hoping to meet someone. Maybe Cleo's message sounded entitled, or maybe it was because she knew the back-story. Nobody else did. Cleo had intended to tell them but then time went by, and it was easier to say nothing about Shannon. Marcus never mentioned her at all, not since the morning they'd gone to clear stuff out of his apartment. They'd gone at a time when Chris should have been at work, but he was home with stomach flu, and launched a torrent of abuse at them. They left with only half of Marcus's clothes, and he told Cleo he wasn't risking going back for the rest, that both Chris and Shannon had mean, unpredictable tempers. He didn't talk about the relationship beyond that, and Cleo wondered if there was more to the break-up than just her.

August turned into September, and they had become used to being around one another. It wasn't like in the movies – it wasn't amazing, but it wasn't terrible either. It was completely fine. But Cleo did wonder if completely fine was what she was looking for. One bone of contention was that Marcus didn't like meeting up with her friends. She didn't mind at first – it suited her to see them separately – but then he started complaining that she was going out too often. When she mentioned it in Norwood Girls, Jude said she'd gone through something similar.

Yeah, Nate was like that after a few months together, and that's why I don't meet up with you guys every time now. And I get it. He doesn't go out with his buddies all that much either. We're hitting 30, it's OK if we don't party every night!!

True. But Cleo didn't like the sense that she was being told what to do, that she was expected to cancel plans on his account.

It was October when he started talking about moving to a bigger place. Cleo's apartment was too small, he said. But she was not for turning – she loved her fourth-floor walk-up in the middle of Brooklyn. Why would they need a second bedroom anyway, she asked? It's not like they had people stay over.

"For kids," he said, without missing a beat.

Kids? This was going way too fast. Cleo didn't even know if she wanted children. She still had plans to take a train around Europe, she told him, no babies for her yet. She expected to see hurt – she'd become used to his hurt expression when something didn't go his way. But this time she saw an unmistakable flash of anger, then just as quickly it was gone. He smiled tightly, and said of course not yet, but no harm in having more space already. Then he kissed her and went out to get bagels.

When the door closed, she picked up her phone and typed a message in Norwood Girls.

Oh my god, Marcus just suggested moving to a bigger place so there's room for our future children. Someone pinch me and wake me up from this nightmare?

Crying laughing emoji from Jude and same from Erica. They'd voted Cleo least likely to have kids enough times to find this hilarious, and she should have been laughing too but she kept thinking about the flash of anger she'd seen.

Sarah was next to reply.

I seriously cannot wait to see you knee-deep in diapers, Cleo. Hey, why don't you come baby-sit for me some night. For practice?

Very funny. They followed with a stream of ideas – how many babies she should have, what their names should be, and what to buy her for her baby shower. Ruth stayed quiet. Cleo was about to ask her how her week had been – she was still having a tough time at work – but Marcus arrived back in and instinctively she put down her phone.

"Hey, you look engrossed – everything okay?" he asked, putting a bag of bagels on the kitchen table.

"Yeah, just checking on some client emails." She wasn't sure why she said that.

"On a Saturday? You work too hard. And you know you don't have to – I earn enough for both of us."

"Sure, but I like my work. Thanks, but no thanks."

"Then why not give up The Cornerstone and focus on the graphic design? You surely don't want to be a waitress all your life?"

Where was this coming from? "Whoa, so you were happy to go home with the waitress after work, but it's not okay now you live with her – is that it?"

She waited for the apology.

"I don't like you working there." He said it casually, but there was a wisp of something else just about audible between the words. "I see customers staring at you in your short skirt and I know what they're thinking." He continued taking the bagels out of the bag.

"Hold up. That's more double standards right there. It was fine for you to look at me in my short skirt, but now you have a problem with other men doing the same?"

He looked up at her and said nothing for a moment. When he spoke, his voice was a too-tight string.

"Yes, I do have a problem with it. You brought me home the first night we met. I didn't have to work too hard for it, did I? I don't want the same to happen with someone else."

Then he walked over to make coffee, leaving Cleo staring open-mouthed at his back.

"Did you actually just say that?"

"I don't want you working there. I earn plenty for both of us," he said, busy with the coffee machine.

"Marcus, you don't get to tell me what to do. Is this how it was with Shannon?"

He turned then, and she saw outrage flash across his face. "Don't you dare mention her name. That's none of your business."

Cleo didn't even try to answer. She shook her head, picked up her purse and walked out the door.

When she arrived back into the apartment that evening, after a long walk in McCarren Park and a coffee with Ruth, Marcus was deeply engrossed in the books on her bookshelf and didn't hear her at first. As she closed the door, he jumped back from the bookcase like he'd just been burnt.

"What's wrong?" Cleo asked, forgetting for a moment that she was still angry.

"Sorry, I just wanted to borrow a book," he said, moving towards her. "I wasn't going through your stuff."

She laughed. "Jeez, I don't mind you looking through my books – take as many as you like."

Then she remembered she was mad at him, and stopped laughing. Taking his cue, he bowed his head, and the apologies came thick and fast – he should never have asked her to give up work, he shouldn't have flown off the handle when she mentioned Shannon, and he'd never do it again. She told him it was fine, everyone gets angry sometimes.

But from then on, she was wary. She avoided talking about work, and started wearing jeans for her shift. Not because he told her to, but because it was easier than fighting. She didn't like this new person she'd become, and it made her question the relationship. On paper, it was hard to find fault – most of the time Marcus was the perfect boyfriend. But it was still there under the surface – just that little bit of tension, the sense that she needed to take care, to anticipate his mood and work around it. She tried explaining it to the girls but, predictably, most of them said it was a normal element of being in a relationship.

Of course you need to be a little sensitive, Cleo – no offence, but you're not known for your sensitivity, said Sarah.

Jude chimed in.

It works both ways. If Nate has a tough day at work, I don't launch into an argument about the trash, and if I have a tough day he cooks me dinner and gives me a shoulder rub instead of bringing up the credit-card bill (so let's just say sometimes I fake a bad day at work).

It wasn't quite the same thing, but she didn't push it.

She didn't tell them absolutely everything either, and that niggled at her, but sometimes it was easier. So when they wanted to meet up in a group, she made excuses to explain Marcus's absence, and when she couldn't think of a credible reason, she said both of them were busy. She was seeing the girls less often, and relying on the text group for contact, but more and more it was just simpler to hide behind a screen.

Chapter 13

Aside from Ruth, the only other person not celebrating Cleo's new settled-down status was her mom, but that was mostly because she hadn't met Marcus and – in her words – couldn't form an opinion. Cleo had held off introducing her; maybe because of their less than perfect back-story, or perhaps because she knew Delphine wouldn't like him. And she was right – things got off to a bad start.

It was the last Sunday in October – one of those perfect crisp fall afternoons in New York, and Delphine was coming for lunch. Just before one, Cleo ran out to pick up a cake from the bakery and bumped into her mother on the way back in. In Delphine's arms was a badly wrapped gift – Cleo could see bits of something gold or brass poking through the pink-and-white candy-striped paper. She offered to carry it up the stairs to the apartment but Delphine insisted on holding on to it – a gift for both her and Marcus, she said.

Inside, Cleo introduced her to Marcus and, after some small talk, Delphine handed over her gift. There wasn't much work left to unwrapping it, and inside was a set of candlesticks, the kind you see in churches – heavy, brass ornaments that would look completely out of place in the apartment.

"They're Romaneseque," Delphine told Marcus, who was tracing a finger over the intricate plaited detail at the base. "They were made in France in the nineteenth century, I believe. Aren't they wonderful?"

Cleo waited for Marcus to say something but he didn't, so she jumped in. "Thank you, Mom, they really are beautiful. I'll make us some coffee while we wait for lunch – Marcus, could you put the candlesticks over at the fireplace?"

Marcus said nothing, but picked them up and carried them across the room, then very deliberately put both of them behind a huge bamboo palm, where they couldn't be seen at all.

"Oh no, I mean out at the front of the fireplace, one either side," Cleo said. "Nobody can see them there!"

But he ignored her and walked over to the stove to check on the chowder. So Cleo moved them herself, already mentally writing her next Norwood Girls message. She and Delphine had very little when she was growing up, but manners were everything, and it was starting to feel like a line had been crossed.

Delphine, to her credit, took no obvious offence, and began quizzing Marcus about his life – his parents, his work, his childhood in Texas. He was as recalcitrant as ever, and while Delphine bravely soldiered on with her questions, Cleo grilled sourdough and seethed.

"Do you know, although I've travelled all around Europe, I've never been to Texas – what part are you from?" Delphine asked.

"Gatesville," was Marcus's one-word answer.

"And do you have family here in New York?"

"No."

Was he this rude to Shannon's grandmother during their Sunday-night dinners, Cleo wondered, as she put chowder in front of each of them, wishing the lunch was over.

Halfway through the meal, Marcus's phone buzzed. Cleo saw him reach into his back pocket and threw him a look to tell him to wait. But he paid no attention and, as he read the text, she saw a flash of irritation. He pushed back his chair and announced he needed to go to the office.

"On a Sunday afternoon?" Delphine said. "Surely they can't expect you to work Sunday afternoons?"

"It's a recurring problem and I need to shut it down," he said, his voice tight.

He pulled his jacket off the coat-stand, and walked over to the coffee table to open his laptop. Swivelling the screen away from them, his eyes narrowed in concentration, he typed something, then closed the laptop and walked to the door.

"Marcus! Can't it wait?" Cleo asked, though in truth she was glad he was going.

"No, I have to deal with this. I'll see you later."

And with that, he was gone.

Delphine and Cleo looked at one another and for a moment neither of them spoke.

"Well," Delphine said in a conspiratorial whisper, "I presume I shouldn't be planning the wedding just yet?"

And because it was all so ridiculous, they both burst out laughing, and Cleo knew then that if she couldn't even begin to defend him to her mother it wasn't looking good.

Marcus still wasn't back when Delphine left, so Cleo ignored the dishes and sat down on the couch with her phone and a glass of wine. She clicked into Norwood Girls to update them on her relationship status.

I know you are all going to kill me, but I'm not sure there's any long-term hope for Marcus and me. My mom visited with us this afternoon and he was SO RUDE to her. I think it's a deal-breaker.

Erica was first to reply.

Nooooo! How could anyone be rude to your mom? She's the sweetest person I know! Was it really that bad?

Cleo typed her answer quickly, glad to have somewhere to vent.

Yes, it truly was. What to do?

Jude was cautious as ever.

Maybe he's just in bad form? Is he out somewhere now?

It struck Cleo that Jude instinctively knew she wouldn't be chatting online if Marcus was there.

Yes, he had to go to the office. Shit, I need help. Do I dump him? How do you break up with someone who lives with you?

Sarah was next.

I think if he's not for you, there's no point in wasting any more time. It's one thing when you're 21 but not now when everyone is settling down.

Before Cleo had a chance to answer, Erica was back.

Hold on now! He is a very attractive man and you have been

deeply obsessed with him for months. Don't do anything rash!

Cleo heard the key in the door then and stuck her phone under a cushion. As he walked in, she watched from the couch, waiting for an explanation.

"I'm sorry," he said. "I know I wasn't myself this afternoon. It's this work thing, it's really bugging me."

He sat down beside her, taking her hands. His were ice cold. His eyes were red-rimmed and he looked tired. He never talked about work, so Cleo never asked, and in truth she found it kind of boring even when he did. But maybe he really was finding it stressful, and she'd missed the signs.

"Talk about it when you're having problems at the office – don't just bottle it up and then take it out on everyone, right?"

He nodded and pulled her into a hug. His leather jacket was cold to her cheek, and smelled of October smoke. After a few seconds, she untangled herself and asked if the problem was resolved.

"Not yet," he said, his mouth in a tight line. "But someone needs to learn I won't be pushed. I don't respond well to threats."

She sat up straighter. "Wait, what? What's going on?"

"Nothing. Just work. It's boring. Let me check something on my laptop, then I'll grab a glass and join you." He kissed her neck, the way she used to love being kissed, and got up to get his laptop.

Only she didn't like being kissed that way any more.

Afterwards, Cleo knew she should have walked away that day, but she didn't. Of course she knew it was just putting off the inevitable – procrastinating over a break-up the same way she did with everything. But it was hard to think about leaving him when he was so stressed about his job all the time – he was working late a couple of evenings a week, and still getting texts at the weekend. She had the sense that someone – a boss or a co-worker – was putting particular pressure on him, but he never opened up about it. On the other side, he was constantly asking Cleo about her day – if she'd gone out anywhere, who she'd met – and the double standards bugged her – why, if he wouldn't talk about his day, did he expect her to itemise every minute of hers?

Ten days or so after her mother's visit, Cleo broached the subject of Thanksgiving and it all came to a head. Despite how badly the introduction had gone, she wanted to invite her mom for dinner, but Marcus wanted them to go away instead – fly to Florida for a break. She told him she couldn't leave her mom on her own, and he kept insisting they go away, saying Delphine didn't like him anyway. Eventually, tired of arguing in circles, Cleo took her phone into the bedroom and told him he could sleep on the couch.

She messaged the girls the latest update, and they were sympathetic – maybe more so than usual because anything involving Delphine got their defences up. They chatted online for a while, then Cleo put down her phone and switched off the lamp, thinking *this is it – tomorrow I'll ask him to leave.* She stared out the window into the moon-washed night, watching a leaf drift past, floating gently towards the ground below. The landing would be soft, as it is for insubstantial things. Like already dying relationships.

Chapter 14

The following morning Cleo could hear him in the kitchen making coffee, so she stayed in her room until he was gone – she was pretty pissed at him, but not enough to break up when he was due at the office.

At eleven, Ruth called by with a box of glazed donuts. She'd had a wisdom tooth out and was slightly woozy from the painkillers but happy to keep Cleo company and coach her in the art of breaking up.

"So, today's the day, right?" she stated more than asked, flopping down on the couch.

"Yep. It's happening. Now I just need to find the words. I truly can't bear the thought of sharing a bed with him again. I slept so much better last night without him there. Did I ever tell you about his foot odour?"

Ruth snorted. "Foot odour?"

"Yeah, I never noticed it until he moved in. I'm talking a hold-your-breath kind of odour. Totally gross. I have no idea why – it's not like he doesn't wash. If anything he's a clean freak, kind of OTT on the hygiene front? Like, long showers, and much mirror-gazing – I'm always ready before him when we go out."

Ruth bit into a donut and cupped her hand under her chin to catch the crumbs. "In Marcus's defence, you have an edge on all of us there – you don't even need make-up. I take a lot longer than you do to get ready. I might be on Team Marcus for this one."

Cleo punched her lightly in the shoulder. "No, seriously, he's too much. I had no idea when I first met him that he was so into his looks – it all seemed very casual and thrown together. Who knew it took hours to perfect that floppy hair. But yeah, despite all that, his feet stink."

She picked a Boston Cream from the box and broke it apart on the plate to let the gooey yellow cream ooze out.

"So what are you going to say?" Ruth asked. "I mean, you need a better reason than feet."

"I don't suppose I can just change the locks and hope he goes away?"

She shook her head. "Sorry, you have to be a grown-up about this one. He's not just one of your flings, he lives here."

Cleo took a sip of her coffee, staring at the bookshelves by the fireplace, at the rows and rows of books, like narrow coloured houses. "You know, he doesn't own one single book on that shelf. Isn't that odd? When we met, he always had a book at the bar with him. But, since he moved in, I haven't seen him read a single thing."

"Well, maybe he's just the kind of guy who likes to read books specifically in bars but nowhere else?" Ruth suggested, getting up to wander over to the shelf. "Actually, could I borrow a few of these?"

"Sure, take your pick. Yeah, I'm wondering now if the book in the bar was just an affectation – a way of seeming more interesting. He probably wasn't reading at all."

"Oh, come on," Ruth said, turning back to look at her. "That's a step too far. I'm sure you'd know by now if he'd gone to that level of subterfuge."

"No, seriously. I don't think I know him at all. I've never met his friends, and the only time I saw where he lived was when we went to clear out his apartment – and were practically chased out of there by Chris – Shannon's brother. At the time I assumed he was just being protective but now I'm starting to wonder what else went on. And Marcus hates it if I bring up Shannon."

Ruth walked back to the couch, three books in hand. "That's not unreasonable though – nobody likes to talk about their ex."

73

Cleo shook her head. "No, there's more to it than that – mentioning her name at all sets him off – it's weird. None of it helps me with my break-up speech though – I can't say 'I'm dumping you because you get agitated when I mention Shannon'."

"Well, give me all the reasons you are dumping him, and let's find one that works?"

"Sure. So, he's secretive, but wants to know everything about my day to the point of interrogation. He doesn't like hanging out with my friends," She looked at Ruth. "Sorry. He was incredibly rude to my mother, and is refusing to have her over for Thanksgiving. He is not the intriguing man I thought I met in the bar – he's possessive, cloying, and actually not very interesting at all once you scratch the surface. At this point, the thought of touching him makes my skin crawl. How's that?"

Ruth let out a low whistle. "Right, we might leave out the bit about making your skin crawl . . . how about we focus in on the situation with your mom? You could explain that you two are exceptionally close and, when he didn't quite bond with her, it made you realise the relationship wasn't going to last."

Cleo nodded. "That's good actually. Oh God, the sooner he's gone, the better. I feel like I've just woken up. Did you see this all along?"

Ruth did a head-tilt before speaking and Cleo knew the answer.

"Well, I didn't love him the night we met, and maybe because Shannon is a friend of a friend, I kinda felt for her in all this too." She paused, but looked like she wanted to say something else.

"Go on, spill, I can take it."

"I didn't want to say it to you before, but I've heard Shannon isn't doing so well. She's drinking a lot apparently, and staying home alone, and I heard something about an overdependence on prescription drugs."

"Oh God, I feel bad now. I never really thought about it from her side, and when Marcus implied the break-up was coming long before it happened, I just took him at his word. I should never have gone near him, should I?"

Ruth shook her head and threw up her hands. "Hey, it is what it is. You couldn't have known, and you're getting out now anyway. What time will he be home?"

Cleo looked at the clock above the fireplace. "Six o'clock. Six hours to go. Maybe we should get out somewhere to distract ourselves?"

"Sorry but I have to go home and get some work done. My boss doesn't really believe in wisdom-tooth pain. Will you call me when it's done? Do you want me to come over tonight?"

"Oh do, please. If you could come about nine, hopefully he'll be long gone by then?"

"But where will he stay tonight?"

Cleo shrugged. "I'm sure he has friends he can crash with. I can't bear the thought of having him here even one more night." She shivered, dreading what was ahead, but certain now that it was the right thing to do.

Chapter 15

The long hand ticked toward the top of the clock as Cleo watched, feeling sicker by the second. It was too early for vodka, but she'd poured one anyway, and it sat untouched, glittering on the coffee table.

Two minutes past six. She closed her eyes, willing him to walk through the door, but dreading the turn of the key. Why had she ever let it get this far?

Half past six came and went, still no sign. She checked her phone, no messages, though he rarely let her know when he was working late.

Seven o'clock. The ice in the vodka was long gone now, absorbed into a watery, tepid drink she didn't want. Her legs were stiff when she stood up to pour it down the sink, so she walked around the room, tracing her finger on the brick around the fireplace, running her hand over the books. The bamboo palm needed watering and it gave her something to do for two more minutes. She checked her phone again. A message from Ruth to say she hoped it was going okay, and one in Norwood Girls about meeting up the following night, but nothing from Marcus.

At eight, she switched on the TV. Local news had a story about a child left alone in an apartment while her parents went to Miami, and a woman who'd fallen from a fourteenth-floor window. How completely depressing – she switched channels until she found a rerun of *Parks and Recreation* but it didn't help. She couldn't get her mind off what was to come and, the longer it took, the sicker she felt.

Finally, at half past eight, the key turned in the door. Cleo's stomach flopped. She took a deep breath, ready to make a speech, but when Marcus walked in it was clear something was wrong. His face was pale, his eyes agitated, flitting around the room. He had a laptop she hadn't seen before under his arm, a rose-gold coloured Mac.

"Are you all right?" she asked, not moving from the sofa. "Did you get a new laptop?"

"I'm fine, I just need to do a few things." He picked up his old laptop from the kitchen table, walked into the bedroom with both devices, and shut the door behind him.

Cleo wondered if she should follow him, but something about his demeanour made her stay on the couch. Fifteen minutes later, he came out of the bedroom, and sat down beside her. His face was still pale, with a slick sheen to it, but he seemed calm. More than calm. Something had changed.

"So, Cleo. How was your day?"

She swallowed. "It was fine. Marcus, we need to talk."

He raised his eyebrows and waited.

"It's about us. I don't think it's working."

"Really?"

She swallowed again. "Yes, I've been feeling that way for a while, but this thing about my mom and Thanksgiving really made me see things clearly. I don't think we're right for one another."

He looked at her coolly. There was no sense of surprise and none of the hurt she'd expected to see. And suddenly she knew she really wanted to see something predictable like hurt.

"So I think it's best if you move out. Maybe you could stay with a friend tonight? I'm sorry, I thought you'd be home earlier and have more time to sort something . . ." *Don't cave now, don't invite him to stay.*

Finally he spoke. "Is it really about your mother, Cleo? Is there anything else you want to tell me?"

Shit, did he think she was cheating on him? "No, nothing else.

We're simply not suited. I'm sorry."

He moved a little closer to her on the sofa, and put his hand on her knee. Her stomach did a somersault.

"Anything about how long I take to get ready?"

Her skin went cold.

"Or being possessive and cloying?"

She slid along the couch to move away from him, nausea rising in her stomach. How could he know?

"What about being rude to your mom? Or – " his hand shot out and grabbed her by the hair.

She screamed as he stood up and yanked her off the couch. He pulled her across the room by her hair, then slammed her face against the bookshelf. She slipped to her knees, stunned and dizzy.

"Or about my lack of reading? About not having any books on *your precious bookshelf*?" He spat the words, hissing in her face, still holding her hair.

She wanted to speak but the pain was too great. Something wet slipped into her mouth – blood?

"You think you're so smart, Cleo. You think because you read lots of books and design your little logos that you're some kind of artist. But take a look at yourself." He pulled her hair again, yanking her head up. "You work in a fucking bar. You wear short skirts and sleep with your customers. You can dress it up any way you like, but you're nothing more than a cheap fucking whore!"

Cleo screamed when he slammed her face against the shelf again.

"You should be more careful when you decide to have a laugh at my expense. See this bookshelf you're so proud of? If you ever thought to clean the fucking thing, you'd have spotted there's a camera behind the books. The feed uploads to my laptop each day, and wow did I see some interesting stuff tonight. But I knew you wouldn't clean the shelves. Cleo the artist, too full of her own importance to do some basic dusting. But not too good to fuck her customers, or to have a good laugh about how to break up with her boyfriend."

He still had her by the hair, and for a moment he stopped talking. Then very deliberately, he swung back his fist and punched her in the face. The pain was like nothing she'd ever experienced, crunching, stinging, blinding. Too stunned to scream, she slipped sideways, then she was on her back on the floor, looking up at him.

His face came closer – he was kneeling now. And before she knew what was happening, his hands were around her throat. She reached up to grab his wrists but couldn't prise them off. Pinpricks of light danced in her eyes and the air she desperately wanted to breathe wasn't there any more. She kept pulling but couldn't loosen his grip. In his eyes, there was nothing – not love, not hate, just nothing. This couldn't be happening, she couldn't end like this, lying on her apartment floor. The room started to swim and the walls were closing in, and then out of the corner of her eye, she saw it. She took her hand off his wrist to grab the Romanesque candlestick and with everything she had left in her body she smashed it down on the side of his head. As if in slow motion, she watched his face change. Rage gave way to surprise and his fingers unlocked from her throat, then so slowly it didn't seem real, he slipped to the floor beside her and lay still.

It took Cleo a moment to grab her breath, then she was scrambling, turning, crawling across the apartment floor, not stopping to look back. At the door, she pulled herself up to her knees, just as someone knocked on the other side. When she pulled it open, still on her knees, Ruth was standing there with a smile and a bottle of wine.

"Oh God, oh my God ..." Ruth's smile faded to horror, her eyes taking in Cleo's battered face. "Cleo, what happened? Did he do this? Don't try to answer ..."

She knelt down to pull Cleo into her arms.

"He's still in there – I hit him – he might be dead," Cleo whispered, too shocked to cry.

Gently, Ruth put her sitting in the hallway and, with the bottle of wine still in her hand, went in to look. She was back almost immediately.

"He's unconscious. Even if he wakes, I don't think he'll be able to move any time soon." She pulled out her phone to call 911. "Ambulance and police," she confirmed, giving Cleo's address.

"He heard us," Cleo whispered, when Ruth finished the call and sank down beside her. "He had a camera in the bookcase the whole time. He watched it on his laptop when he came home and heard everything I said to you today."

"Shush, we can talk when you've been seen by the paramedics."

"Is it bad?"

Ruth put her arm around her shoulder, and Cleo saw blood pool on her white shirt. "It's not so bad," she said, but she was crying.

"Am I in trouble, Ruth? Will they think I tried to kill him?"

"I don't think so, Cleo. Not when they see your face. And not when they watch the footage on the camera he's got, right?" She hugged her. "I don't think you have anything to worry about now."

LAUREN

Chapter 16

I'm early and Cleo isn't here yet. I take a table by the window and order a skinny cappuccino, waving away the menu. It feels odd to be meeting Cleo back in Dublin, but I haven't been able to get her story out of my head all week. And how I'd misjudged her. Taking her photo, envying her life, assuming I knew what that might be like, and yet less than a year ago she was literally fighting to save that life. My marriage break-up seems so amicable in comparison, and I've promised myself to lay off the self-pity. Dave can be childish, but he's not violent. Jesus, not that that should be any kind of benchmark. *Man held up as shining example because he never beat his wife.*

My thoughts are interrupted by Cleo's arrival. She's just as striking as she was in Italy or perhaps more so now we're back in Dublin on a grey, rainy September morning. She stands out among the crowds of Saturday-morning coffee-drinkers – taller than most, her auburn hair swishing down her back, her bemused smile hiding so much.

I rise to greet her and she pulls me into a small hug, like we're old friends, and not people who met under the shade of an apology. To that end, I apologise again for taking the photo but she brushes it away.

"No, I need to apologise to you – if I'm right, and this is about

Marcus, then you're caught up in something that has nothing to do with you."

"But if I hadn't posted the photo, none of this would have happened," I pointed out, as the waitress arrives with my cappuccino.

"I'll take an espresso," Cleo says to her, then turns back to me. "Well, let's just say we're in this together now, and we'll figure it out."

I nod, and take a breath before speaking. "Can I ask you something? Why didn't you guess it was Marcus when I told you about the messages in Italy? I think it's the first thing I'd have thought of if it was me?"

She shakes her head. "Oh, but it's not Marcus, I know that. The part I told you is just the first half of the story – there's more to it. That's why I suggested we meet up in person."

"How can you be so sure it's not Marcus?"

"Because Marcus is dead."

She says it so calmly.

I stare at her.

"But wasn't he still alive when your friend called the police that night?"

Her espresso arrives and she nods at the waitress. "Oh, for sure I didn't kill him." She raises the cup to her lips and sips. "He recovered and was arrested and held in custody – he didn't make bail. Then back in January, he was stabbed during a fight in prison. He was dead by the time they found him – bled to death in the prison library, beside the crime-fiction bookshelf. Kind of apt, I guess."

My mouth drops open – at the story, and at the ease with which she tells it.

"Hey, it may sound cold, but he's no great loss to society. I can't say for sure, but I imagine I'm not the first person he beat senseless."

"You think maybe he was abusing his ex – what was her name?"

"Shannon. I don't know, but it's possible. What I didn't know that night, as I sat there planning my break-up speech, is that Shannon took her own life."

"Jesus."

"Yeah. On the same day Marcus attacked me, she jumped from her fourteenth-floor apartment."

"Oh my God! So do you think that had something to do with why Marcus attacked you? He'd heard about Shannon and lost it?"

Cleo drains her espresso and raises her hand to ask for another. "Perhaps. But also because he heard for the first time what I really thought of him. I know now that's what he was doing when he took his laptop into the bedroom after he came home that night – he watched the tape from that morning. God, when I think about what I said that day, sitting with Ruth. Stuff nobody should hear about themselves, ever. Up until then, all my bitching was done online, so he had no idea."

I'm still trying to take it all in, and wondering what I got myself into when I posted that bloody photo. My world is very simple compared to this New York story of violence and prison and death. Two deaths. Jesus.

"I guess he must have had some idea you were talking about him, or why would he have put up the camera?"

"Yeah," Cleo says, "when the cops looked at footage on his laptop, it went back to October. He installed the camera after we fought about me working in a bar. So, basic trust issues, I guess. Ironic given he was the one who cheated on Shannon. That poor girl."

I watch as her face clouds over but just as quickly it's gone. I get the sense she's sorry for Shannon but in a detached way – like hearing something bad about a friend of a friend, without feeling personally touched. She's made of tougher stuff than I am, and probably all the better for it.

My phone is ringing on the table – my mother. I reject the call and turn it over. "Sorry, just my mum. She rings me fourteen times a day so I have to screen."

"Are you close?" Cleo asks.

"I suppose. Well, she phones me a lot and likes to have input in every aspect of my life. Not close in the way you and your mum are."

Cleo nods. "Yeah, we're very close. My dad died before I was born, so it's always been just the two of us. She doesn't like to talk about it, she never mentions him. I've asked for photos but she says there are none, so I don't even know what he looked like . . . They weren't married but she gave me his surname and that's really my only link to him. "

"I'm so sorry, Cleo. My dad passed away too, but I was nineteen. I can't imagine never having known him. Your poor mother. And poor you."

"Yes, but I don't feel I've ever missed out – she's like a mom and dad rolled into one. We're closer than ever since the attack. As soon as I came out of hospital, I moved in with her, and I haven't been back to my apartment since. Ruth and Jude boxed up all my belongings and brought them to my mom's, and Ruth took any of Marcus's stuff that the police didn't take. Actually, I guess she still has it. I should probably take it . . ."

She doesn't sound like she really will, but who could blame her?

A waitress rushes past, slowing down just long enough to deposit an espresso in front of Cleo.

"So yeah, my mom and I are close, and she really misses me now I'm here, but it's not forever – when I'm done travelling, I'll be home."

She looks wistful for a moment, and I wonder if she's as cool about everything as she seems.

"You said you know who VIN is," I say, feeling bad for changing the subject. "If it's not Marcus, who is it?"

"Right. Well, when I Skyped my mom last week, she told me that Shannon's brother Chris had been out at her house. Like actually banging on the door, yelling, looking for me. She had no idea who he was at first, but eventually put the pieces together. He'd been drinking, she said, and it was hard to make sense of it, but basically he's been looking for me for months because apparently he wants to confront me about Shannon's death."

"Oh God."

"Yeah."

"Wait, because Marcus broke up with Shannon to be with you, it was your fault that she jumped?"

"Yep. At first he blamed Marcus but then, awkwardly, Marcus went and got himself killed, so Chris needed a new enemy and I guess I was next in line."

The waitress comes over to clear my cup and asks if she can get me anything else. I order more coffee. This conversation isn't going to end any time soon.

"And how did that make you feel?" I find myself asking Cleo, slipping into therapist mode.

"I guess I should feel bad. But, honestly, I don't. Of course I feel sorry that she died, that she was depressed, that she had no help. But I can't take responsibility for another person's actions. I didn't know her, I never met her."

I'm nodding, and inside I'm marvelling at what is either enormous strength of character or a huge lack of empathy. She's right, of course – allowing herself to be eaten up with guilt for something over which she had no control would be pointless – but I don't know many who wouldn't be affected in some way. Perhaps she's just very good at hiding it.

"And how did it end – that night at your mother's house?"

"She called the cops and they took him away. They let him off with a caution but he's not allowed to go anywhere near her. So, yeah, I wonder if he's the one sending the messages?"

"What did you say his name is?"

"Chris."

"And his surname?"

"O'Regan."

"O'Regan! I wonder if the 'O R' in @Vin_H_O_Rus is short for O'Regan? Can you think of any other link between Chris and the username @Vin_H_O_Rus?"

She shakes her head. "No, but then I know very little about him."

"If it's him, why would he be asking me your name? He already knows your name."

"Because he doesn't know for sure it's me in the photo – he's only met me once. He's trying to confirm it's me."

Some of it fits, but I'm not convinced. The messages sound closer to home than some guy in New York.

"But the messages don't sound American," I tell her.

"Sure, but we all speak English, and it sounds pretty much the same when it's written down. If the person is really looking for me and not you, it's the only thing that makes sense."

She has a point. I ask what the next steps are.

"Could you send me some screenshots and the link to some of the tweets?" she says. "And maybe don't bother blocking VIN any more – it's pointless anyway, and it'll be easier to trace him if we have all the tweets. I'll forward everything to a detective back home – he was my contact after Marcus's arrest and he also spoke to my mom a few days after Chris went out to her, so he's a good starting point. I don't know if they investigate stuff like this, but it's worth trying."

"And did your mother tell Chris you're here in Dublin?"

"God, no. She stood on the doorstep, trying to calm him down, sympathising about his sister, and deflecting from me. But he kept roaring that he wanted to know where I was, insisting that she tell him. So she called the cops."

I have to concede it's starting to make more sense now. And perhaps the only reason I didn't hear anything American in VIN's messages is because I wasn't looking for it. I click into my phone to pull up some of my screenshots and send them on to Cleo.

"I guess even if Chris did recognise you in the photo, he thinks you're in Italy – there's no reason for him to consider Dublin, is there?"

"Exactly," says Cleo, picking up her phone when my messages arrive. "And you're the only link. Which unfortunately means he's going to keep bugging you, I guess . . . sorry about that."

I hold up my hands. "No, please, as I've said many times this is entirely my fault. Jesus, even my kids warned me about putting up the photo. And I'm a bloody psychologist! I should have known better."

Cleo smiles then. "Don't beat yourself up. I let a madman move into my apartment. I think I win the 'who's the biggest idiot' competition." She points to my hand. "I see you're still wearing your ring. If I was a psychologist, I'd be thinking it means you're not ready to move on."

I'm about to explain again, but I stop, and twist the ring off my finger.

"You know what, you're probably right," I tell her, dropping it carefully into the zipped pocket in my handbag. My finger looks naked, and I can't decide if what I'm feeling is unease or freedom – perhaps a bit of both.

We chat about other things then – how Dublin compares to Brooklyn, how Irishmen differ from Americans, and the crap tips

Cleo earns at work. And then I need to leave for Ava's basketball match. She stays put when I get up to go and, as I head back out into city-centre bustle, I'm half hoping that it's over, and I'll never see Cleo again.

Chapter 17

Before I even reach my car, there's a new VIN tweet, as though he senses we were talking about him.

Ah. You still think ignoring me is going to work. It's like watching a tiny bird ignoring a giant cat. Why are you holding out?

Is "holding out" an Americanism? It's hard to be objective now. I take a screenshot, and another tweet comes through.

Maybe it's because you're so caught up in your own little life and your little blog? If your blog is a reflection of your life, I would suggest ending it right now. Your life I mean, not just the blog. Ha!

Before I have time to screenshot, the next one arrives.

Seriously though. Why do you think anyone wants to see your photos? I looked through last night. Photos mediocre at best. AT BEST. Some are very poor. Aren't you embarrassed to share them?

They keep coming.

Take my advice and keep your overnight oats pics to yourself. The world is not interested in what you had for breakfast.

Then a final one that makes me freeze as I slide into the driver seat of the car.

And the posts about your scrawny, spotty daughters. WHO CARES?

My face feels hot and my stomach lurches as I start the engine. It takes another minute to slow my breathing. The tweets mean nothing unless I give them power – I just need to keep ignoring.

Gripping the steering wheel, I pull out into traffic.

By the time the girls say goodnight and go to their rooms, I'm exhausted, and the book I was planning to read lies unopened on the couch beside me. The high ceilings and huge bay windows that were so appealing when we bought the house make the room feel cold now. I need company.

I pour a glass of wine and click into Twitter – there's a widespread conversation about a talk-show guest who was rude to his host and, although I didn't see it, I join in and soon get a sense of what's going on. Molly spots that I'm there and says hi – she's just back from holidays so has been offline. Catherine joins in too, and AnnaRose says I seem off form and asks if I'm okay. And suddenly, although it's a terrible idea, I can't keep bottling it up any more, and I'm telling them about VIN.

At first, the consensus is to ignore. Then Molly searches for the VIN tweets, and I can almost hear the collective intake of breath when she tells the others to look too. The responses fly in, swift and sympathetic. Most people tell me it's horrible, and to keep ignoring. Lill isn't sure. She reckons there's a lot to be said for standing up to trolls – why not share the tweets and show I don't care? I'm not convinced but there is something in what she says – if only the lure of sympathy. The debate rolls back and forth; Molly says he doesn't sound Irish, and Catherine wonders if it's Leon from last year. I wonder if VIN is reading, and relishing the attention. Perhaps it's time to change the subject – I tell them I'll think about it and ask Molly about her holiday.

Sure enough, a few minutes later, VIN tweets me again.

I enjoyed that – listening to your pals get their knickers in a twist. The self-importance dripping from the screen.

Then another:

Share or don't share, I'm not going away. And as you sit with your glass of wine, isn't it nice to have me keeping a close eye on you?

Icy pinpricks break out across my skin. My eyes go to the uncovered windows – long black slits to the outside world, like eyes, but for someone looking in. For a moment, I sit there, staring, willing myself to get up, but my legs don't listen. The window frame creaks, making me jump. It's the wind. It's just the wind. It's enough to pull me out of my paralysis – I get up and cross the room. My hand is shaking as I reach out to pull one curtain across, then the other.

Walking back to the couch, I realise I've been holding my breath. The room feels instantly warmer and safer and I'm wondering what I was thinking, sitting here with the curtains wide open. And then I start to feel silly. Of course there's nobody out there. VIN doesn't know where I live. VIN is more than likely Chris who is behind a screen in his New York apartment, not looking through my South Dublin windows.

I tap into the tweets I sent earlier. I had mentioned having switched on the TV too late to catch the chat show, and I'd posted a photo of my half-full glass. So obviously I'm sitting on my couch drinking wine. I'm an idiot. And I'm glad Dave doesn't know what happened – it proves every point he's ever made about social media. I need to be more careful.

Chapter 18

A black cloud hovers over me on the drive to work, dense and unclear. Rebecca was in a horrible mood leaving for school this morning, but Mondays aren't her strong point – especially September Mondays. It was frustrating, not worrying – not the stuff that makes up black clouds. Traffic is horrendous all the way to the city centre and I run my mind's eye over my work diary, wondering if I'll make my 9 o'clock appointment. Then I see what's wrong. Jonathan Oliver is my first client. It's part of the job to deal with all kinds of people – from mildly irritating to truly despicable – but in all my years of practising, I've never met someone who makes me uneasy the way Jonathan does.

With a sigh, I turn into the clinic car park.

Susan is in before me, putting post into pigeon-holes. The coffee machine in the kitchenette is broken, she tells me, so she's going out to the café next door – would I like her to bring me a coffee? I try to hand her a fiver but she won't take it.

"Brian's in a fouler," she says under her breath. "You're going to need all the coffee you can get. My treat."

"Oh. Thanks for that. But what's up with Brian?"

"The new behaviour analyst is gone."

"Who?"

"Oh yes, you didn't even meet her. She started during your

holidays, then called in sick for the last two weeks, and now she's handed in her notice. So we're short-staffed again, and he has to find someone else. Fouler." She nods towards his office.

I can hear his voice coming through the wall; it sounds like he's on the phone. His door handle starts to turn down and I dart for my own office. It's enough to start my day with a cross teenager, I don't need a cranky boss too.

Susan knocks ten minutes later with a cappuccino, and lets me know in a lowered voice that Jonathan is outside. "He's so good-looking!" she mouths.

"You are insane," I mouth back, and signal to her to give me five minutes.

Two minutes later, he walks in without knocking, and carefully closes the door behind him.

I walk around my desk and take a seat in the centre of the room, indicating for him to take the one opposite me. He takes the one beside it instead, which is marginally nearer to me. Maybe he didn't understand my gesture, or maybe he's being defiant. I can't always read him. He's grinning at me, arms folded, knees splayed.

I shift back in my chair.

"So, Doc, how are you?" Before I can answer, he sits up straight and points at my left hand. "Oh! The ring is gone, I see. Trouble with the hubby? Has he run off with someone younger? We're more alike than you thought, aren't we, Doctor Elliot?"

Shit. I clasp my hands and force a smile.

"Now, Jonathan, you know this is about you, not me."

"But I think it's relevant. I mean if you're going through a marriage break-up, maybe you're not in the right frame of mind to help me get through mine. Right?"

I see the escape hatch and I jump at it.

"Absolutely – I should have thought of that myself. I'll suggest another psychologist for you – someone here at Steps to Wellness so you won't have to change clinic."

He holds his hands up in mock surrender. "I take it back! I'll stick with you, thanks, Doctor Elliot – none of the others are as pretty." He tilts his head and looks me up and down.

Dear Jesus, in any other profession I'd walk out at this point.

I push my chair back an inch.

"Jonathan, if we are to continue with these sessions, I need you to take them seriously. It's not about me, it's about helping you get through your break-up. Have you been thinking about Sorcha in the last few days?"

He lets out a big sigh, as though I've just asked him to turn himself inside out and tap-dance across the table.

"Fine, let's talk about me. Yes, I thought about Sorcha and, yes, I drank too much and, yes, I bought a two-thousand-euro suit at the weekend, as part of some kind of midlife crisis. Does that sum it up?"

I'm about to reply, but he jumps in again.

"I saw you actually."

"I'm sorry?"

"In the city centre on Saturday – walking along Grafton Street, in your weekend gear. You looked nice. I like the sexy-secretary thing you have going on here, but the weekend jeans thing kind of suited you too." He pauses to look me up and down again. "Seeing you out of uniform was like seeing you naked in a way."

"*Jonathan!*" I stand up now, and take a step back. "We can't continue like this."

His hands fly to his face, covering it completely, and he says nothing for a moment, then starts to rock gently back and forth. The silence is broken by what sounds like a muffled sob. Surely he's not crying?

"Jonathan?"

He's still rocking, and I'm sure now he's crying.

"Jonathan?" I try again. With anyone else, I would instinctively reach out a hand to comfort, but not here, not with him.

It feels like forever before he parts his hands and looks at me, but it's probably only ten or fifteen seconds.

"I'm sorry," he whispers eventually. "God, what am I like? And I'm sorry for what I said, I shouldn't have."

Sitting back down opposite him, I give him a moment to collect himself before I speak.

"That's okay. If you need to cry, let it out."

He nods, and I pass him a box of tissues.

"I think I might go now, though I know our time's not up," he says, and although I'm sorry for him, I'm relieved.

"Absolutely. Let's pencil something in for next week and start again."

I usher him out, then shut the door and collapse back down on the big leather chair behind my desk. Jesus, that was tough going. I know I should relish the difficult cases and learn from them, but I could do without Jonathan.

On autopilot, I pick up my mobile. There's a little envelope showing me I have new mail in my blog email account. I pull down the notification.

The subject is "**Gotcha**" and the sender is VIN.

Dear Lauren,

I thought I'd say hello on email now too. Twitter is so limiting, isn't it? I have so much more to say to you. About your "photography and lifestyle" blog and your mind-numbing life. By the way, that photo you posted of your new trainers – I thought your legs looked a little chunky? Letting yourself go? Not shifting those holiday pounds?

Speaking of which, I'm still waiting to hear back about your American friend in Venice. Believe me when I say I'm patient.

Yours always,

VIN

Slumping against the back of the chair, my hands drop to my sides and I close my eyes for a moment. I need to stay calm. If it *is* Chris, it looks like Cleo's detective contact hasn't been to see him yet. But this email makes it even easier to prove it's him. So it's actually a good thing. It doesn't feel like a good thing though. I can hear Dave's voice in my head: *Why do you have your email address on your blog?* Because that's what people do. And until today, I've never had anything other than kind feedback about my photos. Maybe I should delete the email address. But then VIN already has it, so what's the point?

Maybe Cleo has news. I send her a quick message and wait, but there's no reply. Opening the email again, I check when it was sent. 8:13 this morning. Which would be the middle of the night in New York. A bad sleeper or one of those guys who plays video games all night?

Susan knocks and pops her head around the door.

"Jonathan is in for Thursday so. I was surprised you wanted him back so soon?"

I put down my phone and sit up straight.

"Did he say that – that I asked him to come back this week?"

"Oh, crap! You mean you didn't?"

I shake my head. "Not your fault, Susan, don't worry. You'd think at a minimum you'd be able to trust clients about their next appointments. Maybe he forgot that I said next week . . ."

"Would you like me to call him and change it?"

I consider it, but then remember him crying in the chair, and tell her to keep the appointment as it is.

"There's just one more thing," she says, looking unsure.

"Go on?"

"It's probably nothing, but he was parked beside you, and he stopped to look in the window of your car. I was holding the door open for another client and saw him. It was just a bit weird so I thought I'd say it, but it's probably nothing."

I smile and thank her, trying to remember what personal belongings are in my car. Mine and Rebecca's library books are on the passenger seat, and there are some empty shopping bags in the footwell – nothing else. My library books are on Social Anxiety, so other than highlighting that I need to step away from work and read some fiction, they don't reveal much.

On Thursday, I'll park around the back of the clinic. And maybe another appointment isn't such a bad idea – the sooner he gets through this break-up, the sooner I'll be free of him.

Chapter 19

Tomorrow's lunches aren't made and the floor's not swept but I'm already thinking about wine and considering leaving everything else until morning. I wonder for a second if I'm drinking more since Dave left – or perhaps it's that I'm always on my own now, and more self-conscious so I notice. It's like my mother is perched on my shoulder, warning me to be careful. *It's a slippery slope, Lauren. Remember what happened to Auntie Maggie?* Poor Auntie Maggie, who was really Great-aunt Maggie to me, brought up seven children on her own, and liked the odd glass of sherry on a Sunday evening. In my mother's teetotal family, this amounted to rampant alcoholism. But that was long before middle Ireland took to opening bottles of wine on Friday nights. Or Thursday nights, I think, as I pull a screw-cap Rioja from the wine rack.

Monday morning's black cloud still hasn't lifted and my cheeks hurt from fake smiling. Brian's still making veiled comments about my hours, and Jonathan was back in this morning full of double-entendres and innuendo – far from the sobbing, rocking husk he was on Monday.

Today's email from VIN was a scathing critique of a dinner recipe I shared last night – apparently I can't cook, my food photography is sub-par, and nobody cares what I eat.

And then when I came home this evening with a new backpack

for Rebecca, she collapsed in floods of tears and stormed up to her bedroom. I followed and found the room in darkness, and Rebecca curled in foetal position on the bed, facing the wall. Sitting on the side of the bed, I touched her hair. Flinching, she pulled away.

"Love, what is it? What's wrong?"

"Mum, the bag is way too babyish," she said, still facing away from me. "I can't take that to school. I'd literally die of embarrassment."

"Surely this isn't about the bag? Rebecca, I can change the bag. It must be something else – come on, talk to me. Is it about your dad?"

"Mum, there's more to life than your stupid marriage break-up. Newsflash – not everything is about you and Dad. You're not *unique*."

I was stung. "Okay. But sometimes when we're upset about something big, we let it show by being upset about something small."

"Stop psychoanalysing me. I'm not one of your clients, and this isn't about Dad. And please take that hideous backpack back to the shop. Can't you just give me the money to pick my own?"

Still mystified, I agreed to return the bag. Maybe we'd go shopping together on Saturday, I suggested. This was met with a shrug, and after a few more minutes rubbing her back, I slipped out of the room.

Now I'm looking at the red-and-black rose-print backpack and wondering what on earth could be wrong with it, as I take a first welcome sip of wine. A tweet notification pops up on my phone and my stomach clenches. But it's not VIN this time – it's Molly asking if there's any update on my troll. I reply, but in the private Twitter group we sometimes use for discussions we want to keep to ourselves.

I'm still getting tweets, I tell her, plus emails now too. Catherine joins the conversation, saying she admires me for not letting it get to me.

Ah you know, I type, **sticks and stones.**

She sends me an applause emoji and I wonder what she'd think if she knew how sick I feel every time VIN makes contact.

Lill joins then to congratulate me for my attitude, and suggests I write a blog post about the experience. I tell her I'll think about it, but I won't – I just want it to go away. Though if Cleo's right and it's Chris, why haven't the police in New York done anything yet?

Cleo still hasn't answered the WhatsApp I sent on Monday – I try her again, and this time she gets back immediately.

Sorry for delay. And unfortunately no update from home. My contact said he will look into it and no need to chase him, he'll get back when he has news, so just waiting. All OK? Lots of VIN msgs?

I type my reply.

Loads unfortunately. And emails now too. I've kept them all, will I send to you?

She says I should, and passes me her email address. Forwarding on the emails feels good, like undoing a too-tight ponytail at the end of a long day. Cleo sends me another WhatsApp.

Got the mails, thanks. Jeez, he's really getting nasty towards you now, not so much about me?

Tell me about it. It's not fair to resent her free pass though – none of it would be happening if I hadn't taken the stupid photo. I send a reply.

Don't worry, I can handle it!

Closing the curtains tight, I turn up the TV to drown the silence, and switch off my phone.

Chapter 20

Dave's mouth is moving and he's saying something about what he's cooking for the girls tonight, but I'm distracted by his cheeks, which are even redder now than they were a few days ago. And when I look down, I can see definite signs of a belly pushing through his shirt. Rubbing my thumb against the inside of my ringless finger, I turn this observation over, and find a nugget of quiet glee. I'm thinking about Nadine and wondering if she's noticed when I realise he's asked me a question.

"Sorry, what was that?"

"Jesus, Lauren, you're miles away! I was asking if you've had any more trouble with the client who was going on about you being in Italy?"

I get up to boil the kettle again. "No, nothing about Italy. Other stuff, but I can't really talk about it because it came up in therapy. More tea?"

He looks at his watch, then up to the ceiling as though he's doing a calculation in his head.

"Are you all right?" I ask, tipping the dregs into the sink.

"Yeah, just working out how much longer the gnocchi bake will be. I don't want the aubergines to dry out."

I burst out laughing and he looks hurt.

"The what? You made what?"

"Lauren, I just told you all about it. Were you listening at all? It's one of Nadine's recipes. Vegetarian. It's very good."

I'm still laughing but I can see he's serious. Two months ago he didn't know an aubergine from his elbow.

"It sounds lovely. I'm sure the girls will really enjoy it. I didn't know you'd gone vegetarian?"

"I'm not really, but Nadine is, and it's not that bad when you try it." His cheeks pinken further. "Anyway, yeah, go on. I'll have one more cup. The girls are probably putting on make-up or something, are they?"

"Finishing homework and throwing stuff in overnight bags. Don't worry, they'll be down in time for your gnocchi bake."

"Cool. So anyway, what were we talking about – oh yeah, your man at work and the social media?"

I give him a look.

"It was one comment about Italy, and it hasn't happened since."

"But even that it happened at all – he obviously found your blog. Aren't you getting too old for blogging and social media?"

Oh Dave.

"Excuse me?"

"I just don't get it. Why talk to total strangers on the internet?"

I'm standing at the counter, pressing his teabag with a spoon to eke out every bit of tea into the hot water, because I know he likes it weak. This isn't a new argument but the 'aren't you too old' angle is.

"Okay, let me explain this one more time. I enjoy taking photos. I share them on my blog because engagement and reaction are part of the enjoyment. I talk to – as you call them – strangers, because that is in fact what millions of people all over the world do, and you might be surprised to hear this but broadening your horizons, engaging in social and political debate, and chatting with a diverse group of people from all over the globe is not in fact a terrible idea. And it only seems to you that I'm too old, because you're so far behind the curve, you're looking at your own arse." I put the tea in front of him with more force than intended and a drop splashes on his sleeve.

"Jesus, Lauren!" Dave's eyes are wide. "Mind the hot tea!"

We're saved from further discussion by Ava, who arrives in

looking for her hair-straightener. Dave wants to know why she needs it, they're just sitting in to watch a film, and she rolls her eyes.

Rebecca comes in then, throws her bag on the floor and flops into a chair with a sigh, burying her chin in her skull-print scarf. Dave and I exchange looks. We both know that sigh.

"What's up, pet?" Dave asks, reaching out to rub her arm.

She jerks away from him and mumbles something into her scarf.

"What did you say?" Dave asks.

"I said is *she* going to be there?"

"Who?"

Rebecca says nothing.

"Nadine, Dave," I say eventually, "she means Nadine."

"Oh right. No, she's gone out for the night. So it's just the three of us."

"Yeah, but I bet she'll be there in the morning," Rebecca says, tracing a circle on the table with her finger.

"Well, yes, it's her house, so of course she'll be there." Dave is getting defensive now. He'll never learn.

"Fine. I'm not going."

"Ah Rebecca, come on. Don't be like that. We've a lovely night planned – I made gnocchi bake and –" he looks at his watch, "and actually I'd better get going or it'll be all dried out."

He stands up but Rebecca doesn't move. I can hear Ava pulling out drawers upstairs, oblivious to the crumbling plans. She'll be disappointed. And worried that we're not making this co-parenting thing work. I walk around to Rebecca and hunker down.

"Hey – why don't you go and enjoy the movie, and then come home early tomorrow morning. I'll be here anyway. Would that work?"

"Before breakfast? Before she gets up?"

"Yes, early as you like."

There's a hint of a nod, and she picks up her bag. Dave's shoulders drop and he mouths a thank-you at me.

Ava bounces back in, hair-straightener in hand, and stuffing it in her bag she looks around at all of us.

"What? What's up?"

"Nothing, let's go," Dave says, leading the way to the front door before Rebecca has time to change her mind.

And then, after hugs and waves, it's just me.

On autopilot, I pick up my phone, and find a new email from VIN waiting for me.

So, Lauren, you like running by the sea I notice. Right along the DART line. Nice of you to share your interesting photos with us. We're so fascinated by your running photos. Because you're the only person in the world who knows how to run, aren't you? You should be on a TV program for people who know how to run. SO UNIQUE. Maybe I'll join you next time.

The phone feels like it's burning me – I stare at it, my mind racing. If VIN is Chris, how the hell would he know anything about the DART line, let alone recognise the backdrop of my photo? I check Instagram – the picture was taken early on Saturday morning and it's mostly me and sky. On the far right of the shot, there's a green blur, and I know it's a DART, but would Chris know that?

I message Cleo to ask if she's free to chat, and my phone rings a moment later. She's getting ready for work, she says, but has a few minutes. I tell her about the latest email, and my rising sense that VIN is not Chris.

"But if he saw a train, it wouldn't be difficult to Google and find out the local urban rail is called DART," she says.

"I guess. Did you hear anything from your detective friend?"

"No – I did chase it yesterday but nothing yet. Relax, Lauren, I'm nearly certain Chris is VIN. Do you want to send me on the email and I'll take a look?"

I agree to do that and she says she needs to go to work. Suddenly I envy her. I waitressed for a summer in New York during college and I was absolutely terrible at it, but I'd still swap places with her now, just to be around people, instead of sitting here staring at the walls.

I microwave some soup and scroll through Twitter as I eat. Molly, Lill and Catherine are all online, talking about a politician who resigned, and I join in, forgetting for a while about VIN. Then Catherine breaks the spell and asks if he's gone away. I'm about to say something breezy, but a spasm of loneliness rips through me, and suddenly I need to share. I want sympathy and hugs and, in lieu of human company, virtual hugs will have to do.

Still there, still doing that really brave anonymous thing, I tell her, replying in our private Twitter group.

Catherine says to keep ignoring, it's the only way to deal with it. Lill is still not convinced – she thinks there's a lot to be said for fighting back. She suggests again that I blog about it, then tags me on a reply to a journalist who is writing about trolling.

@LaurenLePhoto you might be interested in this – @CarolineMcGahernJournalist is looking for contributors – see here:

"Looking for people to chat to me for sensitive article on internet trolling – please RT #journorequest"

Before I have a chance to say I'm not interested, the journalist replies.

Hi Lauren – if you are on for it, would love to chat? Thanks, Caroline

I'm annoyed at Lill for putting me on the spot and so publicly too, and I'm not sure attack is the best form of defence, no matter how often Lill says it.

I tap out my reply.

Sorry, wish I could help but in my case not really troll, it's person with grudge against a friend. Sorry!

She replies straight away.

That sounds intriguing and a bit scary! No worries at all, thanks.

I reply: **Storm in a teacup, sorry can't be of help, good luck with article!**

Then I go back to Molly, Lill and Catherine and ask if they know who is on *The Late Late Show* tonight. I've had enough of talking about VIN.

Much later, Cleo messages me during her break at work. She's looked at the email and says that because "program" is spelt with just one m instead of "programme" it means the sender is American. That hadn't jumped out at me at all, and I try to remember how I spell it. I'm nearly sure I always write program, but it's hard to look at it objectively now. She also says that if you Google "Dublin suburban rail" you find out about the DART pretty quickly. So VIN is still more than likely Chris, she says, and

I don't need to worry about him joining me on my run any time soon. I ask her if she's sure Chris is really in New York – could he have come to Dublin looking for her?

As I type, I realise how dark it is outside and get up to walk over to the window. The poplars at the far corners of the front garden sway in the night-time wind and look almost sinister against the dusky sky. I pull the curtains, without looking out this time.

Cleo replies to remind me there's no reason for Chris to think she's in Ireland – the photo was taken in Italy, so why would he come here?

Unless he's shifted focus, I think. More and more of the messages don't mention her at all now, they're about me. My running, my food photos, my daughters, my blog. What if he doesn't care about finding Cleo any more – what if it was just a random, temporary fixation? It would be a hell of a lot easier for him to find me.

Chapter 21

"Can you put the trolley back for me?" I ask Rebecca and I'm met with a downturned mouth and a sigh, but she starts to pull the trolley across the car park to the bay.

As I'm reshuffling bags in the boot, I sense someone coming up behind me. I swing around and find myself looking straight into Jonathan's grinning face.

He's just inches from me, and I have to step sideways to put some space between us.

"Jonathan, hi, what are you doing here?"

"Oh, just about to do my weekly shop. Much quicker now Sorcha is gone."

Weekly shop? Here? Doesn't he live in Clontarf or Sutton or somewhere on the northside of the city?

"It's always a pleasure to see you in your civvies," he says.

I fold my arms and take another step back.

Rebecca is ambling over, looking at her phone, and suddenly I know I don't want him to talk to her. He follows my gaze.

"Is this your sister, Dr Elliot?"

Rebecca looks up. "Mum, can I go to the cinema tonight?"

"We'll see."

Jonathan is standing at the open boot of my car and I can't close it unless he moves. I reach up and make motions of pulling it slowly down, but still he stands there.

"She's not your daughter surely?" he says, then turns to Rebecca. "Is this your mum?"

Rebecca nods and smiles, her manners instinctive, even in sulky teen mode. Jonathan takes a step back and turns his head sideways to look her up and down.

"I can't believe it – you must be, what, fifteen or sixteen?"

Rebecca grins widely and her cheeks turn pink. "I'm thirteen, but I'll be fourteen soon."

"Rebecca!" I say, louder than intended, and they both look at me.

Rebecca is surprised, Jonathan amused. Fuckwit.

"Rebecca, into the car, please." I lead her by the arm around to the passenger side.

Once she's in, I turn back to him.

"We need to go now, but it's probably best if we keep things professional, even if we spot one another out and about. It's better for your treatment, I mean."

He nods, still smiling, enjoying my discomfort I suspect.

"Sure, I'll see you soon at Steps to Wellness anyway," he says, turning towards the entrance to the supermarket. Then he stops and looks back. "Goodness, I can't remember what I need at all now. Isn't that strange?"

I'm already getting into the car, and I pretend I can't hear his words or the glint of challenge in his voice. As I reverse slowly out of the narrow space, he stands, watching, then I see him walk towards a car. He's not going to the supermarket after all.

"Who was that, Mum?" Rebecca asks, not looking up from her phone.

"Just someone from work. Let's just say, not my favourite person."

"Is he the guy who knew we were in Italy?"

I grip the steering wheel and slow down for an orange light ahead.

"Well yes, it is, but where did you hear about him?"

"Dad told us – he said one of your clients guessed you were in Italy because you put pictures of the holiday on Instagram and on your blog. He said it was a good lesson about over-sharing and why it's a bad idea. Is it true?"

Trust Dave to take a private conversation and turn it into a cautionary tale for our children. With me as the bad guy.

"It's true that someone at work seemed to know I was in Italy," I tell her, choosing my words carefully, "but there are lots of ways he could have known. I had Lonely Planet Venice in my handbag shortly before the trip for example, and my bag was on the floor beside my desk. I had been chatting to Susan our receptionist about mosquitos and whether or not we'd need to take spray with us – it's likely there were people in the waiting room who could hear us." We're still stopped at the lights, and I turn to look at her. "There are lots of ways he could have found out."

The lights change, and we pull off with the traffic. I can feel her looking at me.

"Okay, but Dad seemed pretty sure it's because of the photos. He said we needed to learn a lesson from your mistakes."

I shake my head. "Dad has his own ideas and I can see why he thought that – I'll have a word with him later."

I'm going to kill him later.

The lionhead knocker bangs smartly against the door when I try it a second time, wondering if they're out.

But someone's here – footsteps sound inside, and the door swings open. Nadine's arched eyebrows arch even higher when she realises it's me.

"Hi, is Dave here?"

"Well, yes, but we're just getting ready to go to a party. Is it urgent?"

Give me strength.

"It's important, yes," I tell her, biting down my irritation.

She pulls the door wide and invites me into the hallway, then goes upstairs. I haven't been here since the dinner party last April. It all seems so obvious now when I think back – the eye contact, the giggling. I remember thinking I was being foolish, and worrying I was turning into someone who doesn't like her husband to have female friends.

Muffled voices float from upstairs and Dave arrives down, followed closely by Nadine.

"This is just between Dave and me, Nadine, if that's okay."

She opens her mouth to protest, but Dave says he'll only be a minute and she goes back upstairs.

"What's up – nothing wrong with the girls, is there?"

"The girls are fine, but I've just heard you told them about my client at work who knew I was in Italy."

"Yeah, and?"

"Yeah, and it's not okay. That was a private conversation between us – I confided something in you about my work, and then you went and said it to the girls, painting me as the villain."

Dave looks surprised. He's used to compliant-me, the face-saving peacekeeper, and now for the second time in a week, he's seeing another side.

"Jesus, relax, Lauren. There was no villain. I just used it as an example for the girls. God knows what they're snapchatting and posting online. I want them to understand that there are consequences, even for adults."

"That's fine, but not at my expense. Just because we're not together doesn't mean you can hold me up as a bad example."

Leaning against the wall at the end of the stairs, Dave folds his arms and purses his lips. There's a reek of high-horse coming from him, and I know what he's going to say before he says it.

"Lauren, it's not that long since you were dealing with that guy Leon tormenting you online. Surely that whole ordeal taught you something?"

"This has nothing to do with that. Leon was an internet troll – I still don't know who he was. Jonathan is a real-life client – it's completely different. Anyway, that's not the point. There are many ways we can co-parent, but making examples of one another isn't one of them. All right?"

Dave holds his hands up. "Fine, got it. I won't mention your work again."

"Thank you." I turn to leave, just as Nadine comes back down the stairs.

"For what it's worth," she says, "Dave was just trying to help. He was being a good dad."

Swivelling around, I open my mouth to tell her to butt out, then stop to choose my words more carefully.

"Nadine, this is between Dave and me. There's no reason for you to worry about it."

Dave looks like he's about to say something, but Nadine jumps in first.

"Lauren, I know you don't like hearing this, but I'm with Dave now, and I'm involved in every area of his life, including his relationship with his daughters. And as I'm closer in age to them, I think I can help with some of the issues that come up."

I can feel the heat in my face and on some level I'm aware that my mouth is hanging open but no words are coming out. I look over at Dave, who seems as surprised as I am to hear about Nadine's sudden interest in parenting. Surely he'll say something? But he doesn't. And I'm still standing there with my mouth half-open, and the moment has passed. Nadine ends it by turning on her heel and going back upstairs. I give Dave the most withering look I can muster and march out without saying goodbye.

Next door, Clare is watering two tubs of dead flowers and looks up as I flounce down the steps.

"Lauren, are you okay?" she asks, putting down the watering can and walking over to the dividing wall. She's wearing a long, black jersey dress, which is completely at odds with the purple tie-dye bandana in her hair and the grey slipper-boots on her feet. She catches my look.

"We're going out for dinner, but we're not leaving for an hour, and I have high hopes of bringing these flowers back to life. So tell me – what's up?"

I don't want to stop in Nadine's driveway, so I suggest tea in my house. Clare puts her front door on the latch, calling back to her husband that she's popping in to me, and follows me out. Clare is the only person who has reacted in any kind of normal, human way to the mess with Dave. We've spent many hours analysing and dissecting the affair over the last two months, usually in my kitchen. Clare doesn't have kids and maybe that's why she has the headspace to lend me an ear for my problems, or maybe she's just one of those really good people you come across every now and then.

Inside, once the kettle is boiling, I tell her about the conversation with Dave. When I get to the bit about Nadine saying she's closer in age to the girls, Clare's brown eyes widen.

"She's a complete wenchbag, Lauren, and always has been, and as soon as the Botox stops working and the hair turns to straw she'll be kicking herself that Dave is gone, she has no friends, and the only people left listening to her whinging will be her personal trainer, her life coach and her cleaner."

I snort at the last bit. This is why I love Clare.

"And only because they have no choice," she continues. "They're paid to put up with her."

"Hang on, I thought you were messing – does she really have a personal trainer?"

"Oh God yes – you hardly think Nadine would be bothered getting to the gym herself or just going out for a run. And same with the life coach and the cleaner – they're all in and out of the house, looking after the Queen."

"Jesus, that's kind of bugging me. For years I've been saying to Dave we should get a cleaner in to help with the house, even just once a fortnight, but he always said we didn't need it. Talk about double standards. And your one's house is always gleaming – why does she even need a cleaner? I'm the one who needs help." I glance down at skirting boards that haven't been washed in months. If even.

"Well, that's the point, isn't it," Clare says. "She has a cleaner, so her house is gleaming. And when Dave is gone, her house will still be gleaming. But will she be happy?"

I'm curious about her certainty that Dave's not in it for the long haul.

"Do you really think he'll leave her? He seems so disgustingly besotted."

"He will. Absolutely. He'll keep looking for younger ones – though he'll find it harder to do. That's the consensus among the neighbours anyway."

This catches me by surprise. "Really? Who? What are they saying?"

Clare slides the bandana off her head and shakes her hair free, running her fingers through her dark curls.

"It was at the Residents' Association meeting. So help me God, if I don't get off that association soon I'll end up in an institution. But yes, they were all commenting last week on how well you're looking and how the split seems to suit you, and that it's gone the other way for Dave. There was a certain amount of barely suppressed glee in the room. And – wait for this – two of them were wondering if you're the one who damaged Dave's car, and they said they wouldn't blame you if you did!"

"Wait, what damage? I didn't do anything to Dave's car!"

"Oh listen, I know you didn't – someone tipped off his wing-mirror and it's hanging loose and, honestly, I don't think the RA gang thought you did it – it was a bit of craic more than anything. But nice to know about the solidarity, isn't it? They're rooting for you."

It doesn't tally at all with what I've experienced – polite nods, skeletal small talk, and no mention of the split.

"But that's because they're feeling awkward," Clare says when I tell her this. "They're not used to neighbours having affairs with other neighbours. And they think you'd be embarrassed if they brought it up. That's all."

It takes a moment to absorb this.

"I see your point," I tell her, "but it would be nice if just once someone asked me how I was doing."

"But, Lauren love, you don't give off that impression. People around here admire you, but they don't feel they know you well enough to ask how you're really doing. You always seem to have everything under control. What's the word . . ." She stops for a minute. "Poised. That's it. And you don't give off an air of inviting questions." She stops again. "Have I hurt your feelings?"

"No," I say slowly, getting up to make tea. "That's fine, it makes sense. I just hadn't thought of it like that. The way I was brought up, you don't air your dirty linen in public, so I guess I can't have it both ways."

"That's it. I think if you want people to ask you about it, you need to bring it up yourself. It can't be healthy to keep everything bottled up – you need to let it out of your system sometimes." She sees what must be a look of horror on my face at the idea of spilling all to our neighbours, and rushes to clarify. "I don't mean to everyone and anyone, but I'm always here if you want to have a bitch about Nadine. And I can fill you in on the nice things – like the RA discussion on how well you're looking. Best of both worlds then, isn't it?"

I nod and place a mug of tea in front of her, grateful for one ally on a day that hasn't gone very well at all.

CLEO

Chapter 22

Click, click, click, then nothing. Cleo tries again, but there's no spark. Dammit. She moves the pan of soup to the ring at the back of the stove-top, the only one still working. It's beyond crappy, but there's no way she's calling the landlord again. There's something deeply unpalatable about him, and the way he pauses to lick his lips when he's talking to her. Like he's about to devour a burger.

She checks the time on the microwave clock. 18:11 say the bright green digits, stark and uninspiring against their black background. She misses her vintage wall clock now, with its reassuring pink roses. Actually she misses everything about her New York apartment – the cheery green sofa, the beaded cushions, the kitchen table that always seemed so small until she moved here and discovered what a small table really looks like.

Her Mac chirps to life and she opens it up to answer the call. Her mom likes to think she's very with it, but it took her a while to get used to Skype when Cleo moved here. She's getting better at the technical side but still marvels that she's able to see right into the apartment from thousands of miles away, and says so every time.

"Let me look at you," she says when Cleo picks up. "Step back from the screen so I can see you better. I need to make sure you're not fading away."

"Mom, they have food in Ireland too, and I'm thirty, remember?"

"Sure, honey, but you know when you're busy you forget to eat. Now, walk me around your apartment."

Cleo holds up the laptop and shows Delphine the saggy brown sofa, the ring-marked coffee table, and the boxy TV set like something from *That Seventies Show*. Delphine is impressed at how tidy the kitchen is, and happy to see the pan of soup bubbling on the stove. If she asks to look inside the fridge Cleo is in trouble – there's a bottle of white Zinfandel, a hunk of Brie, and a lemon. But she's satisfied with her cursory tour and Cleo flops down on the sofa to fill her in on what's going on.

"So how is work – are you still in that bar?"

"Yep, still in Nocturn. I'm working tonight, so I'll need to go get ready in a few minutes."

"Saturday night – tips will be good?"

"Nah, I mostly tend bar, and people here don't tip bartenders. But I like it."

Delphine nods and tilts her head to the side, which means she's working up to a question.

"And do you like it enough to stay?" she asks, twisting her watch on her wrist.

"It's fine for keeping me in money while I'm here, but it's not what I want to do forever. I'll be back, Mom – I just need a little more time to explore."

"But there's a whole world to explore," Delphine says, twisting her watch faster. "Why get stuck somewhere tiny and backwards like Ireland?"

"Backwards – that's a little harsh! Where did that come from?"

Delphine purses her lips. "Well, there are better places you could be."

Cleo looks into her mother's eyes, three thousand miles away, trying to work out where this antipathy towards Ireland is coming from. But today they're impossible to read.

"Well, sure, I intend to explore other places," she says eventually. "I'd like to try living further south too – maybe Spain."

Delphine stops twisting her watch and nods. "I think you'd love Spain."

"And don't worry. I'll be back to New York eventually. You know this is something I've always wanted to do and, after everything that happened with Marcus, I realised I needed to stop dragging my feet. Carpe Diem and all that, right?"

Delphine sits up straighter at the mention of Marcus, her mouth set in a tight line.

"Okay, Mom, what is it?"

"I got *this*," Delphine says, holding up a piece of paper.

Cleo's squinting but can't see what's written on it, so Delphine holds it closer to the camera on her tablet.

"That's too close now, Mom – just tell me instead – what is it?"

"It's an email from that guy Chris. I printed it out."

Damn. "What does it say?"

"He says '*As soon as your daughter took Marcus, she killed Shannon. She's an entitled narcissist, a –*'" She stops reading and looks up at Cleo.

"Go on, Mom, it's okay."

"He says '*She's an entitled narcissist, a whore who thinks she can take what she wants and stamp all over anyone who gets in her way. You tell her I will find her one way or another, and then she'll face up to what's she's done*'."

Cleo realises she's rocking back and forth with the laptop on her knees, nodding at Delphine – perhaps to reassure her that she's fine with this. But inside she's reeling. Does he really hold her responsible? It's ludicrous. What Shannon did was tragic but she was an adult, in charge of her own actions. And thinking about what Marcus did that last night, who knows what he did to Shannon over the years?

"Honey, are you okay?" Delphine has crumpled the print-out into a ball and is moving it from one hand to the other, crushing it smaller and smaller.

"I'm fine. The people responsible for everything that happened are Shannon and Marcus. But they're both dead, so Chris is looking for the next best thing, and that's me. It's understandable, but I'm not letting it get to me. I'm just sorry you're caught in the middle."

She shakes her head. "Don't worry about me, I can handle an email, and he's not allowed to come near my house."

"Mom, can you forward me the email? I'll send it on to

Detective Murphy. We need to report it – Chris shouldn't be contacting you at all after what happened on your porch that night. Also Detective Murphy is investigating some messages that a friend here is getting about me, and he might be able to see if they're from the same IP address or whatever."

"Wait, what messages?"

"Just some social media stuff, a troll."

"A what?"

"It means someone who's deliberately nasty to someone else online, but anonymously."

She puts the ball of paper down on the table. "Do you think it's Chris?"

"I'm not sure. Maybe. That's why I need you to send me the email. Can you do that?"

She promises she will. As Cleo says goodbye and starts thinking about work, she realises she forgot to put on the water for a shower. She smiles, thinking about trying to explain an immersion to her mother.

As the water slowly heats, she takes her bowl of soup to the window and pulls aside the yellowing net curtain. Outside, Saturday-night partygoers weave up and down Aungier Street. Taxis snake along the road, busy already at six-thirty. There's an atmosphere that's palpable even through the glass, a buzz she hasn't felt anywhere else. Immersions and crappy tips aside, Ireland's not such a bad place to be.

LAUREN

Chapter 23

It's twenty minutes since I pulled out of the clinic and I'm still less than a mile along the road. It's like this every year in September – somehow back-to-school congestion seems to cascade into the rest of the day, and Monday is always the worst.

My eyes are itchy with tiredness, and Jonathan's appearance at the supermarket on Saturday is still jabbing at me, nudging a knot in my stomach.

My phone rings and I see "Mum" flashing up on screen – I think about not answering but she'll just keep trying every five minutes until I do.

"Hi, Mum, I'm driving, but I have you on Bluetooth. How're you?"

"Lauren, I saw something very strange today. And it has to do with you."

Oh God, this could be anything. "Yes, what is it?"

"Well my neighbour showed me a picture on her phone, and I'm nearly sure it was you. But how could she have a picture of you?"

"Maybe it wasn't me, just someone who looked like me? Where did she get the photo?"

"That was the strange thing – she said it was a website. Someone is putting pictures of you on their website."

My hands clench the steering wheel and a shiver runs down both arms. "What was the site, Mum? Did she tell you the name?"

"Yes, she said it's called LePhoto. Maybe a French website or something? Could it be *pornography*?" She whispers the last word.

I burst out laughing and my hands relax on the steering wheel, but just as quickly I stop – much as I'm relieved that my photo isn't on some porn site, I'm now faced with explaining my blog to my mother.

"Lauren, what's so funny? This could be quite serious."

"Sorry, Mum. LePhoto is my website. I write about photography and bits and pieces of my life, and I take photos and put them online."

"I'm sorry, you do what?"

"It's a blog – remember the scrapbooks I had as a kid? It's just a grown-up, digital version of a scrapbook."

"But why?"

"Because I like taking photos and I like writing, and people like reading."

Silence.

"But doesn't your boss mind? Surely it's at odds with your professional work?"

"My boss doesn't know. It's anonymous – my surname isn't on it and I don't give much away. That photo your neighbour found is unusual, I don't share many pictures of myself. So chances of someone at work recognising it are low." Even as I speak, I wonder if I'm fooling myself. If my mother's neighbour spotted me, it's not a huge leap to assume that Jonathan or anyone else has found me too. Maybe I need to take a further step back. My mother is talking again and I realise she's asked me a question.

"Sorry, Mum, what was that?"

"I said, even if it's anonymous, I still don't get it. Why would you want to share personal thoughts on the internet for everyone to see? If you've something on your mind, talk to me or to one of your friends. Don't be letting everyone know what's going on with you – surely you can see that's a bad idea?"

"Mum, don't worry. I don't share personal stuff, it's not like I'm blogging about my marriage break-up."

She lowers her voice, as though afraid someone can hear our conversation. "Well, that's it exactly – you don't want the world knowing your business."

I want to laugh again – she's in her hallway in West Cork, and

I'm in my car, and nobody can hear us at all, but still she's worried we're being overheard. Heaven forbid anyone would ever know what's really going on with either of us.

"How are the girls and Dave anyway?" she asks, and I grit my teeth.

"The girls are fine. I don't know how Dave is, I'm sure he's grand."

That's not strictly true. He called me earlier, bored while he was waiting for the garage to fix the wing mirror on his car. He launched into a long-winded story about being ripped off for what was clearly a tiny job, and I made sympathetic noises while scrolling through my work email. My attention snapped back when I realised he'd changed the subject – he'd reached the real purpose of the call. Apparently Rebecca was rude to Nadine when the girls had dinner there yesterday; she'd made some pointed comments about the roast potatoes, suggesting that if Nadine made them herself instead of buying from an expensive deli, they'd taste better. Apparently she'd even mentioned my cooking in a complimentary way – not something I've heard from her before. I told Dave I'd bring it up with her, trying to keep the smile out of my voice.

My mum has gone quiet and I know she's about to launch into something about us getting back together. I tell her traffic has started moving and I need to go, though even after I hang up it takes another forty minutes to get to Monkstown. The girls are home from school ahead of me, and already doing homework in their rooms, but Rebecca comes down when she hears the front door, and drops into a kitchen chair without saying hello.

"Hey, what's up?" I ask, ruffling her curls.

She swipes my hand away. "Don't touch my hair. It's bad enough as it is."

I have no idea what she's talking about but pull my hand away and sit beside her.

"What's wrong?"

"Nothing."

"Dad was on the phone about dinner yesterday – did you say something about Nadine's cooking?"

Faux-innocent eyes meet mine. "Me? I was just trying to save her some money – I told her it's easy to make roast potatoes herself and they cost less too."

"Hmm. Right. Would you like a cup of tea?"

She nods and looks away, going quiet again.

When the tea is ready, I sit beside her again and wait. Eventually it comes.

"I hate my hair."

This is new. Ever since she was small, strangers have been stopping to tell her how beautiful her red curls are.

"Your hair is lovely – where is this coming from?"

"Nowhere. I just hate it. I look horrible. I wish I could chop it all off. I look crap compared to the other girls in school."

"You don't, you look beautiful, but that's not even the point. It's not about appearance, it's about what's inside."

"Oh Mum, stop! You're one to talk. Colouring your hair and going out running – if appearance doesn't matter, why do you pay so much attention to it? You're such a phony!"

It feels like a slap, and at first I can't think of a single thing to say. Then she puts her head in her arms and her shoulders start to shake. When I reach out to rub her back, she jerks away.

"Rebecca, what's going on?"

"Nothing," is the muffled reply. Then she looks up. "I'm dying my hair, and you can't stop me."

With just the briefest pause, Lauren-the-psychologist jumps in to save Lauren-the-mother from saying the wrong thing.

"That's fine, love. If you want to dye your hair, you can. Just check with the school first to make sure they don't have any rules about certain colours, will you?"

Her eyes widen and her mouth opens to say something but she changes her mind and runs back upstairs. Maybe she won't dye her hair, or maybe she'll dye it blue and get us all in trouble but, either way, her step sounds lighter on the stairs.

It's quiet now that the girls are in bed, and I should be reading notes to prepare for clinic tomorrow, but I'm online. Ironically, I had a client today who is worried about his social-media addiction – he'd be surprised if he knew his therapist is unable to go ten minutes without checking her phone.

On Twitter, Catherine and Lill want to know how I'm doing and if there's been any progress with VIN. Nothing so far I tell them, making a mental note to check with Cleo.

Lill joins and makes a suggestion. **I know you weren't sure, but would you consider talking to that journalist? Get it out of your system?**

Catherine replies before I have a chance to.

Yeah but you have to be careful. Everyone says don't feed the trolls, she says, always more cautious than Lill.

Her avatar is a picture of Lisa Simpson and I've never seen a picture of Lill herself, though I've known her online for four years now.

I know, I reply. **I'll think about it.**

Your hubby would go mad too if you talked to a journalist, wouldn't he? Catherine says.

Dave would indeed be apoplectic. I type a question.

@LillGalwayGirl What was the name of the journalist again? Don't tag her, am still just thinking.

She's CarolineMcGahernJournalist. She might have found people by now though. I'll check her tweets, says Lill.

She's back a minute later. **No, she's still looking. You could ask her if you can do it anonymously?**

I tell her I need to think about it. I try Cleo then, to see if there's any update, and she replies to say she'll call me, as it's too long to type out.

"So my mom got an email from Chris," she says, as soon as I answer. "I passed it on to Detective Murphy, and he asked Chris about it. He admits sending the email – well, he signed it so that's not much of an admission – but claims to know nothing about the VIN messages."

"Can the police check if the messages came from the same computer?" I ask her. Maybe we're finally getting somewhere.

"They'd have to get a court order for the IP address and that takes time, so no quick fix unfortunately."

"Really? They can't just like, I don't know, look it up on a database or something?"

"No, I thought so too, it's not that simple unfortunately. But if Chris knows they're on his back now, it might curtail him, right?"

I'm not convinced. "I'm still not sure Chris is VIN. Why is he bothering to troll me?"

"I don't think trolls care who they go after – they just like getting at people," Cleo says. "He's getting his kicks picking on you while he's waiting for you to confirm it's me in the photo."

"Okay, but why would he give his name in an email to your mother but message me anonymously?"

"I guess because being anonymous gives him leeway to be nasty," she says. "Hey – I wonder could we get him to say something he could only know if he's really Chris? I take it VIN has never mentioned my name?"

"No, never. When he's not telling me I'm a useless waste of space, he's asking for details about you. Though I get the feeling he's accepted that I only met you briefly in Italy and he has no idea you're here in Dublin and we're in touch. So that's something."

There's silence on the other end of the phone for a moment.

"Well, how about you try to draw VIN into saying something about me – something that he would know if it's Chris? Like my name, or where I'm from, or about contacting my mother?"

I'm not sure about this at all. Writing about trolling is one thing, but engaging directly with VIN is a much bigger step. It's my turn to go quiet.

"Lauren? Are you still there?"

"Yes, I'm here. I'm just not sure it's wise. It's toxic enough reading – if I reply I'm going to get even more hate."

"Hey, I'm conscious you're getting the brunt of this, so it's totally up to you."

For the second time tonight, I say I'll think about it, and end the call.

An email has come in while we were talking.

Dear Lauren,
Isn't it cosy when it's just the two of us? You on your big couch, me never too far away.
See you very soon,
VIN

My head snaps up and my eyes go to the window. There's nobody here, there's nobody outside looking in. Of course there isn't. He knows I'm on my couch because that's where I am every night at this time. It's a lucky guess. Nothing more.

Chapter 24

The sitting room windows rattle with pelting rain, and everything feels half-hearted and dreary. I pull a throw off the back of the couch and wrap it around me, staring at my glass of sparkling water and wondering how I'm going to fill the next five hours. On the coffee table a stack of notes from the clinic beckons. Depressing though it may be to work on a Saturday night, it will kill a few hours, and take the pressure off next week. Sighing, I pick up the first file. Jonathan's name is at the top, in my handwriting. *Jonathan H. Oliver.* I'd forgotten about the H. Could it have something to do with the Vin_H_O_Rus username? It wouldn't explain the Rus part or the Vin part . . . now I'm seeing things where there's nothing to see. Suddenly I don't want his file in the house anymore and, knowing it's ridiculous, I get up and go outside to put it in the car. It's lashing rain and the file gets wet but I don't care – I don't want any part of Jonathan in my home.

On my way back in, I glance over to Nadine's and wonder what the girls are doing. The lights are on, casting a glow on the garden outside, and faint strains of music drift out – something poppy I've heard on the radio recently. I go up the steps to my own house and shut the door, blocking out the music, and feeling once more the heavy silence of an empty house.

Back on the couch, I open the next file, but my mind is still on

Dave and Nadine and the girls, wondering what they're doing. Picking up my phone, I ignore the little voice that tells me nothing good comes of spying, and click into Snapchat. I search for Ava first, but she hasn't posted anything. Rebecca next, and she hasn't let me down. There's a photo of a frozen pizza, across which she's typed "**Yuck**", then a picture of Dave and Nadine standing together at the sitting-room window. They're facing away from the camera, and have their hands in one another's back pockets, like something out of an 80s teen movie. "**Ugh!!**" is what Rebecca has typed on this one, and I nod in quiet agreement. I shouldn't be spying, and she shouldn't be sharing photos of her dad and his girlfriend, and I definitely shouldn't be enjoying Rebecca's disdain, but as I put down the phone and pick up the file from work, I feel better.

It's almost ten by the time I put down the last file and switch on TV. *The Snapper* is on, and I go to Twitter to see who else is watching – most of the country it seems. Molly, Catherine and Anna are sitting in tonight too, tweeting all the best lines – there's a virtual clinking of glasses when I join in, and some virtual raised eyebrows when I tweet them a photo of my sparkling water.

Anna is surprised. **Never had you for a sparkling water girl, Lauren. Just when you think you know someone!**

Maybe I'll have a glass of wine later, I reply. **Or chocolate. Or both. Girls not here, so feeling sorry for myself!**

The commiserations come then, and I'm glad to have these friends – these people I've never met in real life – keeping me company. Actually I did meet Molly once – we were both at a women's networking event and we went for a drink after. She was exactly like she is online – outspoken, direct, but with a warm streak that pokes through regularly, much as she tries to hide it on Twitter. We said we'd do it again, but it hasn't happened since. Her kids are much smaller than mine, so she can't get out as often, and sometimes chatting online is easier. You can do it in your pyjamas for starters. With that in mind, I go upstairs to get changed for bed. And it's only half past ten. It really doesn't get much more rock'n'roll than this.

The Snapper is over and I've switched off the TV with every intention of going to bed but my body isn't listening – one more flick through the entire internet, and then I'll go. The rain is still battering the window, loud now that the TV is off, drowning out even the ticking of the clock. I get up and move towards the window, switching off the lamp as I pass. The room is dark, save for the sliver of street-light that slinks between the curtains and across the wooden floor. Peeking out, I crane my neck to check if the lights are still on in Nadine's. I can't see, even with the curve of the bay window. The poplars at the end of the garden are swaying in the wind, and the rain is beating against the path, bashing down into the already formed puddles. At the end of the garden, over the wall, I see a sudden movement. Is someone there? The small fir tree beside the gate is darting over and back like a crazed puppet and it's hard to see what's shadow and what's real. Gripping the curtain, I try to focus. Something dark moves on the ground, then just as quickly it disappears. I take a small step back, my eyes still on the garden. My heart is tight in my chest and my breath is gone; nothing's coming in or out as I watch and wait. There it is again, but for a fraction of a second longer this time and I'm sure now it's just the shadow of the tree. I'm almost sure.

A noise bursts through the silence, making me jump. It takes a second to register that it's my phone, buzzing on the coffee table. I pick it up, pulling down the envelope notification, sensing already that it's be VIN.

Dear Lauren,
Are you all alone in that big house of yours tonight? It must be very quiet with the girls not there. You can hear every creak, can't you? You look lonely. Would you like me to come inside and keep you company?
Yours forever,
VIN

The phone skitters across the floor and my hands fly to my mouth. Is he outside? I'm frozen in the middle of the sitting room, my brain shouting at me to do something. But what? Call the Guards? What would I even say to the Guards?

Out in the hall, I step over moving shadows towards the door –

it's double-locked and the chain is on. I'm sure the back door is locked too – I turned the key when I got dressed for bed. Didn't I? Jesus, now I don't know. I need to check, but I can't make myself open the kitchen door. Surely I locked it? I'm trying to remember but my thoughts are knotted. *Breathe. Breathe.* Okay, I came downstairs, and went to the kitchen to get more water. I turned the key then, I know I did. The windows are all closed too, there's no way to get in without breaking them. But what if he smashes one? Is anyone going to hear? Dave is too far away, and Clare is probably fast asleep next door.

Alarm. I need to put on the alarm so it will go off if someone breaks a window.

Nobody is going to break a window. It's just an internet troll. I say it over and over in my head, like a mantra to ward him off.

I cross the hall to the alarm panel beside the front door. My fingers are numb as I hit the buttons and hear the reassuring robot voice tell me the system is arming. The stained glass on either side of the front door lets street-light and tree-shadows in, but little else – nobody watching can see me here, I'm sure of it. And the logical part of my brain knows there's nobody there, he's playing with me. But still, I feel exposed, and when I go upstairs, I'm half-running. It's only when I'm there, standing with my back against the closed bedroom door that I remember my phone is still in the sitting room. For half a second I think about leaving it there but I can't. What if someone breaks in and there's no way to call the police? I close my eyes and take a breath, then turn the handle of my bedroom door again.

Downstairs, my phone is where I dropped it, lying on the floor, blinking up at me. I stare at its little green light, and my breathing starts to slow. I reach down to pick it up and logic kicks in. He's not here. He knows I'm on my own because I said so on Twitter. He doesn't need to break into my house, I let him in through my phone.

There's another email from VIN. It's just one word.

BOO

Chapter 25

When the girls arrive home on Sunday afternoon, Dave comes with them.

"I think they can manage the walk on their own," I say with a grin.

"I need to talk to you," he mouths, watching as the girls go up the stairs, then making his way to the kitchen. I follow, but don't sit down. I'm not in the mood for one of Dave's monologues.

"What's up?"

"It's Rebecca – the attitude is just non-stop now."

"Oh look, Dave, she's a teenager, her parents have just split up. Nadine is going to have to suck it up sometimes. What was it this time?"

"She was taking photos of Nadine's paintings and sniggering to herself."

I want to snigger now. Nadine fancies herself as an artist, and has framed her own artwork and hung it all over the house. I'm not any kind of expert, but I don't think her landscapes and bowls of fruit are destined for the National Gallery just yet.

"Right, I'll tell her to lay off."

"And she was rude to the cleaning lady yesterday morning too – Grace was mopping the kitchen floor, and Rebecca spilled some milk. It was an accident, but she completely ignored it and got up to leave the kitchen. I told her to clean it up, and she pointed at Grace and said, 'That's her job though, isn't it?' and walked out of the room."

I feel something squeeze my heart – this isn't how I raised Rebecca. Laughing at Nadine behind her back is one thing, but this is another level entirely.

"Okay, that's not on. I'll have a chat with her," I tell him, sinking slowly into a chair. "God, she's lashing out in every direction – it's so bloody draining."

"Well, you need to get tough with her – there's only so long you can keep saying it's because of the break-up."

There's no parent so wise as the one who doesn't have to actually do most of the parenting. He calls a goodbye to the girls and lets himself out, and I ready myself for the next battle.

"Rebecca, do you want to tell me what went on at Nadine's yesterday?"

She looks up from her phone, a guilty look crossing her face.

"What, about the dumb paintings? Mum, they're so bad – you've seen them. The hideous one in the kitchen with the mud-coloured fields and the grey sea – how is that art?"

"I'm no fan of Nadine's artwork either but you can't be rude about it, it's not nice," I say, sitting beside her on the couch. "Imagine how you'd feel if someone did that to you? And your dad said you were rude to the cleaner as well – what was that about?"

Her cheeks flame and the bravado slips away.

"Sorry," she mutters, looking down.

"So it's true?"

"I didn't mean it. It just slipped out"

"Hmm. And did you say sorry?"

"She was gone when I went back in."

My own cheeks are heating up now. If I saw another child behaving like that I'd be horrified.

"Right, well, next time she's working, we need to go down and apologise, okay?"

She sighs, but doesn't argue. I take a breath, ready for the next battle.

"Now, do we also need to talk about Snapchat?"

There's the guilty look again.

"What?" she says.

"Remember what we agreed. I said you could have it as long as I can see what you're sharing, you don't share any photos of yourself that you wouldn't like your gran to see, and you don't post pictures of people without their permission."

There's the guilty look again. I can see her trying to work out which rule she's broken or, more likely, which one I've discovered.

"I don't know what you mean?" she says with a smile I haven't seen in a while.

"The photo of your dad and Nadine last night? 'Ugh!' was the term you used, I think?"

The smile disappears and she's hunting for an answer. She's obviously forgotten she posted it.

"Well, you're one to talk. You put the picture of that woman up when we were on holidays. At least Dad is someone I actually know."

Touché.

"This isn't about me, it's about you." *The Nine O'Clock News* is starting, and instinctively I reach for the remote to turn up the volume, then remember I'm still in the middle of a parenting lecture.

"Well, that's a handy one to use, isn't it?" she says. "Kind of gets you out of everything. I must remember that if I ever have kids."

I take her hand and she pulls it away.

"Look, I'm not cross. I probably would have done the same thing if Snapchat was around when I was your age. But think before you do it next time, okay? Dad would be upset if he saw it." Even as I say it, I wonder why I'm protecting his sensitivities.

"Mum, Dad's hardly going to be on Snapchat. He thinks it's exclusively for stalkers and naked selfies."

I smile at that, and despite herself she smiles back. Oh, what I would give to hold on to that girl – the smiling one who still engages.

"You're right. But what if someone else sent it to him? Someone could screen-grab it, don't forget that."

Her face changes then, and there's something there, but I can't tell what.

135

"Rebecca, are you okay?"

"Yeah, Mum. I'm going to bed." She gets up, and taking her phone with her, goes upstairs to her room.

Jesus, who'd be a parent of a teen?

I text Dave to tell him I'll bring her down to apologise to the cleaner whenever she's there next. As I hit send, I notice a new email notification.

Dear Lauren,

I'm getting tired of you now. Let's get back to where we started – you give me the details I want about the woman in Italy, and I stop. Nobody telling you your photos are crap, your daughters are ugly, and your thighs are a little on the wide side for those leggings you wear running. Tell me what I want to know, and I'm in the wind.

Yours,

VIN

As if on cue, a gust of wind outside blows the door-knocker against the door, and the bang makes me jump. And for a minute, I'm tempted. What if I reply and tell him something – anything? It doesn't have to be Cleo's real name, he's never going to know anyway. If it's Chris, he'll think he's made a mistake and the person in the photo is not Cleo, and if it's *not* Chris, maybe he'll leave me alone, believing he has the information he needs.

I start to type, then stop – Cleo needs to okay this.

Switching to WhatsApp, I message her my idea and wait, but there are no blue ticks to show me she's read it.

There's another bang. I listen for the wind. Was it actually someone at the door this time? Nobody would call at half nine on a Sunday night, not without checking first. I walk over to the window and reach out to pull the curtain aside but my hand stops in mid-air. The thought of looking out and actually finding someone looking back at me is too much – it's easier to stand here not knowing. My hand drops to my side, and I wait, transfixed. A gust of wind whips up and the knocker bangs again. It must have been the wind all along. Jesus, I'm losing it.

Suddenly my phone starts to ring, clanging loud in the silent house. At first I don't move – I watch as the phone jerks on the coffee table, demanding to be picked up. I don't want to answer but I need the noise to stop. Forcing one foot in front of the other, I reach down to pick it up. It's my mother. And then I'm laughing, with the relief and the silliness. God, I need to get a grip.

Chapter 26

It's Tuesday night before Cleo finally sees my WhatsApp – she likes the idea of me giving a false name to VIN to see where that leads, but as soon as I see her reply my stomach turns. It was a great plan when it was just a plan. Now that it means actually engaging with VIN, I'm not so sure. I tell her I need to consider it. She's going to think I'm a lunatic, all gung-ho one minute, backing out the next, but then she's not on the receiving end of the messages.

As though reading my mind, a new email pops up.

Dear Lauren,

While you're deciding what to do, let's chat some more about you. I feel I'm getting to know you better. I see your running photos, your attempts at "arty" ocean shots, and your fascinating (yawn) breakfasts. But I have questions. Why, for example, do you pay a fortune to send your girls to St Catherine's private school, when they could just as easily go to another school for free? Is it a status symbol? Dress your daughters in the most expensive uniform around to show everyone how successful you are? Oh, did I mention? People like you make me want to PUKE.

VIN

Pinpricks of cold sweat break out across my forehead. How could he know what school the girls go to? Christ. My fingers grapple to open my camera roll – there are dozens of pictures of the girls, but I haven't put any online since that first VIN message in Italy. And I don't think I've ever shared anything from inside or outside their school – I'm certain. How could VIN know anything about St Catherine's?

I need to speak to Cleo. She answers on the first ring, her lazy drawl at odds with my hyper state.

"Hey, Lauren, what's up?"

"Cleo, I really don't think it's Chris. VIN knows the name of the school my girls go to – it must be someone local."

She doesn't miss a beat. "Relax, Lauren, it's Chris. I know it is. My friend Ruth back home told me she bumped into him in a bar one night recently. He was drunk, and talking non-stop about what I'd done to his sister and about confronting me. He demanded she tell him where I am, but she just called security. When he was being put out, he yelled something about Italy to her, and said 'I bet she's sitting on a beach somewhere, and doesn't give a shit about what she's done'. So I'm even more sure now he's the person who's been messaging you."

I rub my fingers against my forehead, pushing back against my hairline, trying to ease the tension headache I can feel building.

"Cleo, it just doesn't make sense. How would Chris from – where, Brooklyn? – know about the school my daughters go to?"

Silence for a moment.

"I've noticed a lot of kids here wear uniforms – do your girls? Maybe you've posted a photo of them in uniform, and he googled to find out which school it is?"

I shake my head at the phone. "No, I never have. I wouldn't, for exactly that reason. And since I started getting the messages, I haven't shared a single photo of the girls. Not one."

"But isn't it possible you posted some random picture in the past that has a school uniform or a school photo or a team sweater in the background?"

That forces me to stop and think. Could I have done that? Ava has a basketball hoodie with the school name on the back – would I notice if it was hanging over the back of a chair and inadvertently in a photo? I don't know.

"I suppose, but it's a long shot. Chris would have to go back through hundreds of photos on the off-chance that I'd done it. Is that likely?"

More silence.

"Okay then," she says eventually. "I think the best thing you could do is give a false name, and see how he reacts. If he believes it, he might go away. If he doesn't, then it's further proof it's Chris. Right?"

My stomach flips.

"Okay, I'll do it," I tell her, feeling sick. "I'll let you know how it goes."

Before I can back out again, I finish the call and open my email to tap out a reply.

Fine, you win. The woman is called Giulia, and she's Italian as far as I know. I took her photo, we chatted briefly, and I never saw her again. Now you have what you want, please leave me in peace.

I hit send and sag back on the couch, stuffing the phone under a cushion. It feels like I've just run ten kilometres and done five hours of clinic sessions back to back. Dear Jesus, please let this be the end of it.

It's not though – within minutes there's an email from VIN.

Giulia. I like that. I'm not sure it's likely though, from what I know about the woman on the beach, and I still need her surname – that's more important. Are you telling me the truth, Lauren? I hope you are. Things will get very messy for you in your leafy South Dublin suburb if not. Those crumbling Georgian walls won't protect you if you make me mad.

I'll be in touch.

VIN

Chapter 27

"Mum, do we have to do this? I don't think she'll even remember," Rebecca whispers as I knock on Nadine's door on Wednesday afternoon.

"We do. Well, you do," I whisper back. "I didn't raise you to treat someone differently just because they clean houses for a living." Getting a glimpse of life inside the house when Dave and Nadine aren't here is appealing too, but I brush that thought aside. It sounds a little too much like spying.

A small, dark-haired woman opens the door. She's wearing a wipe-clean housecoat like my granny used to wear to protect her clothes – I haven't seen one in years. She looks surprised at first, then her face lights up with recognition.

"Ah Rebecca love, your dad's not here – do you want to come in out of the cold and wait?"

She pulls the door back and we step in.

"I'm Lauren, Rebecca's mother," I tell her, putting out my hand. She shakes it.

"I thought as much – you can see the likeness. I'm Grace. Come on in – it's chilly out there this afternoon."

The house is warm and, most unusually, there's a smell of baking. Grace beckons us through to the kitchen. I haven't been further than the hall since Dave moved in – this feels illicit, but I don't hesitate.

The kitchen is huge, bigger than I remember, and I can't help looking around for signs of Dave. But there's nothing – not just nothing belonging to Dave, nothing anywhere. The counters are clean and clear, there's none of the clutter I have in my kitchen. It's pristine and soulless. I wonder if Dave notices the difference, and which he prefers. The only personal touch of any kind is a painting on the wall above the table – I recognise the mud-coloured fields and grey sea from Rebecca's description of Nadine's artwork. It is indeed uninspiring.

"I've a tea brack that's just out of the oven – will you have a bit?" Grace asks us, pulling me from my thoughts.

Rebecca nods and reaches for plates, then boils the kettle and takes out three expensive-looking cups and saucers, while Grace cuts the brack.

This isn't how I pictured our apology going.

I clear my throat.

"Grace, you're probably wondering why we're here . . ."

Soft brown eyes meet mine, eyebrows raised in an unspoken question.

"Rebecca has something she wants to say."

Grace looks over at Rebecca who has her back to us, busy with teabags. I will her to at least turn to face us, and she does.

"Sorry," she whispers. Then a little louder, "Sorry for what I said on Saturday morning – I didn't mean it."

"Not at all! Sure I knew you didn't, love. Don't mind it." Grace puts a plate of sliced tea brack on the table.

I'm not as quick as she is to let my daughter off the hook.

"She wasn't brought up to leave other people to clean up her spills, it really isn't okay."

"Oh listen, don't worry – sure it was a welcome break from dusting light-bulbs or whatever it was I was doing." There's a twinkle in her eye and I wonder if Nadine really gets her to dust the light bulbs. "Sit down and have some tea and brack, and we'll have a chance to chat while the house is quiet."

"So Dave and Nadine are both at work, I guess?" I ask as I pull out a chair, though I already know they are.

"They are indeed. He works long hours – but sure you'd know that yourself. She has it a bit easier – none of the late nights he does, though you'd think working in computers would mean longer days. She's right too – isn't that the way we'd all have it if we could?"

She has a lovely accent. I can't place it – somewhere in the south-east of the country maybe – I could listen to it all day.

"God, yes. I work half days but I feel like I'm always on, running between work and kids and house."

Rebecca puts tea in front of us, then wanders off with her own cup and her phone, bored already. Instinctively I want to follow, to see more of Dave's new home, but I stay put.

"Do you work in other houses too?" I ask Grace, while trying to guess her age. She looks older than me, but it's hard to tell if her weathered skin is down to lifestyle or the passage of time.

"I do, and a few small offices, but this is my biggest job – Nadine likes me to come as often as she needs me, sometimes at short notice, so I have to be able to move other things around."

That sounds like Nadine all right, everyone at her beck and call.

"God, that must be difficult to organise?"

"Ah, it is and it isn't. But Nadine pays well, so I can't complain. My husband has a bad back and can't work – I'm not going to turn down good money. Even from someone who likes her radiators polished and her skirting boards shone twice a week."

There's that twinkle again and I still can't tell if she's joking or serious.

"You should see my skirting boards, they could do with a shine." As soon as the words are out, my cheeks start to feel hot. Does it sound like I want her to clean my house too? But she looks unperturbed.

"Oh listen, same in my house – I'm so busy cleaning everywhere else, I've no time for my own."

Immediately I feel better. And I see the parallel – I'm so busy helping clients with their woes, I have no time for my own either.

"Do you have far to come?" I ask. "From home, I mean?"

"No, just down the way in Dún Laoghaire, near the centre."

"Oh that's handy for work – I take it you grew up somewhere outside Dublin though? I've been trying to place your lovely accent."

Her cheeks pinken and she smiles. "I don't know about 'lovely' – I grew up in a tiny village in Waterford. A one-shop, one-pub place. Blackthorn Bay. I do miss it sometimes." She looks wistful for a moment.

"Especially when Nadine's got you polishing radiators?" I chance, grinning at her.

She lets out a burst of laughter.

"Now, you're a woman after my own heart," she says, pushing the plate of brack towards me.

I take a piece and bite in – it's divine. What would Nadine think if she could see me now?

"So, do you see much of Dave and Nadine," I venture, "or are they usually at work?" I wonder how much I can ask without sounding nosy.

"Oh, I'd see them a fair bit – her more than him now, but I'd be here on a Saturday morning sometimes, especially if they're having people over for dinner. I do a lot of the cooking."

My jaw drops. My God, all those nights I slaved over dinners for Dave's friends. Now he pays someone to do it.

"Ah now, nothing fancy," Grace says, reading my reaction. "But Nadine isn't confident about cooking, especially for big groups, and your husband can't boil an egg, if you don't mind me saying so. I just do up a curry or a stroganoff – something they can heat up that night and pretend they made themselves. With the homemade mango chutney from the jar and the homemade raita dressing from the deli."

That makes me laugh.

"And what about during the week – I thought she was all into gnocchi bakes and aubergines?"

"She knows how to open jars and throw everything together in a pot all right," Grace says. "He's never home till late anyway so she eats on her own a lot of the time."

That's interesting. He used to be home relatively early when he lived with us. I wonder what's changed.

Grace reads my mind. "You'd nearly think he was avoiding her sometimes," she says, giving me a wink. "Ah no, he works hard, no doubt that's all there is to it. But if I was living with someone who was as exacting as she is, I might work late more often too."

"Oh really! So she's tough on him, is she?" I ask, ignoring the little voice telling me this isn't quite ethical.

"I'm probably not being fair now. She likes the house neat and he's a bit messy – leaves his cups of tea all over the place and it drives her mad. He likes the TV volume up loud but she doesn't and she always gets her way. Sure it's her home really, isn't it? Hard to get past that. But the house is like a morgue sometimes when they're both here – she's not one for small talk either. Sometimes I feel a bit sorry for him." She looks up at me. "I hope you don't mind me saying that."

I shake my head. "Not at all. I nearly feel sorry for him myself now!" Nearly, but not quite.

"Will you have another cup of tea?" she asks.

I tell her I'll make it.

And I know it's childish, but as I walk over to the kettle I can't help feeling a little gleeful about sitting in Nadine's kitchen, drinking Nadine's tea, listening to gossip from Nadine's cleaner about the man who is still technically my husband, and may not be quite as happy with his new life as it appears.

Chapter 28

Three minutes to ten. I straighten my shoulders, ready for Jonathan. It's warm in my office but I put back on my suit jacket. Armour.

There's a knock, and Susan shows him in.

"Hi, Dr Elliot," he says, smiling, and takes a seat. "I'm feeling really positive about everything and I think I'm finally starting to process that Sorcha has left me. I'm ready to do some good work here today."

The session is far and away the most productive we've had to date. Instead of skirting around issues, he's open and constructive; he says he's accepted that Sorcha is gone, and he's not as angry anymore. I'm starting to wonder if I've completely misjudged him. Maybe the raw stage he was at made him act like a dick, and this is the real Jonathan. Jesus, separation can really screw people up.

When our session comes to an end, I walk him to the door and suggest he leaves it two weeks before booking his next appointment. He turns back to me and smiles.

"You know, you remind me of her."

"Who?"

"You remind me of Sorcha. She was always accusing me of following her too. *Bitch*."

He walks off then, and I'm reeling and spinning, wondering

which one is the real Jonathan, and who he is calling a bitch.

"I need to get my winter coat," Dave says, hopping from one foot to the other on the doorstep, pulling his light jacket around him for full effect. I'm tempted to tell him it's not convenient and that he should have texted first, but I pull the door wide.

"Cheers, are the girls here?" he asks, walking ahead of me into the kitchen as though nothing has changed.

"Yes, both upstairs doing homework. Or at least that's what they're supposed to be doing – they're probably on Snapchat. I'll tell them you're here."

"Bloody Snapchat – I just don't get it," Dave says, shaking his head and looking suddenly like an old man.

I suppress a smile.

"Shouldn't you make them leave their phones down here?" he says.

"I'm only joking. They're doing homework."

He shakes his head again. "And what about you and your man from work – any more trouble there? All okay?"

And because it's been on my mind since the session this morning, and because nobody has asked me how I'm doing all day, I let it out.

"Yeah . . . no, not really. He's still . . . unpredictable. At the end of our session today, he said something that freaked me out a bit, and now I can't figure him out at all. Some psychologist I am."

"What did he say?"

I pull out a chair and sit down heavily.

"I think he obliquely called me a bitch. Except he might have meant his ex-wife. I don't know."

Dave shakes his head. "Jesus, that's awful."

"I know. I wish I could tell you the full story, but even letting out a bit of it, I do feel better. I need to talk to Brian about organising a session with a therapist myself I think, if I can find the time."

"But, Lauren, you know you brought this on yourself. He saw your photos online and now when he's crossing boundaries you're surprised."

"Jesus, Dave, I thought you were on my side."

"I am, but surely you can see this is your own fault? This is exactly like it was when that guy Leon was harassing you. You have to ask yourself is it them or is it you?"

"*Dave.*"

He doesn't pick up on the coiled spring in my voice; he's too busy being right.

"Remember what it was like back then, Lauren – you were miserable. And we still don't know who Leon was. Maybe he's not gone away. I don't understand why you didn't shut down all your accounts back then. Always on that bloody phone, always chatting to your friends online. What's so bad about the real world?"

I walk to the sink to fill a glass of water. If I answer him now, I'll say something I can never take back. I watch as water rises in the glass, then spill it out and go again. Only when I'm sure I'm in control do I turn to face him.

"The reason I didn't shut everything down is because that's giving in. People need to stand up to bullies. You don't understand that, because you've never taken a minute to think about anything more important than where your next beer or your next shag is coming from." I slam the glass of water down on the counter. So much for being in control.

Dave stares, eyes wide. Then he turns towards the hall. "I'll get my winter coat when you're not so bloody cranky," he says, and walks out.

I slam the water down a second time though there's nobody there to hear it, and grab my laptop from my bag. On Twitter, I go straight to search for @CarolineMcGahernJournlist and my fingers fly over the keys to tap out my question.

Are you still looking for people to interview about trolls?

While I wait I go into VIN's Twitter account, and that's when I spot something new. His account bio has a link to a website – that definitely wasn't there the last time I looked. Vinhorus.com. My finger hovers over the link for just a second before pressing it, and then I'm through to what looks like a standard blog. Except it's not a standard blog, it's VIN's. My breath is coming a little faster now as I scan the home page for information. There's no biographical detail, but there is a blog post, just one, titled *The Beginning*.

My stomach tightens as I start to read.

Would you like to hear a story? A history really – a history of actions and consequences and the sins of the father. Pay attention now – there may be a quiz.

Back then, even though I was young, I always knew when it started again – I'd see it in my mother's tight lips and red-flecked cheeks, and her voice that sounded like nothing. He hadn't been home. He was with her. The Whore. That was a word I'd only ever heard the older kids in school using, and I never knew what it meant until she came into our lives.

Of course he'd come back each time, and they'd sit in silence, my mother's eyes red and my father's face white. And I used to listen after they sent me to bed to hear the front door. Or the bedroom door.

Sometimes he'd stay a week, then he'd be gone again. And they thought nobody knew, but of course people knew. The lady who who lived next door used to whisper to her daughter when I'd walk by. People in school knew too. The older kids used to laugh at me. I knew because they'd stop when I got near, then start again when I'd gone past.

I remember towards the beginning of the end there was one night when everything was okay again. He was back from a business trip and I heard them talking and laughing in the living room after I went to bed. I crept down the stairs to listen, but the laughing had stopped by then. My dad's bag was still in the hall – a brown holdall he used when he went on sales trips. I opened it quietly and put my hand inside to feel around. My hand closed around a small, flat box, wrapped in silver paper. Jewellery. It could only be jewellery in a box this size. If he'd brought my mother a present, maybe he was staying. Carefully I opened the wrapping to look inside. I didn't know anything about jewellery but I reckoned she'd like it, and she'd smile again. I put it back the way I found it and ran up the stairs before they heard me.

The next day, my mother didn't have the present and she wasn't smiling. I checked her room, but there was nothing there. I looked in the bag while he was having his breakfast and the box was still in it, zipped into the side pocket. He took the bag with him when he went to work, and said it might be a few days this time. And then I understood – the present was for the Whore. That was the beginning, and this, dear reader, is the end.

My chest feels tight and my breath is short as I read it a second time. Is this VIN's life? Or just a story – an attempt to freak me out? I'm about to read it a third time when Ava comes into the kitchen looking for food. Snapping the laptop shut, I force a smile and start dinner.

It's late by the time I get a reply from the journalist – the girls are in bed and I'm re-reading VIN's story when her message comes in.

Yes, still looking, would love to interview you if interested?

Can I be anonymous? I ask.

Ideally we want people willing to be named, to make a point about standing up to trolls, but I can ask my editor, she replies.

Sure. How does it work? Do we meet? I am in Dublin.

Me too. I can email questions then we could meet in city centre at time that suits? she says.

Great. I will message you my email address, thanks

I follow her account and message her my details privately, then sit back to let it sink in. Am I taking control? Or is it the worst idea I've had yet? I don't know, but VIN has made his next move, and maybe this is mine.

CLEO

Chapter 29

Slate-blue dusk slips like smoke through the window and fills the apartment. It happens so slowly that Cleo doesn't notice until she's sitting in almost perfect darkness. For the third time, she picks up her cell and thinks about calling her date to say she's sick. Back home, she'd never have gone on a date she didn't want to, but there's something about Irish guys . . . a kind of self-deprecating shyness she's not used to, and it's harder to knock them back. Maybe she'll do this one date, then let him down gently.

A Skype call flashes up on her laptop – Delphine doing her usual Saturday check-in. Her face fills the screen when Cleo answers, her hair glinting in the kitchen window sunlight.

"Hey, Mom, your hair looks good – did you colour it?"

She pats it down. "Is it too red?"

"No, it looks great."

"Thank you, honey. How are you doing? Staying in tonight?" She's nodding towards Cleo's tatty sweater.

"I'm going out actually, on a date. I thought I might escape without changing?"

"Sure, whatever you think." She's laughing now.

"Fine, I'll change before I go. How are you doing?"

"I'm good. A little chilly – fall is really setting in now. Is it like that in Dublin too?"

"It's beautiful at this time of year," Cleo says. "You should come some time. Maybe while I'm here – you know, that's a great idea, you should definitely come over!"

"Don't push me like that!" The answer slices through the air between them.

Cleo sits back from the screen.

"Jesus, Mom, don't hold back, tell me how you really feel – what's up?"

Delphine shakes her head and pulls on a smile, but her eyes betray her, like an anxious, choppy sea.

"Mom, what is it?"

"Nothing at all." She shakes her head, harder this time, like she's dislodging an unpleasant image. "I was thinking about last fall, and everything that happened with Marcus. It must be on your mind. Are you doing okay?"

"I'm good. I'm a little pissed about Chris and all that stuff, but I haven't been thinking about Marcus."

She looks at me as though she doesn't believe it, but it's true. It's done and he's gone.

"It's okay to talk, you know."

"I promise you if I need to, I will, but I'm fine. It would be good to solve this thing with Chris and the messages though."

"Any update on that?"

"Yeah, he's started writing a blog now – the VIN person, I mean. And he seems to be hung up on an affair his dad had. I've checked with Ruth, and she's never heard of Chris and Shannon's parents having marriage trouble, but then she wasn't all that close to Shannon. And she doesn't know Chris at all."

"And you think it's definitely him?"

"I'm almost certain. Lauren replied to an email on Tuesday and said my name is Giulia and I'm Italian. She sent me the reply – basically, the person says he doesn't think that's very likely, bearing in mind what he 'knows' about 'the woman on the beach'. If he's unconvinced about the name Giulia, it really seems like it must be Chris. A total stranger would believe Lauren."

Delphine sits back on her chair and Cleo can see the kitchen window behind her. With a whoosh, a first ever wave of homesickness surges through her, catching her off guard. Where did that come from? Just for a moment, she'd give anything to be sitting in her mom's small, bright kitchen in Long Island, solving the world's problems over coffee and cake.

"Cleo, I just don't know. The man I met on my porch that night was raw and broken about the death of his sister – angry at anyone he could blame for what happened. And while of course it's not your fault, it's very human to want to confront you."

"Jesus, Mom."

"Sweetheart, I don't mean it's right. But he's grieving, and he thinks speaking to you is the answer. He didn't seem like someone who would send anonymous messages to a stranger in Dublin."

Cleo doesn't say anything.

"But isn't that a good thing?" Delphine continues. "Why do you want it to be Chris?"

Cleo lets out a long breath. "Because if it's not Chris, then we have no idea who it is, or why he's targeting us. Better the devil you know."

"Ah," is all she says to that, and Cleo can see her turning over what she's said. "Well, who am I to say? It could very well be Chris. But look after yourself, won't you, honey?"

Cleo nods and tells her she needs to get changed to go out. She closes the laptop and, after a beat, calls her date to tell him she's come down with stomach flu. He's so lovely about it, she almost feels bad for lying. But she doesn't, because life's too short for mediocre dates and bouts of misplaced guilt.

LAUREN

Chapter 30

"God, I always forget how much I like your kitchen until I'm here on a sunny day. I'd love if mine was bright like this."

Clare is being kind, my kitchen is falling apart, but natural light and pale colours make it look bigger and brighter than it really is.

"You only got yours done up a few years ago, will you stop! Tea or coffee?" I ask, glancing at the clock. "Too early for wine. Ava and Rebecca would sign me up for AA if they came down and found us drinking wine at four o'clock on a Monday afternoon."

Clare nods and opts for tea. She's head of IT for an IFSC bank and is on a rare day off but says she's bored out of her mind – she was in here almost as soon as my car pulled up.

"How are they doing anyway, the girls?" she asks, lowering her voice.

I sit opposite, waiting for the kettle to boil.

"Ava's okay, Rebecca not so much. She mostly pretends she's fine, but I can see it written all over her. Literally."

"Literally?"

"She dyed her hair. Though the weird thing is, I was worried about her dying it pink or blue and getting in trouble with school, but she dyed it brown."

Clare's mouth drops open. "No! Her beautiful red hair?"

"I know. As rebelling goes, it's a bit odd, isn't it? And she's been rude to Nadine, and even to their cleaner, which is really out of character for her. I know it's all an attempt to get attention but I'm giving her the attention and she's pushing me away."

The kettle trundles to a stop and I pour hot water into two mugs.

"That sounds hard for Rebecca. And how about you, Lauren – how're you doing?"

"Same as ever. You know, totally fine except for the broken marriage, the falling-down house, the troublesome client, and the small matter of the internet troll."

"The who?"

"My own personal troll. This person who goes by the name VIN and sends me horrible messages on email and Twitter and has started a creepy blog now too."

Her eyes widen as I fill her in on VIN, Cleo, and Chris, and show her some of the messages and the blog post.

"What does 'Vin H O Rus' mean?" she asks, looking at his profile.

"I don't know – possibly a shortened version of his name or his initials."

She shakes her head. "Jesus, you poor thing! Can I help in any way?"

"Thank you but no. I'm taking back some control though – I've agreed to meet a journalist for an article on internet trolls. It'll be good to vent a bit."

She puts down her tea. "Seriously? I know I'm always saying you need to talk, but maybe a journalist is a step too far?"

"It'll probably be anonymous. I won't do anything I'm not comfortable with."

She looks at me, lacing and unlacing her fingers around the mug.

"I suppose if you're not named and if it makes you feel like you're taking control, it's not a terrible idea. But be careful, won't you?"

I nod, and I can feel my throat tighten.

"And what about the rest of it?" she continues. "Are you sure there's nothing I can do? I'm not great at DIY but I could stick my foot out and trip Nadine when she's tottering past some evening – would that help?"

That makes me smile. "Ha, she doesn't even wear heels. She doesn't need to, she's tall and gorgeous without them. The cow."

Clare snorts. "You're ten times more gorgeous than she is. There's nothing of substance there – it's all fake tan, fake hair, and enough Botox to fill the Irish Sea."

I shrug. "She's not exactly natural-looking, but she's also ten years younger than me, and nothing can change that. I'm moving on."

That gets her sitting up straighter.

"Oh! Someone new?"

"Jesus, no! I just mean ready to move past Dave."

Her voice softens. "Are you not past him? Would you take him back?"

It takes a moment to find the right words.

"Mostly the answer is no," I say eventually, "but, God, sometimes the loneliness gets to me. Sitting here at night with nobody to talk to. . ." I trace my finger across a biro mark on the table. "But nobody is allowed to talk about the loneliness – nobody wants to hear that someone they know is lonely, because it makes them uncomfortable. So we have to plaster on smiles and pretend we're fine, for fear we'll push people even further away." I stop and smile at her. "Have I frightened you off yet?"

She reaches across the table and puts her hand on mine. Her skin is warm and unfamiliar – I can't remember the last time I was touched by anyone other than my children.

"Not at all. Keep going, this is good for you," she says softly and I'm sorry when she gently releases my hand.

In the middle of the table, there's a napkin holder, filled with yellow daisy-print paper napkins. They've been there since spring, untouched since Easter Sunday. I remember trying to decide between daisies or polka dots. As if that mattered. I pull one out and examine it.

"And we're not allowed to say we don't like being on our own." I tear off one of the little daisies and drop it on the table. Then another, and another, until the napkin is gone. "We all have to embrace being independent, and we can't admit we'd rather be in a couple."

Clare laughs. "Hey, I can absolutely see how you'd rather be in

161

a couple. The world is bloody made for couples. But not with the wrong man surely?"

I look down at the old, scratched, wooden table, a testament to years of marital tea and family dinners.

"I know it's not okay to say this, but when things are going really badly wrong –" I look up, and she's staring back at me, but I see no judgement, "yeah, sometimes even with the wrong man."

I sweep the little pieces of napkin, with their tiny unknowing daisies, into my hand and throw them in the bin.

Chapter 31

"Would you like a coffee while you're waiting?"

I look up from my phone at the ponytail-swishing waitress and order a cappuccino. The journalist won't be here for another ten minutes, and I'm reading over the questions she sent by email. There's nothing at all wrong with them, but still they're making me squirm.

Can you tell me the back-story – how did the first message come about?

No matter what way I look at it, there's no getting away from admitting I shared a photo without permission.

What does the person say in the messages – can you give some examples?

That makes me uncomfortable too. Putting it out there publicly that my troll thinks I'm pathetic with my running selfies and my overnight oats just makes me feel, well, pathetic. I'm not sure how empowering this is going to be.

My cappuccino arrives in an oversized cup the colour of egg yolk and, as I stir in the chocolate flakes, I see a woman come through the door. A girl really, she couldn't be more than twenty-two or twenty-three. Long hair tumbling over her shoulders, a slogan sweatshirt with something about unicorns, and a Mac peeping out of her oversized cross-body satchel. I smile up at her though inside I'm suddenly nervous.

But she swishes past and joins a woman at another table. I'm still looking over at her, wondering if she got it wrong, when a voice interrupts me.

"Lauren?"

I look up to see someone my age or perhaps older, with honey-coloured hair tied back in a low bun. A pair of dark-rimmed glasses slip down her nose as she inclines her head towards me, and she pushes them back up, waiting for me to confirm that I am indeed Lauren.

"Hi, yes, Caroline?"

"That's me," she says, pulling out a chair and sitting down.

There's no laptop peeking out of her bag – instead she pulls out a notebook and pen, and a recording device.

"Thank you for meeting me," she says. "Nice to say hello in person!"

It's Saturday, but when she takes off her coat I see she's wearing a smart black dress, the kind I often wear to work. She reminds me suddenly of Clare, and the knot I didn't know was in my stomach starts to unfurl. I smile back.

"You too. I went ahead and ordered," I tell her, nodding towards my coffee.

She raises her hand and orders the same, then opens her notebook.

"I won't keep you long, but I'm delighted we could meet – it's much easier than a phone interview," she says, fiddling with a button on her recorder. "Okay, grand, that's set to record." She looks up at me. "It's safer than relying on notes. So, thanks for this – no doubt you've plenty of other things you could be doing on a Saturday morning!"

"It's no trouble – I work near here, and I needed to pick up some files from the office anyway."

She writes something in her notebook and I try to read but her handwriting is too scrawly to follow upside down.

"Let's start with that – a bit of background – what do you do for a living?"

It's such an easy question but I'm struggling already.

"I'm a counselling psychologist with the Steps to Wellness Clinic – but actually, don't put the clinic name in."

164

She scribbles something again.

"And what about family – do you have children?"

I shift in my seat.

"Yes, two daughters, fifteen and thirteen."

"And their names?"

"Ava and Rebecca, but do you mind if we keep their names out? I'm happy to tell the story, but wouldn't like anyone to identify me or the girls."

Caroline taps her pen on her lip, and for a moment she's elsewhere.

"I'll talk to my editor. I completely understand why you want to be anonymous, but I think it will be a better, more relatable story if we give your details – you're not just some nameless, faceless victim, you're any of us, you're all of us."

I nod, and take a sip of my coffee. "I absolutely see that, but it would be great to keep all options open. Would that be okay? Hopefully your editor will understand. It's for *IrishNewsOnline.ie,* right?"

The pen is still tapping against her lip and for a minute I wonder if she's going to call it off, but then she smiles.

"Absolutely, nothing off the table for now. And do you have a partner?"

Jesus, I'm not cut out for this. These are the most basic questions and still they feel like pulling plasters.

"I do, I have a husband, but . . ." she's looking at me, waiting – there's no impatience there, only interest. "He's gone," I say finally. "He moved out a few months ago." And to my surprise, it feels good to confess to a stranger. I make a decision. "And actually, regardless of whether we go with anonymous or not, you can put that in. It's not like we're the only people in Ireland with a failed marriage, is it?"

"Oh, tell me about it," she says, putting the pen down, "My husband and I separated about six years ago. I get it. We are definitely not alone. Well, except for the fact that we are alone, so to speak."

That makes me laugh. And in a world of happy couples, I'm glad to be sitting here with a kindred spirit.

"And it's good if we can include it," she continues, "because I think it's part of the story. I imagine the fact that you're getting used to being single makes dealing with your troll more difficult – if your husband was still around, you'd have someone to talk to about it?"

"Yeah, that's part of it. And the messages tend to come at night, when I'm on my own, so that's kind of scary. Do you think it's okay to have that in there, that it's scary? Or am I just giving the troll what he wants?"

She stops to think about this. "I know what you mean. I'd say we can find a way to show readers that it's even tougher when you're on your own, but at the same time we'll avoid giving your troll his kicks – we won't make you sound like you're cowering in the corner. If you like, I can send you what I've written, so you can read over and make sure you're happy with it?"

Sinking back in the seat and picking up my coffee, I nod and thank her. Getting final approval on what goes out will make the world of difference.

"Listen, don't worry – we're not looking to run anything controversial. To be honest, *IrishNewsOnline* are getting a bit of stick about their comments section and this feature is their way of showing they don't condone trolling. So neither I nor they have any reason to be controversial and get ourselves in more trouble."

It's starting to sound more appealing.

"Do you work for them full-time?" I ask her.

"No, I'm freelance. I write for whoever pays me – women's magazines mostly. The most exciting thing I do is a Sunday newspaper social diary, but it's under a pseudonym – I think my editor there knows that readers are unlikely to believe a middle-aged introvert is up to speed with what's going on with Ireland's glitterati."

The ponytail-swishing waitress comes back and Caroline orders an Eggs Benedict. I go for avocado and poached eggs, and another cappuccino. I have a feeling we're going to be here for a while.

"It's the invisible age, you see," she continues, once the waitress is gone. "I find people see me less and less. I remember once when I was younger watching a woman at the meat counter in the supermarket. She looked tired, and she was wearing something brown and beige, and ordering the housekeeper's cut. And she was invisible. I remember promising myself I wouldn't let that happen to me, and yet here I am. I'm the invisible woman at the meat counter."

It's like she's inside my head – it feels like I've known her for a lot longer than fifteen minutes.

"Yeah, I know what you mean. It's hard to keep up with the younger generation," I say, glancing over at unicorn-sweatshirt-girl.

"Is that why you blog?" Caroline asks.

"How do you mean?"

"Well, blogging and social media might be seen as a young person's game – so I was wondering if you do it as a way of staying young?"

Caroline writes something in her notebook as she waits for me to answer and I'm reminded to choose my words carefully, no matter how friendly she is.

"No, I don't think so . . . There are bloggers in all age groups. I have a great network of online friends and they're from every age and stage. In a way that's what I like about the internet – it gives you access to people you might otherwise never meet."

She's writing, and then looks up and indicates I should keep talking.

"In real life, we spend most of our time with people like ourselves – people from the same background, same school, same row of houses. Whereas online, you could be talking to a twenty-year-old gamer from France or a fifty-year-old teacher from Leitrim, and that age and location is largely irrelevant, other than adding texture to the relationship. Does that make sense?"

She nods, still writing.

"So I guess I don't see it as a way of staying young, but maybe that's a by-product. I feel engaged in a wider conversation – life isn't just about work and home." She looks up. "Not that there's anything wrong with that," I say in a hurry. "I don't want your readers to think I'm saying my life is more interesting than theirs. It certainly isn't."

"Well, except for the troll," she says with a smile.

"Yeah, except for the bloody troll."

"So talk to me about that – how did the whole thing start?"

I tell her about the morning on the beach in Venice and putting the photo of Cleo online. She's scribbling furiously as I talk, and I wonder why, when the recorder does all the work, but maybe it's a habit.

"And what made you use the hashtag 'how I wish I spent my twenties'?" she asks.

The food arrives, giving me a chance to think about the answer.

"I suppose she just stood out," I say, carefully cutting my toast. "She looked so relaxed, at ease with the world. At Cleo's age, I already had two children. I love my kids, but part of me wishes I spent more time sitting on a deckchair in the waves . . . shit, don't put that in! My kids will think I'm wishing them out of existence."

"That's fine," Caroline says, putting down her pen to focus on her Eggs Benedict. "I'll make a note to leave that out." She doesn't make a note, but I assume she'll remember.

"The irony is, while I was imagining that Cleo had this really chilled, exotic life, spending all day reading in the sun, she was just on holidays like we were. She actually lives here in Dublin, and has a very normal job in a bar – don't put that in the article – so I guess appearances can be deceiving."

Caroline nods, swallowing a forkful of food before she replies. "Absolutely, and we all do it – make snap judgements about people. So, if I remember correctly from what you said in your email – after a few messages from the VIN account, you told Cleo about it? How did she react?"

I tell her about our conversations, and without going into all the details, I tell her about Cleo's eventual suspicions that the messages are possibly from someone she knows in New York.

"I get the sense you don't feel the same?"

I push a piece of avocado around the plate with my fork.

"Yeah, I don't know. One minute everything she says makes sense but then I get a new message from VIN and I can't picture it being some guy in Brooklyn. Plus VIN seems more interested in me than in Cleo. Sometimes there are two or three emails in a row that are just directed at slagging me off, and don't mention her at all."

Caroline taps the fork to her lip, like she did with the pen earlier. "So do you think he's transferred his obsession from her to you?"

"Maybe, but he does still want to find her and still asks about her too. Then there's this weird blog post – I don't know where that fits with any of it." I pull it up on my phone and we go quiet while she reads.

"Interesting. And did you ask VIN what the blog post is about?"

"God no! I don't want to engage with him at all if I can help it. I never reply to anything. Oh, except I did tell him Cleo's name is Giulia and that she's Italian in an effort to get him off my back, but I'm not sure he believes me. We'll see."

She looks at me over the top of her glasses with unreadable brown eyes. My seat feels hard and uncomfortable now, and I want to get up and walk around.

"This is difficult on you, isn't it?" Her voice is softer, sympathetic. "Tell me what it's doing to you. Let readers know what happens if they allow their fingers tap out hateful messages behind the shield of a screen."

I feel put on the spot. No matter how I word it, crying over what's happening isn't going to be acceptable, because I brought it on myself. That's how the internet works. I shake my head, unable to come up with an answer, and there are tears at the back of my eyes.

"It's okay," she says, softer again. "You're allowed to be upset. What's happening to you is horrible and, whatever you may think, nobody deserves this. You may feel you brought it on yourself, but you didn't. The person at fault here is the troll."

I nod, holding back the tears.

"Just throw any words you like at me, I'll turn them into sentences – how about that?"

I nod again and take a deep breath.

"I feel stupid. Lost. Vulnerable. Old. Foolish. Cross. Angry more than cross. Upset. Scared."

Her head is down, her honey-hair greying at the roots.

"That's good, that's what I'm talking about. What else?"

I sit back in the seat and look at her through the blur of tears.

"Powerless. More than anything, I feel completely and utterly powerless."

Chapter 32

"Oh hiya, Lauren, how're things?"

I shift both bags of groceries to one hand and reach up to close the boot. Dave is coming towards me, jiggling car keys in his hand. Even in the dark I can see he's in one of his "good" shirts, the ones he keeps for nights out. Their front door is open; Nadine must be still colouring in her eyebrows.

"Grand. Just heading in with the shopping," I tell him, opening the garden gate. I'm not in the mood for chit-chat but Dave's not great at picking up on subtle cues.

"Here, give me the bags, I'll carry them in for you."

"I'm fine, Dave, I can manage a few groceries." His face falls. "But thanks for the offer."

We both look up to the sound of his front door closing and see Nadine coming down the steps in a strappy black dress and newly blonded hair.

"Are you ready, hon?" she asks Dave, eying me up and down.

I wish now I'd stayed in the smart top and blazer I wore this morning to meet Caroline, instead of changing into running gear. I never even went for the run.

"We don't want to be late for Georgina and Noel. You know how Georgina fusses."

Suddenly I feel hot and slightly sick, and I want to go inside instead of standing here looking at this woman in her cloud of heavy perfume, taking my place at the dinner table. Georgina and Noel are our oldest friends and, for years, the last Saturday of every month was spent in their house or ours, eating colossal steaks and knocking back expensive red wine. And here we are on the last Saturday of September, but I'm standing here in my running gear, and Nadine is going in my place. And I have no idea if Georgina and Noel care.

Dave holds his hand up in a coming-now gesture to Nadine, and looks at me with something close to an apology, then turns to get into the car.

I watch them drive off.

"Want to talk about it over a bottle?"

Clare's voice catches me off guard.

"Jesus, you're like a cat! Aren't you going out tonight?"

"No," she says, walking towards her own gate and pushing it open. "it's just some of the golf crowd – I told himself to go ahead without me. Will I grab a bottle and come in to you?"

It's not dinner in Noel and Georgina's but it's a million times better than sitting on my own.

Rebecca is staying with a friend, and Ava is at a disco, and I'm grateful to Clare and her bottle of wine for saving me from a too-quiet house.

When I fill her in on the Georgina and Noel story, she starts to laugh.

"What – what's so funny?"

"I know you never said as much, but I have a sneaking suspicion you didn't actually enjoy those dinner parties, and am I right that you can't stand Noel and Georgina?"

I stare at her for a beat, then start to laugh too. It's absolutely true. I can't bear Noel with his casual racism disguised as some kind of post-modern humour, and Georgina is a complete snob. I remember once she told a story about their nanny from China, and I nearly choked on my wine when she started mimicking the woman's accent. Of course Dave and Noel thought her mimicry was hilarious.

"I don't know how you spotted it before I did but, Jesus, you're absolutely right. Noel is a racist dick, and Georgina is the worst kind of snob. And they have no interest in anything outside their own lives. I remember bringing up homelessness one night. They all just looked blankly at me, then Noel shrugged and carried on talking about the apartment they were buying in Croatia."

Clare opens the giant pack of tortilla chips she's brought with her, and I go into the kitchen to look for a bowl and a tub of salsa that's still in date.

"Practically a party now," she says when I sit back down.

"Yeah, a pity party for me so far – sorry. I shouldn't keep going on."

"Hey, it's totally allowed. But just think of Nadine sitting there, fake-laughing at Noel's jokes – you're better off here, aren't you?"

She's right. Clare is always right. Nadine will be bored to tears – the boys prattle on about work, and Georgina goes on and on about her daughter's sporting achievements. My attempts to bring up any topic beyond the radius of our neighbourhood were always met with complete disinterest.

"You know, I met that journalist today and she asked me why I started blogging – I reckon it was those dinner parties, and life with Dave in general. They all acted like as long as we were okay, nothing else mattered. They never cared about what was going on anywhere else. I guess that's how I got interested in Twitter and chatting to people online – a desperate need to talk about something beyond our South Dublin bubble."

Clare pours more wine for both of us, nodding. "That makes sense. We all need an outlet. But surely at home Dave talked about other things?"

Pulling my legs up under me on the couch, I take a sip before answering.

"To be honest, not really, and as the years went by, it all started to feel a bit shallow. Of course he couldn't understand it at all. He used to ask me constantly why I was talking to strangers online – I think he took it as a personal slight."

Clare is smiling. "But he was right, wasn't he? Not defending him, but he could obviously sense he wasn't enough for you?"

"I suppose. He was always going on about it, giving out every time he caught me on my phone. And when that guy Leon started sending me horrible messages – remember the troll last year?" Clare nods. "I reckon Dave felt like his point had been proven."

172

"I'm going to go out on a limb here and suggest something," Clare says, looking suddenly serious. "I'm going to suggest we get a takeaway, because we have much to discuss. Deal? And I'm going back in next-door to get a second bottle of wine." She holds up her hands. "No arguments – this is your therapy session, Lauren – think of me as your personal psychologist, armed with Pad Thai and Rioja."

While she's gone, I check my phone and find an email from VIN.

Missing your daughters tonight, are you, Lauren? Just think of it as practice for when you're older, sitting on your own in your big house with nobody at all around you. Not long to go now.

So VIN knows the girls aren't here, but doesn't know Clare is, or was up to a moment ago. As I turn that over in my mind, I hear the front door close quietly. Clare doesn't have a key – could it be Ava? No, she's not being dropped home for a few hours yet.

There's no sound now, no footsteps in the hall. Just silence and the ticking of the sitting-room clock. I realise I'm holding my breath and I need to get up from the couch and see who's there, but I can't. I stare at the sitting-room door handle, willing it not to move. I try to listen, but white noise is pounding in my ears. Is there someone in the hall?

The room begins to swim in front of my eyes and I close them to make it stop but it makes everything worse. My phone starts to ring, loud in the stillness, and I grab it, fumbling, cursing myself that it's not on silent. Now they'll know I'm here. Christ. My mother. Rejecting the call, I hold my breath and listen. Silence. Then a creak in the hall.

I sit up straighter but my body still won't move off the couch.

Then all of a sudden, there's a knock on the door.

Everything is suspended and I'm paralysed, my heart battering in my chest. I wait for the door to open, dreading what's coming but completely unable to move.

The knock comes again, but now I understand it's not the sitting-room door, it's the front door. Clare?

Scrambling to open WhatsApp, I type out a message to her.

I think there's someone in the house. In the hall.

Her reply is immediate.

No, nobody there – am outside and can see through the glass at front door. Hall empty. You're OK. Can you open the front door?

My legs are shaking when I stand up. At the sitting-room door, I reach out to touch the handle and it's cool in my hand, but not reassuring. I twist it and with everything I have in me I yank the door open and look into the hall. Empty. Looking to my right, I can see Clare's outline through the glass. To my left, the kitchen door at the end of the hall is closed. Did I leave it closed? I can't remember. Clare's face is pressed against the glass.

"*Lauren, I'm here, it's okay. There's nobody else in the house – can you open the front door?*"

I let her in, and tell her we need to check the kitchen. She walks ahead of me down the hall and pushes the door wide.

"See? Nobody here."

Upstairs, the rooms are quiet and empty too. When we go back to the sitting room, my hands are still shaking and it takes a moment to get my breath back. When I do, I tell Clare about hearing the door close.

"Oh Lauren, that was my fault – I left it ajar so I could get back in – it must have closed in the wind. You're after getting an awful fright. I should have known better."

I shake my head. "No, just me being jittery. I got a message from the troll while you were gone and he said something about being alone, so when the door closed I thought he was somehow here." I shake my head. "God, I'm losing it. I need to do something about this guy."

"Well, hopefully talking to the journalist will help. Did you tell Dave about her?"

I shake my head again. "No, Jesus, he'd go nuts! He already thinks I share far too much online – talking to a journalist would be a whole new level. And he doesn't know about VIN anyway."

Clare doesn't say anything.

"What?" I ask her.

"Well, it's not my business, but don't you think it would all go more smoothly if he hears about the article from you beforehand?"

"It'll be anonymous, he won't ever know about it."

She laughs, then stops. "Sorry, I don't mean to laugh, but come

174

on! Is it going to say you're a psychologist?" I nod. "And that you have two teenage daughters, live in Dublin, and have a blog?" I nod again. "And are you mentioning your marriage break-up?"

"Yeah, I decided it's time get my head out of the sand."

"Lauren, Dublin is small. It won't take much to work out who it is, and even if Dave doesn't see it himself, someone will tell him. Don't you think?"

She's right. Again. Oh for God's sake, I'm going to have to tell Dave.

Chapter 33

It's ironic that the first birthday message I get is from Cleo, the person I've known for the shortest time. Her WhatsApp is waiting for me when I wake up.

Hey, our cop friend back home visited Chris again. Says no proof or suggestion it's him. But really hard to prove either way without IP address, court order etc so I'm not convinced. Any word from VIN re name Giulia? And btw, happy birthday

My eyes are still blurry with sleep as I type my reply. Actually VIN hasn't said anything more about Giulia all week, one way or the other. I wonder what's going on behind the scenes – does he believe me?

PS thanks for the bday wishes and how did you know? I ask, after updating her on VIN.

It's on your Facebook, she replies.

Of course. And soon there is a flurry of birthday wishes, most indeed on Facebook, and I'm glad as I make myself a quiet coffee downstairs that the internet still cares. My real-life family members are fast asleep upstairs, and one – though I don't know if he's still my family – is asleep two houses away. He's insisting on taking us out for dinner tonight to celebrate. I think it's a little odd that we'd go out together but it's probably good for the kids.

Caroline emails too, to ask if I'm free to meet again. I thought one meeting was enough but I realise I'm looking forward to chatting – it's therapeutic, talking while she listens and takes notes. We agree to meet on Tuesday afternoon for Part Two.

At eleven, Ava comes down with a present for me, but we have to wait for Rebecca, she says, as it's from both of them. Rebecca has been sleeping later and later and it's almost impossible to get her up on school mornings, so I leave her to her Saturday lie-in, and it's after twelve when she comes down, her newly brown hair in a curly nest around her head, her eyes blinking in the sunlight. In a stage whisper, Ava reminds her it's my birthday, and she gives me a half-hearted hug, then rummages in the cupboard for food. Rolling her eyes, Ava gives in and presents me with my gift. They've got me nail varnish, a book voucher, a beautiful grey scarf, and my favourite Molton Brown Bushukan shower gel. I'm touched by how much effort they've gone to – I hug Ava, and Rebecca doesn't flinch when I put my arms around her – I'll take what I can get.

At six, Dave calls to collect us, and insists on driving so I can have a glass of wine. He's booked a table in Firebird Pizza in Bray and when we first sit down conversation is stilted – it's a long time since the four of us went for a meal. I can't resist saying it's kind of Nadine to let Dave out with us. He throws me a look, then says she's out with her friends, and he can't stand them. All they talk about is clean eating and spray tans, and they make him feel old, he says. The girls laugh and I find myself laughing too, and just like that, the ice is broken. We slip into family mode, and by the time our main courses arrive, part of me has forgotten we'll be going home to separate houses. The waiter tops up my wine and then Dave orders me a birthday Mojito, and I'm enjoying letting go of the reins, not being the only one in charge. When dessert arrives, there's a candle stuck in mine, then Dave orders me another Mojito, and I'm floating now, in a good way.

I'm only half-listening to Rebecca when she asks Dave if she can do her homework in Nadine's sometimes – because it's warmer there, she says, giving me a look. I'm about to say something, but decide against it. Choose your battles. Then the conversation moves on, and Rebecca looks disappointed. Ava is talking about a big basketball match she has on Tuesday, asking Dave if he can come.

He says he will, and suggests we go together. I remember my meeting with Caroline then. Shit, I should have checked with the girls before agreeing.

"I just need to move a few things around – I've arranged to meet Caroline that afternoon. But it's fine, I'm sure she'll switch to Wednesday."

"Who's Caroline?" Dave asks.

"Oh yeah, I saw that written on the kitchen calendar – who's Caroline?" Ava echoes.

I'm about to say she's a friend from work but, actually, this is as good an opportunity as I'll get to tell him the truth. Clare is right, he's going to find out one way or another.

"She's a journalist with *IrishNewsOnline.ie* and she's writing about internet trolls. She's interviewing me for it."

Dave's mouth falls open. "Are you serious? You're going to talk about Leon? Lauren, I really don't think you should. Just let it lie – he's gone now anyway."

Ava and Rebecca are listening intently.

"Well, I don't know if he's gone. I'm getting tweets and emails from an anonymous account called VIN. And there's a chance it's Leon."

Dave pushes back his chair and folds his arms. "All the more reason to leave it, for God's sake. Why do you do these things? Why on earth would you speak to a journalist about your personal life?"

My arms are folded now too, and the girls exchange looks. I keep my voice even.

"It's cathartic. It helps to let it all out."

"But everyone will read it! You can't do this. Will there be pictures? Will you be mentioning the girls?"

"Relax, it's anonymous. Well, probably anonymous."

"What does that mean?" he asks, his voice going up a notch.

I never noticed before how squeaky he gets when he's cross.

"Caroline's editor wants me to be named, though I'm not sure yet. I'll see how I feel when it's written."

Dave scratches his head, and looks at me like I've just told him I'm moving to Goa to find myself.

"But how do you know she won't just use your name anyway,

whether you like it or not? She has all your details now – what's to stop her?"

I look at him, then over at the girls. Ava's eyebrows go up in a 'he's got a point' way. Rebecca is half-smiling, enjoying the drama.

"I met up with her, and I trust her. It's grand – relax!"

It's the "relax" that does it. He gets up from the table, throws down his napkin, and storms off towards the front door of the restaurant. It's not at all funny but suddenly I burst out laughing, and then the girls are laughing too. There are tears streaming down my face, and the waiter is giving us a curious look, but it's like a dam has burst and I can't stop.

A minute later, Dave is back. He's forgotten his keys. He sits down, and mutters that he'll still drive us home, and something about not leaving the girls stranded just because their mother has lost her mind. Ava and Rebecca exchange an eye-roll and Ava winks at me, and all of a sudden, I think I might cry.

Curled up on the couch once the girls go to bed, I pick up my phone. There are lots more birthday wishes on Twitter and Instagram, plus a pointed comment from Rebecca on a bathroom-mirror selfie I posted before we went out.

What happened to "I rarely post selfies", Mum? she'd written and, though it's a dig, part of me is happy to hear from her on any medium.

Dave messages to say he's sorry for the way my birthday dinner ended, but he still thinks I need my head examined. I reply that it's lucky I'm a shrink so, and put my phone screen-down on the coffee table. It beeps again a minute later and I turn it over to see what Dave is saying now, but it's an email from VIN.

Happy Birthday, Lauren. Mmmm. You smell nice. Molton Brown Bushukan. It suits you.

I stare at the message, reading it over and over. My skin crawls with imaginary ants and I swipe at my arms, trying to wipe them away. How could he know what shower gel I used? Has he been in the house? Is it someone who knows the girls?

Upstairs, Rebecca is asleep but Ava is still awake. I ask her if she bumped into anyone when she was buying the presents and she says she didn't. She's confused and asks me why, but I need to go back downstairs and message Cleo.

Cleo's response is as laid-back as ever – she says I probably posted about my presents online. I know I didn't, but I go through my photos anyway, then go back to tell her so.

It's probably in the corner of some picture somewhere if you look, she replies.

I go back through the photos, and then I see it. It's in the photo I put on Instagram while I was getting ready in the bathroom – at the very edge of the mirror reflection, you can just about make out the bottle of gold-coloured liquid. Even when I zoom in, it's difficult to read the label, and half of the name is completely out of sight. Is it enough for someone to work out what it is? I'm not sure. But I don't want to think about alternatives.

Chapter 34

My laptop clock shows 14:13, and a familiar sick feeling sets in as I wait for Jonathan's knock. It's two weeks since he's been in, and I can't stop thinking about his parting shot – when he called me or his ex-wife a bitch. Surely he meant Sorcha? We made some real progress that day, but now my stomach is a ball of anxiety again. Notes of Brian's faux-concern about self-care ring in my ears and I make a mental note yet again to book a session with the therapist we use for clinic staff.

The knock comes and I greet him with what I hope is a neutral and professional hello – he looks well and seems at ease. Instead of the tailored suit he normally wears, he's in jeans and a check shirt. The casual look softens him and, as we get started, there's no hint of the aggression I saw two weeks ago.

He starts to talk about feeling less angry now when he thinks about Sorcha's new relationship, and about making changes at home – he went shopping at the weekend for paintings to take the place of the ones she took when she left. He goes into lots of detail about one painting of a rowboat emerging from the sea and seems quite taken with it. He wonders if he's the rowboat, coming out of the drowning feeling he's been experiencing. Then he smiles, looking almost shy, and says he should leave the analysis up to me. I'm about to reply when my phone rings in my bag. I reach to stop it ringing.

Switching off the phone, I look up to apologise. But Jonathan's face has changed – the smile is gone.

"Someone more important than me? Am I not worth your full attention?"

The sudden transformation catches me off guard and it takes a beat to find an answer.

"Sorry, I thought I had my phone on silent. I am absolutely here to listen to you."

He slumps in his seat and folds his arms. Petulant Fish-eye is back.

"Who was it?" he asks.

"Don't worry about that – let's just get back to you. Talk to me about the rowboat again."

"Fuck the rowboat."

"Tell me why you're angry now."

"You're just like her, only half-listening to me. So quick to jump up and answer your phone. Sorcha was like that. And now I know they were calls from *him*."

Okay, now we're getting somewhere.

"So she was seeing him before you split up?"

He doesn't answer. He's staring into the distance, his eyes glassy and his cheeks flecked pink and white.

"Do you want to tell me about that – how you found out?"

"It was her phone. She never paid any attention to it, then all of a sudden she was rushing every time it beeped, shielding it when I was nearby."

I nod.

"So then I started to follow her."

I sit up straighter.

"I followed her one night when she said she was going out with two of her friends. I asked her who she was meeting, and her face gave everything away." He's looking off into the distance again, as though not conscious of me at all. "She stuttered, then came up with two names. Said she'd met them at the gym." He looks back at me. "Who meets friends in the gym?"

I nod again, and make a note.

"So I followed her. She drove to Howth and I drove a bit behind. I watched when she went into a restaurant on the West Pier. A few minutes later I followed her in – I couldn't see her at first, but then

I spotted her in a corner. With him. I didn't go over, I just left. And smashed my fist into the windscreen of her car when I walked past. It didn't break, but my hand was bruised for weeks."

He's looking at me, waiting for some kind of response. I write notes, buying time.

"And did you confront her that night?"

He shakes his head. "No. I needed to plan. And to move some things around."

"What kind of things?" I'm genuinely curious.

"Well . . . let's say money, mostly. She's the one with the money, and the house was in her name too, so I had to deal with that."

It's clear he's holding something back

"How do you mean 'deal with that'?"

He smiles, showing all his teeth, and suddenly I'm thinking of sharks.

"By being smarter than she is. Like a rowboat emerging from the sea."

Then he starts to laugh at his own joke, a joke I don't understand at all, and I'm glad it's five to three and I can call an end to our session, and look forward to six whole days free of Jonathan Oliver.

My peace is short-lived, interrupted by an email from VIN just after the news starts at nine that night.

Oh Lauren, is this your life now, slumped in front of the TV like the couch potato you really are? What would your Instagram followers think if they could see you? They can't see the real you, but remember, I am watching you.

I'm not falling for it this time. I had just tweeted that I'm looking forward to collapsing on the couch after a long day – he's throwing my own information back at me. But something sticks out. *I am watching you.* That's what Leon used to say. Something shifts in my memory then – a night just like this one, about a year ago, when I told Dave I'd see if Clare could ask someone from work to look into Leon's account. Dave had said he had a friend in IT who might trace Leon's IP address for us. But he never came back on it, and the messages stopped soon after.

I hit Dave's number.

"Hey, what's up?" he says as soon as he answers, his voice low, almost whispering. I can just about hear the TV in the background.

"Why are you talking so quietly?" I ask.

"Nadine's asleep, I don't want to wake her."

At quarter past nine? I wonder if she does that every night. There's something about that – Dave sitting on his own watching TV there and me sitting on my own here.

"Is everything okay?" he asks.

"Yes, it's about those messages I mentioned when we were out on Saturday – the ones from VIN. I'm wondering again if VIN is actually Leon, and I wanted to ask you what happened with your friend who was going to trace the messages for me that time?"

A pause.

"What friend?"

"Remember, you said you had a friend who'd be able to trace the IP address and find out where Leon was. Back when I was going to ask Clare for help?"

"Oh yeah, I forgot about that. When the messages stopped, I didn't bother asking him again."

"Could you chase it up now?"

"But there's no point, Leon is gone."

"Yes," I say, injecting patience I'm not feeling, "but Leon and VIN might be the same person. Proving the messages come from the same IP address would be something – even if we still don't know who it is or where they're physically located."

"I'll ask, but it's a long shot – the guy has kind of moved out of IT now."

"Right, well, see what you can do – I can ask Clare if needed."

Dave says goodbye, and I go into Leon's Twitter account to see if I can spot any similarities to VIN's. There's nothing though – the account is still there, but he's deleted all his tweets. I try VIN's then, and again nothing jumps out – his only tweets are to me, and there are no other details. Just the link to the website. I click into it, and realise there's a new blog post.

The Plan

What my parents didn't know is that I used to see her around sometimes. I knew exactly who she was. She used to walk along, happy in her world, not caring about the lives she was ruining. One day I spat on the ground as she was walking towards me, hoping she'd walk in my spit. But she just looked at me like I was dirt, and walked around it.

That's when I decided to try the voodoo doll. One of the kids at school had told me how to do it. I needed something of hers to make it work – a piece of her hair, or some of her clothing. So that was my plan. I'd follow her and see where she lived, and find a way to get something that belonged to her. Then I'd stick pins in her eyes until she understood that it's not okay to ruin people's lives just because you have lipstick lips and long legs and smile more than my mother did.

To be continued

I read it a second time, then message the link to Cleo – maybe there's something there that will link it to Chris, though I can't see anything at all. Switching on the news, I pause only to block VIN on Twitter. It doesn't do any good in the long-term, but it might annoy him to have to set up another email address. Choose your battles and take your little wins.

Chapter 35

When I push through the door of the café on Wednesday afternoon, Caroline is already there at a small table down the back. A man in a suit is reading a paper by the window and an elderly woman is cutting into a scone, focussing on making tiny, even slices. There are no other customers, and the girl behind the counter looks blankly at me as I walk past, then goes back to her magazine.

Just as before, Caroline is wearing a black tailored dress, and today her glasses hang from a chain around her neck. The Dictaphone is out on the table already, and she presses the record button as I sit down. There's a cappuccino waiting for me, still hot, though I'm a couple of minutes late.

Caroline gets straight down to the interview. She wants to hear about the messages – to get a better sense of the kind of things VIN says. She tells me she's started writing up the background but feels giving real examples of what VIN is sending will help readers understand just how serious it is.

I ask her if I can see the draft about the background, and something flickers across her face. Irritation?

She smiles then. "Absolutely. You can see it all when it's written up – but we'll wait until I have everything in. No point in toing and froing piecemeal, is there?"

I nod, dismissing the little voice in my head that's telling me to insist. It doesn't matter whether I see it now or later, as long as I see it.

Her pen flies over the page as I tell her about the first messages – the ones in Italy that were all about Cleo. On my phone, I click into my screenshots folder and feel a shiver across my shoulders as I see the one from the last night of our holiday – the one that made it seem like he was outside our mobile home. She squints when I hold my phone up to show her, then puts on her glasses to read it.

"And do you think he was there?"

"No, he couldn't have been. Even if he was in Italy, he couldn't have known which campsite we were in or which mobile home was ours."

"So then how did he know what you were doing – isn't it remotely possible he was there? This is all good stuff by the way, this is the kind of thing the readers want to hear about." She writes in her notebook again.

My throat feels dry. I pick up my cup to drink, and when I put it back down it hits the side of the saucer. Some of the cappuccino spills out on the table and the spoon clatters to the floor.

"Are you all right?" Caroline asks, concerned eyes peering at me above her glasses.

"Yes," I nod, reaching down to pick up the spoon. "It just got to me a bit – I've been avoiding thinking about that night." I sit up straight. "But it's better to talk about it and move on. And I'm certain he wasn't there. He probably took a lucky guess – chances are I'd be sitting outside on the deck with a glass of wine, like I did every night."

She nods. "Sure, and maybe you had put something online that night."

I hadn't, I'd checked the next day. But it's easier to agree that she must be right than to face any uncomfortable alternatives. I show her some more messages on my phone, and keep talking as she writes.

"So, I know we touched on this before,' she says, 'but I want to go back to it – over time, the questions about Cleo lessen, and there's more of a focus on you and your family?"

I nod a yes.

"So how does that make you feel? That shift from Cleo to you and your family?"

It takes me a moment to find the right answer, but there's no sense of impatience from her.

"It's fine. I put the photo up in the first place, so I can't complain."

"Really? Don't you feel any resentment at all? You're getting these horrible messages, and she's just getting on with her life . . . "

"As she should. She didn't bring any of this on herself. I'd be horrified if she was more directly involved – this way it lessens the guilt."

She makes a note. "But she's worried for you, I presume – it must be upsetting her?"

"I wouldn't say she's upset, more curious than anything. She's like Nancy Drew, trying to solve the mystery. But no, not upset. I suppose I'm the shield, protecting her from any real emotional involvement. She's just fixated on proving it's that guy in New York, and other than that she gets on with her life."

Caroline sits back in her seat, pen to lip.

"You know," she says, "perhaps it would add to the story to have Cleo contribute too. Do you think she would?"

"I don't know. She's not really someone who looks for the spotlight. Then again, I presume she could be anonymous too?"

Caroline hesitates, then nods. "Sure. Will you ask her?"

I tell her I will and we get back to scrolling through screenshots on my phone. There's a familiar nagging voice in my head warning me, reminding me not to share too much, but it's being drowned out now by something sticky and addictive – the balm that comes from sharing the load.

When the doorbell rings just after six, I'm surprised to find Grace, Nadine's cleaner, on the doorstep, holding what looks like Rebecca's black skull-print scarf.

"Sorry to interrupt your evening, but Rebecca left this in her dad's and I thought I'd drop it back in case she needs it," she says, handing it over.

"Oh you're very good, and there was no need – Rebecca's up and down between the two houses all the time, but thank you."

She nods, then opens her mouth and closes it again. There's clearly something else she wants to say.

"Will you come in for a quick cup of tea?" I ask on impulse. "I've no tea brack now, but I can rustle up a fairly good pack of Jaffa Cakes?"

She hesitates for a moment, then steps in.

In the kitchen, she stays standing, and while I busy myself with tea, I can almost feel the air quiver with indecisiveness.

"So how's everything going up in Nadine's?" I ask, pulling out a chair for her.

"Grand now, no complaints – well, no more than usual." I watch her making up her mind. "Actually, there was something I wanted to tell you, only I'm not sure it's my place."

My hand flies to my mouth.

"Crap, was it Rebecca again?"

"No, no, nothing like that."

"Oh, thank God!" I sit down opposite. "Sorry, that must seem very melodramatic. It's just been a tough few weeks, and I don't think I can take any more drama!"

"Ah, I'm sorry to hear that, but no, Rebecca hasn't done anything. She's a good child – you're lucky with your girls."

"God, it doesn't feel like it sometimes, she's been a nightmare for ages now. And despite how much time she spends slagging off Nadine –" I meet Grace's eyes, "she's started going over there to do her homework, because it's warmer than here. Which is true, but I wonder if it's just a way to get at me. God, sometimes I feel like she's slipping from my grasp." I don't know where that came from but Grace doesn't look surprised.

"It's hard for sure, and I remember it with my own daughter when her dad first put his back out and I had to go out to work. She sulked for months, but she came around eventually, and now we're closer than ever. Kids don't like change, and we can bend over backwards trying to fix everything, but sometimes all we can do is wait for them to come back to us."

Despite coming from a relative stranger, this is more reassuring than anything I've told myself or read in a parenting book since all of this trouble with Rebecca started.

"And I wouldn't worry about her spending time in Nadine's," Grace continues. "If you try to pull her back, she'll want to be there even more."

"You're absolutely right. I'm just so conscious of Nadine taking my place. I mean, that's ridiculous – Rebecca can't stand her – but that could change. And I'm supposed to *want* it to change, to want her to like Nadine, I know. But then I think of that and get all worried . . . it's so bloody complicated!"

Grace smiles. "I know it is. But listen, you're her mother. There's nothing in the world like the bond between mother and child. Sure, maybe there'll come a time when she doesn't hate Nadine and they actually become friends. But you grew her and birthed her and raised her – nothing changes that. There's a quote I like: 'A mother is she who can take the place of all others but whose place no one else can take.' I think a cardinal said it. I used to think about it a lot when my daughter was younger. She came back to me, and Rebecca will come back to you – I promise."

There's a lump in my throat and I take a sip of tea to compose myself.

"You're right," I manage after a moment. "I need to stop panicking. And look at me, loading all my woes on to you, and you only came to drop back a scarf. And sorry, what was the other thing you wanted to say?"

"Oh no, it was nothing at all," she says. "Just that Dave and Nadine are looking at holidays and they might forget to tell you. What I mean is, you might be relying on them to mind the girls and they wouldn't be here."

I nod slowly and thank her, though something tells me it's not what she originally intended to say.

"Where are they off to this time?"

"Somewhere in Ireland, I think," Grace says. "They need quality time together, those two. I don't think they see each other except when they go out to dinners and parties – and sure that's always with other people."

"Oh really?" I prompt.

"Ah yeah, it's because of work mostly, it's not anyone's fault. But she's cross that he works long hours, and he's cross that she's often in bed asleep when he gets home. I don't know if either of them really and truly wants it different though, you know?"

I nod again. I think I do.

"They must have some time together, just the two of them

though – at weekends maybe, during the day?" I ask, wondering what I'd say if a client told me they were quizzing an ex-husband's cleaner about his new relationship.

"I'm sure they do," she says, not sounding sure at all. "I'm there on Saturday mornings when she's getting her hair done and he's playing golf, but maybe they go for a nice walk together in the afternoon."

We both grin at that. There's no way Nadine goes for a nice walk anywhere on Saturday afternoons.

"I'll tell you when they spend time together," Grace continues, lowering her voice "– when there's someone else around to see. Then they're the perfect couple, in each other's pockets. God, I'll be struck down for saying things like this."

I shake my head. "Oh listen, I'm having a crappy time at the moment, and this chat has given me just the lift I need – nobody will strike you down for that."

There's silence for a moment as she sips her tea, tucking a strand of greying hair behind her ear.

There's no doubt she still has something she wants to say, and I wonder if I stay quiet will it spur her to fill the silence, but it's a nice kind of silence. Companionable, not awkward.

And in the end, it's broken by Ava rushing down the stairs to see if dinner is ready, prompting Grace to take her leave.

"It's lovely to hear the sound of family," she says as she heads down the steps. "It can be very quiet up in Nadine's."

And as I close the door, I think about that, and wonder if it's time to stop focusing on what's going on up the road and appreciate what I have here.

Chapter 36

Jesus Christ, I know he's here to talk about himself, but this is excruciating. Jonathan doesn't notice when my eyes slip to the clock on the wall behind him – he's mid-flow, ranting about his ex-wife again. This is my job, I remind myself, digging my nails into my palms as he drones on.

"Towards the end, she tried harder to hide the affair, but the damage was done. I knew everything about him, her plans, where they met – everything."

Now I'm interested again.

"Tell me about that – how did you know her plans?"

He sits back in the chair and folds his arms, his face creasing into a smile.

"Ah, I can't tell you that, Dr Elliot. Then you'd know all my spying secrets. It might be counterproductive."

Smug. And baiting me.

"I think it would help you to get everything off your chest. Did you sneak a look at her phone?"

He laughs. "Come on. She was stupid but not that stupid. She had a PIN on it, and she never let the bloody thing out of her sight either. No, I was smarter than that."

"You listened in to her conversations?" I think about Marcus and Cleo. "Or maybe you had a webcam set up?"

"Jesus, you're hardcore. Is that what you used to do, before your husband walked out?" He holds his hands up. "Sorry, too far. But no, I didn't have a webcam. I traded on her stupidity and her big mouth. So to speak."

It makes no sense at all, and I'm more curious than I'd like to let on, but he doesn't seem ready to do anything more than skirt around it. I'll leave it for now. His need to show off will win out eventually.

"And did she catch you – the thing you did to find out her plans?"

He stops, as though he hasn't considered this at all until now.

"No, actually, she never did find out. I kind of wish she did. It's too late now."

He sounds wistful, almost sad.

"I'm sure you could still tell her – have you been in contact with her recently?"

The sad look is still there and when he speaks he's almost whispering.

"No, not recently."

Lucky Sorcha, I think, then check myself.

"Well, it's probably for the best until you reach a place where you feel more at ease with the break-up."

He looks up at me. "Is that how it is for you?"

"Sorry?"

"Are you at ease with your break-up? Or do you sometimes dream of stabbing your husband?"

My mouth opens but I can't think of a thing to say.

"Jesus, chill, Dr Elliot. It's a joke. I wouldn't stab anyone." He pauses, then grins. "Too messy."

My head is pounding by the time I get home, and all I want to do is lie on the couch, but my mother rings just as I'm walking through the front door. She fills me in on her latest bridge-club drama and her friend's daughter's new job (A dog-walker! Imagine, she says, how is that even a job?). The girls aren't home yet and I curl up on the couch with the phone on speaker so that I don't have to hold it so close to my throbbing head.

"What's wrong?" she asks, eventually realising she's done all the talking and I've said almost nothing at all.

"Ah, I just have a headache. Work stuff. And Rebecca's giving me headaches too."

She's not interested in my work problems, but immediately wants to know what's wrong with Rebecca. I tell her about a new top I bought her at the weekend, a treat because she seems so down. She'd worn it to the cinema on Saturday night, but then on Sunday morning I found it stuffed in the bathroom bin. I went to her room to ask her about it but, as soon as I held up the top, she burst into tears and shouted at me to get out. Later on she came downstairs and gave me an awkward sideways hug of an apology, but when I tried to ask her about the top, she clammed up. I left it hanging on a kitchen chair but later, when I was pouring potato peels into the kitchen bin, I spotted it. Under eggshells and teabags, definitely irretrievable this time.

My mother is horrified by the story and says she'd never have put up with that kind of behaviour from me, missing the point completely.

"But, Mum, it's totally out of character. She's clearly upset."

"Just because your parents split up doesn't give you an excuse to throw good clothes in the bin," says my mother, and my head aches even more. "For goodness sake, your father *died* and you never carried on like this."

My mother doesn't believe in displays of emotion, even in mourning.

"It's a sign that she's upset, Mum, that's what I need to focus on. She's a good kid, acting out because of everything that's going on. Which if you think about it, is a positive thing, because now I know there's something up."

"Parents today are too soft. You never did anything like that as a child, and you'd have been in trouble if you did."

"Oh, don't I know it!" I roll my eyes, but it hurts my head. I need to end this conversation. "Listen, my headache is getting worse – I think I need to sleep it off," I tell her, disconnecting the call while she's still saying goodbye.

The pain is screaming at me now, and I lie down flat on the couch. There's paracetamol in the cabinet in the bathroom but I don't have it in me to walk up to get it, and now my eyes are closed.

When I open my eyes, everything is dark. A tiny shard of fear flicks through my stomach in those first seconds when I don't know where I am or why I'm asleep. Then it comes back. Sitting up, I put my hand to my head, bracing myself for pain, but it's gone. How long have I been asleep? And where are the girls? I pick up my phone to check the time. After six. Jesus, I've been asleep for two hours. There's a noise upstairs, then a laugh. Ava, on the phone I think. I flop back on the couch, still disoriented after the unexpected sleep, and click into my email to find a message from VIN.

Hello, Sleeping Beauty. Did you have a nice nap? Shall I send a handsome prince to wake you? Or perhaps, for you, a Huntsman.

I sit up, shaking, blood pounding in my ears. How could he have known I was asleep?

Suddenly the room is far too dark, suffocating. I pull myself off the couch and run to the light switch, half afraid of what I might see, but desperate for brightness to fill the corners. The curtains are open – was someone looking in while I was asleep? Has he worked out where I live? Even if he's figured out that LePhoto is Lauren Elliot, surely there's no way to find out my address. Could he have he pieced it together from pictures I've taken in and around the house, like a digital jigsaw puzzle? My mind races ahead of my hands as I fumble to close the curtains.

Upstairs I can still hear Ava's laugh, but I haven't heard Rebecca yet. Something prickles across my skin.

"Rebecca?" I call, walking to the kitchen, but it's in darkness.

Taking the stairs two at a time, I check her room. It's empty, and she's not in the bathroom either. In Ava's room, I signal at her to hang up the phone. She covers it and asks what's up.

"Where's your sister?"

"*In her room, I guess – Mum, I'm on the phone!*" she says in a loud whisper.

"Can you tell whoever it is you'll call back. She's not in her room – didn't you come home from school together?"

"Yes, of course we did," she says, after disconnecting her call. "She was just behind me, I left the door open for her."

"Well, she's not here now – did she say she was going back out anywhere? Did she go up to your dad's?"

"No, Nadine's there this afternoon, so she wouldn't. But what's the panic? She's thirteen, not three!"

With the Huntsman email still ringing in my ears, I lower my voice and try to sound calmer.

"I know. But I'd feel better if I knew where she was."

"Well, I heard the front door open and close about ten minutes after we came home, but I thought it was you."

"No, I was home before you, I fell asleep on the couch. Are you sure she didn't say anything?"

"Yeah, I'm sure. Here, try her on the phone," she says, handing me her mobile.

I call Rebecca's number and wait, willing her to pick up, but it rings out. Could she be gone to a friend's house – maybe she asked me and I forgot? I go back down to get my own phone to search for numbers, trying to work out where to start. *Shit, shit, shit.* What if it has something to do with the message from VIN – was he outside our house while I was sleeping? Could he have convinced Rebecca to go with him? Jesus Christ. I need to think clearly but everything is blurring now, dizzy and hot, and I'm spiralling, staring at the useless phone in my hand.

The doorbell rings, and my head snaps up. It only takes a fraction of a second to register the dark hat and high-vis jacket through the glass. I yank open the door. My stomach flops and my knees loosen and I have to lean against the door-jamb. Oh please God, no.

"Are you Rebecca Elliot's mother?"

My eyes go past his face and out to the road outside where I can see a Garda car, with a second Guard inside. I look back at the man standing in front of me.

"Yes. Please, just tell me Rebecca's okay."

"She will be. We found her down on the rocks below the East Pier in Dún Laoghaire. I'm afraid she's been drinking. A passerby saw her stumbling close to the water's edge, and thought she looked intoxicated, so gave us a call. We went down and picked her up. Obviously, as she's a minor we needed to make sure we got her home safely. Did you know where she was, Mrs Elliot? Or where she got the drink?" The guard holds up a Lucozade bottle. "It's gin or vodka inside, I can't tell which," he says. "Is it from your house?

It's a good idea to keep drink under lock and key."

I nod but I'm hardly listening. Rebecca is okay.

"Is she in the car? Can I go out to her?"

He steps aside and I run out. The guard follows and opens the back door of the car for me. Rebecca is lying back against the seat, with her eyes closed.

"Rebecca!"

Her eyes open but it takes her a moment to focus. Then she smiles.

"Hi, Mum, I'm so tired. Can you take me to my bed?"

Reaching in, I help her out of the car and into the house. Behind me, I hear the Guard follow, but he stays on the doorstep.

"Best to keep a close eye on them at that age. No harm done this time, but it could have ended badly if she'd slipped in. On a dark evening like this, nobody would notice at all."

Nodding my thanks, I close the door, and let out a deep breath. Rebecca is sitting on the bottom step of the stairs, with her head against the wall, muttering something about neighbours and Doctor Who.

"What are you talking about?" I ask.

She looks blankly at me, then her eyes open wide. "Mum, I feel a bit sick," she says, and before I can do anything, she vomits all over the floor.

Distracting though it is to manhandle a drunken teen to bed, I can't get the Huntsman message out of my mind. Everything he's said to date could be gathered from what I've posted online, but even I didn't know I was going to nap until it happened. I'm sitting in bed mulling it over when a text comes through from my mum, asking me if the sleep helped clear my headache. A tingling feeling takes hold in the pit of my stomach. I'd told her on the phone I was going to sleep it off – was somebody listening? Could he have somehow hacked into my phone to eavesdrop on to my calls? Wondering if I'm losing it and glad nobody can see me, I type 'Can hackers tap mobile phones and listen to calls?' into Google. And the answer, according to a full page of search results, is an overwhelming yes. The tingling sensation grows as I click through the links, one after another. If the articles are to be believed, all any hacker needs is a mobile-phone number in order to listen to calls and read texts.

But how could VIN have my mobile number? I know it's not on any of my social-media accounts, but I check anyway, going through all my profiles. It's not on my website either. So how could he have it? Then it dawns on me. It's in my email signature. I click in to check and there it is, along with my social-media contact details – when I replied to tell him Cleo's name was Giulia, my signature was automatically attached to the email. VIN has my phone number – I handed it to him on a plate.

Chapter 37

It's Friday night and the girls are getting ready to go for an overnight in Dave's. He insisted on calling down to get them – I suspect it has something to do with rubbing salt in the Rebecca-on-the-rocks wound. Sure enough, as soon as he arrives on the doorstep, he starts.

"Do you think we should search her bag?" he stage-whispers when I beckon him into the hall.

"What?"

"For drink, I mean. We've locked everything away in our house – well, Nadine doesn't keep much drink in the house anyway – but she might have taken some from here again? Or have you got rid of it now? Or at least hidden it?"

There it is. The blame. As though the house is teeming with bottles of vodka, tempting curious teens.

"No, Dave, we don't need to search her bag. She was so sick on Wednesday night, and again yesterday morning, I don't think she'll drink again for a long time."

He glances up the stairs. Music wafts down – the girls are packing, and can't hear us. He whispers anyway. "Still, you never know. Maybe best to just get rid of whatever's in the house so she isn't tempted again? I know you like a drink at night but this is about what's best for the kids. We need to think of them now."

"Oh now, come on! You know she didn't steal vodka and go drinking down by the sea on a Wednesday afternoon because there was vodka in the house – she did it because she's desperately upset that her parents have split up, and she's crying for help in any way she can."

His face turns a wonderful shade of red and his hands are on his hips, and it takes everything in my power not to go one step further and point out that the split is on him. I change the subject instead.

"But listen, on another note entirely, I heard the rumours about the hospital board and the guy that got fired – is it true?"

His colour subsides and his hands slip into his pockets, and I spend ten minutes feigning interest and nodding in all the right places.

The girls are still upstairs when Dave gets to the end of his saga, and we stand in silence for a moment. I can see my breath, smoky in the half-light – the old floor tiles don't retain any heat. Half-heartedly I suggest tea. Dave says he was just about to say the same, and strides on through to the kitchen to boil the kettle.

"*Girls, hurry up, your dad is here!*" I yell up the stairs, and follow him.

He's searching through cupboards for teabags, confused because I rearranged everything last week.

"By the way, I got a new phone today and a new number," I tell him, pulling out the sleek device that made my eyes water when I heard how much it cost.

"A new number?"

"Yeah, just a precaution really, but I think the person stalking me online might have managed to tap my phone too."

"Surely they can't do that – it's illegal, isn't it?" Dave says, finally locating the teabags.

"Sure, but I don't imagine internet trolls are all that worried about legalities. My old phone was in bits anyway after one too many falls – it needed replacing. The new number is a bit of a pain, but it won't take long to give it to people who need it. Maybe I won't tell my mum."

He smiles at that, and for a moment it's like old times.

A stack of work files clutters the table and I move it over to the counter.

"How are things going in work for you – with that guy who was being difficult?" Dave asks, glancing at the files. "Do you think he's the one sending you the internet messages?"

"I don't know. He's definitely interested in creeping me out, but the VIN messages don't sound like him."

Dave carries the teapot to the table, remembering for the first time ever to put a stand underneath it. Nothing like stable doors and horses bolting, I think, running my finger over one of the countless rings burnt into the surface.

"But surely it's a reasonable conclusion – he's fixated on you, and he knows how to find you on the internet. Who else could it be?"

I really don't want to get into the Cleo story with him, so I say nothing about Chris.

"I suppose it could be Leon – that's probably the most logical explanation, since he did it before."

Dave is shaking his head. "Ah, it couldn't be. Sure he's long gone. I really don't think it is. Tea?"

I look up at him. Something in his tone transports me to another Friday evening, when we were sitting right where we're sitting now. It was bright, with May sunshine streaming in the window – I remember Dave was about to make tea and I suggested a glass of wine in the garden instead. He got up to get a bottle of white from the fridge, while I filled him in on the gossip I'd got from Clare. She'd heard that Nadine was cheating on Ollie, her fiancé – the neighbour on the far side had heard a screaming match the night before. Ollie had walked out in the end, yelling something about searching nursing homes for her next affair.

I remember it so clearly now, Dave sitting back down with the bottle and the glasses, shaking his head.

"Nah, I can't see it happening. They seem solid. I doubt she'd cheat on him. Wine?"

At the time I was surprised he wasn't interested in my gossip, but nothing more. Jesus, that seems like another world now.

"Any word from your friend in IT?" I ask.

He stops mid-pour, his forehead creased.

"Yeah, he doesn't work in IT anymore so it's tricky."

"Is it not something he could do at home on his own PC?"

"I don't know. I can ask him . . ."

"Thanks," I say, despite his distinct lack of enthusiasm. "Look, I might see if Clare can help in case your friend can't."

Dave shakes his head. "I doubt there's anything she can do – you can't trace an IP address just like that. Don't ask her yet – leave it with me for now." He pushes his chair back, forehead still creased. "Right, I'll go check on the girls – I don't know how much packing they could need for a one-night stay."

"Aren't you going to drink your tea?"

"I better leave it. Nadine's trying a Moroccan Tagine recipe and she told me not to be long."

"Homemade?" I ask, holding back a grin.

"Well yes, mostly. Grace put something together earlier to get her started but she's doing the rest of it herself tonight. Why do you ask?"

"No reason. God, she sounds like a great cook." I smile at his retreating back, and tonight it's not even fake.

By ten o'clock, the house is deathly quiet, and my good humour has slipped away. My mind keeps wandering up the street to Nadine's house, where she's filling my daughters with Moroccan Tagine and notions about Botox. Curiosity beats common sense, and I click into Snapchat. Rebecca hasn't let me down – there's a photo of Dave and Nadine sitting side by side on the couch, arms folded, both gazing at the TV.

Living the dream on Friday night, it's like being in a not-funny Gogglebox episode, is what Rebecca's chosen as a caption, and it makes me smile. On my own TV screen, a red-haired actress is being interviewed and, as she pushes a strand out of her eyes, it reminds me that Cleo never replied to my last messages. My fingers hover over WhatsApp, but in the end I opt for an old-school phone-call – a little bit because it's easier than typing and a lot because the house is too quiet.

She picks up after three rings, sounding uncharacteristically hesitant, and I remember then that she doesn't have my new number. As I explain who it is, I can hear the TV in the background – we're all living the Friday-night dream.

When I remind her of the messages I sent last week, she says she'd prefer not to contribute to Caroline's article, and the second blog post didn't really illuminate anything for her.

"No voodoo dolls lying around when you went to Chris's apartment that time then?" I ask.

She laughs at that, or maybe she's laughing at something on the TV.

"Speaking of Chris," she says, "I'm flying out to New York on Monday night. It's mostly to visit my mom, but I'm going to call to Chris's apartment and have it out with him."

"What? Are you crazy?"

"We want to know if he's VIN, and the police are taking too long. If I go there and talk to him, we'll know for sure. I imagine people who hide behind keyboards are taken aback when challenged in real life. So that's what I'm going to do."

I'm shaking my head into the phone, trying to find the right words to talk her out of it.

"But he could be dangerous – I really think this is a bad idea."

"We each have our ways of dealing with it, Lauren. For you, talking to the journalist is the solution. For me, I need to face Chris head on. Whether he's VIN or not."

And as I hang up, I wonder how often I get her wrong – this complicated but curiously straightforward woman I've inadvertently let into my life.

CLEO

Chapter 38

Nothing has changed. The sidewalk is slithery with rain and the sky is gunmetal grey and the footfall is just as it always was, multi-coloured ants marching the New York streets to start the day at work. Ruth's apartment is only two blocks from the subway, but to Cleo it feels like ten – pushing against the early-morning crowd, dragging her suitcase behind. Ruth's left a key in her mailbox and when she lets herself in Cleo flops on the sofa and lies there, inhaling the familiarity.

Her mom can't understand why she's staying with Ruth tonight, instead of with her. In a bid to avoid the truth, Cleo said Ruth is going through a break-up. Then Delphine was annoyed that she didn't know Ruth was in a relationship. It didn't last long, he was a bit of a creep, Cleo explained, feeling bad for Ruth's fictional boyfriend.

There's a note on the table – there are fresh bagels in a bag on the counter, Ruth says, and Cleo is to help herself to juice and coffee. She'll try to get off work at five so they can grab dinner. That gives Cleo eight hours to do what she needs to do.

Outside, the sidewalk is quieter, and she sets off on foot, retracing steps made on a different day in a different time. The street name is gone from her memory or maybe it was never there, but she's pretty sure it was between Lorimer and Union, a few blocks before Grand Street. She'll know it when she sees it. She makes her way along Lorimer Street, walking by the laundromat, and the bakery on the corner, its blue awning sheltering morning smokers from the unsure rain. Narrow clapboard homes in every shade of sand and sea-blue line the street, interspersed with brownstones and taller red-brick offices, looking down on their squatter neighbours. She didn't miss it while she was gone, but now she's here, there's a dull ache. At Sol's Pizzeria, she turns west onto a quieter street. Uncollected garbage topples out of trash-cans that line the sidewalk and every third house has been tagged in blue by someone called Skil or Skll.

Half a block down, she comes to it. A mint-green clapboard-fronted building, stuck between an auto-repair shop and a boarded-up construction that used to be a mini-mart, according to a faded sign still visible above the window.

She walks up the steps, scanning the front door. White paint peels off the edges and rust seeps from the handle. The stained-glass window looks too pretty for its surroundings, like a last gasp attempt at keeping up appearances. Peering inside, she can make out dark-green flooring and mud-coloured walls, and a bank of mailboxes at the far end of the entrance hall. To her right, outside the front door, there are two columns of buttons. She's pretty sure Chris was on the third floor, and the two buttons in the middle are N. Diaz and C. O'Regan. Her hand hovers over the bell before she presses it – he's probably not home at ten o'clock on a Tuesday morning. But she's here now, and she really needs to make this stop. She presses and steps back, wondering what she's setting in motion.

And nothing happens. He's not here. Or he's asleep. Or he doesn't open the door to unannounced strangers. She sits on the stoop, deflated. Maybe Lauren was right – it's a bad idea, and this is her out.

Then the door behind her opens, and a middle-aged man in sweats comes out of the building. She smiles as she gets to her feet.

"Forgot my key again," she tells him, rolling her eyes. She watches him taking in her sheepskin coat, her green knit dress, her flat black boots. She doesn't look like a burglar or a terrorist. In a single movement, he returns her smile and pushes the door to let her pass through. She has to squeeze to get by and she can't tell if it's deliberate. He smells of too much deodorant and not enough air, but she's inside now, and he's gone, and she's facing up the dark threadbare stairs.

On the third floor, the first door is ajar, and Spanish words filter out – a mom cooing over a baby. There's only one other door.

With Lauren's misgivings still ringing in her ears, Cleo raises her hand and knocks.

Footsteps. She realises now she didn't expect him to be here and for a moment, turning back and racing down the stairs is the most appealing move. But she stays. It needs to end.

The door opens, and she's standing face to face with him. He's taller than she remembers, six foot two easy. Red-rimmed eyes blink at her from under dark heavy brows. His skin is greyish white, like oatmeal that's been let go cold, and his lips are a deep, fleshy red, a bright scar through stubble that seems more accident than design. He's wearing a white T-shirt stained with salsa or ketchup, and dark-blue check pyjama pants. He runs a hand through thick black hair, still blinking like a mole coming up in spring.

It's clearly up to Cleo to speak first, but she holds off, expecting recognition, then guilt. His face shows only mild confusion and much disinterest.

"I'm not buying anything," he says, and starts to close the door.

"I'm not selling anything," she tells him, and waits.

"Sure, well, maybe you have the wrong apartment." He runs his hand through his hair again. He looks like he hasn't slept in weeks.

"You're Chris. I'm Cleo. Remember me?"

His face changes. A flicker of understanding, and something else.

"Cleo. What do you want?"

"I want to talk to you, face to face. Unlike you, I'm not afraid of direct confrontation. I don't need to hide behind anonymous accounts and nasty messages to make my point. If you have something to say, say it to my face." The last word is a dart, whizzing towards a bullseye.

"I have no idea what you're talking about, but who do you think you are? Turning up at my door, berating me for God knows what, after what you did?"

"After what I did? I met a guy. It's not a crime. What you did is criminal. What you're still doing. And believe me, the cops are on to you. This is literally your last chance to stop, before they catch up with you."

He shakes his head. "Cops? What are you talking about? That night at your mom's? I haven't been back since. I was drunk, and grieving. Jesus Christ, even your mother understood that." He stops for a moment and scans her up and down. "You look exactly like her, but you're clearly cut from a different cloth."

"But that's just it," she tells him, her voice calmer. "Turning up to shout at my mom is something I get. Sending vicious messages to a complete stranger is an entirely different thing."

He pulls the door wide and she thinks for a moment he's going to invite her in. But he steps forward and pushes his face towards hers. The smell of last night's beer mixed with stale coffee hits her, and she steps back.

"I have no idea what you're talking about!" he hisses.

She steps back again, searching his eyes. They're haunted, but it's all there, raw and open. If he's hiding something, he's very good at it.

"Okay, maybe we can start over," she said. "Someone has been sending anonymous messages to a friend of mine – someone who saw a photo she posted on social media. A photo of me. And that person has been trying to find me. If it's you, then here I am – you can stop messaging."

He looks blankly. "I haven't been messaging anybody." Then he sighs. "Let's talk inside." He pulls the door back, and Cleo steps in. The heavy drapes are drawn although it's mid-morning, and she can just about make out a battered red sofa and an overflowing ashtray. The air is stagnant with stale cigarette smoke and unwashed skin. Empty beer cans line the floor beside the sofa. A fly buzzes from one end of the apartment to the other, over and over, trying to get out but finding no chink.

Chris pads across to the window and pulls the drapes. October sky lightens the room but only just. The furniture is dark and mismatched – an IKEA end-table beneath what looks like an antique lamp. A sleek flat-screen TV beside a vintage bookcase. He sees her looking.

"I took some of her stuff. Shannon's, I mean. We had different tastes." He doesn't explain who had which taste.

He indicates that she should sit, and she does, wondering what Delphine would say if she could see her now. He drags a chair over from the table and puts it opposite the sofa, as though they're in a therapy session.

"You don't have work today?" she asks, lifting a stack of PR magazines off the couch and putting them on the floor.

"I left my job a few months ago to work for myself," he says in a way that doesn't invite further questions.

She imagines he doesn't meet clients in his apartment. If he has any clients at all.

She takes a breath. "I'm very sorry about your sister. I should have said that first."

He accepts with the briefest of nods.

"And I'm sorry for turning up at your mom's that night," he replies. "I was so angry when Shannon died, and I needed someone to blame. For a long time, I focused on Marcus, imagining what I'd do to him once he was let out of prison." He sees her face change. "Obviously I wouldn't really do anything. And I know it's not the healthiest way to deal with things, but –" he shrugs, and doesn't finish.

"And then, when Marcus died?" she prompts.

"Yeah, when Marcus was killed, I should have been relieved or even sorry for him, but I was just angry that I never got to confront him. I needed a new focus." His chin is down, and he looks up at her through lowered lids.

"A new enemy," she says softly.

"Yes," he says, almost whispering, "someone to blame."

"Except you couldn't find me."

He nods. "I tried your apartment but there's someone else living there now. I asked around among people who knew Marcus, but nobody seemed to know anything. Then I remembered Shannon saying he'd met you in The Cornerstone on Lorimer Street, so I went there one night. I asked the manager about you – I said I was an old friend."

He pauses, waiting for her reaction but she doesn't say anything.

"The manager was cagey at first but when I said I heard what

211

happened with Marcus and was worried about you, she opened up. She said she wasn't sure exactly where you were but that anyone would deserve a year-long vacation in Europe if they'd been through that. I could feel my blood pressure go up as she said it – my sister was lying in her grave, and you were swanning around Europe getting a suntan."

He looks up at Cleo, accusation in his eyes. For having an affair or taking a vacation, she's not sure.

"Chris," she says softly, "it's not a vacation. I moved there after Marcus tried to kill me. You know that, right? That he tried to kill me?"

The accusatory look is gone, replaced with something else, but she's not sure what. Empathy? Or resentment, because she's still here and Shannon is gone?

"Yes, I know all about it. And I'm sorry – what you went through is horrific. But –" he stops again.

"What, I brought it on myself? Chris, nobody brings someone like Marcus on them – not me, not Shannon."

"This is hard to explain," he says.

She nods for him to go on.

"You had cuts and bruises, you were in hospital, police interviewed you, he was arrested. You were a victim in the truest sense. The proof of it is in your hospital reports and his mugshot and in your old boss talking about how you deserve a year-long vacation." He stops to swallow, and she doesn't interrupt. "But Shannon took her own life. She's a victim too, but there's no acknowledgement. There's shame and there are whispers and there are lowered eyes when my parents go to Mass on Sundays."

"So you wish she could have had my ending?"

He nods.

"And I hers?"

"No! No, because . . ." He looks up at her, and his eyes are the saddest she'd ever seen. "Because even with what little I know of you, Cleo, I know you wouldn't have done it. You'd never have jumped from a fourteenth-floor window over someone like Marcus. But Shannon did, and I can never get past that."

Chapter 39

Neither of them says anything for a while, as the truth of his words hangs between them. His head is in his hands, and if he looks up he may cry, so Cleo lets the silence linger long after uncomfortable.

Eventually he straightens up, ready to talk again.

"She'd been drinking a lot and taking Valuim. I feel like I should have seen it coming, and yet I never dreamed she'd do something like that. Even looking back, even with all the guilt and the what-ifs, I still don't think I could have guessed it. It's just such a leap – drinking too much one minute, to jumping out a window the next. Leap. Bad choice of words." There's a ghost of a smile, then it's gone.

"Did she leave a note?"

"An email. Very twenty-first century, right?" He searches on his phone for a moment, then passes it to her. "She sent it to my dad, and he forwarded it to me."

Cleo clicks into an email with the subject line **Marcus** and reads.

Dear Dad,
Something is eating me up inside and I can't go on any more.
Goodbye,
Shannon

Her skin prickles. She's never read a suicide note before, and didn't imagine something so clinical and short. She looks up to see Chris watching.

He nods. "Yeah, not much there, is there?"

"What does she mean when she says something is eating her up inside?"

He shrugs. "The break-up with Marcus. Clearly. It's in the subject line."

"Yes, but why the word 'something' – doesn't that suggest it's more than the break-up?"

Chris shifts in the chair and sits up straighter. It's an old office chair, and doesn't look very comfortable. His or Shannon's, she's not sure.

"Who can guess what was going through her mind that day? Like I say, she was drinking too much – she wasn't very coherent in those final weeks."

"Do you have Shannon's cell phone? Maybe there's something there to explain what the 'something' was?"

Wordlessly he walks to a room off the kitchen – his bedroom presumably, and comes back with a cell phone and charger. It takes a minute to charge enough to power it on, then he hands it to her, and she starts to go through Shannon's email inbox.

"Sorry, do you mind if I do this?" she asks, glancing up at Chris.

He shrugs. "Knock yourself out. I've already looked – it's all spammy newsletters. She was always signing up for things."

There are hundreds of newsletters from dozens of online stores, and Goodreads notifications still arriving every day. Cleo shakes her head. It's odd to think of all these messages flying into the inbox of someone who has been dead for a year now.

"Shouldn't you unsubscribe from all these mailing lists?" she asks Chris.

Another shrug. "Does it matter either way? I don't use the email for anything, and she's gone."

"Do you mind if I take a look through what she was sending and receiving towards the end?"

"Sure, go ahead."

She scrolls back to November, to the day Shannon died – the last time she read any of the newsletters or notifications. There's a PayPal confirmation showing a refund from an online clothing store, more Goodreads messages, an out-of-office reply from someone called Hayley with a *New York Sun-Herald* email address, and a message from a Jessica at *NurtureUs.com*. Cleo glances up at Chris, then clicks into the email.

Dear Shannon,

Thank you for contacting us here at NurtureUs.com. We'd love to help you through this beautiful time as your baby grows inside you. We can teach you about nutrition, exercise, and what to expect. We have a Deluxe Mama package that would be just perfect for you, for $199.99. It includes videos, newsletters, and three Skype calls, plus a beautiful baby-shower gift two weeks before your due date. If you'd like to proceed, just click here to register.

My very best wishes,

Jessica

Whoa. She looks up at Chris again. Surely at the autopsy they'd have noticed if she was pregnant? Maybe only Shannon's parents were told? Cleo clears her throat.

"Did you find something?" Chris asks.

"Maybe. Did you . . . did anyone suggest at any point that Shannon was pregnant?"

Pain crosses his face.

"No. But she couldn't have been – the medical examiner would have told us. And she wasn't seeing anyone, not since Marcus left her." There's still a hint of accusation there. "Why are you asking?"

She holds up the phone so he can read Jessica's email. He shakes his head, baffled.

"I don't get it. Why would she consider something like this if she wasn't pregnant?"

Cleo's not sure either. She keeps scrolling, flicking past little bytes of Shannon's life, the before and after looking very much the same. She goes back to the clothing refund. Two sweaters and a pair of pants. Did she think they wouldn't fit any more if she was pregnant? But there are other refunds dotted around her inbox. Maybe she was just an impulse night-time shopper – buying drunk and returning sober.

An idea forms. Cleo goes to Shannon's Sent Items folder, and searches for *NurtureUs* – she might have contacted them directly through their website, but with a bit of luck, there'll be an email. And there is.

Hi,
My name is Shannon, and I think I might be pregnant. I can't tell anyone in real life, and was wondering what kind of information you can provide?
Regards,
Shannon O'Regan

She *thinks* she might be pregnant. So she hadn't tested yet. Maybe that's what happened – maybe by the time Jessica replied, she already knew she wasn't? Could it be the 'something' she referred to in her suicide email to her dad? Marcus had said they were strict Catholics – maybe she couldn't tell them about her pregnancy. Jesus, surely that's not what made her jump?

"Would she have told you or your parents if she thought she was pregnant?"

Again pain flashes across his face. "I don't think so. We were close, but there was some stuff we never talked about. And she'd never have told my parents – they'd have lost their shit completely. They'd have disowned her. They'd literally have thrown her out." He stops, realisation dawning. "No, that's not it. That's not why she jumped. No fucking way. She wasn't even pregnant, for God's sake!"

"But what if she thought she was?"

He stands up and starts pacing, pushing his hand through his hair, over and over. The room is small, and he reminds her of the fly, buzzing up and back. He stops then.

"No. I can't accept that. She jumped because she was heartbroken about Marcus, not because she was afraid of our parents."

She changes tack. "Does Shannon have a laptop we could look at?"

"She did, but we never found it – it wasn't in her apartment after she died. I guess she loaned it to someone or left it in to be repaired."

216

"I imagine all her emails and messages are on her cell phone anyway," Cleo says. "Actually, do you mind if I look at her text messages?"

He nods, but there's nothing of interest – her mom confirming lunch plans for the following weekend and some messages with friends arranging a night out.

Cleo swipes through the screens on Shannon's phone, and in among the apps on the third page, she spots a WhatsApp icon.

"She used WhatsApp to message too?"

"No, just the text on her phone," Chris says. "Why?"

"She has the app installed – is it okay to have a look?"

He nods and she clicks in.

That's where she strikes gold. There's a long chain of messages with someone called Taryn, right up until the morning after Shannon's death, when Taryn suggested they meet for coffee, not knowing her friend was in the city morgue. Jesus.

Cleo scrolls back and starts to read.

Shannon: I fucked up, I think I'm pregnant.

Taryn: No! Did you do a test?

Shannon: Not yet. It might be too soon. It's just a very strong feeling right now. Everywhere. I feel sick, I'm tired all the time, my boobs hurt a little.

Taryn: You know that could literally be tiredness and PMT. Plus you have been hitting it hard with the booze lately – that'll take it out of anyone.

Shannon: Maybe. Anyway, still on for dinner on Friday?

Cleo skips past dozens of messages about dinner and what they're watching on Netflix, looking for more pregnancy conversation.

Shannon: My period is late.

Taryn: How late?

Shannon: Two days.

Taryn: Come on! Two days is nothing. Just do a test already!

Shannon: I will. Soon. I feel a bit weird about it.

Taryn: Because of who it is?

Shannon: Yeah. What kind of a moron gets knocked up by an ex who's now living with his new girlfriend?

It's too hot in the apartment and Cleo wants to take off her coat but she's stuck staring at the phone, scrolling through the life of a dead woman. This was always coming – of course it was Marcus. She should feel anger, or at the very least hurt, but there's nothing. It's like watching a story unfold on a screen, one that has nothing to do with her life.

She keeps reading.

Taryn: Don't be so hard on yourself. You're not the first, and you won't be the last.

Shannon: I've asked him to call tonight, and I'm going to tell him.

Taryn: WTF?

Shannon: I'm sick of going through this on my own.

Taryn: But you're not even sure if you are! If this is a way to get him to go back with you, it's not going to work. Please don't do this. Not until you test.

Shannon: I have a back-up plan. I have some other stuff I need to discuss with him, something way bigger than a poppy-seed-sized fetus.

Taryn: ???

Shannon: I'll fill you in sometime. It's not something I can talk about easily. Coffee tomorrow?

Taryn: Sure. But think about what you're doing tonight. It could backfire x

It's Shannon's last message, sent the day she died. The next one is from Taryn the following morning, chasing up the half-made coffee plan.

Chris is sitting down again, lost in his own thoughts, but when Cleo looks up, he snaps out of it.

"Did you find something?"

She passes him the phone. "Yeah. I'm guessing she wasn't pregnant, but she certainly thought she was." She stops and wonders for a second about the can she's opening. "And she was telling Marcus. The night she died."

Chapter 40

Chris is pacing again, but now he's a bull, not a fly. When he punches the wall, Cleo jumps. He turns back to her.

"You think he did it? He pushed her?"

"I don't know, but I think it's a possibility. What was her apartment like – was the window high up off the floor?"

He shakes his head. "No, it was a glass door, leading out to a small balcony with a railing."

"And if she was out there with Marcus, could he have pushed her? Logistically, would it work?"

He winces. She needs to choose her words more carefully. Lauren or Ruth would be a hell of a lot better at this kind of conversation.

"I'm sorry. I just mean could he have done it?"

Chris sits again, dazed.

"She was tiny. Five feet tall and weighed not much more than a hundred pounds. If he wanted to, yes, he could have pushed her over the railing. Oh my God." He looks at Cleo. "What do we do?"

"We call the police. That's what we do." It sounds like she's taking charge, but her mind is reeling. She wants to sit still, to make the world stop spinning for just a minute, but Chris is up again and rummaging through a drawer, flinging sheets of paper on the floor.

"Chris, are you okay?"

"The number for that cop – the one who spoke to me after I sent an email to your mom. He was good to me, understood about grief. He gave me his card, but –" he sits down on the floor, "I can't find it."

"Detective Murphy. It's okay, I have his number – he took on the case when Marcus attacked me." Cleo walks over and sits on the floor beside him. His hand is on the ground and she covers it with hers. "I'll call him for you."

Chris closes his eyes and nods, then listens as she makes the call.

Detective Murphy doesn't pick up at his office, so she tries his cell. That goes to voicemail too. She leaves a message, giving Chris's number.

For a while, they sit, saying nothing. Cleo has cramp in her leg, and needs air, but can't leave him like this. The fly is still here, buzzing through the silence. There's no air in the apartment. Outside, an uptick in car horns and slammed doors remind her that it's lunchtime, and she hasn't eaten for hours. But still she waits.

Her phone rings, startling them, and Chris raises his eyebrows in an unspoken question – Detective Murphy? But it's Ruth, checking that Cleo got in okay, and confirming dinner plans.

"You should go," he says, when she finishes the call.

"Are you sure?" She tries to keep relief from her voice.

"Go. I'll let you know if Detective Murphy calls. Though what good it will do with Marcus dead, I have no idea."

"But if she was pushed, wouldn't you want to know?"

He picks at the carpet, not answering at first, and suddenly it's clear – there's a part of him that doesn't want to know.

"I can't decide which is worse – imagining her so lost that she takes her own life, or thinking of her horror, knowing he was going to push her over." His voice breaks on the last word. He swallows.

"I think truth is important," she says softly, and he nods.

Cleo stands up awkwardly, shaking out pins and needles, still not sure about leaving him.

"What do you think the 'something else' was?" he asks.

"I'm sorry, what?"

"In her messages to Taryn, she wrote that there was something else she wanted to discuss with Marcus – something much bigger."

He looks up like he's waiting for her to tell him the answer and make everything okay.

"I don't know what it could be – but I didn't know Shannon."

Chris looks confused, then shakes himself.

"Of course. I forgot. It feels like you've been here forever."

It feels like that to Cleo too, though it's only been a couple of hours. She really needs air.

"Maybe you have a think while we're waiting for Detective Murphy to call, and I'll think back too, in case there's anything that happened when Marcus was living with me?"

He nods, and this time she's really going, making her way to the door. She hears it close softly behind her as she runs down the stairs, and out into the flinty October light.

Ruth's mouth forms a perfect "O" when Cleo gets to the bit about the last message to Taryn, and she puts down her fork. They're in Danté's, Cleo's favourite Italian restaurant, because Ruth is the kind of friend who remembers details like that. The chat and the wine are working in tandem like a salve and Cleo is starting to unwind. She hasn't heard from Chris yet, so Detective Murphy must not have called. It's only six though, she thinks, checking her phone again.

"Jesus. Do you think it's possible that Marcus . . . I mean, he couldn't have, could he?" Ruth asks.

"Killed her? I don't know, but when I consider it, it doesn't seem impossible. And that says something, right? I mean, if I asked you could your dad or your boss or your creepy colleague who always hugs you too hard at office parties have killed someone, what would you say?"

"No! Of course not."

"Exactly. That's the reaction you'd expect. But if you ask me if Marcus did it – or could have done it, I can't give you an emphatic no. That's telling in itself."

Ruth nods slowly, her fork still lying on the table. "Jesus, that's . . . I don't even know what to think. That you could have been living with someone capable of that?"

Cleo signals to the waiter to bring more water. Jetlag is kicking in and her mouth feels like sandpaper.

"Well, I guess the bit where he tried to beat me to death in my apartment was an indication – right?" She smiles at Ruth, but Ruth doesn't smile back.

"My God, that poor girl. What she must have gone through that night. One way or another, I guess."

Cleo's cell beeps, but it's not Chris – it's Lauren, wondering if she's had any luck proving Chris is VIN. That's going to be a long story, and not one she'll be overjoyed to hear. Cleo turns the phone face down.

"I know. It's shit. All of it. And there's nothing we can do right now, so let's talk about you instead. How's work?"

Ruth is an analyst in an investment firm, and works insane hours most of the time. She rarely takes vacations, she gives the job two hundred per cent all the time, and as far as Cleo can see she gets no recognition for any of it. Her boss is lazy and a bully, and no matter what Ruth does she finds fault. So when Ruth puts her head in her hands at Cleo's question, she's not surprised.

"That bad, huh?"

"Worse," comes the muffled response from behind her hands.

"Go on, spill, what's she done now?"

Ruth looks up. "It's not what she's done – this time it's me." She sighs. "You know I told you before that when I get really mad at people at work, I type out an email telling them exactly what I think of them, but I never send it?"

Cleo nods. It's not a therapy that would lend itself to bar work, but she can see how it could help in an office environment.

"Well, this morning, she wanted a report that she'd asked me to have ready for tomorrow. When I said it wasn't due yet, she peered at me over those tiny glasses she wears to try to look more intelligent, and said, 'You know Ruth, if you spent less time eating donuts and more time on your reports, you might be able – just once – to deliver something sooner than the very last moment it's due.' Obviously, I wanted to stab her on the spot but instead I nodded and walked back to my desk, bright red, with everybody watching me. Of course there was a donut on my desk, sitting there, mocking me. And this is the worst bit – I put it in the trash. Isn't that the most stupid thing you've ever heard? I mean, the report's not due till tomorrow, and still she managed to embarrass me in front of everyone, and make me throw away a perfectly good cinnamon donut." She laughs, but it doesn't reach her eyes.

"She's a bitch. Forget her. And I'll buy you ice-cream on the way home. Deal?"

She shakes her head. "That's not it. I was so mad, I just started typing. Nothing I haven't written before really. Just telling her exactly what I think of her, her lack of ability, how she lets us do all the work while she takes all the credit, and at the end, as always, I told her that her glasses fool nobody, that we all know she's going to get caught out for the fraud that she is."

Ruth looks down at her bowl of congealing carbonara. Cleo waits, but it's clear where this is going.

"And you . . .?"

"One of my colleagues walked over to my desk, so I had to close the screen. The email auto-saved to my drafts, and when I went back in to delete it, I pressed send by mistake."

"Oh Ruth. Oh my poor Ruth."

"I know. What kind of idiot does that? What kind of idiot drafts emails like that at all?"

As Cleo reaches across the table and puts her hand on Ruth's, something stirs in her mind, but slips away again before she can get hold of it.

"So what happened then?"

"I realised what I'd done as soon as I hit send, and I tried to recall it but it was too late. She'd seen it. Nothing happened for an hour – I basically sat at my desk, trying not to throw up. Then she emailed me and asked me to come into her office. There was a woman from Personnel there with her. She'd reported me. Can you believe it?"

Cleo shakes her head. "Wow. What did the woman from Personnel say?"

"She could hardly get a word in. My boss started by reading out my entire email – believe me, I wanted to die on the spot – then, get this, she started to cry. Actual tears. I don't know what black magic she used to conjure them up, but she did. She said she's extremely self-conscious about her glasses, and that comment in particular really hurt. And that she's going through some medical issues, and finding it difficult to cope generally, and my email had pushed her over the edge. Cue more tears, and Personnel-lady handing her tissues."

"What medical issues?"

Ruth throws her hands up, almost knocking a tray from a passing waiter. "Who knows? None is my guess. It's very easy to throw around vague comments about medical issues and being hurt when you want to play the victim."

"Ah Ruth, I'm so sorry. It's just shit, all of it. So what happens now?"

"They're considering what action to take, I'm due to hear from them next week. It's so over the top. I know I should never have written the email, but my God, taking action over it?" She looks like she's going to cry.

"We need something stronger than wine now," Cleo tells her. "This is a tequila situation."

Ruth makes a supreme effort to blink back the tears, and a watery smile breaks through.

"I'm back in to face her in the morning – I'm not sure tequila is going to help me."

"Ice cream then. Right?"

She nods, digging her fork into her pasta and pushing it around the dish.

"I'm done with this – let's get the check."

It's only when they're walking back towards her apartment with two pistachio ice creams that Cleo works out what's flitting in and out of her memory. Taking out her phone, she excuses herself and calls Chris's number. The background noise when he picks up tells her he's somewhere else – a subway maybe, not his apartment. He starts to tell her Detective Murphy hasn't been in contact and she cuts him off.

"Shannon's drafts – we never checked them. We looked at her sent items, and her inbox, but what about her drafts folder? If there was a 'something else' she wanted to discuss with Marcus, could it be there?"

Chris is quiet for a moment.

"I'm not so sure. If she was going to talk to him about something, I don't know that she'd put it in an email to him?"

"But maybe not him. There was an out-of-office response from someone called Hayley working at the *New York Sun-Herald* – is that a friend of hers?"

"Not that I know of."

"So maybe Hayley is not a friend, but a contact at a newspaper – maybe there's something she was going to tell? Something about Marcus and how he was treating her?"

Silence again. They've stopped at the corner, a block from Ruth's apartment. Ruth is finishing her ice cream, Cleo's is starting to melt in the cup.

"If he was. . . mistreating her in some way," he says eventually, his voice low and hard to catch in the echoes of the background noise, "I don't think it would be newsworthy."

"Not news, but for a feature, maybe. Journalists write about human stories all the time for features – challenges people have come through. Hey, it's worth checking anyway, right?"

"Sure thing."

She imagines him running his hand through his hair. He says goodbye and Ruth looks at her expectantly.

"I just asked him to check Shannon's draft emails, which will take like two seconds, but he doesn't seem enthusiastic."

"I don't imagine it's down to the effort or the time, Cleo. I imagine it's about what he might find there," Ruth says, throwing her ice-cream cup in a trashcan. "You're suggesting his sister had been through something so horrible that she might tell a journalist about it, and that ultimately her ex-boyfriend murdered her. I'd say his reluctance is understandable?"

Nodding, Cleo throws her melted ice cream after Ruth's, and as they make their way back to the apartment, the rain starts, sharp and heavy, pelting them, warning them that something is coming.

Chapter 41

An hour later, Cleo is in yoga pants and an oversized sweater, warm and dry on Ruth's sofa. Ruth inherited the apartment from her grandmother and hasn't changed a thing since she moved in. It's like something from the middle of the twentieth century, but somehow it works. The small mahogany kitchen table has hosted numerous pizza nights over the years, and the green-velvet pintuck sofa was often Cleo's bed for the night afterwards. The gold jacquard wallpaper would be deemed far too fussy by today's standards, but it makes the room cosy and comforting, tonight more than ever.

As she attempts to reply to Lauren, Cleo's phone jumps in her hands. Chris.

"You were right," he says as soon as she picks up. "It was in her drafts." His breathing is rapid, his voice cracked. "She had written it all down to send to that person, Hayley. And she'd written one to my mom too. And –" His voice breaks then and he stops.

"It's going to be okay, Chris. Truth is better than not knowing. What does it say?"

Silence.

"Do you want to copy and paste the email and send it to me? Don't press send on the draft – the police need to see that. Just copy and paste the text, and send it to CleoRHolloway@gmail.com." She spells it for him. "Did you get that?"

There's a muffled sound that she takes as confirmation.

"Chris, whatever it is, it can't be worse than thinking she took her own life if she didn't. We'll figure it out, we'll talk to the police, we'll get through this. Okay?"

"Okay."

She hears him take a breath.

"I'll send you that now. Call me back." He disconnects.

A minute goes by and she refreshes her inbox twice, but there's nothing. Ruth comes out of the shower and suggests putting on a movie. As Cleo is filling her in on her call with Chris, the email comes through, and the movie is forgotten.

Ruth sits down cross-legged on the rug and waits while Cleo silently reads the email.

Hi Cleo – this is the draft email she had written but never sent to my mom. Most of it is the same as what she'd put in the email to the journalist, but there's more at the end.

Dear Mom,

Something is eating me up inside and I can't go on any more – if I'm ever going to get better, I need to get it out. It's about a party I went to with Marcus, back when I was sixteen. It was all college kids, I was the youngest person there, and when they started passing around beers, I took one. So did Marcus – more than one. He had maybe three or four, and when I asked him if he'd be okay to drive us home, he said they were only small beers. There were jello-shots too, and I didn't think there was much alcohol in them, so we had some. We were just doing what everyone else was doing, and I know we weren't the only ones driving home after.

When it was time to leave, Marcus was fine – he showed me he could walk in a straight line and count backwards from ten – so we got in the car to drive home. The party was about fifteen miles out of town. It was out by Brighton Falls, so nothing around but farmland and empty roads. We had the music on loud but I was feeling sleepy, from the beer I guess, and after a while I closed my eyes.

Then it happened – we hit something. I remember screaming, and the car skidding to a stop. I remember Marcus saying it was

227

probably a deer, and getting out of the car with a torch. I remember hearing him swear, and I got out to see too. It wasn't a deer. It was a man.

He was lying on the side of the road, cheek down, eyes open. A middle-aged man in a heavy coat, with mud on his brown loafers. There was a hat lying nearby, one of those old hats they used to wear back in the fifties. I don't know why that sticks in my mind – maybe I stared at the hat to avoid looking at the man.

I remember Marcus swearing again, asking what the hell anyone was doing on the road at that time of night. I took out my cell phone to call emergency services, but he grabbed it out of my hand. It was too late, he said, the man was dead.

I screamed then, and Marcus shook me, and told me to shut up. I told him we had to call the police, but he said we couldn't, because we'd both been drinking. We had to go, he said. I begged him to stay but he told me we'd both end up in jail for underage drinking and DUI. I know it sounds so bad, but I believed him, and on that night in the dark, his eyes half-wild, I was a little afraid of him too. The poor man was already dead, so – may God forgive me – I did what Marcus said. I got in the car again and let him drive us home.

I thought about calling the police that night, after Marcus dropped me off, but I was too scared. And the next day it was in the news, and they called it a hit-and-run, and said that police were looking for a couple seen driving erratically north of Gatesville that night, out near Brighton Falls. I talked to Marcus, told him we needed to turn ourselves in, but he said under Texas law a hit-and-run is a felony and we could both go to jail for a long time. So I stayed quiet.

For twelve years, I stayed quiet.

But now I think it's time we talked about it and let the poor man's family finally have some peace.

Mom, I'm so sorry. It was a terrible thing we did that night, and we should have stayed with the man. We should have called emergency service. Maybe he wasn't dead at all – maybe if we'd stayed, they could have saved him.

I should never have listened to Marcus. And I understand now that I would never have gone to jail – he lied to me. I was a minor. But he was eighteen – he did it to protect himself, scaring me into silence. And I let him, and I stayed with him all those years, and I thought I could make it work, but I can't keep it inside any more. And now that he's left me, I see him for what he really is.

So I'm going to see him tonight to tell him first, to give him a chance to arrange a lawyer and go to the police himself. I think once he's heard everything I have to tell him, he'll do the right thing. I have something to show him too, to help him see sense.

After I've told him he needs to confess, I'll send you this email, so if it gets into the news, you know about it already. And I'll send a copy to Dad too. If Marcus doesn't cooperate, I'll send the story to a newspaper contact I have, and to the police.

I hope you can find it in your heart to forgive me, and may the Lord have mercy on Marcus when he faces up to what he's done.

With love,

Shannon x

Without speaking, she passes the phone to Ruth who reads it quickly, then looks up, shaking her head in disbelief.

"And she doesn't mention his name – the man they killed . . ."

"No – I wonder if it's in the draft to the journalist. I can ask Chris. Jesus, I can't believe she stayed with him all those years after that. He's a monster."

Ruth is chewing at the corner of her lip.

"Well, she's hardly whiter than white herself – she was involved too. I guess they were wrapped in it together."

"But she was only sixteen, she'd never have been held responsible. Even under Texas law, right?"

Ruth shrugs. "Yeah, I guess, but there's something in the way she writes about it – it sounds kind of skewed towards a 'poor little frightened girl' picture of things," she says, pulling herself up off the floor and walking over to the kitchen. "It's extraordinarily easy to play the victim and make everyone else seem like the bad guy. You know?"

Behind her, Cleo can hear the sound of glasses and a wine cork popping as she rereads the email, trying to see what Ruth sees.

Ruth hands her a glass of wine, and sits back down on the rug with hers. In the lamplight, her face is pale, and there are shadows under her eyes that Cleo hadn't noticed until now.

"She wasn't entirely innocent, true, but I don't know that any of us can defend Marcus – you saw me that night, Ruth, after what he did to me – he's not the good guy here."

"Of course not. I'm just curious about the tone of the email and why she wrote it, and why she was going to discuss it with him first. Plus she hadn't told anyone about the pregnancy but that has to have been a factor in whatever she was planning. There's something more to all this."

Cleo reads the email a third time, stopping at the line about talking to Marcus.

So I'm going to see him tonight to tell him first, to give him a chance to arrange a lawyer and go to the police himself. I think once he's heard everything I have to tell him, he'll do the right thing. I have something to show him too, to help him see sense.

Does the "everything" refer to the pregnancy? The thing she wants to show him might be a pregnancy test? But if she was potentially sending him to jail, and wanted nothing more to do with him, why tell him about the baby at all? Or had she already found out she wasn't actually pregnant?

Her head is spinning.

Ruth puts her wine on the floor and stretches her arms above her head. "Perhaps she told him about the baby and that's what happened? They fought about it and he pushed her?"

"I don't know. I'm not sure Marcus would care that much if she was pregnant. It's not like he was married to me. Our relationship was very much on the rocks at that stage, and he was already spying on me with the camera."

Ruth says nothing but she's looking at Cleo strangely.

"What?" Cleo asks.

"Nothing, I'm just tired after all that shit with my boss today, and my brain is addled trying to piece together this jigsaw."

"Come on, it's me you're talking to. What is it?"

Ruth gets up off the floor again and walks over to the kitchen, and Cleo watches as she opens one cupboard door, then another. She's not looking for anything but the right words.

"What if we caused it?" Ruth says finally in a small voice.

"What if seeing our conversation on camera made Marcus so angry it caused a fight with Shannon, and ended with her death?"

"No, he didn't see our conversation until he came back from Shannon's that night – she was already dead by then. I'd even seen it on the TV news – I just didn't know it was her." Cleo gets up and walks over to Ruth. "But even if it had been prompted by something he saw on camera, that wouldn't make it our fault. He was spying on me. We're entitled to have a conversation without the presumption that we're being watched, and we can't control what someone like Marcus chooses to do. Okay?"

Ruth nods, then her face changes.

"Hey, you don't think he might have had a camera in Shannon's apartment too? If he was spying on you during your relationship, maybe he did the same with her?"

Cleo pauses to think about that. It was entirely possible. Would the police have searched for something like that – possibly not in a suicide case? Would Marcus have removed the camera if he was there that night? Presumably yes, but it's worth checking. She needs to call Chris.

He picks up after one ring, sounding calmer. He thinks the police had a look around Shannon's apartment but he never heard anything about a camera – maybe Detective Murphy will be able to check. He wonders if it's worth searching for the video files rather than the camera, but Cleo doesn't know where Marcus's laptop is now. The cops took it the night Marcus attacked her, and she hasn't seen it since. Another question they can ask tomorrow. She's saying goodbye when Ruth starts waving at her to stop. She's mouthing something. Cleo excuses herself to Chris and covers the phone with her hand.

"I have Marcus's laptop – remember I took his stuff from your apartment? It's here in mine!"

"No, the police have it – they told me they took it that night and they never gave it back. It was part of the evidence against him."

Ruth looks confused. "Then whose laptop do I have – is it yours?" She walks over to a closet by the door, and rummages around in the bottom of it.

"Hang on, Chris," Cleo says into the phone.

Ruth turns around from the closet, holding a rose-gold Mac.

"That's not mine," Cleo says, "but I've seen it before – Marcus had it under his arm when he came home the night he attacked me."

They stare at each other for a beat, then Cleo puts her cell phone back to her ear.

"Chris, what kind of laptop did Shannon have?"

His voice is rasping now. "A Mac. A kind of pink-gold colour. Why?"

"It's here. At least I think it is." Cleo holds the phone to her ear with her shoulder and takes the laptop from Ruth. "I'm just opening it now. Would she have had a smiley sticker at the top of the screen near the camera, and more smiley stickers down the left-hand side?" There's an intake of breath on the other end of the line. "There's a post-it stuck to the right-hand side with lists of passwords and PINs, and the number 0316 comes up over and over. Does that mean anything?"

"That's her birthday. March 16th."

"Okay, I'm going to charge it up and log in to have a look around – is that okay?"

A pause.

"Could you wait for me?" Chris says. "Could I call by your friend's apartment?"

Cleo looks over at Ruth and mouths "He wants to come over". She nods.

"Sure, grab a pen and I'll give you the address – we'll wait."

Ruth finds a charger and starts to power up the laptop while Cleo passes her address to Chris. When the call ends, they sit together on the couch, staring at the black screen.

"There's probably nothing there we haven't already found in her emails and her messages," Cleo says, when the power gets to 5%. She sits forward and starts to type, trying the first password on the post-it note.

Ruth puts a hand on hers.

"Maybe leave it till he gets here. This is a huge deal for him – let's do as he asks."

Cleo sits back.

Fifteen minutes later, Chris arrives at Ruth's apartment, looking like a shadow of the person Cleo met that morning. Without speaking, Ruth and Cleo get up from the couch to let him sit down at the laptop. His hands are shaking as he types in the first password and screen opens on her email account, the one they've already looked at on her phone. There are other websites open in her browser, but nothing unusual – Facebook and some news sites. The deflation in the room is palpable. Ruth moves back towards the kitchen and throws Cleo a *give him some space* look. Cleo follows her.

"It's a shame it's not Marcus's laptop like you thought," she whispers to Ruth. "If he had a hidden camera in Shannon's apartment too, I imagine he'd have taken it with him that night, but there would have been something in the video files."

She nods. Then she stops and her eyes widen. "Wait, what if there's a video on Shannon's laptop? Remember the 'thing' she was going to show him – the one she mentioned in the draft email to her mother? What if it wasn't a pregnancy test, but a video – what if she was planning to record her conversation with Marcus that night, in case he backed out of turning himself in?"

"I don't know … it's worth a shot, I guess." Cleo turns to Chris and raises her voice a little. "Can you check for a folder with video files?" He looks confused. "We were wondering if perhaps Shannon recorded her conversation with Marcus. That night."

Understanding washes over his face and he turns back to the laptop.

Ruth is shaking her head.

"What?" Cleo asks.

"If she did record him that night, she wouldn't have been able to save the file anywhere afterwards, because she was *dead*." She glances at Chris. Then out loud she says, "It would just be there in the video-recording app on her laptop. Look for PhotoBooth or QuickTime apps. If she used one, it should still be open."

"This is a long shot," Cleo whispers to Ruth. "I don't know if she'd have gone to this trouble. He's the one with the spy-camera history, not her."

"They've been keeping a huge secret for twelve years, and they share responsibility for killing a man then leaving him alone on the roadside," she whispers back. "I'd say there's a reasonable chance some of his habits have rubbed off on her. It's worth a look."

Cleo walks back towards the couch to look over Chris's shoulder, just as he minimises the web browser, and that's when they see it.

They're looking at themselves, on a video screen – Chris to the forefront, Cleo and Ruth behind. There's a red "stop" button at the bottom of the screen.

"It's her Photo Booth app," Ruth whispers. "It stops recording a minute or two after you close the laptop – it restarted when we opened it. It's recording us now."

Chris turns to her.

"What do I do? How do I see what she recorded?"

"Press stop but don't do anything else. The video should still be there."

He does as she says, and a row of photos and video clips appear across the bottom of the screen.

"Click on the last one on the right," Ruth says, still whispering. He does.

The video screen is dark at first but they can hear voices. A woman's voice Cleo doesn't recognise at all, and a man's voice that's all too familiar, rising like a spectre from the grave.

Chapter 42

As a trio they freeze, staring as the image comes up on screen – an apartment Cleo hasn't seen before, with glass doors looking out onto the night sky, and two people. One she recognises from her Facebook profile picture. The other is Marcus.

Shannon is nearer to the screen than Marcus – it looks like she might be sitting at a desk or table, about to use the laptop. She's turned sideways to speak to him, her dark ponytail swinging when she moves her head. He's a little further away, but in shot.

"Won't he see himself on the screen if he comes closer?" Cleo whispers to Ruth.

"She probably has her web browser open to cover the video screen," Ruth whispers back. "As long as the camera is on, that's all she needs."

It's hard to tune in to what they're saying at first, and Chris turns up the volume. Marcus is speaking.

"Shannon, this has to stop – the texting, the calls to the office. We're not together anymore."

To Cleo, he sounds uncharacteristically sad. Maybe they have it all wrong, maybe she did jump?

"I think when you hear what I have to say, you'll see things differently."

Shannon's voice is harder than Cleo expected, but then she's not seeing her in any kind of normal circumstance.

Marcus shakes his head.

"I'm sorry, but I can't keep doing this."

Shannon reaches to pick something up.

"I suspect you'll change your mind when you see this."

"What is it?" he asks.

"You know what it is. And it's positive."

She stretches her arm towards him. He hesitates at first, then comes closer to look.

"See the two lines? That means I'm pregnant."

Cleo watches as his face changes, a cold anger she knows so well, replaced in a heartbeat by something more neutral. He takes it from her, holding it up to look.

"What are you playing at, Shannon?"

"There's no playing. We're going to have a baby. You and me."

"Hold on, it's hardly mine. We've only slept together once since we broke up."

Ruth reaches over and squeezes Cleo's hand, as Marcus keeps talking.

"You've been overdoing the Valium and vodka for months now, and I'm sorry but that baby could be anyone's. Shannon, I don't even know if this test is real – I can't deal with this right now. I need to go."

Cleo watches Shannon's face, waiting for pain or surprise but seeing none. She sits up straight, nodding slowly, the hard smile fixed in place. It's clear now that she expected this.

"Don't go, Marcus, there's something else."

His shoulders fall and though he's too far from the camera to catch the sigh, the watchers sense it.

"What now?"

"You see, being pregnant has given me a new perspective. Now that I'll have my own child, it's made me wonder about other children – the ones who never saw their dad because he died on the side of a road one night in Gatesville."

Marcus's arms drop to his side and he takes a step closer to her. To the watchers.

"Shannon. Leave it."

"I can't leave it. Not any more. That man's children deserve to

know what happened to their father, just like our baby will know what happened to you."

"What happened to me?" Now he looks confused.

"For sure. Our child will know the truth either way. Maybe that truth will be that you're in prison for killing a man then walking away, or maybe that truth will be that you're at work and you'll be home by six for dinner and a bedtime story." She smiles. *"The truth will be yours to make and mine to tell."*

He takes another step closer.

"Shannon, what are you saying?" His voice is soft.

"You know what I'm saying. It's your call. We can make a family together, you, me and this little guy."

They watch as Shannon reaches down – it's off-screen but clear she's patting her belly. Her empty belly. Did she know?

"Shannon, we can't be a family." There's a tightness to his voice now, a taut string Cleo knows so well, but he keeps his expression neutral. *"Even if this baby is real, we're not together anymore. You know that."*

"Then on your head be it."

Shannon turns back to the laptop and pulls it towards her. She's typing something, her brow furrowed in concentration. Does she even remember the camera above the screen? Marcus moves closer, he's right behind her now.

Instinctively, Cleo steps back. Chris flinches.

Shannon and Marcus fill the screen, and for a moment, it's as if they're both in the room, both back from the grave. And one just minutes from her death.

"What are you doing?" Marcus asks.

Shannon looks back at him and nods towards whatever is on screen – something she and Marcus can see but the watchers can't. He leans in over her shoulder, narrowing his eyes to read.

"You're telling your dad about that night? Are you insane?"

A smile plays on her lips. *"Not insane, Marcus. In fact, I haven't felt this clearheaded in a long time."* Her hand goes down towards her belly again. *"I haven't finished the email yet, and I don't have to. It's your call."*

"You want me to turn myself in? I don't get it." The anger is gone for a moment and he seems genuinely confused.

"*It's not my preferred option but it's up to you.*"

"*Meaning?*"

"*Marcus, it's pretty simple. You can move back in tonight and we can start planning our future, or I finish writing this email to my dad. You've got about sixty seconds to decide.*" She's looking directly at the screen now, as her hands fly across the keyboard.

Behind her left shoulder, Marcus comes closer, reading as she types. He inches back again, and now his face is bone white, his eyes furious. The mic on the laptop doesn't pick it up but Cleo can see his breathing. In, out, in, out, faster and faster, his chest moving, his gaze staying still – never straying from the words on the screen. He closes his eyes and puts a hand either side of his head. Shannon is still typing and doesn't look back. His eyes spring open, and Ruth lets out a gasp. He puts a fist in his mouth – to stop himself shouting? He shakes his head slowly, then drops his hand to his side and takes a visibly slower breath.

Still Shannon types, oblivious to what's going on behind her. There's a knowing smile on her lips, and Cleo wants to scream at her to turn around but it's too late.

His face changes again. As they watch from the future, he composes himself, unfurling his brow, relaxing his arms, breaking into a smile. Only his eyes hold a hint of what they've just seen.

"*Shannon.*" His voice is soft.

Her smile grows wider. "*Yes?*"

"*I used to think about this, you know – about what it would be like to be parents. It's what you always wanted for us, but it's taken me my –*" he pauses, searching for a word, "*my affair to understand that it's what I want too. Let's do it, let's raise this child together.*"

"*And Cleo?*"

"*She was a distraction.*"

Ruth squeezes Cleo's hand again, but she's way beyond any sensitivity about their relationship

"*The baby changes everything,*" Marcus says quietly. "*What you said about coming home by six for dinner and story-time? That's what I want.*"

"*Then I guess I don't need to finish writing this email to my dad,*" Shannon says, turning to him.

She stands and reaches her arms out to him. He hugs her, his face towards the screen, towards the watchers. And it's there. The fury. Determined and pitiless.

Chris puts his hand to his mouth. "Oh Shannon, go! Please just go!" he whispers.

Beside Cleo, Ruth has tears rolling down her cheeks.

The futility is beyond comprehension, as each of them silently begs this girl from the past to run.

But she doesn't run. She hugs and she smiles and she stays.

Marcus pulls back then and kisses her forehead.

"*Imagine – a baby,*" he says. "*Do you think it's a boy or a girl?*"

Shannon is still facing away from the laptop and they can't hear her reply but he smiles in response.

"*I think we need to make things a little more official. Especially for your parents. Here –*" He reaches, and they can't see, but then she raises her hand, and he's taking a ring off her finger. "*Do you mind if I borrow this for a moment? There's something important I need to do.*"

He stands, looking around the room for a moment.

"*We need somewhere more romantic, I think – how about looking out at the New York sky?*"

He switches off the lights inside the apartment and it's harder to see now, but they can still make out what's happening. He walks towards the glass door to the balcony and pushes it open, then turns to beckon her out.

"*No,*" Ruth whispers, but Shannon can't hear her and she follows Marcus out onto the balcony.

It's dark and they're in the distance now; the watchers can just about make out shapes.

Cleo hears a strangled sob from Chris and moves around to sit beside him. Gripping his hand in hers, she asks if she should stop the video now.

"Let it play," he whispers, and she does.

As they watch, helpless to change what's already done, they see one dark shadow kneel before the other. They see Shannon's outline against the moonlit sky, clasping her hands together. And still they watch as he stands again and picks her up and swings her around, her ponytail swishing in the night breeze. She's tiny in his arms, and he lifts her again with ease, her lower back against the railing. It's too dark to see her expression, but all of them can feel it, every inch of it, as they understand what's coming. He kisses her again, then lifts her higher, so the railing is now at the back of her knees. And then it's easy. Far too easy. One flick, and she's over. One release, and she's gone. Like a dying autumn leaf, floating to the merciless ground below.

Chapter 43

At first there is nothing. No movement, no sound. They stare at the screen, trying to take it in. Cleo is still holding Chris's hand, and when she turns to look at him his face is immobile. She searches for words but there are none. Then Marcus saves them – the movie unfolding in front of them continues, dispensing with the need for speech.

He's back inside the apartment, the glass door still open behind him. He draws nearer to the laptop, sitting down in front of it, so his face takes up most of the screen. Again there's the urge to step back, and Cleo has to remind herself that he's not really there, he can't see them. He's pressing something on the keyboard now, his eyes moving from one side to the other.

They hear the click of keys being pressed. He's typing something, his mouth moving as he does so, but they can't hear the words. Then he pushes back from the laptop and closes it. The screen fades to black.

This time Cleo is ready to break the silence.

"Chris, we need to call the police."

His hand slips out of hers. "I think I need a minute." Trance-like, he stares at the blank screen.

Cleo looks back at Ruth – she has tears in her eyes.

"I keep thinking we should call 911 and try to save her," Ruth whispers. "Like it happened just now."

"I know," Cleo whispers back. "There's nothing we can do for Shannon, but let's keep a watch over Chris."

He's poker-straight on the couch, his face blank.

"Can I get you anything? A drink?" Cleo asks.

He shakes his head, then clears his throat. "I don't even know where to start with telling my parents about this. I don't think they should ever see that video – there's so much there that they'd hate, not just the . . . end. Jesus, we didn't know Shannon at all."

Cleo takes his hand again. "Don't look at it like that. She's still your sister. All that time with someone like Marcus would warp anyone."

Ruth throws her a look but Chris just nods.

"What was he doing at the end, when he was at the laptop?" he asks.

"I think he was deleting the email she'd written to your dad," Cleo tells him.

Understanding washes over his features.

"The suicide email to my dad – it was never about suicide. And she never sent it, Marcus did. Oh my God." He rubs his face with both hands. "So he deleted most of her email to Dad, but left that first line about something eating her up inside?"

Cleo nods. "And all he had to do was type 'Goodbye, Shannon' and hit send. I'm guessing he never noticed that the subject line included his name. Or maybe he did, and wanted your dad to think she killed herself because she was heartbroken."

Chris winces, but carries on. "Do you think she really believed she was pregnant? Could the autopsy have missed it?"

Ruth shakes her head. "I don't think an autopsy could miss something like that, but if she was taking Valium like Marcus said, it can cause a false positive pregnancy test. Maybe that's what happened."

Cleo nods. Poor Shannon. Planning a future based on a twelve-year-old secret and a baby that didn't exist. She tells Chris she's going to try Detective Murphy again – it's late, but they need the laptop off their hands. She reaches over to close it and without thinking, starts to pick at the smiley-face sticker that's stuck beside the camera.

"No, don't touch that!" Ruth says and Cleo pulls her hand away.

"Why, what is it?"

"I'm guessing she put it there to cover the light that comes on when the camera is operating – we should probably leave everything as is."

Cleo nods, and pulls up Detective Murphy's number. This time he picks up and, without a word, listens to the story. Cleo's not sure how it works when a murderer is dead, but he says it's still murder and will be investigated. He promises he'll come by to pick up the laptop, and she passes the message to Chris, but he's gone back into a trance-like state. Ruth gets up to put on coffee, the agreement between them unspoken – for now, Chris stays here.

Silver-grey light filters through the gap in Ruth's heavy living-room drapes, drawing Cleo out of a dream about frantically trying to call home. She pulls the patchwork quilt up over her shoulders and closes her eyes again, but sleep is gone. What time is it anyway? Her phone has slipped under the couch and, when she slides it out, the screen shows four missed calls. Three from her mom and one from Lauren, plus two messages from Lauren. And it's almost eleven. Shit.

She sits up, blinking in the half-light, then slips off the couch and knocks on Ruth's door. There's no sound from inside, but a note on the kitchen table says she's gone to work. God, poor Ruth. Chris was there until three this morning, then they were up talking for another hour when he left. Now Ruth has gone in to face her horrible boss, and Cleo won't even be here when she gets home – she needs to get out to her mom's. Everyone needs a friend like Ruth, and nobody needs a friend like Cleo.

She switches on the coffee machine and calls her mom to let her know what's happened – it takes some time to get through the whole story and Delphine is upset on realising that her daughter was living with a murderer.

"But it's over and he's gone and at least we got to the truth. That's important, right, Mom?"

There's silence on the other end of the phone.

"Mom, are you still there?"

"So, I guess the messages were never from Chris?" she says eventually.

"No, nothing to do with him. So we're right back to the start trying to solve that one."

"Cleo, did the messages ever mention the name Barbara?"

Cleo switches the phone from one ear to the other as she pours her coffee.

"What? Who's Barbara? Why would they mention Barbara?"

"Oh, it's nothing. A friend got some hoax messages, you know, one of those ones about winning the lottery or something, and I thought she said it was from someone called Barbara. Don't mind me."

Something in Delphine's dismissal seems off.

"Mom, are you sure? You sound weird."

"I'm sure. Ignore me!"

Cleo nods into the phone as she swallows the too-hot coffee and winces.

"Mom, I gotta go, I need to message Lauren – I'll see you later, okay?"

Cleo disconnects and sits back down to look at Lauren's messages.

Did you go to Chris's apartment? Please let me know if you are ok?

Then another:

Cleo, I'm getting worried. He might be dangerous. Please get back to me?

It seems so odd now that this time yesterday she was confronting Chris about VIN. And inside, she knows now she's glad he's not. But Lauren won't be happy, there's no relief for her – if it's not Chris, it's wide open again. Pressing the call button, she takes a deep breath.

LAUREN

Chapter 44

Oh my God. I say goodbye to Cleo and sit perfectly still, except for my hand, which is shaking, still holding the phone.

Chris is not VIN. Cleo's ex threw Shannon over a balcony, and they killed a man in a hit-and-run twelve years ago.

But mostly, Chris is not VIN.

And even though I've been telling Cleo it's probably not him, I realise now how much I desperately wanted it to be. Because then it's about her, and I'm just caught in the middle. And Chris is a real person, with a face, and a name, and an address. VIN is still faceless and nameless and who knows where.

On cue, my phone buzzes, and the little white envelope tells me I have mail.

Dear Lauren,

Do you like when the house is quiet and your kids aren't there, *needing* you? People like you have children to tick a box – it's nothing more than a vanity project. Get married, have two-point-four children, buy a big house. Though it's falling down around you, isn't it? Those cracks in the ceiling and in the tiles in the hall – they're only going to get bigger, you know. Like the cracks in your life – your big, fake, pretend life. It's all going to come crashing down, Lauren. Wait and see.

VIN

Like a sleepwalker, I pull myself off the couch and walk to the hall. Eyes down, I search, and it doesn't take long to find them. Two white tiles near the front door with hairline cracks through their centres. When I look closely, I can see cracks in the black tiles too. And above me, high in the vaulted ceiling, there are spider lines, snaking their way out from the light fixture, hiding in the plasterwork. Part of me wants to laugh – my troll is spotting my domestic flaws before I do. But there's no mirth in it – it's the kind of laugh that precedes hysteria. Like clockwork, I scroll through my photos, looking for some taken in the hall. There's one from last month – a new-shoe photo – though I can't see any crack. Going back further, I find another – a photo of a package on the hall table. And when I zoom in, I can see the two cracked tiles. *Result*. That's how he knew.

The glimmer of satisfaction is short-lived. What's the point in all this? What is VIN trying to prove, and why am I still chasing clues every time he sends me something? I'm running around in circles, panicking with each email, then reassuring myself when I work it out. But for what?

Sitting on the bottom step of the stairs, I close my eyes. The answer is immediate and blunt, and really, it's always been there – either I stop posting photos, or stop caring that he can see them.

My mum and Dave would say it's obvious – stop posting. My Twitter friends would say stop caring, but it's easier said than done. What would Cleo say? She'd shrug, and tell me it's my call. Thanks for the help, hypothetical Cleo.

I click in to Twitter to see what I've posted today – a tweet about hospital waiting lists and one about a politician. The same kind of stuff everyone tweets, nothing that gives much away. But in a sense, no matter what I write, no matter how innocuous, it says something about me – gives him clues. Maybe I need to turn the tables on him.

I go to his Twitter account to read through his tweets. All of them are directed at me, and there's no location given on any of them. Nothing new. No clues. I click through to Vinhorus.com then, and there's a new post up, called *And Then He Was Gone*

Still sitting on the bottom step of the stairs, I start to read.

My mother couldn't keep him. It wasn't her fault, it was the Whore's. He left, and she locked herself in her room. I sat outside her door for two days, listening to her crying, then she stopped and there was nothing. I banged on the door and she said to go away. So I knew she was okay.

On the third morning, through the locked door, I told her I was taking money from the jar in the kitchen and going out to buy food. At the shop, I got bread and milk, but instead of turning for home, I walked to the Whore's house. The last of three cottages at the end of the street, all white on the outside with flowers in the window-boxes, as though good people lived there. I was able to get right up to the window and look inside. Even through net curtains, I could see them. My dad was kissing her and she had her arms around his neck. Slut.

At the corner of the house, there was a little gate leading to the side passage. Opening it, I sneaked around to the back and peeped in the kitchen window. Nobody there. The backdoor was right in front of me, inviting me in. I pulled down the handle and inched it open, then crept inside her kitchen. And what happened then? Well, you'll have to wait and see.

Scrunching up my eyes in the low evening light, I read it again, slowly. "*Cottages with window-boxes*" doesn't tell me much – they could be anywhere. The word "*shop*" does though – if the sender was American, he'd say *store*. But then Cleo's just told me it's not Chris, so it's a moot point.

I'm reading it a third time when a knock at the front door makes me jump. Clare is on the step, hugging herself to stay warm and she launches straight into something about working from home and needing a break, then stops.

"Lauren, what's wrong? No offence, but you look like shit. Did something happen?"

Pulling the door wide, I invite her in and she follows me through to the kitchen.

Clare sits down, still hugging herself, as I switch on the kettle, then the heating.

"Will I put on the light too, or is this a Halloween-themed idea – having tea in the dark?" she asks.

"Very funny. Yes, please turn it on."

Light floods the kitchen, and we sit opposite one another at the table, wrapping our hands around our mugs of tea.

"So," she says. "What's up?"

"It's this stuff with the messages again. I've just found out it's not the person we thought it was, so I'm back to square one. He seems to know so much about me, but then when I check it's usually because I've posted some picture or detail online. I'm going around in circles and it's exhausting."

I stop and wait for her to tell me to get off the bloody internet, but she doesn't.

"So do you think that's it – he's finding everything from what you post online? Was there ever anything that couldn't be explained away?"

I take a sip of tea and try to remember.

"It's hard to say. Like, he mentioned a shower gel I got as a birthday present, and when I looked, I found it in the corner of one photo, but I'm not convinced he could have worked out what it was. And he knew where the girls go to school."

She raises her eyebrows at that.

"I'd never put up photos of them in uniform but, as Cleo said, maybe there was a jumper on a chair with a crest showing. I guess if you go far enough back through anyone's photos, you can piece stuff together . . . "

"Right," Clare says, in her wonderfully pragmatic way, and without even knowing what's coming next I'm glad she's here.

I have a sudden image of her at work, dealing with a big IT crisis, rolling up her sleeves and putting everyone at ease with a single "*Right*".

"It sounds like he's gleaning everything from photos and blog posts and tweets – he could be miles away, couldn't he? Is there anything you absolutely cannot explain away? Anything that shows he can't be some faraway randomer?"

"Kind of . . . last Wednesday I fell asleep on the couch after work, and I woke to a message asking me if I enjoyed my nap." I lower my voice to hide the shake.

"Okay. And could you have said anything online about being tired or looking forward to a sleep – could it have been a lucky guess?"

I shake my head. "Not online, but I had told my mother I needed to sleep. On the phone, I mean. I wondered then if maybe he'd hacked my phone, so I got a new phone and a new number."

I look up, expecting disbelief or ridicule, but she just nods. "Good idea."

"And I should feel safe but I don't. I'm only guessing he tapped my phone, or maybe hoping, because that's easier than thinking he was outside my house looking in while I slept." Imagining it sends a shiver across my chest and down into the pit of my stomach.

"Well," she says gently, "whether he listened to your call or looked through the window, isn't it time you went to the Guards?"

"You see, we did – the police in New York were dealing with it, because Cleo was certain it was this guy Chris. But as of her phone-call ten minutes ago, I know it's not. And I get the feeling in some perverse way she's glad it's not Chris. But now I'm left with this mess on my hands, and yeah, I do need to go to the Guards." I let out a deep sigh. "It's sounds so obvious but when you're actually faced with doing it, it's daunting."

She reaches a hand across the table. "I'm sure Dave would go with you?"

Dave. Oh God, he'd get on his high horse about this. No doubt he'd come with me to report it, but he'd get far too much 'I told you so' ammunition out of it.

Clare reads my mind. "Or your mum?"

"My mum would be completely baffled by the whole thing, or she'd think we're all going to be murdered in our beds. No, I need to keep my mum out of this."

"Right," Clare says, draining her tea and pushing back her chair. "Where are the girls?"

"At basketball, then going straight to Dave's. It's Nadine's birthday so they're celebrating with a broccoli quiche or something." I catch her eye. "I'm joking. It's probably a really nice sugar-free butter-free cake."

"Well then, get your coat and I'll get mine and meet you out front in two minutes. I'll drive. And put a bit of blusher on. You don't want to scare the Guards."

"You're hilarious, Clare," I tell her, leaning down to rummage in my handbag for nothing at all, as my eyes fill up with tears.

Chapter 45

There's an unmistakable lightness to Thursday morning and even the knowledge that Jonathan is my first appointment can't dispel it. I just wish I'd gone to the Guards sooner instead of waiting for Cleo to prove it was Chris. They took a statement and asked me to send on copies of the emails and some screenshots of the tweets, and details of the new blog. They said they might need my laptop and phone for forensic analysis but they'll let me know. It could take months to investigate, they said, especially if the servers and sites are outside of Ireland, but they took the whole thing a lot more seriously than I expected, and as I walked back down the steps of the Garda Station, linking arms with Clare, I felt better than I had done in weeks.

All of this is rumbling through my head when Jonathan ambles into my office.

"Dr Elliot, you look well. Sleeping better?"

I search his face for amusement or guile, but there's nothing disingenuous in his expression. Sitting down, he folds his arms and stretches out his legs.

"How are you, Jonathan, how have things been this week?" I ask, coming around to sit opposite.

"Good. I think our sessions are really helping."

The words are innocuous but I don't trust him. Our eyes meet. I'm right.

"You were telling me last week about your ex-wife, and how you were able to spy on her. Do you want to talk about that some more?"

"Really, Dr Elliot? Is that relevant to our therapy?" But he's smiling and I know he wants to show me how smart he is.

"I think you need to get everything out if you're really going to move past this. What did you do?"

He leans forward and lowers his voice. "I didn't have to do much at all. She told me everything herself, so to speak."

He sits back, smug.

"She told you? About her affair?"

"You could say that."

Oh, for God's sake.

"Go on?"

"She joined a closed Facebook group called Trophy Wives, for women with more time and money than sense. That's not actually their definition but it describes it perfectly. And, Jesus, you should see some of the stuff they post in there – it's like a window into a girls' night out, except they don't know anyone is watching." He licks his lips. "It's ironic really because, if anything, I was the trophy husband. I was the one with the mid-level job and the loaded wife. But she didn't like that – she liked the idea of being a kept woman and didn't want people to know it was Daddy's money, not hubby's. You know?"

I nod and pretend to take a note.

"So yeah, Sorcha kept them all up to date on her affair – when she was meeting him, how she felt about him . . . some of them were egging her on, telling her to leave me. Sluts."

I sit up straighter.

"But how did you know what she posted?"

"Because I was there too," he says matter-of-factly, as though it's the most obvious thing in the world. "I saw it as a suggested group in my own Facebook feed, so I set up a fake profile with a woman's name and requested to join. They don't pay any attention – as long as you're a woman, you're in."

Oh my God. So he knew everything she was doing, and she had no idea. A familiar chill flicks across my skin.

"The gas thing is," he says, leaning in again as though he's sharing a bit of harmless gossip, "she's gone now and I'm still there. Still listening."

"She left the group when your marriage broke up?"

"Let's just say her account is dormant."

His fish-eyes are fixed on my face, a half-smile on his lips, and I know he's waiting for more, waiting for me to ask him something else.

"Jonathan, do you think it's healthy to stay on in that group under a fake profile? Wouldn't it be better to make a clean break?"

His face changes and he looks confused. "But they're my friends now. Why would I leave?"

There are dozens of Facebook groups called Trophy Wives or with the words Trophy Wife in the name and, without knowing his fake profile, working out which one is Jonathan's is impossible. After ten minutes, I'm lost in a world of women who want to marry older, wealthy men. Most of them are US-based and I wonder if Jonathan made it all up, but then there's no reason why Sorcha's group wouldn't be American.

Engrossed in my laptop screen, I don't hear Ava come into the kitchen until she's right beside me.

"Here," she says, holding out her phone. "Gran wants to talk to you – she couldn't get you on your own phone. *She sounds cross.*" She whispers the last bit.

Oh, here we go.

"Hi, Mum, how're you?"

"Why won't you answer your phone – I thought you were dead!"

My mother generally thinks people are dead if they don't pick up after two rings.

"Sorry, I forgot it in the car when I came in from work – I'll pick it up in a bit or send one of the girls out."

"Your brand-new phone? For something you're so attached to, you're very careless, normally you can't let it out of your hand for a second."

Nice two-pronged attack there, thanks, Mum.

"Well the car's right outside and it's locked," I tell her, scrolling through more Trophy Wife groups. "And this street isn't exactly a hotbed for thieves."

"You should get a landline. It's not a good idea to rely on mobile phones. What if someone broke in and your mobile wouldn't work?"

"Mum, why would a landline be any more reliable than a mobile?" I ask but, even as I say it, I know I'm being unreasonable. Possibly the most annoying thing of all about my mother is that she is sometimes right.

After a twenty-minute rundown of all her neighbours' ailments and what the priest said about gambling last Sunday, I say goodbye and get back to the trophy-wife research. Changing tack, I try googling Sorcha Oliver but nothing comes up – maybe she never took Jonathan's surname. I look again at the members in one of the larger Trophy Wives groups in my search. The names are all distinctly American, and the profile pictures mostly show beautiful young women, but some show couples, and others babies. One is a picture of a teacup with a love-heart on it, and another is a gerbera daisy. Could one of them be Jonathan? I click into the teacup but her privacy settings are high, and I can only see her cover photo and name. The gerbera daisy is equally private, as are most of the others I try. And suddenly it strikes me that any of them could be Jonathan, or any middle-aged man getting his kicks from joining a women-only group. The beauty and the fatal flaw of the internet – being anyone you want to be.

I switch to Twitter, and search for LillGalwayGirl first. My face is hot, but she'll never know I did it. I study the familiar photo I've known for years, then take a look at her most recent tweets: a chat with two book bloggers, and disdain for last night's episode of a BBC crime drama. Oh for God's sake, what am I doing? I *know* Lill. You can't converse with someone online for years without knowing them, and nobody keeps up a fake persona for that length of time.

"What are you doing, Mum?"

Rebecca's voice startles me.

"Nothing. Something for work. Are you okay?"

"Just getting a glass of water."

I pat the chair beside me.

"Sit down for a minute and have a chat. I feel like we haven't talked in ages."

She rolls her eyes. "Um, we talked at dinner, like three hours ago. Anyway, I'm wrecked, I need to go to sleep."

My face stays neutral while she fills her glass and walks out of the kitchen. I call goodnight to her and she mumbles something I don't catch.

Then my head is in my hands, and suddenly I think if I don't hold myself on this chair, I might just slip to the floor and lie there in a sobbing, miserable heap. For all of it – the stupid marriage and my broken girl and the messages that won't stop no matter how many photos I delete. And all the pretending we're fine when we're not fine, and the cracks that are everywhere, not just in the tiles in the hall. That's the thing about cracks – once they start, there's no way to reverse the damage. Painting over them only works for so long, then they're back, longer and wider and deeper than ever, and no matter what I do I can't seem to stop the spread.

Chapter 46

The doorbell rings, clanging loud in the silent house, and I curse myself as I do every Halloween night for not being organised. I'm tipping packs of jellies into a bowl when the doorbell rings a second time, impatient now.

It's not a trick-or-treater though, it's Dave.

"Hey, can I come in?" he says, already stepping into the hall. He takes a pack of jellies from the bowl and grins at me. "Cheers. There are no goodies in Nadine's."

"Dave, what are you doing here? The girls are both staying with friends – I told you that."

"Yeah, I know," he says, sitting down at the kitchen table, tipping a handful of sweets into his mouth. "I just don't want to answer the door to trick-or-treaters. You know I hate it."

"Why don't you let Nadine do it?"

He folds his arms and presses his mouth to a perfect sulk. "She's gone out to a Halloween Ball with her girlfriends. I wasn't invited."

"But what difference does it make whether you're here or at home? There'll still be trick-or-treaters calling here."

His eyes open wide. "But sure you'll answer the door here, you always do."

There's no hint of irony, just Dave being Dave. I sigh and open a pack of jellies myself.

"Nice witch's hat by the way, Lauren. I see you went all out with your costume this year."

"Very funny. Anyway, my jeans and jumper are black – it's a fine costume. And the girls aren't even here – I'm not sure why I bothered. God, I kind of miss all those years of homemade costumes and too many sweets now."

But Dave's not interested in a discussion on the passage of time or nostalgia for years gone by.

"So what's new – how's work?" he asks, his mouth full of sweets. The chewing makes a squelchy sound and reminds me there are things I don't miss.

"It's fine –"

The doorbell interrupts me, and I go out to a ballerina and a Spider-Man. Their mother is hovering halfway down our front path and I recognise her from one of the barbecues in Nadine's last summer. I wonder what she'd say if she knew Dave was in my kitchen. I wave and smile, and she waves back, then hurries the kids down the path.

Inside, Dave is leafing through a magazine. He skips past an article on gender balance in the media and one on US politics, and stops on a city-centre restaurant review.

He looks up at me. "Why are you smiling?"

"I can't decide if the fact that you never change is a good thing or not."

"Probably not, to be fair. What's the latest on the article *you're* doing – the one about the internet stuff?" he asks, closing the magazine.

"Going well, I think, though I haven't seen it yet. I met Caroline – the journalist – a couple of times and we're due to meet again on Saturday morning for the final interview."

"Hang on," Dave says. "You haven't seen it yet? But sure she could be writing anything!"

Oh Lord, here we go.

"I get to see it before it goes in to the editor. And she's not some total stranger – I've met her, remember, twice now. She's very nice."

"All I'm saying is, if I was a journalist, my greatest trick would be to convince everyone I'm nice."

He actually taps the side of his nose as he says it, and I want to throttle him, even if there's a tiny part of me that knows he has a point.

We're both saved by the bell – this time there's a pirate and a witch, and no visible parent, though it's hard to see much in the dark.

When I go back to the kitchen, Dave has finally given up waiting for me to make tea and is boiling the kettle himself.

"Listen," he says, turning around, "you haven't said anything about me to the journalist, have you? Anything about us, or Nadine? It's just that it'd look bad at work."

"Yeah, Dave, it's all about you – everything is about you."

He looks confused. "What?"

"I'm joking," I sigh, "though it clearly missed its mark." I mutter the last bit.

He's busy pouring water and doesn't hear.

"And in the messages you've been showing Caroline for the article, there are none about me?"

"No, because the troll doesn't mention you."

He gives me a funny look – surely he's not feeling left out? It would be exactly like Dave to feel left out.

He sits down with two mugs of tea and opens a second pack of jellies, tipping the entire contents into his mouth in one go.

"Actually, did you ever get your friend to look into finding Leon's IP address? You said a couple of weeks ago you were going to ask again?"

He points at his mouth – it's too full of jellies to answer. I wait. His chewing is the only sound in the kitchen now, and I get up to boil the kettle again, though I haven't touched my first cup of tea. Finally he swallows.

"Oh shit, yeah, I forgot to tell you. He said he can't, because it's illegal. You need a court order to get an IP address."

"Dave, I know you need a court order to do it the official way, but I thought your friend could kind of work around that?"

He holds up his hands. "No, no can do. Sorry."

I sit back down and face him. "Fine. It doesn't matter anyway, the Guards are dealing with it now."

"Really?"

"Yeah. I thought it was someone in particular – this guy in New

York – but it turns out it wasn't. So Clare came down with me to the Garda station last week and I reported it, and sent them all the emails and screenshots from VIN, and the ones from Leon too, in case it's the same person."

"Really?" he says again. "But what will they do?"

"They'll investigate obviously. Try to find out who sent both sets of messages and if they're the same person."

"But, like, I presume internet trolls are careful about deleting all their sent items afterwards. It'd be some job to find them."

A laugh escapes before I can stop it. "Dave, deleting doesn't do anything. He can delete all he wants from his sent items, but nothing really disappears."

He pushes back his chair.

"Anyway, I'd better go."

"I thought you were going to hide out here till the trick-or-treaters finish up?"

"Yeah but if Nadine phones and I'm here, there'll be trouble."

And then he's gone, whirling out of my kitchen and into the night, leaving his mug on the table, because some things don't change at all.

The bowl of sweets by the front door is almost empty, but there haven't been any callers for twenty minutes – figuring I'm home free, I go out to the hall to take it away. On cue, the doorbell rings again and on the doorstep three boys Rebecca's age silently hold out plastic bags. All three are wearing clown masks but no costumes. I tell them they'll have to split two bags of sweets between them. They take my meagre offering and turn to leave without a word.

I'm about to close the door when a noise out on the road makes me look up and I spot a dark-coloured car outside my front gate. The engine is idling but the headlights are off. I can see someone in the driver's seat – the boys' dad maybe? Though they're too old for chaperones. The boys continue down the path and out onto the road, heading for Clare's house. I stare at the car, trying to make out who's inside but it's too dark. Suddenly I get the sense that he's staring back at me, and I don't want to be there any more, standing in my doorway, lit by the porch light. I close the door, lock it, and after a moment's hesitation, I put on the chain.

In the sitting room, I peek through the gap in the closed curtains. The car is gone. Now there's just black moonless sky and the outline of the trees at the end of our garden, swaying in the night-wind. Maybe it was a parent after all.

I draw the curtains tighter and switch on a lamp, pulling my too-thin cardigan around me against the chill. In the fireplace, there's an unused candle – a fat orange one Rebecca picked up to mark Halloween. I light it and the small flame works hard to dispel the cold atmosphere but doesn't quite succeed. Water gurgles in a pipe somewhere and I wish the girls were here tonight. My laptop beckons from the coffee table; online company will have to do.

Molly and Lill have changed their names to Molly-ween and LillWitchGirl for the night that's in it. Catherine is having a glass of wine to get over her youngest throwing up all over the carpet after too many sweets. Anna is watching *Nightmare on Elm Street* with her teen son. And I'm on my own, half missing my husband, but only because the house is too quiet. I type that out in a tweet, but then delete it. Instead I tell them Dave is here and we're watching a film with the girls. Molly and Catherine immediately zone in on Dave's presence and I feel bad for lying. But safer.

Catherine moves to our private Twitter group to ask how it's going with the article, and I tell her it's nearly done.

Did you go for anonymous in the end? she asks.

I will. The journalist said I could decide for sure once it's ready, but I already know I will go anon. My gut tells me it's the easier path.

A niggling thought pops up. What if VIN tries to expose me as the anonymous contributor after the article comes out – could he do that? Then again, there's nothing controversial in what I'm saying. And I don't think he has enough followers on Twitter to do any kind of exposé. I go into his account to check, but his follower count is zero and the only person he's following is me. The link to the blog is still there and, taking a breath, I press it. There's a new post up, called *Backfire*. I sit up straighter, and start to read.

It was dark in the Whore's kitchen, and messy. Breakfast dishes still on the table, and a buttery knife stuck in a jar of marmalade. My mother would never have let my dad do that. Half-eaten toast sat on plates, and cups with dregs of tea stood beside them, the kind of mess a whore leaves. On the counter, I saw a hairbrush – I pulled out some hair, wrapped it in a tissue, then slipped out before anyone caught me. Now I could make my voodoo doll. The Whore was going to be sorry.

Only it didn't quite go to plan.

I took some candles from the sitting room, and a box of matches from my dad's old pipe box in the shed. I waited until my mother was watching TV and then I lit the first one. I let the wax drip down onto a piece of paper I'd laid out on the carpet. The wax kept spilling over the lines I'd drawn, and the candle burned very slowly. The wax drips made a sound every time they hit the paper. It was too hot to hold after a while and I wriggled my wrist to get the sleeve of my jumper down over my hand.

Then I heard a door open downstairs and it made me jump. The candle dropped onto the floor, and the flame snaked along the carpet, leaping forward, so much faster than I'd ever have imagined. For a moment, it was beautiful.

But I didn't want the house to burn down – I got up and ran for the door, shouting for my mother. I heard footsteps on the stairs, and then she was inside my room, shouting at me to get out. I watched as she grabbed a blanket and threw it on the carpet, smothering the flames. She stamped on it, and I remember wondering if she could feel the heat through her slippers. There was a smell then, a horrible smell that hurt my eyes and my nose. I watched as she lifted the blanket to check underneath, then rolled it in a ball and put it in the corner of the room. I craned my neck to see the carpet. It wasn't dark blue any more in the bit that got burnt – it was brown and black and horrible. My mother came towards and looked at me for a second, then lifted her hand and smacked me, hard across the face. My cheek stung like it'd been cut with a whip.

"Don't you think I have enough to be dealing with?" she said, and went back down the stairs.

It was all the Whore's fault And I knew second time round, I'd get it right.

Is this really VIN's childhood? And if so, why is he telling me? I check the About page on the website but there's no information, and an online search to find out who owns the website *Vinhorus.com* yields nothing – it's hosted on Wordpress, so there's no personal information available. I slump back on the couch, trying to make sense of it all. Clearly VIN has a grudge against the person he calls the Whore, but what the hell does that have to do with me?

Chapter 47

As I'm clearing away dinner on Wednesday evening, the doorbell rings, and at first I don't recognise Grace – she's muffled up in a giant parka, far too big for her tiny frame. She pulls the hood back from her face and half-smiles as she says hello, but she's visibly uneasy.

"Come in out of the cold," I tell her, closing the door against the early November chill. "How are you, is everything okay?"

She nods but looks anxious.

"Could I speak to you about something?" she says.

I beckon her in to the sitting-room and close the door behind us.

"This is awkward," she starts, as she sits down on the couch.

Something squeezes my heart. No good comes of any conversation that starts with *this is awkward*.

"I should have told you this the last time I called," she continues, "but I wasn't sure it was my place to intrude, and you seemed like you had enough on your plate."

Now I feel sick. "Is it about the girls?"

She shakes her head. "No. It's about your husband."

I let out a slow breath. "Okay, what's up with Dave?"

"It might be nothing at all, but I think it's better if you decide that. The first time it happened was about three weeks ago. I was cleaning on the Wednesday morning, and he was at home a bit later than usual. He was in the study – I don't think he knew I was in the house. I'd used my key, thinking he'd be at work already."

She pauses.

I have no idea where this is going, but I'm starting to feel sick again.

"I was dusting the little table in the hall and I heard him on the phone in the study. At first I couldn't make out what he was saying and . . ." she looks up at me, "obviously I wasn't trying to listen. But then he got … I supposed you'd say agitated, and his voice went up a bit. That's when I heard it."

She stops again.

"What did you hear?"

"He said something like, 'I didn't realise there was any harm in it, I was just trying to teach Lauren a lesson. But if she finds out I'm Leon, I'm screwed'. I don't know who Leon is, but . . ."

Grace is still talking – I can see her mouth moving but I'm not listening anymore. *Dave is Leon.* A cold breeze flicks the back of my neck as my eyes watch Grace's mouth. It makes no sense, and I shouldn't believe it, yet somehow immediately I do. And perhaps that's the saddest thing of all.

"Are you okay?" Grace is saying.

I nod and swallow.

"I'm sorry, I missed what you said just there," I tell her.

"I didn't know what he meant by 'I'm Leon' and it might not have been anything but the bit about 'teach Lauren a lesson' had me worried. I came here that night to tell you. Then I didn't say it in the end, but it was on my mind."

"Of course. I can see it was a difficult situation for you – what else did he say on the phone that morning? Do you know who he was talking to?"

"Well, I stopped dusting and listened at the door." She looks up at me and I nod to tell her it's okay. "But he started to say goodbye so I slipped into the kitchen. I'm afraid I don't know who it was or what it was about."

I get up to fill a glass of water and bring one back for Grace too. When I sit, she starts talking again.

"I went home that night and told Tom – my husband. He said it might be nothing, but the best thing would be to keep an eye out for anything that would explain it, and then tell you if I had something more concrete. That seemed sensible." She smiles. "He's not much use with the housework but he's good in a small crisis."

There's more coming, I can feel it.

"So did you keep an eye out?"

"I did. I don't mean I was spying now or anything, but I'm in the house a lot and they tend to forget I'm there. And for a while there was nothing. But then this morning when I let myself in, your husband was there, again in the study. I knocked and went in, because Nadine's note said I was to hoover in there. He closed the laptop really quickly when I opened the door, and I wondered if it was just work stuff or something else. He looked flustered, but said he was heading in to the office and rushed off. And then I –" She stops, again looking for some kind of retrospective permission. I nod. "I opened his laptop. I know it's a terrible thing to do, and I'll be fired if they find out but there was just something wrong with the whole thing. I could feel it in my gut." She pauses. "So I opened it, and it was just a Google page, but then I saw what he was searching – look, I took a photo for you."

She pulls up a photo on her phone and passes it to me. The search entry is clearly visible in her photo of Dave's laptop screen: 'Can gardaí find IP address of anonymous troll?'

"I don't know anything about what an IP address is but I know what a troll is. And I suppose it has something to do with what he said before – the Leon thing he mentioned. And I told it all to my husband this afternoon and showed him the picture and he said it'd be safer to tell you and let you decide, so here I am." She pauses. "Only I've probably gone and got myself fired now, haven't I?"

Jesus Christ. All this time. He sat in my kitchen last night, casually drinking my tea, then he's at home this morning, scrambling to cover up what he did. Fucker. The absolute fucker.

"No, you haven't got yourself fired, Grace. I need to confront Dave about this." Her face falls. "But I won't mention you at all. I'll think of something, but I won't breathe a word about this conversation." She still looks nervous, and now I'm even angrier with Dave for putting her in this position too. "I promise you I won't involve you. I appreciate you coming to tell me this – lots of people would have stood by and said nothing. I'll tell him I found out how to trace it myself online. Okay?"

She nods, but still looks only slightly reassured as I walk her out to the door.

I take her hand as she turns to say goodbye.

"I really mean it, Grace, I won't involve you, please don't worry. And thank you."

And then she's gone into the night, and I hesitate for just a few seconds more, before running down the path.

At Nadine's door, I press the bell, and wait, trying to slow my breathing. What was he thinking? Why would he do that to me? The door stays stubbornly shut, and I try again, pressing the bell twice more.

"*Dave!*" I half-shout, hammering on the door with my fist now. Still nothing. They're probably both still at work.

My hand touches my back pocket, but I've left my phone at home on the couch.

I try calling his name again. Nothing stirs. Part of me wants to pick up a stone and fling it through their front window. But I don't. Instead I walk back around to my own house, and lock the door.

In the sitting room, I try phoning him, but it goes to voice-mail. At the end of the beep, I take a breath, but I have absolutely no idea where to start. *Were you my troll?* It's insane. And why? Jesus Christ, no wonder he's anxious about the Guards dealing with it.

Then the doorbell rings, and I rush to answer, ready to let him have it, but it's not Dave, it's Clare.

"Hey – I saw you at Dave's house – is everything okay?"

"No, it's not okay. Come in."

She follows me to the sitting room and sits beside me on the couch. She's wearing pyjama bottoms with boots and a cardigan, and I'm so glad to have this friend it almost hurts.

There's no roundabout way to say it. "The troll I had last year was Dave all along."

"Did he tell you that?"

"No. Nadine's cleaner overheard him on the phone talking about it – she was just here telling me. Bloody petrified she'll get fired for talking out of turn, which is making me even more angry with Dave. I promised her I wouldn't involve her." I sigh. "How could he do this?"

I'm waiting for Clare to tell me there must be a simple explanation, but she doesn't. She sits back and folds her arms.

"Let's have a glass of wine," she says.

I watch as she treads a familiar path to the wine rack in the kitchen, and when she comes back she busies herself with the corkscrew, still saying nothing. She pours me a huge glass and a slightly smaller one for herself, then sits beside me.

"Clare, why aren't you surprised?"

She lifts the wine to her lips and looks at me over the top of the glass as she drinks. Her eyes are darker than ever in the low lamplight, and I can't read them.

"I had an inkling," she says finally.

"What? You knew?"

"No, nothing concrete. God, no. I'd have told you for sure. Just a hint of something that stayed at the back of my mind. It was too ridiculous to even verbalise to myself, but now that you say it I'm not as shocked as I would otherwise have been."

Shifting on the couch, I turn to face her.

"But why? What hint?"

"It was last summer. You were talking a lot about your online friends – trying to get me to join Twitter, remember?"

I do remember. God, I must have been a pain.

"And – you might not like this – but often when I was here and you were on your phone, Dave was a bit eye-roll-y about it. He'd look at me, nod towards you, and throw his eyes up to heaven – that kind of thing."

I can feel colour filling my cheeks and I'm glad it's too dark for her to see.

"Then one night we were all in mine for dinner," she continues, "and you'd got the first couple of messages from Leon, and you were telling everyone – remember?"

I do. I wasn't too worried at that stage – it was dinner-party anecdote material and nothing more.

"I remember you were laughing about it but I was kind of worried for you, in case it would get out of hand. I glanced over at Dave to see what he thought, but he wasn't looking at me, he was typing something on his phone. Then a moment later, you got a message from Leon and showed us all – do you know the time I mean?"

I nod. It was a response to an article I'd shared on Twitter that day – something about the gender pay gap. Leon had said if women worked as hard as men, they wouldn't need to keep wittering on about being paid less.

"For some reason," Clare continues, "I was looking over at Dave when you were reading the tweet, and he was still looking down at his phone, but he was smiling. Not smiling – smirking. And something tiny lodged at the back of my mind. And I thought of it on and off since, but always told myself it was ridiculous. Until tonight when you said it, and it didn't seem ridiculous anymore."

Silence now. A car passes outside, and the wind picks up, making the bay windows rattle and the candle flicker in the fireplace. I stare at the flame, watching it dance. Clare's eyes are on me, waiting for me to speak, but I don't know what to say, partly because I'm no longer shocked that Dave sent the messages and that in itself makes me indescribably sad.

"Do you think he went to all that effort just to get me offline?" I ask her eventually.

"Perhaps. Or maybe it was a way to get your attention – to engage with you?"

I let that idea sit for a moment. A way to get my attention. Like a toddler having a tantrum.

Clare clears her throat and I turn to look at her.

"Oh God, what now?"

"I'm just wondering if he started again – is VIN his way of staying close to you even though he's gone?"

"No, he couldn't. Could he? The VIN messages are even nastier than Leon's. I don't think Dave would go that far."

"Well, until half an hour ago, you didn't think he was Leon either . . ."

"I know, but this is a whole other level. He couldn't be VIN, could he? What would be the point?"

Clare shrugs and throws up her hands. "To teach you a lesson? To show you he was right all along and being online so much has a downside?"

That makes me wince, and she qualifies it.

"I don't mean I think you're too caught up in it, but he clearly does – he's said it often enough. Or maybe it's a way of seeking your attention – albeit in a completely fucked-up manner – the bold schoolboy who keeps pulling your hair?"

"Jesus Christ, there are better ways of getting my attention – like continuing to live here and not sleeping with the neighbours, you know?" My voice is louder than I intended, and Clare reaches out to touch my arm.

"I know. And maybe I'm completely wrong. In fact I probably am. More wine?"

I don't want more wine, I want a clear head for when I get hold of Dave. I pick up my phone to try him again and see a message from Cleo.

Back in Dublin, exhausted after my trip home but kinda missed Ireland a little too. Any more messages from VIN?

Yep, still loads. So, so tired of it now. I hit send.

Ah, I'm sorry to hear that. I was thinking, should we go to the police here in Ireland now that Chris ruled out?

Already done, reported it to Guards last week when you told me wasn't Chris.

Her response is immediate.

Great. Actually – has VIN ever mentioned the name Barbara?

No, never – why? I ask.

Just something my mom asked me when I was back home. I think she was confused about hoax messages in general, but I thought I'd check with you.

Sure thing, I reply. **I'll keep you posted about any new messages anyway.**

Cool, she says. **Let's do coffee soon and see what else we can do?**

Sounds good xx I type.

I glance at Clare and try calling Dave again, but there's still no answer. He couldn't possibly be VIN, could he? Clicking into the VIN account, I look at the profile again. There's still no avatar, but he's added a cover photo – my picture of Cleo on the beach. There's no new blog post, but where the Twitter bio has always been blank, there's now one word: **VINDICTA**.

"Vindicta. I guess that's what VIN means!"

I turn my phone to show Clare, then type the word into Google. The search results all refer to a game – maybe the troll is a gamer? The game seems to involve dragons and an army general called

Vindicta but none of it links in any way to what VIN has been messaging.

"It sounds a bit like the word 'vindictive' – does that mean anything?" Clare asks. "Could he be calling you vindictive for some reason – to get at you?"

I shake my head. It doesn't add up. Nor does it make sense that VIN is calling himself vindictive – it's not a compliment in any form. Unless it means something else – in a different form . . . back in Google, I try **"vindicta meaning"** and a Latin-English dictionary comes up. According to the page, **vindicta** is a Latin word, and in English it means "revenge".

I show it to Clare and she examines it for a moment, then shakes her head.

"A flair for the dramatic no doubt, a deliberate attempt to scare you. Don't worry about it."

"No, I think it's real – I think he's talking about revenge on the person he calls the Whore in the blog posts. I just don't know what that has to do with me."

I turn my phone screen down and cover my face with my hands.

Clare sighs. "Ah Lauren, this must be horrible. I'm here for you, okay?"

I nod but don't speak, because I know if I do I'll be crying, and if I start I don't know how I will stop.

Chapter 48

Thursday morning, sitting at my desk, I still don't know what the Vindicta reference means and I still can't get hold of Dave.

When I knocked on the door before leaving for work, I got a very curt response from Nadine – he was gone to a conference in Bristol and wouldn't be back till the weekend. So I left him a voicemail, short and to the point: *I know you're LEON. We need to talk.* He ignored that and my next two calls, so I tried using Rebecca's phone – he's never ignored a call from either of the girls. But this time he did.

He's probably petrified, though I don't know how he thinks he's going to manage living two doors away and maintaining a relationship with his daughters while avoiding me.

And, in ten minutes, I'll have the weekly hell that is a session with Jonathan. Dear God, why didn't I become a teacher like my mother told me to?

With Vindicta still playing on my mind, I go into VIN's Twitter account and click through to his website. He's published a new blog post overnight, this time called *The Doll*.

So in the end, I used pipe cleaners to make the second doll – my mother would have killed me if she caught me with candles and matches again. I made the head with a ball of white wool, I glued the Whore's hair to the top, and stuck buttons on for eyes. I remember thinking 'black eyes to match her black heart'. I took a knitting needle from my mother's room, closed my eyes, and thought about what I wanted to happen – it was simple really, I wanted her to die in grotesque pain for what she did to us. I opened my eyes, and plunged the knitting needle into the head. Right between the eyes. I did it again and again, then sat back, and waited.

And it worked, but not the way it was supposed to. Did I take the wrong hair from the hairbrush? I couldn't have, it was long hair – it wasn't my father's. But either way he was gone. Dead as a doornail. My mother was back in her bedroom, and I spent most of my time sitting outside her door, listening. There was a funeral, but we didn't go. My mother said she couldn't go through it and that I was too young. I asked what happened to him but she just looked at me and shut the door of her room. I went back to look at the voodoo doll. The hair wasn't Dad's, I was sure of it. But I needed to know how he died – if he was stabbed in the head. It was like a ball of fire inside my stomach and it wouldn't go away.

On the fourth day, my mother got up and made tea, then sat down at the table with her hands wrapped around the mug, staring at nothing.

"Mam?" I touched her lightly on the shoulder and she jumped.

"What is it?"

"What happened to him? Did the Whore do it?"

Her eyes were black and empty. She turned away from me before she answered. When she started to speak, her voice sounded strange to me – empty like her eyes.

"She may as well have killed him," she said, still not looking at me.

"Did she stab him between the eyes?" I asked, afraid of the answer.

"No." She sighed, but her voice didn't change. "You see, what happened was, he was driving home from a party. Because that's the kind of thing they did together – went to parties. And they were supposed to walk home, but she said it was too far, and her heels were too high."

She turned to me then, and I was glad, even though I'm not sure she really saw me.

273

"Imagine. Her heels were too high. Why didn't she just wear proper shoes? So he drove, because she made him drive."

She stopped and looked away again. I waited, not knowing what was coming but praying that nobody was stabbed in the head.

"And of course your dad had had a few whiskeys. He never did that when he was here either. So he had a few whiskeys, and she wouldn't walk home, and he drove the car, and sure you know what happened then – he crashed it, didn't he?"

She turned suddenly back to me, and I jumped. Her eyes flashed, no longer empty, and that should have been good but somehow it wasn't good.

"He died on the spot, and she walked away." She slammed her teacup down on the table and it cracked in two, tea spilling out all over the table. She didn't notice. "That woman did it to him, and he did it to himself. Isn't that a neat thing now?"

I didn't know what she meant but one thing was clear – nobody got stabbed, and I had the right hair on the doll. I just needed to try harder.

The door opens, pulling me away from VIN, and in comes Jonathan, smiling a little too widely.

"How was Halloween, Dr Elliot – did you get dressed up yourself?" he asks as he sits down. "Or did you just stick on a witch's hat with your normal clothes?"

My head jerks up. Was that his car outside my house?

"Sorcha always just put on a witch's hat," he continues. "But then again, we didn't have kids. You might be under more pressure to wear a costume?"

Now he sounds genuinely curious, a normal man making normal small talk. Or a good actor, messing with my head.

"We're past that stage in our house now. But talk to me about that – did you want children? Did Sorcha?" I ask, sitting down.

Let the games begin.

His face darkens. "She didn't. I did. It's one of the things we fought about. She'd have been a terrible mother in fairness. That's one thing we can all be thankful for – no chance she'll ever procreate."

"But I guess she might have children with her new partner – how would that make you feel?" I wonder if I'm going to enflame something I shouldn't, but he must know it's a possibility.

He looks at me for a moment and I can almost see his mind working behind his eyes, trying to decide on something.

"She won't ever have children," he says in a low voice, "because she's gone. She's not with a new partner. She's in the ground, in a pine box, in the family plot."

Sorcha is dead? How could I have missed this? He's been talking for months about their separation but never once mentioned she'd died – this doesn't make any sense.

"I'm so sorry, Jonathan. When did this happen?"

"A few months ago. I suppose I'm still in shock."

My mind rolls back over his intake interview, the notes and the forms – there was nothing to suggest we were dealing with a grieving widower. How did I not spot this? But then, he never said it – not once. He's always spoken of her as though she's very much alive.

"Was she ill? Was it sudden?" I ask, scrambling to understand.

"It was very sudden. An accident at home."

A rash of goosebumps breaks out on my arms.

"What happened?"

He crosses his legs and leans back in the chair, half closing his eyes.

"She was taking a bath one morning, and she had her radio in the bathroom with her – she used to plug it into a socket in our bedroom with an extension cord. I told her over and over there's a reason bathrooms don't have sockets, but she still did it."

He pauses and opens his eyes wider. My skin is prickling cold, though the heating in my office is on high.

"And that morning, she must have been trying to change the channel and something went wrong – it slipped into the bath water, and that was it."

He clicks his fingers, and I jump.

"She was electrocuted, there and then in her own bath. There was a burn mark on her stomach – they reckon she dropped it on herself. The doctor told me it would have been quick, but I don't know if he was just trying to make me feel better." He gazes at me. "I don't think it would have been that quick, do you?"

My hands are on the arms of my chair and I'm sitting rod straight, trying to take it in. I swallow. "Jonathan, again, I'm so sorry to hear this, it sounds traumatic. So if she was still living with you when this happened, does that mean there was no marriage break-up and no affair?"

"Oh, there was an affair all right – all of that was true. I think telling you she left me was my way of coping with her death – it was easier than saying she died. I'm still having trouble with those words: *she died*. So horribly final."

"I understand," I tell him, though I'm not sure I do. "Of course it changes things here for us too – we're dealing with bereavement and not a marriage break-up, but I didn't know. In a sense, we need to start over now. Do you see that?"

He smiles. "I've got all the time in the world, Dr Elliot. I can keep coming to see you every week forever."

"Well, ideally you'll feel better after treatment and you won't need to come forever," I tell him with a small laugh that comes out sounding nervous.

"I know, Dr Elliot, and I trust you to get me better. I'd trust you with anything. I know you. And everything we discuss here is confidential, isn't it? Anything I tell you about Sorcha?"

"Of course, Jonathan, you can speak freely."

And as he goes on to talk about Sorcha, and how he felt coming home that day to find her electrocuted body in the bath, I wonder if any of it really makes him feel better, and I wonder too if it damages me, to sit here taking all of it in. If reducing his pain somehow increases mine – if it's stacked up inside me, like a deck of cards, growing taller as his grows shorter, until it's so big inside my chest I can no longer breathe.

It's later than usual when I get home from work, and the house is dark and quiet. Ava is in her bedroom studying, but there's no sign of Rebecca.

"She's gone down to Dad's house to do her homework," Ava tells me. She turns back to her history book, and I go downstairs to phone Rebecca. She doesn't pick up and I try again, but still no answer. Memories of her drinking session down at the pier flood back and my stomach tingles. She wouldn't, would she?

I have to ring Nadine's bell three times before Rebecca answers, and when she does she looks at me as though I'm interrupting something important.

"Why didn't you answer your phone?" I ask, trailing behind her as she walks through to their kitchen."

"It's on silent. So I can study." Innocent eyebrows arch.

"You know your dad's in Bristol, right? He's not even here?"

"Yeah, what difference does that make? He'd still be at work if he wasn't away. Anyway, Nadine always says I can let myself in whenever I want. I told her it's usually freezing in our house."

I dig my nails into my palms but say nothing. And it's hard to argue – it's a lot warmer here than our house, and her books are spread out all over their big kitchen table – she really does seem to be studying. As I'm searching for reasons to bring her home, I hear footsteps behind me in the hall.

"Oh, Lauren. I didn't expect to see you here?"

Nadine looks me up and down, like a spider who's just caught a fly.

"Sorry, I was just worried about Rebecca – she wasn't answering her phone so I called up. We're going now."

I step towards the table and start to gather Rebecca's books.

"I'm fine here, Mum, I'll head home in about an hour."

Rebecca has her arms folded, and her eyes meet mine, waiting for me to push back. I can feel Nadine watching and I know she's hiding a smirk even without turning around. I'm not taking the bait. Not today.

"If that's okay with Nadine, then I'll see you at home for dinner at six."

Rebecca deflates a little and Nadine fake-smiles at both of us – sorry perhaps to have an unexpected visitor now that the gauntlet lies untouched. It's a bittersweet win, but I'll take it.

Chapter 49

"I was surprised you asked him to come back so soon," Susan says when I walk into the clinic on Friday morning.

"Who?" I ask, but even before she answers I know.

"Jonathan Oliver." She nods towards the door to the waiting room. "He's there already."

I close my eyes briefly, too cross to speak, and take a deep breath in through my nose.

"Lauren, are you okay?" Susan asks, standing up from her seat. "Can I get you a glass of water?"

I open my eyes. "I'm fine. Send him in."

If Susan is surprised at my abrupt reply, she doesn't show it, and I make a mental note to run out for coffees later.

Before I can shrug off my blazer, Jonathan is standing in my office.

"Jonathan, I didn't ask you to book for today. Was there some confusion?"

He takes his usual seat and crosses his legs.

"Oh sorry, my mistake. It's just we made so much progress yesterday, I thought you wanted to keep going?"

"I think it's best if we discuss decisions like this together and let me decide on the schedule – is that okay?"

"Of course." He smiles. "But you want to hear the rest of the story, don't you?"

"I'm sorry?"

"I could see it in your eyes yesterday. You know that wasn't the full story, and there's a part of you that's horrified, but there's part of you – the voyeuristic part – that really wants to hear it. You're not so different to the rest of us."

"Jonathan, I have no idea what you mean." But I do.

He looks around the room, his eyes roaming over walls and ceiling.

"Everything I say here is confidential, isn't it? You can't tell anyone – like the guards for example?"

"Of course, everything is confidential," I tell him, keeping my voice steady.

"So will I say it, or do you want to guess?"

"Why don't you just tell me?" I say, feeling strangely calm.

"How about I tell you what I did, then you guess how I got away with it – play detective. I suspect you like having a little mystery to solve – trying to work out how people know the things they know. You do, don't you?"

"Go ahead, Jonathan." I don't take my eyes off his.

"You see, Sorcha didn't want me any more. I was an interesting toy she played with for a few years – something she used to annoy her dad. But then she got bored, and she met someone else, who was even better fun – a personal trainer in a gym. I can't imagine what her dad would have said if things had gone as far as a meeting. Which would have happened – she was going to divorce me. And that would have meant losing everything – not just her, but the house, the two cars, the holidays, the bank accounts – everything. Her father made me sign an agreement before we got married – little good it did him in the end." He stops to smile, then goes on. "But I couldn't let her take it all away, so I put a stop to her before she could leave me. You should have seen her face when I arrived up the stairs that morning, wondering why I was home from work. And how her face changed when I picked the radio up off the bathroom floor and held it above the water and waited for her to understand. The realisation crossing her face – it was profound. I'll never forget it." His eyes glaze over for a second, then he shifts in the seat and starts again. "The next part wasn't very nice. At one point I had to look away. But it worked, and she's gone, and I still have everything. Everything except a wife to share it with me." He stops again and smiles at me.

I'm rooted to the chair, my eyes fixed on his, aware that on some level I knew this was coming.

"Are you okay, Dr Elliot, have I shocked you?"

My mouth is too dry to answer. I shake my head, just a fraction of an inch.

"Now it's your turn," he goes on. "You have to tell me how I did it without being caught."

I see triumph in his eyes – he's thrilled at having shocked me, and desperately wants to show me how smart he is.

I swallow and think about the bottle of water in my bag, but my limbs are deadweight.

"Tell me," I manage eventually, in a hoarse whisper.

"Ah, come on. Won't you even try?"

"I guess maybe you got someone to lie for you? Someone at your work?"

He shakes his head, a playful smile on his thin lips.

"They'd hardly lie for me to cover up a murder – come on, Dr Elliot, I work in medical sales, not the CIA."

"I don't know then – you have a friend in the Guards?"

"Ah listen, you're not even trying. Give me something more creative."

He leans forward and is just inches from me now. I can smell the aftershave and toothpaste and a hint of stale coffee breath.

"Why don't you just tell me, Jonathan." My voice is stronger now. "I'm not as creative as you, it seems."

He sits back and folds his arms again, stretching out his legs, so I have to move my feet to avoid his.

"So, I was due to host a webinar that morning at eleven. There were customers dialling in from all around Europe – fifty-seven of them, I think. At a quarter past ten, I slipped out of my office carrying a stack of files, as though I was going to the photocopying room. I left my coat on my chair in my office, and closed the door behind me. Our receptionist never notices internal staff coming or going, so it was easy to slip out. I went home, surprised Sorcha, and well, you know what happened next – I've explained that."

I nod, wondering if this is really happening.

He continues. "This is the smart bit. I went back downstairs and brought in my stack of files I'd taken from work. Inside one of them was a picture that normally hangs on the wall behind my PC at work." He grins. "I took down a picture in our kitchen, and put my work painting up instead. It's a painting of a rowboat emerging from the sea."

He stops, and I nod, though I'm not sure why.

"Then I switched on my laptop and hosted the webinar, with the painting behind me. On a plain white wall, it looked exactly like my office at work. And I was wearing a suit, and looked like I was sitting at a desk. So when the Guards asked me where I'd been at eleven o'clock, I could show them a recording of the webinar. I have fifty-seven witnesses who all dialled in to it and saw me do it from my office. Smart, right?"

I nod again, aware that it's a million miles away from the correct response, but it's exactly what he needs me to do.

"And nobody even questioned it. Everyone believes what they see in front of them. It looked like my office, so it was my office. So what do you think, Dr Elliot? Are you impressed?" His eyes are wide now and his hands are gripping the arms of the chair. There's something manic about him as he waits to hear my reaction.

I choose my words carefully.

"To be honest, I'm shocked, as anyone would be. But as a counselling psychologist, it's not my place to judge – I'm here to help you get through this. In time, you may find that the best way to heal is to tell the truth yourself. But it's not for me to make you do that – I will do my best to help you get to that place yourself."

The short speech takes it out of me and I just want him to leave now. The clock shows we have four minutes left.

"Perhaps you can think about that between now and our next session – I'll book you in for next Wednesday. Don't worry about stopping with Susan on the way out – I'll take care of putting it in the book. Does that sound okay?"

"You're one of the good ones, Dr Elliot. I feel bad now for some of the stuff . . . well, for messing with your head a bit. You were spooked at times, weren't you?"

He doesn't look like he feels bad; he's almost salivating. I swallow and nod, unable to summon up any more words.

He smiles, pulling himself out of the chair, and as he turns towards the door I quietly, quietly let out a breath. He waves and smiles as he leaves, like someone saying a casual goodbye to a friend. I'm still sitting, unable to move, but when the door closes, it's like a spring, and life comes back to my limbs.

I rush across the office and open the door again, just a crack. There's another client at the desk talking to Susan, and Jonathan is hovering behind. Just go, I tell him in my head, and he must hear me, because he turns and walks out of the clinic.

Darting out to reception, I go to the window beside the front door, and look out. Jonathan is getting into his car, and I watch as he pulls out and onto the road. I sag against the window then, conscious that Susan and the client have both stopped talking.

"Are you okay?" Susan asks, standing up.

"Yes, but I have to do something urgently. I'm sorry, but can you cancel my next session?"

In all my years, I've never cancelled anyone at such short notice but Susan must see something in my face because she just nods and sits back down. Back in my office, I stop only to grab my bag, then I'm out in the early November sunshine, wondering if this will finally bring it to an end.

The ice-cubes crackle as the gin hits, loud in the quiet kitchen. The ring-pull makes a satisfying snap when I open it, and the tonic fizzes as it fills the glass. The first gulp hits the back of my throat and I take another, not tasting anything. *Drinking at lunchtime? It's a slippery slope, Lauren.* That's what my mother would say if she was here. But then I'd tell her that I've just spent two hours in the Garda station reporting a murder, and maybe even my mother would understand.

Two Gardaí took my statement, one male, one female. I could see them exchanging looks every now and then, and trying to keep their faces neutral when I got to the bit about the radio and the bath. I asked them if they have any death like that on their files – someone called Sorcha Oliver from Sutton? They couldn't confirm, they said, they'd have to look into all of it. But then one of them got up and brought in a Detective Sergeant to speak to me, and I knew they were taking it seriously. Three pairs of eyes widened when I told them about the webinar he did from home, and about the painting of the rowboat. I wished then I'd googled it before I came in, to see if it really happened. I told them that Jonathan turned up in my local supermarket car park and that he might have been outside my house on Halloween night. They asked me if I had reported any of it and I felt myself going red when I told them I hadn't, but they didn't seem surprised. I told them about the messages from VIN, and that I'd reported those to Dún Laoghaire Garda Station. One of them left for a few minutes, then came back in and nodded to the other two. I wondered if they'd contacted Dún Laoghaire. I showed them some of the screenshots and messages from VIN, and the blog posts, and told them about the picture from Venice that started it all, and that Jonathan knew I was there. They wanted to know if he'd admitted he's VIN. No, I told them, but it's the only thing that makes sense.

"What do the blog posts mean?" one asked me, but I didn't have an answer. Maybe it's the true story of Jonathan's childhood, and he's been fixating on and blaming women in his life ever since then? Or maybe it's all made up.

"And why did he tell you all this about his wife's death and his alleged part in it?" the Detective Sergeant asked, after I'd told the entire story twice. "That's what I don't get. Obviously we need to investigate to see if there was in fact a death such as you describe –" looks were exchanged again, suggesting they'd already checked, "but why confess, when he'd got away with it?"

"I think he wanted to show off, to show me how smart he is. And to shock me – he got a thrill from shocking me."

"But surely he knows he's likely to be investigated now? And, if it's true, he could end up charged with murder?"

Three curious faces wait for my answer.

"Not at all – he believes that everything discussed during a session is confidential – that the relationship between psychologist and client is protected under law in the same way as that of a solicitor and a client. Lots of people think that, mostly from watching US TV shows. But of course, as you yourselves know," I nodded at all three, "psychologists are required by law to disclose information relating to crimes."

Sitting in my kitchen, I wonder if on some level Jonathan also knows that, or does he truly think I can't tell anyone, and that he'll be back for another session next Wednesday? I swish the ice cubes in my glass and take another gulp. The gin starts to work, a numbing settles in. The Guards promised they'd let me know as soon as they'd spoken to Jonathan, and he has no reason to believe I'm here rather than at work, but I can't help walking through to the sitting-room window to watch for cars. Friday afternoon traffic is heavy on the road outside, but nobody stops, and nobody looks like Jonathan.

"What if you speak to him but don't arrest him today – I'll be at risk, won't I?" I had asked as I was leaving the interview room.

"You don't need to worry," the Detective Sergeant said. "I can't say too much, but I don't think he'll be going anywhere near you for a long time, Dr Elliot."

Still. What if they're wrong? What if he's not there when they go to his office or his home, or what if they make a mistake and can't arrest him for some reason? My hands are shaking as I pour a second gin. That'll be the last. I need to think about what to tell the girls, if anything, and I still need to talk to Dave about Leon. As I take a first swallow of the fresh drink, I hear a car pull up outside. My legs feel suddenly sluggish, but I make it to the sitting-room window to look out. A taxi, and it's stopped outside my house. I can't see who's in the back but as I watch it starts to move again, then stops outside Nadine's – Dave, coming home from his conference in Bristol. Without thinking, I race outside and get to him just as he finishes paying the fare. His eyes widen.

"Lauren. Shit. Why aren't you at work?"

"I think we need to talk, don't we, Dave?"

He opens his mouth to protest, to make an excuse, but then his shoulders slump and his head goes down.

"Fine. In our house though, Nadine doesn't need to be involved."

Our house. I don't say anything. Pick your battles.

In the kitchen, he looks at the gin bottle in surprise.

"What's going on?"

"It's a long story, but I want to talk about Leon. Sit down."

He does, and I stay standing.

"Well?"

I wait for him to tell me some story about trying to trap Leon or to deny any knowledge of the account, but he just looks down at his hands. Somewhere, there's a tiny shred of relief that at least this part is out in the open.

"Oh my God, Dave."

"I'm sorry."

"But why?"

"I really am sorry, I wish I could take it back. It was a shitty thing to do. And when I realised how much it was upsetting you, I stopped. But at first you made light of it, and it felt like a game. I didn't think there was any harm."

"But I still don't understand why?"

"Because you were never off the damn phone. I was sick of competing with your online world and losing. Leon got your attention." His mouth sets in petulant line, and the small shard of sympathy that had nudged its way in trickles away.

"Jesus Christ, Dave. I don't even know where to start with this. How could you do that to someone you're supposed to care about?"

He shakes his head, still looking down at his hands. "I know." It's so low I can hardly hear.

"And now the Guards are investigating – how's that going to look if they find out it was you? The good doctor preying on his own wife, getting his kicks out of scaring her?"

"*It wasn't like that! I never meant to scare you!*" he shouts, and it's better than whispered apologies I can't forgive.

I want to fight.

"*You're not an imbecile! Don't play dumb!*" I'm shouting too. "*You knew fucking well it scared me and you kept going anyway. Did it give you a thrill, that power to hurt me?*"

He flinches and it feels good.

"No! When I saw it was getting to you, I stopped."

"Sure, then you started again."

"What?"

"You were Leon, and now you're VIN."

"What? Jesus Christ, Lauren, that's a whole different ball game." His face is flushed. "I'm not VIN – you know I'm not."

"How can you expect me to believe that? I had a troll, and it turned out to be you. Now I have another one – of course it's you. And that's the conclusion the Guards are going to come to as well."

Until now, he's been like the child caught with his hand in the biscuit tin, but for the first time I see fear.

"It wasn't me, I swear to you. I don't know anything about this VIN person. And we're not even together any more – why would I bother?"

His words are like a slap. I slip down onto a chair, and suddenly, the air is gone, I have no fight.

"Lauren," he says, his voice quieter now, "I swear to you on our daughters' lives, I'm not VIN. Please tell me what I can do to prove it to you."

I look over at him, anxious eyes pleading to be believed. Something slides inside me and I can't do this anymore.

"You're off the hook. I know it wasn't you. The Guards are arresting a client from work for something much more serious than cyber-stalking, but it looks like he's VIN."

He lets out a long breath, like an untied balloon. "Is it the guy who was bothering you," he asks in a small voice, "the one who knew you were in Italy?"

"Yes, it seems so. But the point is, it's not so different – what you did to me last year is just as bad. You could easily have been VIN. Don't you ever do something like that again to anyone! Okay?"

He nods and his high colour slips away in a tide of relief.

"How did you find out?" he asks eventually.

"I figured out how to trace an IP address online, and it led back to my own house," I tell him. "Can you imagine how I felt?" If he pushes me on how exactly I did it, I'm in trouble.

He looks away. "Do the girls know?" he asks.

"No. Only you, me, and Clare."

"Oh for goodness sake, why did you tell Clare?"

"Dave, I'd tread carefully if I were you. You're not in any position to lecture me. I told Clare because I needed to talk to someone, and I will continue to tell Clare or anyone else I choose if I need to talk. So maybe the onus is on you to not be the talking point. Understand?"

He nods again and this time I think maybe he does.

By the time the girls get in from school, the gin is back on the shelf, the glass is washed, and Dave is gone. As soon as the key turns in the front door, I come out to the hall and pull both of them into a hug at the same time. Rebecca pulls away first, heading for the stairs, phone in hand.

"Will you stay down for a few minutes, Rebecca?"

"Why?"

"Ah, nothing really, I just feel like chatting with my girls. Come on."

Ava follows me into the kitchen, but Rebecca stays where she is and moments later I hear her go up the stairs.

"What's up?" Ava asks, pulling open a cupboard door and stretching up to the top shelf.

"Nothing much. I wasn't feeling great and left work early, and it's been a long day here on my own. I just felt like sitting down to chat."

She gives me a look now too, and I wonder when I last asked them something like this. She sits down with a biscuit and her phone, glancing at me one last time before clicking into something online.

"Hey, I'm right here. Can we not talk for two minutes without your phone between us?" I sit down beside her. "What's so interesting on there?"

"Nothing, sorry, Mum. Just wanted to see something . . ." she trails off, lost in another world. Then she claps her hand over her mouth.

"What is it?"

She looks up at me, her hand still covering her mouth.

"Ava, what is it – just show me."

She doesn't move, so I take the phone from her, and then I'm looking at a Snapchat photo of Rebecca. She's in her school uniform, in her bedroom, and she has a quarter bottle of red wine in her hand. **Friday Afternoon Tipple** is captioned across the photo.

I look up at Ava.

"Is this from just now?"

A tiny nod. "I think so."

I take the stairs two at a time and burst into Rebecca's room. She's lying on her back on the bed, propped up with pillows, looking at her phone. The wine bottle on her locker is half-full. Defiant eyes meet mine.

"Mum, you're supposed to knock."

"Are you seriously going to speak to me like that when I've just found you drinking in your room?"

She shrugs. "Who cares?"

"I care! And you should too. What has got into you?"

She rolls her eyes at me, and looks back down at her phone.

Red mist descends and I grab it out of her hand.

"*Look at me when I'm bloody talking to you!*" I roar at her, and I know it's not going to help but I can't stop now. "What were you thinking? And posting it on Snapchat, and in your uniform!"

"Oh, because that's what's important, Mum – not the drinking, but the fact that I'm in uniform. God forbid the nuns would find out we're not perfect. Somehow I don't think the nuns are on Snapchat."

"That's not what I meant. Give me that bottle now!"

With an exaggerated sigh, she hands it to me.

"Where did you get it?"

"In the cupboard with all the spices."

"Rebecca, that's been there about four years –" I sniff the bottle and wrinkle my nose. I can't tell if it's age or just bad wine. "Right, we need to talk about this, but first of all let's delete it from Snapchat." I click into her account and start to scroll through the pictures she's posted in the last twenty-four hours.

There's one of me sitting on the couch, head down, engrossed in my laptop. She's captioned it **The Silent Mummy** and something uncomfortable simmers inside me as I stare at it. Is that what she thinks of me?

Then there's a close-up of our kitchen calendar – she's drawn a circle around my few appointments and written **Exciting times – work, coffee, dentist, repeat.**

The next one shows me putting on lipstick at the hall mirror. Across it she's stamped **All dressed up and nowhere to go.**

"Rebecca, why are you putting photos of me online?"

She shrugs but the defiance doesn't quite reach her eyes. There's a hint of nervousness now.

"Why not? It's not about you, it's just whatever I come across. That's how it works, Mum. Jesus, not everything is about you, you know! Now can I have my phone back?"

I sit on the bed. Something is flitting in the corner of my mind.

"Have you posted other photos of our kitchen calendar?"

She shrugs again. "I guess. It's just a calendar."

"Yes, with all my private appointments, letting anyone who wants to know see where I am at any given time – what were you thinking?"

No answer.

"Rebecca, I need you think carefully about this – have you ever posted a photo of me asleep on the couch – in the afternoon, I mean?"

Another shrug. I grit my teeth and keep my voice even.

"Come on, Rebecca, it's a simple question. Maybe the day the police brought you home – before you went out? I had a headache and fell asleep on the couch after work – did you take a photo and put it on Snapchat?"

"Maybe. Yeah, I think so. So what?"

"And what about on holidays, on our last night in the mobile home – did you put a photo of me on Snapchat that night?"

"Oh come on, that was ages ago!"

"Please, Rebecca, you're not in trouble – I just want to know."

She pulls at a curl, winding it around her fingers. "Yeah, I think so." She looks up again. "But what's the big deal? The account is private, it's not like anyone other than friends can see."

I click into her profile to see her friends. She has 476. The back of my neck tingles as I scroll through them, a sea of names and avatars that mean everything and nothing.

"Rebecca, who are all these people?"

"Friends."

"Over four hundred friends? Do you even know four hundred people? Rebecca, most of these are surely complete strangers!"

I choose one name – OrangeBoy94 and point at it. "Who is that?"

"Just a guy." Her voice is smaller now.

"Who? Where is he from? What's his real name?"

She mumbles something.

"What?"

"I said I don't know. Look, I don't know all these people in real life, but that's how it works. Isn't it the same for you?"

I have a million things in my head right now about why it's not the same and why it's not okay but I can't verbalise any of them. Instead I'm running through the list, looking for a name that might be VIN or Jonathan Oliver. I scroll and scroll but there are so many, and I don't know if he'd use the same name everywhere.

Then I find it. VIN HO Rus.

"Look," I tell her, pointing at the screen. "That person has been stalking me for the last two months. Ever since Italy. Messaging me, telling me he could see me and knew what I was doing. And this is where he got it from – all from you. My God, I thought some creep was watching while I slept on the couch, or hacking my phone, and it was you on bloody Snapchat!"

She sits up now. "You're just saying that to make me feel bad, to teach me a lesson."

I pull my own phone out of my back pocket and show her the Huntsman email.

"That still doesn't make sense. I didn't put your name on it – there's no way anyone could have known it was you."

"Of course they could, Rebecca! Anyone looking at my Instagram account would find you in a heartbeat through your comments on my photos. It's simple then to trace you through to Snapchat. But, look, that's not the point – the point is you posted pictures of me without permission and I've spent two months thinking someone was watching me."

I watch as comprehension sets in, then guilt. And I know I need to stop now, before it goes too far. I take her hand and, for the first time in a long time, she doesn't pull away.

"Okay, you didn't know, and you didn't mean for any of it to happen. But you can't share photos of me online, or any photos you wouldn't be happy for me to see. Understand? And you must stick to connecting with people you know in real life. Can we go through this list together and delete the people you don't know?"

To my surprise, she nods.

"And the drinking . . . Rebecca, I know this is all down to me and your dad separating but this isn't how to deal with it, love."

She snaps her hand back.

"Oh, for God's sake, Mum!" There are angry tears in her voice. "It's not about that. Jesus, people split up all the time, I get that. It's bloody Kayleigh in my class."

"Who?"

"Kayleigh. Ollie's sister?"

I feel like we've switched TV channel and I have no idea what we're watching. "Who is Ollie?"

"Mum, you know this – Nadine's ex-fiancé. His sister is in my class – I told you that months ago."

Did she? I have no memory of it whatsoever.

"She's been a complete bitch to me ever since Dad shacked up with Nadine, and she's got three other girls in the class at it too – snarky whispers in the corridor, screen-grabbing and doctoring my snaps, bitchy comments on Instagram about my clothes and my hair . . ." She trails off and tears spill down her face.

I look at her anxious eyes and her dyed brown curls and I think about the top in the bathroom bin and the backpack she hated and mostly I think about what an idiot I've been, missing every single red flag.

I reach for her hand again. "You're being bullied?"

Her eyes close as a sob escapes and I can almost see the relief running through her body.

"Rebecca, why didn't you tell me?"

Her eyes open again and I can see all of it – hurt and pain and loneliness – and it's so blatant now. I slide my hands under her shoulders, one on each side, and scrape her up towards me, pulling her into a hug. She doesn't resist, and after a moment, she lets herself sink into me, her body shaking. I close my eyes, rocking her back and forth, wondering about all the things I thought I knew, all the things I tell my clients, and all the things that are right in front of me but too close to see for what they are.

Chapter 50

By ten o'clock, a low-lying headache has dug in, and my lunch-time gins are a distant memory. Rebecca and I talked for over an hour once she stopped crying – longer than we've talked in months. We worked on a strategy to deal with the bullying and, despite Rebecca's reluctance, we agreed to tell Ava about it too.

At six the Guards rang to tell me Jonathan had been taken in for questioning and subsequently arrested and held. I sank against the kitchen door, trying to hold back tears while thanking the detective. I sat for a while, waiting for relief to set in, but it was too soon. Everything still felt jangled and frayed.

For dinner, we ordered in pizza, and the three of us ate straight from the box, watching *Gilmore Girls* reruns. Rebecca looked happier than I'd seen her in a long time, and when she went to her room just after nine, she stood behind the couch to kiss the top of my head, and whispered "Thank you".

And now I'm sitting here thinking about missed signs and lost months and how I could have helped her so much sooner if I'd seen the wood for the trees. Could I have kept Dave if I'd seen those signs sooner too – would I have wanted to? Should I have worked out that he was Leon? And Jonathan . . . a shiver runs through me, and my headache nudges louder.

Then at the back of my mind, something clicks. I sit up straight, slide my laptop on to my knee, and start to type.

Hi Caroline,

I know we're due to meet tomorrow, but I'm just getting a little anxious about the article and the anonymity side of things, and the pieces of the interview that were due to be left out, like my daughters' names, clinic name etc. Sorry if I sound dramatic, but I think I really need to see a draft at this stage. Would you mind sending it on to me tonight so I can make sure I'm comfortable with it?

Best regards,

Lauren

I hit send and sit back, wondering if it sounds rude or demanding. I reread what I've written, and as I do, a reply comes in.

Hiya,

TBH I haven't written it up yet – I just have rough notes and segments done, but not the whole article. Are you still OK to meet tomorrow for the final interview? After that I can send? Trust me! It will be fine.

Caroline xx

Slowly I blow air out of my mouth, reading through her reply a second time. It might be fine, but what if it's not?

Hi Caroline,

Sorry if this sounds OTT but I think I really need to see it at this stage. Can you send me through your notes and the parts you have done? Happy to read those in advance of first draft. Will confirm re meeting tomorrow once I've gone through them.

Regards,

Lauren

She is going to think I'm a paranoid lunatic but I'm past caring. Her reply when it comes is less friendly.

OK. Give me an hour to type them up.

Caroline

No kisses. But fuck it. I'm not taking any more chances.

It's almost midnight by the time her next message comes through, a long email with quotes and comments from me, going back to our first meeting last month. At the beginning, she has a section called **Personal Details** and she's made a note that Ava and Rebecca's names shouldn't be used, nor Steps to Wellness. She mentions VIN and I'm wondering now if I should ask her to change that – to make up a name instead. A tight knot forms in my stomach while I'm skimming through notes on different types of messages I got from VIN. She's also mentioned my separation from Dave, but in bold she's noted that no personal details should be included. There are more transcripts of our interviews and my VIN messages below, but everything is pretty much what we discussed. Just like she said. I let out a breath as I type a reply, confirming our meeting tomorrow. Jesus, I'm getting paranoid. Jonathan is in custody, there will be no more messages from the VIN account, and not everybody is out to get me. Caroline is just doing her job, and did everything as she said she would.

I close the laptop and lie back on the couch, waiting for the knot to uncurl. But there's something not quite right with the picture. I fall asleep, dreaming not of Jonathan but of kind eyes and false smiles.

Chapter 51

When I walk into the café, Caroline is already there, pen and notebook out on the table, cappuccino in hand. She stands to give me a light hug, then steps back to look at me, her eyes sweeping me up and down.

"You look tired – is everything okay?" she asks, raising a hand to beckon the waiter.

I sit and order a coffee and a BLT without looking at the menu.

"Just about. I had a very challenging situation with a client at work but I think it's on its way to being resolved." I stop and look at her notebook. "This isn't for the interview, right? Obviously I can't talk about anything work-related for the article – I'd be fired on the spot."

She shakes her head, her hair immobile in a perfect low bun. "Definitely not, I'm just worried about you. Is everything else okay?"

"You know what, maybe it is. I think I'm coming out of a tunnel."

"And VIN – any update on the American guy?"

"Yes, actually. We know now that Chris – the guy in New York – is not VIN. Cleo was over there and met him and it's a long story, but it's not him."

Her eyes light up at this. "Tell me, I have time."

"I can't, I really can't. It's not my story to tell. It's a tragic, horrible mess of a thing where nobody wins."

She looks disappointed, and I wonder what it's like to be her – does the story matter more than the people behind it?

"That's fine, I understand. I'm just worried about you – it's only a few weeks since our last meeting but you look a lot thinner and paler."

I run a hand through my hair and make a mental note to take more care with my foundation.

"Yeah, there's been a lot going on . . ."

"Tell me more," she says, picking up her pen.

I imagine for a moment telling her about Dave – how good it would feel to let it out that he was Leon. And I imagine Dave's face, reading the article. His cheeks going red, his fingers digging into his scalp, apoplectic with horror, and I smile. But then I imagine Ava and Rebecca reading it, and my mother reading it, and perhaps recognising the details and I know, no matter how much Dave deserves this, they don't. I don't. So I tell Caroline it's all just small stuff, and has nothing to do with the trolling.

"Okay, so back to VIN then – it's definitely not Chris?"

"It's not but it seems fairly certain now that it's somebody else."

"Oh! So who is it?"

"I can't really say. It's with the Guards. Actually maybe pretend I didn't say we may have found out who it is, and just carry on with the article as it was? I'm thinking now that legally I probably shouldn't say anything at all."

"No problem," she says but I can hear disappointment. "So what are the next steps now that you think you know who it is?" she asks as the food arrives. "How does Cleo feel about it?"

My mouth is full of BLT and I cover it, swallowing before answering.

"Actually she doesn't know yet. I meant to call her last night but I had a splitting headache. I'll message her when we finish up here. She wanted to meet for coffee soon, but I guess we might not need to now, if it's all over. That's sort of odd in a way, that I might never see her again."

Caroline nods. "Yes, I can see that that would be strange after what you've gone through. Perhaps you'll stay friends?"

I stop to consider that. "I don't know. We're very different. I'm not sure we have anything other than VIN in common." Somehow, despite every frustrating moment of the last two months, this leaves me feeling sad.

I excuse myself to go to the bathroom, and take a moment at the sink to gather myself together. It reminds me of the first time I met Cleo, in the bathroom in Italy, when she asked if I was okay and made me sit down to catch my breath. It seems like a million years ago, and with sudden clarity I know, despite everything, I'm going to miss her.

Outside, Caroline is scribbling in her notebook but closes it as I return to the table.

"Do you mind if we finish up soon," I ask her, looking at my watch. Quarter to twelve. "My headache is coming back and I should check on Rebecca too."

If Caroline is wondering why I need to check on Rebecca she doesn't ask.

"Of course – I have everything I need now anyway, and can go ahead with writing up the article." She stops, and looks hesitant. "Was everything okay with the notes I sent you last night?"

"Absolutely. I didn't get through them all, but they look great. And sorry for pushing you to send them on, it's just – I got worried for a minute that I was making a mistake."

She smiles, and the laughter lines around her eyes crinkle. "No problem, I completely understand. It's a very human reaction – most of us feel vulnerable putting ourselves out there. But I think when the article goes out you'll feel better."

I nod and say goodbye, leaving Caroline with her notes. At the entrance, I stop to message Cleo.

Hey, looks like VIN caught, someone from my work, no link to you, long story.

I hesitate, then type another line.

I can fill you in over coffee?

I hit send, wondering if she'll hear the vulnerability. I message Rebecca then, to ask if I should bring home doughnuts, already knowing the answer, then I'm rushing out into the Saturday morning crowds, thinking about fresh starts.

Chapter 52

The fresh start is short-lived. Before I even get through the front door, Rebecca tells me Dave called in a few minutes earlier, and seemed really angry but wouldn't say why. Sweet Jesus, what on earth could possibly be so important, I wonder, walking down to Nadine's. When he opens the door, his cheeks are a now familiar strawberry shade and I feel myself tensing.

"We need to talk," he says and walks through to the kitchen, leaving me to close the door and follow.

Grace is at the sink, polishing wineglasses. She glances up, looking nervous. I smile over, but she's already looking back at the wineglass in her hand. Then I remember that Dave doesn't know we've met.

"Grace, could you give us a minute?" Dave says, and she nods, moving through the doorway on the far side of the kitchen, into the dining room. She pushes the door so it's almost but not quite closed.

Dave gestures for me to sit down, and I'm apprehensive now, like I'm being hauled in front of the principal.

"What's up?" I ask, putting my bag down on the impossibly shiny floor tiles.

"I need to know how you found out about it," Dave says, sitting opposite.

Shit. With impeccable timing, my phone buzzes from my bag. It's an auto-text from my dentist but I open it and frown at the screen, buying time.

"Lauren."

I put the phone down on the table.

"Found out about what?"

"About Leon," he says, glancing behind him at the dining-room door, and lowering his voice. "How did you know I was Leon?"

Over his shoulder, I see the door move a fraction of an inch – Grace is listening from the dining room.

"I told you," I say, keeping my voice even. "I researched online and found out how to do it."

"I don't believe you. I talked to my friend in IT – he says there's no way a normal person could do it. You'd have to be a hacker. You might find the IP address, but you'd never trace it back to a physical address. So how did you do it?"

"Dave, are you seriously going down this road? Have you forgotten that you started this – *you* trolled *me* – how on earth are you trying to turn this back on me?"

"Prove it then – show me how you did it," he says, reaching across and grabbing my phone.

"*Jesus Christ, Dave, don't you dare!*"

He puts it back down in the middle of the table.

"Well, what are you hiding?" he asks.

"I'm not hiding anything but you have absolutely no right to take my phone like that." I stare at him, daring him to try again. He keeps his hands flat on the table.

"Then I have to ask. Did you log into my laptop?"

"Sorry, what?"

"Nadine told me you were here on Thursday afternoon when I was in Bristol – were you snooping on my computer?"

Fucking Nadine.

"Yes, I was here Thursday, because Rebecca was here and wouldn't answer her phone. But no, Dave, I wasn't on your laptop – I can't believe you'd even suggest that! Anyway, I already knew you were Leon on Wednesday night, so how would snooping on Thursday even be relevant?"

"Well, maybe that's just the first time you were caught – how do

I know you haven't been here other times?"

"Sorry – *caught*? What do you mean caught? I came here to collect our daughter – you make it sound like I was doing something wrong. You're being ridiculous."

Dave sits back and folds his arms.

"So show me how you did it."

I fold my arms too.

"I'm not even going to entertain this. Dave, how would I even log in to your laptop if I wanted to – I don't know your password."

"I don't have a password."

"Of course you do – you always did when you lived in our house. Or is it that you don't need it any more because you're not a troll now?"

He winces. Strike one for me.

"I never had one, there's no password."

"There is – you're probably just entering it on autopilot."

"There isn't."

"Fine, show me your laptop and you'll see that you do have a password and I couldn't have gone into it."

Pushing back his chair, Dave gets up.

"Right, come with me. I'll show you I'm right."

I hang back for a second when Dave stalks out of the kitchen. Grace pulls the dining-room door back slightly and peers through, uncertainty all over her face. I shake my head, and mouth: "*Say nothing, I'll sort it*". She nods, but doesn't look convinced.

In the study, Dave already has the laptop open and is looking at me triumphantly.

"I told you, I don't have a password. You could easily have looked at it when you were here."

"Dave, whether you have a password or not isn't actually the point – I've never been in this study in my life, I wouldn't dream of logging in to your laptop, and to be honest, I cannot believe we're even having this conversation after what you did to me. You trolled me. You sent me horrible messages anonymously to freak me out. That I managed to work out it was you is upsetting you now more than anything and you're lashing out, trying to push back on me. I will *not* accept this." The words come out in a hiss. "*You* did wrong, *you* got caught. *So man the fuck up and stop trying to get out of it!*" I roar the last bit, then turn on my heel and march out of the study and through the front door.

He doesn't come after me, and I wonder if perhaps for now he'll stop trying to solve the mystery of how he got caught.

CLEO

Chapter 53

Gerbera daisies the colour of butter and yams vie for attention as Cleo stops at a flower stall to read Lauren's message.

Hey, looks like VIN caught, someone from my work, no link to you, long story.

I can fill you in over coffee?

So it's over, and in the end it had nothing to do with her. How odd – why was someone from Lauren's work so interested in *her*?

Absolutely let's do coffee – just tell me where and when, she replies.

Cleo chooses a bunch of daisies, and crosses Grafton Street to the bookstore opposite. Inside, she runs her hands over paperbacks, inhaling new-book smell. It's crowded with Saturday-morning browsers, but not as busy as the street outside, and she stays far longer than the time it takes to choose two titles.

It's after one when she emerges, blinking in the winter sun, her new books tucked under her arm, and when her phone beeps she fumbles to pull it from her pocket. The number isn't one she recognises, but the message is from Lauren.

Hey, texting on Rebecca's phone, mine fell in water. In hotpress drying it out but think it's dead. Do you want to get that coffee this afternoon? Say four o'clock outside Metro Café on South William Street? Lauren

Cleo replies to tell her that works, and realises she's glad they're meeting, even if it's just to say goodbye. Messaging her mom to say she may be late for their weekly Skype call, she wanders over to Powerscourt Townhouse to get some lunch and start her book.

It's five after four when she arrives outside Metro, but Lauren isn't here yet. The city sky darkens above the buildings, and dotted lights slip on one by one as she pulls her coat around her and wishes she'd worn a hat. Five minutes tick by and still Lauren doesn't show. Using her teeth, Cleo pulls off one glove and fishes in her coat pocket for her phone. No messages. She types one out to Lauren.

Hey, just me. I'm outside Metro – are we still meeting? Am I in right place – 4pm Metro on South William Street?

She hits send, before remembering Lauren's phone is languishing in her airing cupboard. Sighing, she types out another message, this time to Lauren's daughter's phone.

Am outside Metro. Are you still good to meet?

She waits, stamping her feet against the cold, and a minute later, Lauren's reply comes in.

So sorry, problem with Rebecca, can't meet now. Need to drive back home asap. Really sorry. Will explain later.

Pocketing her phone, Cleo heads south towards Aungier Street, a little irritated at the late notice but mostly – surprisingly – disappointed they didn't get to catch up. Realisation hits – she was looking forward to it. What would Delphine think about that – putting down roots in Dublin?

But back in the apartment, it's freezing cold, and even ten minutes after switching on the storage heater, Cleo can still see her breath. And she misses her cosy New York apartment again and reckons her mom doesn't need to worry.

A few chapters into her book, Cleo's phone buzzes with another message.

Crisis averted, didn't need to go home after all, am outside your apartment block with apology cake and coffee – I know you're on ground floor but not sure which apartment is yours, can you buzz me in?

Jeez, what is up with her today? Cleo presses the buzzer with one hand, typing her reply with the other.

Yes, ground floor, apartment 2, buzzing you in now.

She opens the apartment door then walks across to the living-room window to take a last look before closing the drapes and accepting nightfall. There's something magical about Dublin on Saturday night – the shoppers and workers going home, crossed with the partygoers going out.

The door creaks as it's pushed open and she calls out, "In here, Lauren!"

She hears her walk into the room and turns to say hello but the smile slips from her face when she sees a stranger in her living room.

"You must be Cleo," the stranger says. "It's about time we met. You probably know me as VIN."

LAUREN

Chapter 54

The last doughnut is winking at me from the box on the coffee table, and I call upstairs to Rebecca to take it away, but she doesn't hear. It's dark outside and time to pull the curtains but I'm too tired to move off the couch. Opening my laptop, I go on to Twitter to see if the VIN account is still there. I wonder will the Guards take it down or will it just sit there, a testament to the last two months of hell? Rebecca arrives into the sitting room and looks over my shoulder.

"Who's Vin-Horus?" she asks.

"It's not 'Horus' – it's a set of initials – H. O. Rus. My troll. Though I still don't know what the letters mean."

"But is it not Horus, the Egyptian guy?"

"Who?"

"The Egyptian God – in mythology?"

I twist around to look at her.

"You know, the son of Osiris? He spent most of his time in battle with Set – Osiris's killer – trying to avenge his father's death," she continues, as though everyone knows this. "I wonder why your troll chose his name?"

I have no idea. Jonathan's never mentioned anything about his father. Could it have something to do with Sorcha's father – he seemed to have issues with him? Maybe it has nothing to do with a god called Horus and really does represent someone's initials or an acronym. I must ask the Guards.

"Rebecca, have you seen my phone anywhere? Did I leave it in your room?" I ask her, sticking my hand down between the couch cushions to check for it there.

"No, do you want to ring it from mine?" she says, passing me her phone.

I hit call on my own number, but there's no ringing sound anywhere in the house. Then I hear Dave's voice on the other end of the line, and it hits me – I left it in his kitchen when I stormed out earlier. Shit. If he looks at my picture gallery, he's going to see the photo Grace took of his laptop.

"Sorry, it's me, I guess I left my phone there – can I pop down to pick it up?"

He says he'll drop it over. There's nothing in his voice to suggest he's seen the photo, but still I'm transported back twenty-five years, watching my mother search my room for the naggin of vodka I knew was under the bed.

As we wait, I ask Rebecca if I can take a look through her Snapchat. That earns me an eye-roll.

"Mum, I said I was sorry last night, you need to trust me."

"Yes, but you need to rebuild that trust, and I have to keep a much closer eye on your social media until you do."

We do indeed turn into our mothers, I think, as I scroll through her most recent snaps. There are no more photos of me, just two selfies and one of the book she's reading. She's standing behind the couch looking down at me with a 'see, told you' look on her face, and I nod to let her know so far, so good.

Instagram next. More selfies, pictures of her friends, and some from her last basketball game. I scroll back further and find some from Nadine's house – one of Ava standing beside the front door making a face, one of Rebecca in the garden, and then a close-up of an unfamiliar painting. It looks like a vase of dying flowers. The caption is "**Who are we to judge?**".

"Where's that from?" I ask her.

Her cheeks flame. "It's my room in Dad's house. One of those pieces of art that Nadine's got all over the place – well, not art, her own paintings. *She* thinks it's art."

"Ah Rebecca, we've talked about this – you can't be putting up stuff like that. What if Nadine saw it?"

I scroll back further and find another one – this time I recognise it as the grey and brown seascape in Nadine's kitchen. Nadine has signed it in dramatic script, and titled it too. **"Blackthorn Bay at Dawn"**.

How odd. I'm nearly sure that's where Grace said she was from. Why would Nadine paint a picture of it? Or are they from the same place? I glance up at Rebecca.

"Do Nadine and Grace come from the same village – is that how they know each other?"

She shrugs. "I don't know where either of them is from."

The doorbell rings and she goes out to answer, arriving back with Dave trailing behind. As he nods hello and hands over my phone, there's nothing at all in his expression to suggest he's seen Grace's photo.

I check for messages – one from my mum, and one from Cleo.

Hey, just me. I'm outside Metro – are we still meeting? Am I in right place – 4pm Metro on South William Street?

Were we supposed to meet? I know I said earlier we'd catch up for coffee but we never made a concrete plan. How does she think we're meeting today? Maybe she sent it to me by accident. It's after five now, so she'll be long gone. I type a quick reply.

Hi, sorry, did you send this to me in error? Don't think we were due to meet today?

Dave clears his throat.

"Sorry, just a strange message from a friend. Cheers for dropping it over, Dave. Actually, out of curiosity, do Nadine and Grace come from the same place – Blackthorn Bay in Waterford?"

He looks confused. "No, what made you think that? Nadine's from Dublin and I don't know where Grace is from."

"She's from Blackthorn Bay in Waterford – the place in Nadine's painting in the kitchen."

"That's not Waterford – it's some place in Australia Nadine visited years ago. What made you think it was Waterford?"

"Oh right, that's funny. Grace said she's from there. How odd. Where is she from then?"

Dave shakes his head. "No idea. I don't really know her. She had

313

two good reference letters, she was way cheaper than anyone else, and she was desperate to make up for hitting the car, so we hired her. I didn't ask too much about her background."

I sit up straighter. "What do you mean hitting the car?"

Dave walks around and sits on the arm of the couch. "She hit the wing mirror off my car one night and called in to apologise and pay for it. She was worried we'd want her to put it through the insurance and said she couldn't afford to lose her no-claims bonus. She stayed for ages, Jesus I thought she'd never leave. And in the end it cost way more than I thought it would – sure wasn't I on to you from the garage that day?"

Rebecca sits down on the rug opposite, interested now.

"But is she not Nadine's cleaner for years?" I ask Dave. "I got the impression she's been there a long time?"

He shakes his head again. "No, only a couple of months. I didn't think we needed a cleaner, but she was so upset that night – going on and on about being a widow and needing work, and she was offering to do it for next to nothing. So we said yes. Why?"

None of this makes any sense. What happened to the husband with the bad back – why would she say she's a widow? And why say she's from Blackthorn Bay – did she pluck the name off the wall in front of her when I asked?

Pulling my laptop onto my knee, I open Google.

"What's her surname?"

Dave scratches his head. Surely he knows her surname. He catches my look.

"I know it, it was on the reference letters, I'm just trying to remember. Meaney. That was it, Grace Meaney."

I type it in to Google and find dozens and dozens of entries for different people of different ages, none of whom look like the Grace we know.

"Hang on, I don't think you have that right, Dad," Rebecca says suddenly, shaking her head. "I saw her name on an envelope in her handbag once."

We both look at her.

"Okay, I see how that sounds, but I wasn't snooping! I was looking for my scarf – you know, the one with the skulls on it? And when I moved Grace's bag, I thought I saw a scarf like it inside –

underneath an envelope and some letters. I didn't want to go poking around in her handbag obviously, and anyway it might not have been my scarf. But I remember seeing her name on the envelope. It was funny, because it's the same name as a character from a *Doctor Who* movie from years ago, and Grace is nothing like the character. Anyway, it wasn't my scarf in the end – I found mine here on our kitchen table that night."

Because Grace brought it here, telling me Rebecca forgot it. My God.

"Can you tell me her name?" I ask quietly.

"Holloway. Grace Holloway."

Something loosens inside me.

"That's Cleo's surname. She's Cleo Holloway."

Chapter 55

The woman standing in Cleo's living room looks like a very ordinary woman – slight in build, early forties, unremarkable brown hair going grey, intelligent eyes, but Cleo has never seen her in her life. And yet she's in her apartment, and she's just said she's VIN.

"Um, I just got a message on my cell from Lauren to say she's outside – is she with you? What's going on?"

The woman holds up a phone in her left hand.

"You didn't get a message from Lauren. You got a message from an unknown number." She smiles. "From me, saying I was on Lauren's daughter's phone."

It isn't making any sense, but Cleo knows she really wants Lauren to walk in behind this woman now and say *this* is the long story she mentioned earlier, and it's all just fine. The woman closes the living-room door behind her and faces Cleo, a smile still on her face. It's odd and awkward and Cleo doesn't quite know how to ask her to leave. It's the kind of thing you think you'll do easily, until you find yourself in the situation. She clears her throat and tries.

"I'm afraid I don't understand what's going on, but I'm due in work soon, so perhaps I can catch up with Lauren directly to hear more about it?"

The woman shakes her head, still smiling, and takes a step

towards Cleo. Her parka jacket looks far too big for her and beneath it she's wearing a plain black top and jeans – she looks decidedly normal. Then Cleo sees it glinting in the overhead light – the woman has something metallic in her right hand, just visible below the sleeve of her jacket.

A knife. *Jesus Christ.* A knife like you'd use for chopping vegetables, except it's in a stranger's hand and she's standing in Cleo's apartment.

"I really need you to leave now, please," Cleo tells her, realising too late that she's taken a step back towards the window.

"I've waited a long time to meet you, Cleo, and I'm not going anywhere." Her voice is smooth and confident, her smile still in place.

"Okay, so if you're VIN, why don't you just tell me what you want with me and Lauren, and we can go our separate ways? How about that?" Cleo sounds confident too but, inside, her mind is a scattergun, trying to pull pieces of information together. Her eyes skim the apartment – where's her cell? On cue, it beeps from the table across the room, but there's no way to reach it without passing the woman. The window behind her is nearer, but locked. Her laptop is sitting on the arm of the couch. Could she grab it and smash the window? The woman follows Cleo's eyes with hers.

"As it happens, we'll need your laptop. But keep your hands off it for now. Will we sit down?"

Cleo stays where she is as the woman takes a seat on the couch, and pats the cushion beside her.

"Cleo, I'm not sure why you think you have a choice in any of this – I didn't go to all this trouble to be ignored. *Sit.*"

This time Cleo does as she's told. Now she's only six inches from her. As the woman speaks, Cleo's eyes fix on her mouth, on the creased lipstick, the colour of overripe plums.

"You can call me VIN but my name is Grace. I don't imagine Lauren has mentioned me – I'm her ex-husband's cleaner. Much as she's enjoyed hearing snippets of his new life from me, I doubt I come up in her conversations."

Cleo finds her voice. "Why are you here? And if Lauren isn't with you, how did you find me?"

"I messaged you to meet at Metro, then waited across the road watching. When I messaged you to say I couldn't make it after all, you left, and I followed you here. It was simple once I had your phone number."

Cleo's mouth falls open as the pieces slot into place. My God, she'd led the woman straight here.

"But that's not the interesting part, Cleo," Grace continues. "I want to tell you a story about your mother, and a man who sold out his family, dumping them for a whore. Did you know Delphine stole my father – that he was mine before he was yours? And then I lost my mam too. Your whore-mother took my whole life away from me, and I've been waiting for a very long time to show her what that's like."

Cleo shakes her head; none of it makes any sense.

"Don't shake your head at me," she snaps, and Cleo stops.

"I think you've made a mistake," Cleo tells her, whispering. "My mother *is* called Delphine, but she's American. She's not from here. She's not with your father or with anyone. My dad died a long time ago, and she never met anyone else."

The thin lips part and a burst of laughter comes out.

"Is that what she told you? That he died, as though it was some kind of passive event? He didn't just die. He drove her home after a party, because she refused to walk, and he crashed the car and lost his life, and she walked away, free to live hers. Is that fair?"

Cleo has no idea what she's talking about, but finds herself shaking her head.

"And then I lost the one person who mattered more to me than anyone. My mother took her own life when my father died – did you know that? By killing my father, she killed my mother too." A flash of anger crosses her face. "Did the whore ever tell you that?"

Cleo shakes her head again, searching for words to appease her, but her mind is still reeling, grasping at things she's saying, and trying to find a way out. Carefully, without moving her head, she looks down. The knife is still in Grace's right hand, the phone is now in her purse on the floor. Could she risk grabbing the blade?

Grace shakes her head as though Cleo had said it out loud.

"Don't even think about it." She nods towards the knife. "This will be deep in your ribs before you know what's happening. Understand?"

318

"Yes." Cleo takes in a breath. "Can I ask, why do you believe my mother did this? Have you maybe mixed her up with someone else?"

Cleo braces herself for another burst of anger, but this time there's none. Grace reaches down to her purse and takes something out – an old Polaroid of a woman sitting on a beach reading a book. Delphine. It must be years old – her hair is longer than Cleo has ever known it. A photo from some time before she was born, and not one she's ever seen. Grace holds it up to her face.

"Like twins, three decades apart. She was about your age when this was taken, I'd say – what are you, thirty?" She asks it as though making small talk in a coffee shop.

Cleo nods.

"Where did you get this photo? Where was it taken?"

"My father took it. On a beach in West Cork, when he was supposed to be on a business trip. I found it in a notebook after my mother died. I knew the whore was American but I didn't know if she'd gone back or not after he died. But of course she did, leaving everyone else to deal with the debris she'd left behind, including me, the motherless child nobody wanted. I knew some day I'd see her again, and then I did. In a photo taken on a beach."

"Lauren's photo? You thought that was my mother?"

"At first. But when I zoomed in, I could see it was someone who looked exactly as she did back then, only far younger than she could possibly be now. It had to be her daughter."

"But you can't have been sure – there's no way you'd remember her that clearly – you were only a child!" Cleo's voice is louder than she intends, and Grace shifts the blade in her hand.

"I knew. Believe me, I'll never forget her face." She looks at Cleo, moving closer again. "*Your* face." Then she grabs her wrist, and Cleo jumps, caught off guard. "And there was *this*." She's got Cleo's wrist in her hand and she's rubbing her thumb over the elephant bracelet. "I saw it when I zoomed in. You got it from your mother, didn't you?" Cleo nods. "He bought it for her, did you know that?" She nods again. "I found it in his bag that night, and thought it was for my mam, but it was for the whore."

"I knew it was from my dad, but I didn't know this story . . ."

"*Your* dad," she spits the word. "He was *my* father – you're just the bastard child he never knew – you shouldn't even exist."

"If what you say is true, then we're sisters," Cleo says quietly. "Half-sisters."

Grace grips her more tightly, digging her nails into the thin skin of Cleo's wrist.

"You're the product of an affair, worth nothing more than a stain on a sheet. I don't see you as my sister, believe me."

The knife is still in her other hand and Cleo tries to pull her arm away but Grace's grasp is too strong.

"Don't worry, Cleo, this isn't how it ends. There's something else we have to do first."

Cleo's cell phone starts to ring, and Grace's nails go deeper into her skin, as a warning or on instinct, Cleo's not sure. They both look over at the phone, chiming out from the kitchen table, and wait as though it's somehow rude to keep talking while it's ringing. As Grace turns back, the cell starts to ring a second time. And again they sit, waiting for it to ring out, the ringtone chirpy and surreal in the deathly quiet air.

LAUREN

Chapter 56

"No answer from Cleo. She could be at work though – she works in a bar on Saturday nights." I put my phone on the counter and boil the kettle a third time,

"The whole thing might just be a coincidence," Dave says, sitting down at the kitchen table.

Rebecca sits opposite him, a sceptical look on her face.

"If it was just the surname, then yes, maybe," I reply, "though Holloway's not exactly a common name. But what about the lies Grace told?"

Dave doesn't answer, but his expression tells me he's not convinced.

"Mum, if Grace has some connection with Cleo, do you think she could be the person who's been trolling you? Isn't that how it all started – when you put up the photo of Cleo?"

I'm about to tell her no, that it was Jonathan all along, but I stop. It's like I've been forcing a shape into the wrong hole, and she's handed me the right one.

I turn to Dave. "When did Grace start working for you?"

"September, I think. First or second week of September maybe?"

"My God, she did it on purpose!"

"I don't get you," Dave says.

"The car – don't you see how easy it would have been to hit your wing mirror on purpose?"

"But why would she do that?"

"To wangle her way into our lives – to get to me, and for whatever reason to get to Cleo." And, my God, I fell for it – I was so busy enjoying tidbits of gossip about life inside their walls, I never doubted her for a second.

Dave leans back on the chair, lacing his hands behind his head.

"But how would she have found my car or my house, or have any idea I know you?"

I glance over at Rebecca who is studying her fingernails.

"Through what we – what I posted online. Pictures of the house, the car, the surrounding area . . ." Dave is going to love telling me I brought this on myself. "Between all the photos on all the social media accounts, there was enough to put it together. A digital jigsaw puzzle."

He looks perplexed. "Hang on, your pictures are of *this* house – I can see how someone would find you fairly easily. But how would they find me?"

Rebecca is still examining her fingernails.

"Yeah . . . I'm not sure . . . I –"

"It was me, Dad."

He looks over at Rebecca.

"I've been putting up photos. Stuff from outside and inside Nadine's house, from school, from around the road. I didn't really think about it – I didn't imagine anyone using it like this."

I walk over and put my hand on her shoulder.

"Ah Jesus, I've told you so often –" Dave starts, but I cut him off.

"We know, we get it, and it's stopped now. But we need to understand why Grace did it, and how this is linked to Cleo. Okay?"

I pick up my phone and go into the VIN account on Twitter. Was it really Grace all along? But if she's related to Cleo in some way, why is she trying to find her – wouldn't she already know where she is?

On autopilot, my finger touches the link to VIN's website.

"Oh. VIN has a new blog post up, and it's called *The End*."

Swallowing, I start to read out loud.

"'And then my mother was gone too. It was just me left, all alone in Auntie Peggy's house in the middle of nowhere. Your mother died of a broken heart, she told me. I wanted to see my mother's body but she said it was already gone. Not suitable for children. I wasn't stupid. Even then I knew people didn't die of broken hearts. I knew all about Peggy's neighbour found dead in the barn. No note, they said. No note from my mother either. We had to leave before people started talking, she said, and packed a bag. And then there I was, in the tiny cold bedroom in Peggy's falling-down house, with nobody left in the world.

There were no other houses beside us – only fields and broken walls. Peggy said I'd have to get a bus to school. I said I didn't want to go to a new school, and she shrugged and went back to her knitting. I knew then that I did want to go to school, and the stone in my stomach just got bigger and hotter as I watched her knitting, not listening.

Later, after I went to bed, I went downstairs to get a glass of water. On my way back from the kitchen, I stopped at the living-room door. She was in a chair by the fire, still knitting. She didn't see me or hear me. The glass of water slipped out of my hand on to the floor and smashed, and then she heard me. She screamed.

"Oh God Almighty, you gave me a fright – I forgot you were in the house at all. Clean up that mess and stay upstairs, do you hear me?"

I stayed up upstairs then, in the freezing cold. I remember looking for an extra blanket, the wardrobe door creaking when I opened it, finding nothing but empty hangers inside. The bedside locker had three drawers, all lined with blue-and-white paper. In the top one, there was a bible, and the other two were empty. Auntie Peggy had left my bag on the floor beside the bed, and I lifted it up to look inside for a jumper to wear to bed. It was the old brown holdall that used to belong to my dad when he went away with work. All my clothes were in it, but no toys or books. In the zip pocket on the outside of the bag, I could feel something. Maybe she'd packed a book for me? I opened the zip and reached inside. It was a notebook, one that belonged to my dad. Inside there were numbers and words, and I knew I've seen it before. It was the notebook he used to write down his sales when he was *away. As I paged through, something fell from the back, and I picked it up from the floor. It was a Polaroid of a beach. I wondered if it was from one of our holidays, but no, it wasn't. There was only one person in the photo, not me, not Mam. It was a woman, sitting on the sand, reading a book. Her knees were bent up, her book resting on them. Her feet were bare. A green dress covered the tops of her legs, going almost as far as her knees. Long, red hair flowed down her back, almost touching the yellow sand behind. She was focused on her reading, not looking at the camera but I didn't need her to look at the camera, I knew exactly who she was. The Whore.*

I made a promise that day to that silent woman in the photo, that if I ever saw her again, I'd show her what it means to lose everything.

And then there she was, 30 years later, with still not a care in the world, and I knew our time had come.'"

I looked up at Dave and Rebecca.

"What the hell is that all about?" Dave asks.

"My troll has been posting bits of this story for the last while, but none so far have been as detailed as this one. If it's true, I guess VIN – well, Grace if we're right – lost both parents as a child and blames the woman she calls The Whore. Though if it all happened thirty years ago, it's hardly Cleo."

"Mum, you don't think Grace is dangerous in some way, do you?" Rebecca asks, looking more anxious than curious now.

I have no idea. The woman I talked to didn't seem dangerous, but then again, she's not who I thought she was.

"I don't know. I'm still trying to take all of this in. But when I think about the lengths she went to in order to find Cleo . . . "

Rebecca nods. "And did you ever mention Cleo to Grace? Like, can she literally find her now?"

I'm pacing again, trying to remember, but I'm nearly certain Cleo never came up in conversation.

"No, we talked about lots of things," I glance over at Dave, "but never Cleo."

"So even if Grace was looking for Cleo, and they're connected in some way, it's still okay, because she has no way to reach Cleo. Right?"

"Exactly." Even as I say it, my mind is scanning back over the conversations with Grace, the photos I've put online, what I've said on Twitter, every photo Rebecca's shared on Snapchat – could any of them lead her to Cleo?

I try phoning Cleo again, but still there's no answer.

Rebecca watches silently from her seat.

"Why don't you try the bar where she works?" she says. "Maybe that's why she's not answering?"

This is why we have kids, because eventually they are smarter than we are. I search for a number for Nocturn and call, asking to speak to Cleo. The person on the other end tells me she's not there – she was due in ten minutes ago, but hasn't shown up, he says. I meet Rebecca's eyes and shake my head as I hang up.

"She's supposed to have started work ten minutes ago, but she's not there."

"She might just be late," Dave says.

"Okay. Does she live with anyone? Does she have a flatmate or a boyfriend?" asks Rebecca, ignoring her dad.

"No, nobody. I don't know who her friends are, or if she's close to anyone at all over here. If something happens, I'm not sure who will know or notice . . ."

I press the button on the kettle again, though tea is the last thing on my mind, and I pick up my phone. Only I don't know who else to call.

"Mum, would you feel better if we drove in to Cleo's place to see if she's okay?"

I'm about to tell her it's ridiculous, that we're overreacting, that Cleo is just running late for work and Grace is nothing more than an internet troll, but when I open my mouth, nothing comes out. Rebecca stands up and takes my car keys off the hook by the back door.

"Come on. Dad can wait here to fill Ava in, I'll go with you. If you keep pacing the kitchen all night you'll wear a hole in the floor. Let's go."

CLEO

Chapter 57

"Now, Cleo, open the laptop and Skype your mother."

Even though she's thousands of miles away and untouchable, every bone in Cleo's body tells her not to involve Delphine.

"She's not there, she's away at the moment."

Grace laughs. "Oh Cleo, what do you think I'm going to say – 'Right so, let's leave it?' Come on." She stops laughing and her voice hardens: "*Now open the fucking laptop and Skype your fucking mother.*"

Swallowing, Cleo clicks into the Skype app and dials her mom, praying she won't answer, but she does. She always does.

"Now put the laptop on the coffee table so she can see both of us, and don't speak. It's my turn to talk."

Cleo does as she asks, and watches as Delphine registers the stranger beside her.

"Hi, Cleo, what's up?" Her eyes dart over and back between her daughter and Grace.

"It's okay, Mom," Cleo says, and Grace moves her hand so that the blade is at Cleo's side now, just millimetres from her shirt and her ribcage beneath.

"I'll do the talking," Grace says in a soft voice, and somehow it's more unsettling than anything she's said so far. "Hello, Delphine, do you remember me?"

Confusion gives way to horror as the knife catches the light and from three thousand miles away it flashes into Delphine's eyes. Her hands go to her throat.

"What's going on? Cleo, are you in trouble?"

"You could say that, Delphine," Grace says. "I'm not surprised you don't remember me, I was only a child when we last saw each other. When my father died, after you took him away. You surely haven't forgotten? You remember my mother I'm sure. Barbara Holloway?"

Delphine's mouth opens and closes again, and recognition flares in her eyes. And in that moment, Cleo understands it's not just a story.

Grace smiles. "Yes, you know who I am. And did you know I lost my mother too? Or were you gone by then? They said she died of a broken heart but we all know what that means. I didn't even get to go to her funeral." She leans closer to the screen. "You took away everything I had and you destroyed it. So I'm going to do the same to you. And just as I had to watch my life unravel in front of my eyes, tonight it's your turn."

She holds the knife up to the screen now, and Delphine puts her hands over her mouth.

Cleo shifts a fraction of an inch to the left, but not enough to make any difference.

"Do you have anything to say before I start unpicking your daughter?"

There's sheer panic on Delphine's face now. "Please don't do anything to her." Her voice is rattling and low. "This has nothing to do with her. This was between me and Barbara. Please, Grace."

"Did you afford me the same compassion when you took my dad, just because you could? With your long hair and your long lashes and your American accent?"

"It wasn't like that," Delphine says, and Cleo sees her hand reaching across the table towards her cell-phone, though her eyes never leave the screen.

Grace sees it too.

"Oh, you can call the police, Delphine, go right ahead. I'm sure the NYPD will be of great service from thousands of miles away."

Cleo's mind is careering, trying to work out how Delphine could call the Irish police – will she even think to do that? She still has her hand on the cell, and she's sliding it towards her. Grace is watching and waiting, like a cat watching a mouse. Delphine picks it up and hits a button, never taking her eyes off them as she speaks.

"I need police, but in Ireland. I don't know the number. My daughter is being held at knife-point in her apartment in Dublin. It's on . . . Aungier Street. Oh God, what's the full address? Cleo, what's the address?"

Cleo opens her mouth to answer, but Grace pushes the blade further towards her and now she can feel the point.

"Ah, ah! It's not that simple."

Delphine is still talking to emergency services, trying to explain where she is and what's happening but she's not making any sense.

"That's enough – you can hang up the call now, Delphine," Grace says, moving the blade closer again, and this time it goes through Cleo's shirt, pricking her skin.

Disconnecting, Delphine holds up her hands. "Grace, please, none of this has anything to do with her."

"I know that. But she's here and you're not, and I suspect this will hurt you more than if you were in her place. Nothing like a mother's love, is there? There's a quote that's been ringing in my ears for thirty years now, 'A mother is she who can take the place of all others but whose place no one else can take'."

Delphine sits up straighter and something changes in her eyes.

"That's right. Nothing like a mother's love. Though mothers lie too, don't they?"

Grace nods. "And you've been lying to Cleo all her life."

Delphine smiles then, and for the first time Grace looks confused.

"I mean *your* mother lied, Grace. Your dad didn't die in a car wreck. Do you really not know what happened?" Delphine pauses and Cleo feels something shift. "It happened one evening about a month after your father moved in with me. Barbara told him she was calling in to talk about child-support payments. I went to see a movie on my own, to give them some space. I was pregnant, and we knew your mother wouldn't take it well, but he wanted to tell her that night, in case she heard it from someone else."

Grace stiffens beside Cleo as Delphine keeps talking.

"And nobody saw exactly what happened, but it seems your mother lost it that night, Grace. She picked up a poker and hit him over the head with it. According to the coroner, she continued to beat him over and over, even as he lay dying on the floor, smashing his skull so badly he was barely identifiable. On our living-room floor, bleeding into the carpet, with no chance to say goodbye to you or to me. Barbara did that, Grace. Not me."

Something shifts again, and Cleo senses Grace slipping, faltering.

"That's not true," she says, but her voice is lower now, hoarse.

"Oh, it's true." Delphine's eyes are wide, and Cleo wonders if she's forgotten the knife, or maybe it's all about the knife. "Your mother didn't die of a broken heart, or by suicide. They told you that to protect you. She died ten years ago in prison. They took her away and locked her up for what she did. She chose to do it, not me, not you. It has nothing to do with us."

Grace's fingers slacken on the blade, her eyes still fixed on the screen, on Delphine. Cleo looks at her mom as she holds Grace's gaze, and then back at the knife. Her hand shoots out and she grabs it. Grace tries to grip the handle but she's not fast enough. It's in Cleo's hand now, and she jumps up, back towards the window.

"*Bitch!*" Grace roars at Cleo, or maybe at Delphine.

She stands up too but doesn't come any closer.

The screen is facing the couch and Cleo doesn't know if her mother can hear her but she screams out her address: "*Mom, it's Apartment 2, Lafayette Hall, Aungier Street – you need to call the Irish police. It's 999 from here but I don't know how that works from there – hurry!*"

Grace and Cleo are back to where they started – Cleo's at the window and Grace is facing her. Except Cleo has the knife now.

She turns it over in her hand. Could she use it?

Grace watches, her eyes darting between Cleo's hand and her face. She's wondering the same thing. She makes up her mind and lunges, reaching to grab the knife. Without stopping to think, Cleo grips the handle and drives the blade into Grace's shoulder. She jumps back with a howl, like an animal caught in a trap. Cleo's heart is racing and there's sweat in her eyes and for a minute she can't see anything. When she looks up, Grace is six feet from her, the knife in her shoulder, but she's still standing. Then inexplicably, she smiles, and bends to turn the laptop towards them. Delphine is on screen, shouting into her cell-phone. Grace stands up straight and takes a bottle of something out of her purse – nail-polish remover? The doorbell rings, but Grace pays no attention, fixed on her task. She unscrews the cap and spills the liquid on the carpet, spreading it left to right, all across the space between them. Droplets splash near Cleo's boots and she jumps back towards the window, as the familiar smell of acetone fills the small apartment.

Then Grace pulls out a box and too late Cleo understands. Her mother screams from three thousand miles away, and Grace laughs as she opens the box and strikes a match. For a second, she holds it high, then it's falling, falling like a fiery arrow to the floor below.

In a flash, flames rise up, making a wall between them, licking the couch and the table. Delphine is screaming at Cleo to get out, but the blaze is already too high. The heat is immense, and panic is setting in. Cleo's hands touch the net curtain behind her as she steps back towards the window and thick black smoke swirls in slow motion around her mouth and nose. The first acrid suck of toxic fumes snaps something in her brain and she turns to open the window, pulling at the handle. Locked. It's hard to see now with the smoke – her panicky hands feel around for the key, but it's not in the keyhole and it's not on the window-sill. Clenching her fist, she smashes it into the glass. Nothing. She tries to scream but when she opens her mouth it fills with smoke and she starts to cough. With her arm across her nose and mouth she turns to face the flames. Running through them is the only hope, but they're far too high now, raging from one side of the room to the other. The couch is blazing, weeping black smoke that spirals up and out and into Cleo's nose and throat. She puts her arm across her face again but on some level she knows it's not working and that this is what happens, people die from smoke.

On screen, her mother is crying and screaming something but the fire is roaring and hissing and Cleo is dizzy now and can't hear her. Her back is pressed against the window and she can just about see Grace's face through the blaze, her mouth open in a ghostly, distorted laugh. Black and yellow and purple flames cover the coffee table, angry and rabid, obscuring the laptop. Cleo can't see her mother any more but now she can hear her screams again and the terror they hold tells her Delphine can still see her. She pushes back against the window, but there's nowhere to go. The smoke is burning her throat and it's inside her nose and everything's starting to swim. Grace is a dark shadow now behind the black and orange pyre and there's no sound from Delphine but Cleo doesn't know if it's because she's stopped screaming or the laptop is gone or because she's starting to flit in and out of consciousness. And then she feels herself slipping down towards the floor and she thinks it might be over.

A siren wails, and shouting voices call out things Cleo doesn't understand, and there's something covering her nose and mouth. She tries to reach for it but she can't move her arm – it's trapped under a heavy blanket. Her eyes are still closed, and she doesn't know what's on her face, but then a voice tells her it's an oxygen mask to help her breathe. She hears someone ask if the flames are out and she opens her eyes – her apartment is still on fire, but she's outside now. Someone says to leave the fire blanket on and she realises they're not talking about the apartment, they're talking about her. And with that horrific realisation, red-hot searing pain grips her, screaming and tearing at her skin like nothing she's ever imagined. The blanket is lifted from her legs and someone is talking about gel and she wants to tell them to stop, to tell them not to touch her but she can't speak or move so she concentrates on the apartment and the fire-fighters in front of the window, trying to push back the flames with a hose. Then in the sea of bright lights and uniforms, she sees one familiar face. Lauren.

"I'm so sorry, this is all my fault, this is all my fault," she's saying, over and over. She kneels on the ground beside Cleo, tears rolling down her face.

Someone is asking Lauren if she knows Cleo and she's telling them her name and that she's not from here but she's her friend.

"I'll come to the hospital, I'll be right behind in my car," she says, reaching a hand towards Cleo, but she doesn't know where to touch. "Oh God, I'm so sorry," she says, her face pale and tear-stained.

Cleo wants to tell her it's not her fault, that they are the victims, that they can't control what other people do, but when she tries to speak, no words come out at all.

AFTER

Chapter 58

Cleo is propped against a bank of pillows and raises one bandaged hand in a small wave when I walk into her room. The bandages go all the way up above her elbows, disappearing under the loose sleeves of the oversized grey T-shirt. There's no blanket, just a sheet to her waist, and as I pull a chair to the bed I feel a guilty relief that I can't see her legs. When I came yesterday she was asleep, and I sat by her bed for a while, talking to her mother. The Guards had given me a summarised version of why Grace set fire to the apartment, and Delphine filled in the gaps. We spoke in low voices but Cleo never stirred. The pain relief had knocked her out, Delphine told me. She and Cleo's friend Ruth had flown in from New York the day after the fire, and were staying in a hotel near the hospital – I tried to get them to stay with me, but Delphine wanted to be as close to Cleo as possible, she said. Maybe later, when things were looking better.

Things are not yet looking better. Cleo has third-degree burns on her legs and will need skin grafts. Her arms have second-degree burns and should heal in a few weeks without surgery. She's on a cocktail of pain medication but there's only so much the drugs can do, she says, when I ask her how she is.

I've brought her three new books, a giant bar of Dairy Milk, and an expensive body moisturiser that I now realise she won't be able to use for a long time. I want to hide it in my handbag but it's too late.

"Thank you," she says, putting the books on the locker. "You're a good friend."

The untruth of her words makes me want to cry.

"Oh God, Cleo, I'm not a good friend – I bet you wish you'd never met me, and I don't blame you. If I'd never rambled into the bathroom that night in Italy, none of this would have happened. Or if I'd never posted the photo in the first place."

She shakes her head. "You couldn't have known. Hey, we could say that about anything in life – if only, what if – but sometimes stuff just happens."

"It's odd to think back to that last night in Italy," I say because I can't agree with her. "I don't think either of us imagined we'd see one another again."

"It all seems so long ago," Cleo says, taking a sip of water, the glass awkward in her bandaged hand. "Your daughters were in the corner playing pool, right?"

"Yes, and Snapchatting everything in sight, making it so easy for Grace to know exactly what I was doing at any given moment." I shake my head because it's what parents do, but I'm not cross at Rebecca any more. When I think of all the time she spent dealing with bullies at school while I put it down to her dad leaving, my stomach twists. Once we spoke to the school, they were swift in dealing with it, and we're almost past it now. Things are not perfect, but they're better.

"What do they think of it now – have you told them the whole story, about me, and about Grace?"

I nod. "I did actually. I didn't plan to, but then I figured it's easier to tell them everything than to gloss over parts and make up lies. I'm slowly realising that getting things out in the open is a good thing – contrary to what my mum might say." I take a bottle of water out of my bag and open it. "Anyway, Rebecca was with me that evening, and she's the one who worked out that Grace was VIN while I was trying to call you that night."

Cleo pushes a strand of hair behind her ear and I can see a red welt creeping out from under the bandage.

"That was you calling – I remember wondering who it could be."

"Yeah. I tried a couple of times, and then I tried your work, and I got anxious. I still felt a bit silly about the whole thing, which is a thoroughly Irish response to everything by the way, but Rebecca suggested we should drive into town to put my mind at ease. And you know the rest, I imagine – when you didn't answer the door, I went to the window, and I wasn't certain it was Grace there but I knew there was something wrong. So I called 999, and then the fire started and –" my voice cracks, and I clear my throat. "When they pulled you through the window I thought you were . . . well, I thought you might not wake up."

"And here I am," she says, raising her glass of water. "Thank you for being a warrior."

I raise my bottle and clink. "Maybe more worrier than warrior but the end result was the same."

"So if you only realised Grace was VIN on Saturday evening, what did you mean when you messaged earlier that day to say you knew who it was?"

I tell her then about Jonathan killing his wife, and my assumption that he was VIN too. As I tell her, I'm conscious that even then I didn't fully believe it was him, but it was the neatest answer, the one that made the problem go away. My mother would be proud.

"And what about Grace now? I asked my mom, but she didn't know what happened to her."

"They arrested her and kept her in custody – that's all I've heard so far." I search her face, looking for a resemblance to Grace. There's something there, something around the eyes, but maybe I'm imagining it now that I know their history. "Do you plan to see her?"

"No," she shakes her head. "Her face is burned on my brain – I hope I never see it in real life again."

I can't help but admire her for her certainty. In her place, I'd be agonising and wondering if I should meet my half-sister, but Cleo sees life more simply and is all the better for it, I suspect.

"Will your mom stay over here for a bit? You know you can stay with me when you come out of hospital, right?"

She shakes her head. "Thank you, but I'll go back to my place. My mom is staying, and Ruth too – she walked out on her horrible

boss and says she's going to have a European adventure with me."
She looks down at her bandaged hands. "Although the adventure
might involve a lot of TV in my apartment for the first while . . .
But anyway, what about you – how's the article going – will the
journalist want to tell the whole story now?"

"She doesn't know the whole story," Lauren says. "It's an article
about an anonymous troll, and that's it. The rest of the story is
yours and your mother's, and not mine to tell."

Cleo nods. "And are you happy with it?"

"Yep, it went live on their site yesterday, and it's absolutely
perfect. Reading it felt like taking some power back from trolls
everywhere, not just Grace – it was liberating. Actually talking to
Caroline all through it was therapeutic, but then I got so paranoid
for a while I thought she was out to sabotage me too."

"Hey, it's not surprising – the VIN messages would make anyone
paranoid, and you were dealing with Jonathan's behaviour too.
Don't be hard on yourself."

A nurse comes into the room and I stand to give him space. He
tells Cleo he needs to check her legs and that she could do with
some rest then, nodding towards me. I take the hint.

Picking up my handbag, I tell Cleo I'll be back tomorrow with
more chocolate. As I'm about to walk out the door of her room, I
remember the message she sent me on the Saturday evening about
meeting up outside Metro, and turn back to ask her about it.

"That was all Grace," she says. "She messaged me, saying it was
you on your daughter's phone, and arranged to meet. The detective
I spoke to yesterday told me Grace got my number from your cell-
phone. You left it in your husband's house that morning, when
Grace was there cleaning? The last message you sent that morning
was to me, and once she had my number, the rest was easy."

I clap my hand over my mouth. "Oh shit, Cleo, I'm so sorry.
Jesus, I'm such an idiot."

Cleo shakes her head. "Oh come on, nobody is expected to
think they can't leave a cell-phone on a table without worrying
someone will mine it for numbers. You couldn't have known. You
have to take people at face value or how could you live your life?"

How indeed. Catching the nurse's pointed look, I walk out the
door, thinking about that for a moment. About this woman who

doesn't overthink and can move continent to live on her own in a strange country. About Ava and Rebecca, and the lessons I'm trying and failing to teach them – about independence and strength and being themselves. About Dave, and his increasingly frequent calls and his mournful, hopeful eyes. About the best way to gently but firmly put an end to those hopes. And finally, as I push through the hospital doors, I think of myself, and of being free, and of fresh starts and face value and for the first time in a long time, perhaps being myself.

The End

Acknowledgements

To Paula Campbell, Gaye Shortland, and all of the incredible team at Poolbeg – thank you for your unfailing support and for putting up with my endless questions.

Thank you to my early readers – my dad, John Fitzgerald, and my sisters Nicola Elaine, and Deirdre – you were all editors in your past lives, I'm sure of it, and I owe you a pink-champagne night for being such brilliant people.

To my Irish friend in America, Lucy Hugo, and my American friend in Ireland, Alicia Harmon, who read One Click to make sure my US chapters are sufficiently full of sidewalks and sodas.

Thank you to writer Tric Kearney, whose advice about the people on the chairs is never far from my mind; to Dr Naomi Lavelle – if you want a forensic proof-reader, ask a crime-reading scientist! - and to Cliona Smith, whose advice was spot on when (a bit like Lauren) I couldn't see the wood for the trees.

Thank you to psychotherapist Stella O'Malley who read the book to make sure Lauren is reasonably good at her job, and to psychologist Sinéad Benn who gave me a steer in the right direction way back when the idea was forming.

Thanks to Louise Phillips for loaning me her Garda Detective contact, and to former Chief Fire Officer, Dublin Fire Brigade,

Stephen Brady for his expertise and for generously giving his time to ensure accuracy.

Thank you to Lisa Ryan for her Mac knowledge, Alan Smeaton of DCU for his advice on hacking, IP addresses, and social media, and to Professor Ted Kesik, University of Toronto, for key information on buildings.

I've been fortunate in getting to know many fabulous people in the Irish writing and book-blogging community over the last year, and I'm not going to brave listing names for fear I forget someone, but I will mention Margaret Scott, who nudged me into writing in the first place, and whose support when *The Other Side of the Wall* came out was incredible.

On the same note, huge thanks to my blogger buddies and IWI writing gang who read, shared, reviewed, and supported me all over social media, as did my amazing friends and extended family (including Edel who regularly turns my book to face outwards in bookshops across the midlands!)

Thank you to the wonderful Office Mum readers, who signed up for a parenting blog but have indulged my sideways slip into fiction with consistently brilliant support since this adventure started.

Thank you to my children Elissa, Nia, and Matthew, who are always inspiring – listening to ideas, suggesting plot turns, and being really quiet when I'm trying to work (one of these things is not true.) Elissa came up with the title for this book (true story) and Nia was the first person to hear the plot outline – her questions and excitement spurred me on to go with it. Matthew helped me with a pivotal plot roadblock, and I can't mention it here because it's a spoiler, but ask me when you see me and I'll tell you.

Thank you to Damien, who knows that sometimes I really want an answer and sometimes I just want a hug and a glass of wine.

And thank you to you, the reader, for reading *One Click*.

Also available from Poolbeg Crimson

THE OTHER SIDE OF THE WALL

Andrea Mara

There's something up with the people next door

When Sylvia looks out her bedroom window at night and sees a child face down in the pond next door, she races into her neighbour's garden. But the pond is empty, and no-one is answering the door.

Wondering if night feeds and sleep deprivation are getting to her, she hurriedly retreats. Besides, the fact that a local child has gone missing must be preying on her mind. Then, a week later, she hears the sound of a man crying through her bedroom wall.

The man living next door, Sam, has recently moved in. His wife and children are away for the summer and he joins them at weekends. Sylvia finds him friendly and helpful, yet she becomes increasingly uneasy about him.

Then Sylvia's little daughter wakes one night, screaming that there's a man in her room. This is followed by a series of bizarre disturbances in the house.

Sylvia's husband insists it's all in her mind, but she is certain it's not – there's something very wrong on the other side of the wall.

'A twisting tale of evil lurking behind a suburban hall door'
– *Sinéad Crowley, author of* One Bad Turn

ISBN 978-178-199-8328